KAREN CLARKE is a multi-published author living in Buckinghamshire with her husband and three grown-up children.

Having previously written twelve romantic comedies, Karen has moved to the dark side and now writes psychological suspense. As well as her solo novels, she has co-written two thrillers with fellow author Amanda Brittany.

When she's not writing, Karen reads a lot and loves walking, gardening, watching TV and films, photography and baking (not all at the same time).

Also by Karen Clarke

Your Life For Mine

Books by Karen Clarke and Amanda Brittany
The Secret Sister
The Perfect Nanny

And Then She Ran

KAREN CLARKE

ONE PLACE. MANY STORIES

HQ
An imprint of HarperCollins*Publishers* Ltd
1 London Bridge Street
London SE1 9GF

www.harpercollins.co.uk

HarperCollins*Publishers*
1st Floor, Watermarque Building, Ringsend Road
Dublin 4, Ireland

This paperback edition 2021

1

First published in Great Britain by
HQ, an imprint of HarperCollins*Publishers* Ltd 2021

ISBN: 9780008400415

MIX
Paper from
responsible sources
FSC™ C007454
www.fsc.org

This book is produced from independently certified FSC™ paper
to ensure responsible forest management.

For more information visit: www.harpercollins.co.uk/green

Printed and bound in Great Britain by
CPI Group (UK) Ltd, Melksham, SN12 6TR

This one's for my lovely mother-in-law Edna

Chapter 1

Two days ago

'You can't take the baby, Grace.' Patrick's tone was pleading. 'I need her.'

'Please, just let us go.'

'I can't.' His tone hardened. 'I won't let you. It'll ruin everything.'

'If you don't, I'll go to the press.' My heart pounded. 'I'll tell them the truth.'

He froze, perhaps imagining the implications, what it would mean for his career. He came closer. For a moment, I thought he was going to hit me. I cringed as he punched the wall by my head. 'What am I supposed to say to people?'

I straightened my shoulders. 'You'll think of something,' I said, heart racing. 'You're good with words.'

He stared at me with something close to hatred. 'And if I let you go, you won't tell anyone?'

'I promise.' I kept my eyes on his. 'And you'll leave us alone?'

He was silent for a moment. 'Do I have a choice?'

I bundled Lily into her carrier, opened the door and ran.

Chapter 2

Now

I looked around the busy airport, heart drumming against my ribs. Despite the promise he'd made, I wasn't convinced that Patrick wouldn't come after me or have me followed.

The urge to keep checking hadn't left me since I boarded the plane in New York. When I wasn't feeding or pacifying Lily during the seven-hour flight, I was inspecting the other passengers in case Patrick had sneaked on board, or sent somebody to reclaim his eight-week-old daughter.

My chest tightened with worry, my hand rigid on Lily's back as I scanned the arrivals area once more, while a sea of people surged past. It was both familiar and strange being back in England – the first time since a fleeting visit to my mother's place in Berkshire four years ago. There was no one here to meet me. No one knew where I was. Patrick had probably guessed I'd return to the UK, but would have no idea where I was heading from Heathrow. I hadn't mentioned my aunt when we were exchanging potted life histories a year ago. He didn't know where she lived and I hadn't told him. Morag was a private person and I respected her wishes.

She'd only told my mother her new address in case of emergencies, though her sister was probably the last person Mum would turn to in a crisis, their long-standing rift unhealed.

Unaware of our noisy surroundings, Lily slept soundly at last in the ergonomic carrier Patrick had bought, designed to hold her against my chest like an embrace. Her cheeks were stained red, her long lashes spiky with tears as she nuzzled into me. I kissed the soft fuzz of her fine dark hair as I hoisted her gingham baby bag onto my shoulder. Grabbing the handle of my suitcase, I followed signs to the taxis, inhaling sharply as a blast of cold air greeted me outside. It was mid-March, but the temperature felt Baltic after the overheated journey and milder Manhattan weather I'd left behind.

I tugged out Lily's lemon-coloured blanket and draped it around her as she began to stir. 'Hush, hush,' I murmured, shivers of cold rippling through my cheap, zip-up jacket as I hurried to the first waiting taxi.

'S'cuse me, there's a queue.' A man stepped forward blocking my way. He had wiry grey hair and an aggrieved expression; the look of someone spoiling for a fight.

'Oh, I'm sorry.' Tears rushed to my eyes, anxiety spilling over. 'I didn't … I wasn't—'

'Leave her alone, Len. You can see she's got her hands full.'

A woman – probably his wife – gave a compassionate smile that creased her whole face. 'Take it, love. We're not in a hurry.'

Relief made me gush. 'Thank you, if you're sure? I need to get her home and settled. My husband's expecting us.' *Home.* I no longer had one.

'Shame he's not here to pick you up.' The man's hard gaze didn't soften as he jammed meaty hands in the pockets of his padded coat.

'Stop it, Len.' The woman rolled her eyes. They were large and glassy, like marbles. 'I remember what it was like with little ones, even if this one doesn't.'

The driver had got out of the taxi and was stowing my suitcase in the boot. He slammed it shut and returned to the driver's seat.

'Well … thank you,' I said to the woman, keeping my face averted, not wanting the pair to remember my face.

She was wearing a navy baseball hat, tortoiseshell glasses, no make-up. Plain, I suppose. Early thirties, hard to tell. Had a baby, but covered up. No idea what it looked like.

Lots of women with babies must pass through the airport every day. Maybe some of them were running away too, wearing a cheap disguise; reading glasses that slightly magnified everything; hair thrust into a generic baseball cap to disguise its length and colour; a baggy grey sweatshirt with shapeless jeans and jacket, all purchased at a Walmart on the way to the airport and changed into in the toilets, before I continued my journey in a different cab.

Patrick wouldn't recognise the dowdy, androgynous woman currently climbing awkwardly into the taxi. No one from my old life would.

Heart jumping, I sat back and settled Lily. She was falling towards sleep again, her rosebud mouth making little sucking noises. Love rose like a sickness. *This has to work.*

'Where to?'

I met the driver's disinterested gaze in the rear-view mirror, then took a last look through the window at the dreary grey afternoon, where the couple were now quietly arguing at the pavement's edge. 'Victoria Station, please.'

Once there, I'd buy a ticket and take a coach for the last leg of my trip; to my aunt's home in deepest Wales where, I prayed, no one would ever find us.

Chapter 3

It felt strange at first, being on the opposite side of the road. I kept catching my breath whenever a car drove past in the 'wrong' lane, but after feeding and changing Lily, glad of the empty seat on the coach beside me, I finally dozed, worn out from adrenaline and the flight. My body was still running on a different time zone, aware it was early afternoon in Manhattan.

It was seven-thirty and dark by the time we reached Fenbrith and rain was falling steadily. Lily awoke, blinking her round brown eyes – recently darkened from blue – as she looked about, her tiny fingers splayed out on my chest.

'Hello, little mouse.' I felt an ache in my lower back as I rose. 'Looks like we're here.'

The driver got out and dumped my case on the rain-slicked ground. 'OK?' he asked as I disembarked, as if compelled to question the silent woman he'd just driven for over five hours and two hundred miles.

I forced a bland smile, one hand cupping Lily's head as I summoned my steadiest voice. 'Yes, thank you. It's been a long day that's all. We'll be glad to get out of this weather.'

Long day. Weather. I was speaking a universal code.

'You and me both.' The driver nodded in tacit understanding. 'On holiday, are you?'

'Something like that.'

'Well, this time of year Snowdonia's not too busy so make the most of it.'

'I will.' *Every contact leaves a trace.* I realised afresh how hard it was to truly disappear, to become invisible. Especially somewhere like this, where a stranger was bound to stand out.

Patrick doesn't know where you are.

For a second, as the coach pulled away, I imagined him appearing behind me, saw the flash of anger in his night-dark eyes and felt the grip of his fingers on my shoulder. *You didn't really think I'd let you go, did you?*

I wheeled around, a tremor running through me. There was no one there, just Lily and me on the empty street.

The rain had eased, but Lily was growing restless, flexing against me, unhappy at being back in her carrier. It had been a couple of hours since her last feed, which I'd undertaken in a sleepy haze, thankful I'd stuck to my guns and continued to secretly breastfeed whenever I could, despite Patrick insisting I use formula or *at least pump and freeze*, as if I was a machine – or a cow. It was clear by then that fatherhood didn't suit him. Or maybe it was because Lily wasn't the son he'd longed for.

Shivering with cold, desperate to get my baby to warmth and safety, I moved closer to the pub I was standing outside; a low-roofed building with light spilling from diamond-paned windows. The Carpenter's Arms, according to the sign, which creaked in the breeze like something from a horror film. The pub where I'd arranged to meet Morag. As I bumped my suitcase into a sheltered porch in front of the door, I briefly considered phoning my mother to let her know I was in the country, but it was better she didn't know in the unlikely event that Patrick decided to call her. Then I remembered; she didn't have the same surname as me, had changed it after my father's death, which would make her hard to find. An image of Patrick rushed in again, his lip curled in anger. I squashed it down. The day was taking its toll. I needed to sleep properly, in a bed, and give myself time to adjust to my surroundings.

I hoped Morag was already waiting in the pub. She lived three miles from the village. I could hardly walk in the dark with a baby and a suitcase, and didn't want to attract attention by taking a local taxi – if there was such a thing in this tiny hamlet. It had the air of a place from a bygone era. I wouldn't have been surprised to see a pony and trap clatter past.

As Lily let out a thin wail, I reached for the worn brass knob on the door just as it swung inwards. A wave of beer-scented warmth, the chink of glasses and the sound of laughter hit me. A pungent aroma of food made my mouth water. *When had I last eaten?*

I stood back, a protective arm across Lily, and yanked my suitcase out of the way as a woman emerged, backlit by the brightness inside so I couldn't make out her features. She half-turned, starting at the sight of me lurking by the door.

As Lily began crying in earnest, a tired sound that squeezed my heart, the woman's eyes met mine. I was aware of her comforting scent; laundry powder overlaid with something earthy; the smell of a garden, a hint of rosemary, and when she spoke, I instantly recognised her voice: raspy with a hint of steel, her Welsh accent barely detectable.

'There you are,' she said. 'Why are you hiding out here?'

'Hey, Aunt Morag.' I heard my slight American intonation and knew I'd have to lose it. 'It's good to see you.'

She stared for a long moment, the silence punctuated by Lily's intermittent cries, then let the pub door close behind her.

'We'd better go.' She jerked her head at the tiny car park at the side of the pub. 'You'll catch your death out here.'

Chapter 4

'I haven't been drinking, in case you were wondering.' Morag swiped some clutter off the passenger seat of a dusty blue van, indicating that I get in before throwing my suitcase in the back.

I obeyed with a nod, clutching Lily like a precious parcel. The interior smelt of compost, but it wasn't unpleasant.

Morag drove in silence but I felt her eyes on us a couple of times as she navigated the dark, narrow roads, their surfaces shiny with rain. There was something dreamlike about the situation. I had to keep blinking and focused my gaze ahead.

After turning sharply and jerking the vehicle down a long bumpy track, Morag pulled on the handbrake and switched the engine off. The cooling radiator ticked in the sudden quiet.

'Come inside,' Morag instructed, leaping out before I could speak and slamming the driver's door.

It felt good to be told what to do, like being a child again. I tumbled gratefully onto a muddy patch of earth, adjusting Lily in her carrier. She'd been soothed back to sleep by the rocking motion of the van, but now stretched with a mewling sound and rubbed her nose on my top.

'Wait here a second.' Morag strode into a surrounding blackness so dense it felt like a living thing pressing down. Everywhere was silent, except for a rustle of leaves stirred by a restless breeze. For a second, I felt eyes on me and my mind flew back to a scene of shattered glass on tiles, pain slicing my thumb as I tried to clear away the mess before Patrick came back, blood trickling down my hand. As a prickling sensation crept across my scalp, a security light burst into life, illuminating a clearing outside a small, grey-stone building. I let out a breath and my shoulders slid down. The cottage wasn't the ancient wreck I'd expected; no slate tiles spilling off the roof, or boards covering spaces where windows had once been.

I'd looked for images of the cottage during an internet search at the New York Library, but found nothing, leaving my imagination to run riot. I hadn't even been sure she still lived in Fenbrith until I called Mum to check, claiming I wanted to send my aunt a sixtieth birthday card and perhaps give her a call. Mum hadn't stayed in touch with her sister, but Morag and I had exchanged the odd postcard over the years. Reluctantly, Mum had passed on the landline number for the cottage and I'd called it from a payphone, fingers trembling with anxiety. I hadn't mentioned Lily, or given a reason why I was phoning out of the blue, but if Morag was surprised to hear from me, she hadn't said anything, merely instructed me to let her know when I was arriving and that she'd meet me at the pub in the village.

'Come on.' She was back, lifting my suitcase from the back of the van as though it weighed less than a feather. Leading the way, she pushed open a weathered door and stood aside to let me enter. The first thing I felt was warmth, wrapping around me like a blanket, the smell of wood-smoke competing with whatever Morag had cooked for her dinner. 'You look exhausted,' she said, flicking a switch on the rough-textured wall.

In a pool of brightness that made me blink, I saw we were in an area comprising a kitchen and living room, sparsely furnished with a mix of old and new, the doors, ceilings and woodwork stained dark brown. A set of chunky wooden steps led up to what must be a bedroom, wooden struts like fencing on either side of the gap at the top of the stairs.

'The bathroom's through there.' Morag nodded to an adjacent door, as though she'd intuited that I suddenly desperately needed the loo. 'Here, let me.'

Her fingers were at the carrier, unfastening the sturdy straps with deft movements until it fell loose. She prised Lily from my arms and swung her away. For a second, I could still feel the imprint of her on my chest, a cold draught where she'd been, an echo of her tiny heartbeat.

'She's eight weeks old.' My voice sounded scratchy, as though I hadn't used it for a long time. My old voice; the one that belonged to me before I met Patrick. 'Her name's Lily.'

'Lily.' Morag nodded her approval that I'd chosen her mother's name. 'I'm a great-aunt, then.'

'I … yes, I suppose you are.'

'Congratulations,' she said dryly. 'Does your mum know she's a gran?'

'No, not yet.'

Morag nodded again, as though it was what she'd expected. 'Go on then.' Her gaze was still on Lily. 'If you need to spend a penny.'

The old-fashioned saying tumbled me back to childhood. It was the sort of thing my grandmother Lily used to say. I crossed the room clumsily, bashing my knee on the corner of an ugly dresser pressed against the exposed-stone wall. The bathroom door was low and I had to duck through, pulling the light cord as I entered. The room was clean but basic; bottle-green and white ceramic tiles on the floor and walls, the toilet seat hard and cold beneath my thighs. The frame in the big square window above the old bath was loose, chilly air pushing through the gaps.

I washed my hands quickly and splashed my face with water at the basin before patting it dry with a faded green towel. I was trembling. There was a shaving mirror on the windowsill, angled so I could see my face. My muddy brown eyes looked enormous behind the reading glasses. I looked away and returned to where Morag was standing with Lily pressed to her shoulder, one large hand tracing circles on her back.

'I'll take her.'

As she handed Lily over, a spasm of torment crossed my aunt's face, gone so quickly I thought I must have imagined it. 'She looks like you.'

'You haven't changed much,' I said at the same time, refastening a popper on Lily's sleepsuit as I slotted her back into my arms. 'Your hair ...' I gestured to Morag's springy mop, still mostly jet-black but with iron-grey strands running through it. Her sun-browned face was scored with lines, deeper than I remembered. She wasn't tall, but stood straight-backed, heavy brows and a square set jaw giving her a forbidding air. Her dark, penetrating eyes seeming to look inside me. She was a more defined version of her sister, or maybe my mother was a less vivid version of Morag.

'You have,' she shot back. Her words were harsh, but I could tell they masked concern. 'Since when did you start wearing glasses?'

'I don't.' I pulled them off, blinking as the world shrank back to normal, feeling an ache behind my ears where the arms had pinched. I shoved them into the deep pocket on the front of my sweatshirt and took off the baseball hat, shaking my shoulder-length hair loose. The room tilted for a moment as a wave of dizziness overtook me. 'I was trying out a new image.'

Morag gave me a sceptical look. She must have a thousand questions. I tried to organise the jumble of words pushing up through my chest, but saw she was shaking her head.

'We can talk tomorrow.' She shrugged off her fleece-lined jacket and hung it on a hook by the door before easing out of her mud-encrusted walking boots to reveal blue woollen socks. Her feet were large, not dainty, like Mum's. 'You need food?' she said. 'Something to drink?'

'No, thank you. I ate on the way.' A stale croissant, I remembered now, picked up at the airport. Exhaustion rolled through me as the adrenaline that had flooded my bloodstream for the past twenty-four hours seeped away. 'Just sleep.' I was swaying, Morag a blurry figure in front of me.

She took the baseball hat from my fingers and hung it up with her jacket. Turning, she unexpectedly touched my hair, smoothing the ends through her fingers. I realised she was overcome with emotion. 'Still brown, then.' Maybe she'd expected me to have dyed it. 'You can have the crog loft,' she said gruffly. 'It's not much, but the bed's comfortable. I'll take the sofa.'

'Crog loft?'

'Bedroom in the loft space.' Her hand fell away from my hair. 'I thought you'd know that,' she said. 'Traditionally, the furthest area away from the cooking hearth.' It rang a distant bell from long-ago visits to my grandparents' Welsh home, but my brain felt like cotton wool. 'Be careful going up there with the little one.'

Holding Lily tightly, I followed Morag up the worn, wooden steps to a low-ceilinged room dominated by a wide bed loaded with pillows and blankets, a brightly coloured throw draped across the bottom. 'It's lovely.'

Morag's whole body seemed to soften as she turned in the cramped space to look at Lily, whose eyes were wide open as she gazed around. 'I don't have anything for the baby to sleep in.'

'She'll be fine in with me.'

'Really?' Morag sounded dubious. She had no idea that for weeks, I'd barely let Lily out of arm's reach, keeping her beside me in bed as I fitfully dozed.

'What if you fall into a deep sleep and roll on top of her?' Morag spoke bluntly, one hand on her hip. I'd forgotten that about her. How she tended to say whatever came into her head.

'I won't.'

'You might.' She turned to a heavy, mahogany dressing table carved with roses and tugged out the bottom drawer, emptying socks and sturdy knickers – mostly black and beige – onto the deep-pile rug. 'She can sleep in here.' She pulled a clean blanket from a chest at the foot of the bed, arranged it in the base of the drawer, laid a pillow lengthways on top and arranged a smaller blanket over that. 'This will do.'

'I don't—'

'I'll come up and check on her,' she interrupted. 'You need to sleep properly, Grace.'

'She'll want a feed in the night.'

'Do it now and get her settled.'

Morag's tone didn't invite argument. I felt myself surrender, grateful once more to be given instructions, feeling as if I was dreaming again as I handed Lily to Morag. I stripped to my underwear and climbed into bed, sinking against pillows as soft as clouds.

'Here we are.'

Aware of Morag watching, her expression unreadable, I took Lily back and hoisted up my vest. As she latched on to my nipple and suckled, my eyelids immediately drooped shut. I felt myself being dragged towards sleep. As Lily was lifted from me, I let myself sink deeper, limbs loosening, breath slowing.

My last waking thought was, *I'm home.*

Chapter 5

In the serene space between sleeping and waking, I heard comforting kitchen sounds downstairs. For a moment, I thought I must be at the house in Berkshire where I'd grown up, Mum making sure my father went to his office with a cooked breakfast inside him, preparing his coffee the way he liked it, strong with a heaped spoonful of brown sugar.

It had been a long time before I realised that preparing his breakfast, packing his lunch and cooking his dinner every day wasn't so much an act of love as a way of 'keeping him sweet' as my mother put it when I asked her once why Dad couldn't make his own meals. Andrew Evans had a temper and our role was to stop it emerging; though it didn't always work.

I stirred, feeling the tug of tiredness deep in my bones. Soft light poured through a rectangle of uncurtained window sunk into the wall above the chest of drawers. Prising my eyelids wider, I frowned at the gaping space in the chest. *Lily.* Sleep scattered as I bolted upright, pushing off the heavy blankets. My gaze scoured the drawer at the side of the bed, though I knew already she'd gone. There was barely a dent in the pillow-and-blanket nest Morag had created. What had I been thinking, letting my baby out of my sight and sleeping soundly for God knew how long?

'Lily!' I stood up too quickly. Everything spun. 'Where's Lily?'

'It's OK, she's here.' Morag's voice rose from below. 'She's fine.'

I rushed down the short staircase, turning at the bottom to face what could only loosely be termed a kitchen. Morag was perched on a three-legged stool at a wooden table that might have once been a door. 'She's sleeping,' she said, nodding at the bundle tucked inside her tartan dressing gown. Only a dusting of dark hair and the soft curve of a cheek was visible.

A bottle, half full of formula, stood on the table, Lily's changing bag open on the quarry-tiled floor in front of a stone fireplace with a heap of ash in the grate. No sign of any sterilising equipment, of course. Morag didn't have children, had no experience with babies.

'You should have woken me.' My voice was sharp with anxiety. 'The formula's for emergencies. I prefer to feed her myself.'

'She only took half.' Morag's eyes were like shards of granite as she studied me, standing there in my vest top and knickers, skin pimpled with gooseflesh. The kitchen was cold in the unheated room, my breath misting the air.

'I didn't hear her crying.'

'She wasn't.' Morag's tone was abrupt. 'I came up to check on her and she was awake. I thought I'd bring her down before she disturbed you.'

'Oh.' What must she think of me, standing there barely dressed, practically a stranger in her home, accusing her of … *what?* 'I'm sorry.'

'You talk in your sleep.'

'I do?' A fragment of a dream came back. *A woman yelling, the thud of someone falling, a pale arm flung out.* Pulse skittering, I rubbed my arms, resisting the urge to snatch Lily back as I sat gingerly on a spindle-backed dining chair. 'What was I saying?'

Morag's gaze was steady. '"Please don't, leave us alone", something like that.'

Nausea swirled through me. I swallowed, unsure what to say. 'What time is it?'

15

She glanced at an old Mariner's clock on the dresser. I vaguely recognised it from my grandparents' house. 'Just gone seven.'

'Lily never sleeps all night.' I rose and moved closer, unease sweeping through me.

'Maybe she was as worn out as you were,' Morag said. 'I changed her nappy; it was soaked.'

Nappy. I'd got used to calling them diapers. 'Thank you. I've got some nappy bags.'

'I know, I found them.' She looked at Lily again, still blissfully asleep, rocking her slightly. 'She's a good girl.'

'Yes, she is.' My stomach growled, heard plainly in the silence.

Morag rose, stool scraping on the tiles. 'Take her back to bed and I'll make you some breakfast.' She relinquished Lily with obvious reluctance, one weathered hand hovering after she'd placed the baby in my arms. Maybe she didn't trust me. I didn't exactly ooze maternal instinct, even if I felt it with every cell in my body. My heart had seemed to double in size the second I held Lily, but Morag probably remembered me announcing that I never wanted children, that they were a 'nuisance'. I'd had bigger plans for my life than being a mother. Yet, here I was.

'Thank you,' I said again, noticing half-moon shadows under Morag's eyes, a deepening of the grooves around her mouth. Had she stayed up all night, watching over us? I breathed in Lily as I kissed her velvet cheek, catching a trace of Morag under her milky, talcum-powder scent. 'If you're sure you don't mind.'

She'd already turned to the ancient-looking stove. I was relieved to see it was free from grease and grime and left her reaching for some eggs in a china bowl by the kettle as I retreated to bed. It was still warm where I'd lain and I settled down to feed Lily, overwhelmed with relief as my milk released.

Grace, please, don't do that.

Don't look if you don't like it.

'Here you go.' My eyes flew open, lashes damp with tears. 'I'll put it here.' Morag placed the tray she was holding on top of a heap of magazines serving as a bedside table, her dressing gown gaping to reveal a faded black Guns n' Roses T-shirt underneath. 'Come down when you're ready,' she said, eyes grazing Lily as she moved away as if checking she was OK. 'I've got fresh coffee.'

When she'd gone, feet padding softly on the stairs, I stared at Lily for a long moment. My chest was heavy with love and fear. Sometimes, they felt like the same thing.

The smell of buttery scrambled eggs and crispy bacon wafted from the plate by my side. I lowered Lily back into her makeshift bed, covering her gently. She curled her hand by her cheek and sighed softly, eyelids fluttering closed.

I watched her while I ate, shovelling food in quickly, uncaring it was lukewarm or that the toast was burnt on one side. I remembered Morag marvelling on a visit to my parents', before she was sent abroad by the paper she worked for, that I'd cooked a proper dinner, being 'hopeless' in the kitchen herself. Aged thirteen, I'd discovered the love of cooking that eventually led me to New York, and Patrick.

I wondered what he was doing now; whether he'd tracked me here, to this room in the eaves in a remote Welsh village in Snowdonia. He had the means – contacts, sources, money. He might not trust that I would keep quiet, despite my promise, and I'd given him every reason not to trust me. Even so, he was the one who'd broken his marriage vows. All I'd wanted was Lily, and to make a new life without him in it. As long as he let me do that, I would keep my side of the bargain; leave him free to pursue his dream of becoming New York District Attorney with his reputation intact. Curiosity burned inside me. What story would he spin? One that showed him in the best possible light, of course.

My mouth was suddenly dry and a chill swept through the room. Trying to hold on to the feeling of safety I'd had the night before, I swung my legs out of bed. Checking Lily was sleeping, I opened the suitcase Morag must have placed on the chest at the foot of the bed, and I pulled out some of the clothes I'd bought on my way to the airport – nothing like the dresses I used to wear, patterned with flowers or birds, worn with sandals and bare legs in summer and cardigans, thick tights and boots in winter. I wasn't that person anymore, and dresses were too frivolous for my new surroundings anyway.

I found my toiletries bag and rooted inside for my grand-mother's ring, left to me when she died – a thick gold band, set with a sapphire, that had belonged to her mother and which I'd always admired. It was too big for my narrow fingers, and I hadn't got round to putting it on a chain to wear, but I liked to keep it close.

'I'll watch her if you want to take a shower.' Morag's voice made me jump. I dropped the ring as her head appeared over the top stair, her gaze seeking out Lily. 'It's an old shower but the water's hot.' There was no apology in her voice for the lack of facilities. This place must be a palace compared to the hovels she'd stayed in during her years taking photographs in conflict zones.

'Thanks,' I said with a grateful nod. When she'd gone, I placed the ring on the dressing table, next to a cracked blue vase of dried lavender. There were no items of jewellery in little saucers on the dresser, no tubes of lipstick or foundation, or bottles of perfume; just a basic brush and comb set and a tub of moistur-iser for dry skin.

By daylight, the bathroom looked just as basic, the shower an attachment fixed to the tiles above the bath, but as promised, the water was hot and surprisingly powerful. As I cleaned myself with a slab of lavender-scented soap and supermarket own-brand shampoo, I felt some of the tension wash away with the grime of the last couple of days.

Wrapped in a scratchy grey towel that smelt of fresh air, I looked at the small heap of clothes on the toilet lid, realising in my hurry in Walmart I'd bought the wrong size. The olive-green hoodie was too big. I pulled it on anyway over clean underwear – glad

I'd thought to buy a maternity bra – with the jeans I'd worn the day before, and rolled up the cuffs. A glance inside a small airing cupboard by the washbasin revealed a stack of thick socks. I chose an incongruous pink-and-green striped pair, so unlike anything I usually wore that I instantly felt better – until I caught sight of myself in the mirror of the old-fashioned medicine cabinet on the wall. The hair Patrick once compared to the colour of chestnuts was almost black with water, hanging damply round my pale face, and the dark eyes I realised were the same shade and shape as Morag's had lilac crescents underneath.

I tilted my chin and pressed my fingers to the soft skin at my throat. The bruises had gone as if they'd never been there but if I closed my eyes, I could feel the imprint of fingers, smell the sour waft of coffee breath in my nostrils, sense the frustration in the clench of the hand closing around my windpipe.

My eyes snapped open. 'It's OK, you're safe,' I told myself, softening my jaw. 'You're safe now.'

Maybe if I said it often enough, I'd believe it.

Chapter 6

'Does he know you're here?'

I shook my head, not trusting myself to speak as Morag handed me a mug of freshly ground coffee. There was a gleaming cafetiere on the scarred wooden counter, beneath a pine-fronted cupboard on the wall.

She traced my gaze. 'Can't stand instant stuff. I grind the beans myself.'

I nodded, as if all I was capable of were head movements. I breathed in the fragrant scent of roasted beans as I took a sip, overwhelmed by a wave of gratitude.

'The baby's sleeping. I just checked.' Morag had seen me glance at the stairs, my ears attuned to the sound of Lily's cry.

'Thanks.' I dropped down on the three-legged stool, cradling my mug, disorientated by the awareness of how different everything was; how much had changed in twenty-four hours. Already, the flight from New York, Lily howling on my shoulder as I paced the aisle, had taken on the quality of a dream.

'I've got to drop off some produce,' Morag said, popping the bubble in my head that contained an image of the glossy kitchen, with its freestanding island, breakfast bar and enormous fridge-freezer, where I'd been just days ago.

'Produce?' I managed.

'I supply the pub and the local shop in the village with stuff from the garden.' Morag nodded towards the window. 'I run a market stall there on Wednesdays. It brings in extra money.'

'That's great.' It made sense somehow, even if it was a world away from her old career. Thinking of my aunt in Afghanistan with her camera, surrounded by horrors I'd never know or experience, made me feel small and silly, ashamed I hadn't made more effort to stay in touch, beyond the infrequent postcards that barely scratched the surfaces of our lives.

'I'm sorry for turning up like this, out of the blue.'

'How did you know where to find me?'

I hesitated. 'Mum.'

'I should have known Gail wouldn't keep it to herself.'

'I'm glad she told me.' I felt an urge to defend my mother, despite everything. 'I wouldn't have known where to go otherwise.'

As Morag's face unclenched, I saw a flash of the fondness I knew she'd felt for me when I was a child, before she went away and fell out with my mother.

'Was he violent?'

Her question caught me unawares. I blinked away a memory of Patrick's fist, a blur as he punched the wall by my head. 'He … he could be.'

'So that's a yes.' Morag leant against the sink. Sensing the anger coiled inside her, I felt a pinch of guilt that I couldn't be completely honest. 'Just like your father,' she said.

'No.' My protest was instinctive, even though the mention of him gave me a cold sense of dread. 'Dad wasn't violent, just … bad-tempered.'

Morag made an impatient noise. Unlike most people, she hadn't been taken in by my father's outward charm. By all accounts, she'd tried to put my mother off marrying him, but as Mum pointed out in a furious argument I'd overheard when

21

I was seven, she wouldn't have had me if she'd turned down my father's proposal.

'Is he likely to come looking for you, this man you're hiding from?'

I shook my head. 'He's got a high-profile job over there. In New York.' I realised she had little idea of what I'd been doing for the last twelve years. I doubted she'd been having cosy chats with Mum – not that I'd said much about my relationship with Patrick to her – and the last postcard I'd sent to Morag was before she moved to Wales; a generic snap of the Brooklyn Bridge with a few words about the heatwave on the back. 'Any whiff of scandal could end his career.'

'He's not the President, is he?'

I allowed a smile. 'Credit me with some taste.'

'Not enough, apparently.'

I flushed. 'I made a mistake,' I began, but she held up a hand.

'I'm not judging you, Grace. Believe me, we've all made those kinds of mistakes.'

'Even you?'

For a moment, I thought she wasn't going to answer, then: 'Even me.' She clearly wasn't going to elaborate, her face becoming shuttered. 'Does the baby have grandparents over there?'

I raised my mug, took another sip of coffee, wishing Lily would wake so I'd have an excuse to move from under Morag's gimlet gaze. 'His parents died a long time ago.'

'And it's definitely over?'

'Yes.' I forced myself to meet her eyes.

'Sounds like he got off lightly.'

'I just want a new start.' I couldn't mask the hint of desperation in my tone. 'A quiet life for Lily and me.'

'I get that.' Morag's eyes shifted as if seeing something unpleasant inside her head. 'If it's quiet you want, you've come to the right place.'

'We won't stay long,' I promised. 'As soon as I can find—'

'Stay as long as you need.' She was all action now, reaching for her jacket, pushing her feet into her boots, grabbing a small bunch of keys off the drainer by the sink. 'I know a few people,' she added. 'I'll bring back some things for the baby.'

'Oh.' I half-rose, panicked at the thought of her leaving, even though seconds ago I'd wanted to be alone. 'That's ... thank you.'

She was gone in a blast of cold air as the door opened then closed behind her, offering a glimpse of dense green trees against a delicate blue sky.

For a moment, I felt abandoned. I stared at the unvarnished slab of door, noticing several large bolts fixed to the top and bottom. It was hard to imagine intruders bothering to look this far off the beaten track but my aunt knew all about danger. The bolts must be a reflex, warding off any number of imagined scenarios. She could have PTSD for all I knew, after giving up her career out of the blue. *When it's too late to matter,* Mum had said, sounding hurt.

Coming back to myself, I shot upstairs to check on Lily. She looked as peaceful as she'd ever been in her flounced and fussy thousand-dollar crib in her expensively designed nursery, uncaring that her new bed normally held her great-aunt's sensible underwear.

Resisting the urge to pluck Lily out and strap her to my chest once more, I straightened the bedcovers then crossed to the window, catching my breath at the view of surrounding woodland and cloud-topped mountains, though the tip of Snowdon was invisible.

Below the window was a garden with neatly tended shrubs and bushes, a sizeable allotment, and a seating area beneath a pergola twined with greenery. It looked nicer outdoors than in and it wasn't difficult to guess where Morag spent most of her time, or where her 'produce' came from.

I felt a small shiver looking back at the trees. I found forests frightening, imagining witches and monsters lurking within, probably fired by my grandfather's tales of a five-thousand-year-old yew tree that grew in Conwy, its cleft trunk rumoured to be a portal to the world of the dead. According to mythology, the tree was associated with a spirit who foretold the names of parishioners destined to die at Halloween. I never liked that particular time of year, even now.

As I was about to turn away, something caught my eye: a wisp of smoke, curling above the trees into the sky. Campers, maybe. I watched for a moment but it had dispersed, if it was ever there. Perhaps I'd imagined it, spooked by the memory of the yew tree.

I reached for my bag on the floor by the bed and pulled out the cheap phone I'd bought with the rest of my disguise, leaving my old one behind. There wasn't much battery left. I found the charger and located a socket behind the heap of magazines, realising Morag had removed my breakfast things while I was in the shower. The magazines were old, all to do with gardening. I wondered whether she'd taught herself, had needed a new skill after she gave up her career. I couldn't recall her previously having much interest in anything horticultural, but remembered my grandfather growing prize-winning marrows and gigantic onions he was unashamedly proud of. I also remembered Mum being envious of Morag's close bond with their father.

As I plugged in my phone and switched it on, I wondered whether I was being pulled back to my childhood because I was in Wales, or because it was preferable to thinking about the recent past.

When my screen lit up, I wasn't surprised to discover there was no signal or Wi-Fi prompt. If Morag was living an almost reclusive life in Fenbrith, it made sense that she'd chosen to be uncontactable and virtually untraceable.

It was probably better I didn't look online, but a gnawing sensation nibbled at my edges. I wanted to know what Patrick had told people; how he would frame Lily's disappearance. Because of his campaign to be Manhattan's District Attorney, his private life was up for grabs, but maybe it was too soon for him to have made a statement. In a day or so, I would venture into the village and find a café; use the Wi-Fi there to look him up. I'd only be able to properly relax once I knew for sure he'd gone public with whatever story he'd concocted – one I prayed would put paid to him trying to find us.

Lily began to snuffle, tiny fist rubbing at her eyes. I scooped her from her makeshift crib, nestling her against my shoulder, the sweet scent of her filling my nostrils. 'You're such a good little peanut,' I murmured, rocking her gently. I'd worried the long flight would unsettle her completely, remembering her purple face as she'd howled during take-off and landing. I was terrified the pressure had damaged her delicate eardrums, but she appeared calm now, her wide-eyed gaze flickering around before resting on my face. Still, I would need to register her with a doctor.

With Lily in my arms, I moved downstairs, slamming a door in my mind on the memory of another staircase, much longer, with a woman's body lying at the bottom like a broken mannequin.

I stood for a moment in the kitchen, feeling lost, thinking with a pang of the job I'd loved and the people I'd left behind. Hard to imagine, now, the determination I'd had to own my own restaurant one day. How everything I'd been building towards since my first year in Manhattan had somehow led me back here – to the country where my mother and aunt were born.

As a distraction, I walked slowly around the room with Lily, taking it in. There wasn't much typical country-cottage charm, but it was comfortable in a rustic way. Perfect for one person.

My brain seemed to jolt when I noticed a man's thick coat hanging from the back of a wooden rocking chair. I hadn't considered that Morag might be in a relationship. It seemed so unlikely, given her previous lifestyle and the way she'd always dismissed marriage as an institution she had no wish to enter.

There was a copy of the *Times* on a wooden cask serving as a side table, indicating her desire to keep in touch with the outside world. It was open on the crossword page, most of it filled in.

The dresser against the wall was cluttered with mismatched china on its shelves, as well as bits of string, some scissors and bric-a-brac, an old-fashioned phone with press-buttons, like something from a museum, and a black and white photo of a smartly dressed couple standing in front of Big Ben. I'd seen the picture before, of my grandparents on a day trip to London.

Hanging beside the dresser was a framed souvenir map that must have belonged to my grandfather, who'd been in the Navy during the Second World War.

I wondered how Morag had ended up with her parents' things. She'd been in Afghanistan when my grandmother died, six months after my grandfather, and Mum had packed up their house, furious that her sister had 'got out of it'. My mother must have relented and saved some pieces for her.

There was a painting on the wall in the gap between the window and door. As I moved in for a closer look, trying to make out whether the horse in the scene was galloping away or towards the artist, I noticed a piece of paper wedged tightly between the canvas and wooden frame.

Adjusting Lily, her head resting on my shoulder as she sucked her fingers, I carefully pulled the paper out and unfolded it, one-handed. It was part of a letter, the paper yellowed and worn, creases distorting the writing, which was densely packed in faded black ink. I could just make out … *be together … love … understand … not my fault* and the letter *B* with one kiss beside it, running off the edge of the page.

Lily shifted and yawned.

'Shush,' I soothed, bouncing her as I guiltily refolded the paper and stuffed it back where I'd found it. It must be a letter to one of my grandparents, though *B* didn't fit either name. Maybe it was a love note to Morag.

Either way, it was none of my business.

26

Chapter 7

'Where did you get all this stuff?' I looked in astonishment at the array of baby paraphernalia filling the floor space in the living room. Apart from a padded baby bouncer, a white wicker Moses basket and a Mamas and Papas pushchair, there was a quilted changing mat, and a canvas bag filled with baby clothes. I dug a hand in and pulled out a tiny denim dress as Morag brought in a highchair and baby monitor. 'It all looks new.'

'Belonged to Annie,' Morag said. 'She runs the Carpenter's Arms with her husband Bryn. Their little girl is nearly four now.'

'But what if they have another baby?'

'No chance of that.' Morag's lips tightened and she didn't explain.

'There's so much.' I lowered Lily into the baby bouncer. 'It's too generous,' I said, strapping her in, touched that my aunt had gone to so much trouble. 'I should call and thank Annie.'

A flush stained Morag's cheeks. She seemed pleased by my response. 'No need.'

'I must give them some money.'

Her headshake was fierce. 'It's taken care of. I kept them supplied with food for free when they opened the restaurant, so they owed me a favour.'

My ears pricked up. 'Restaurant?'

'At the Carpenter's Arms. Nothing fancy, just good, home-cooked food with locally sourced ingredients. It's been very popular.' She glanced at Lily who'd instantly fallen asleep in the bouncer, lashes fanning her cheeks. 'Come and look around outside,' she said. 'The little one will be fine for a moment or two.' Morag had got the fire going earlier and reached over to put a guard around it before nodding to a pair of wellies tucked into an alcove by the door. 'They should fit you.'

I reluctantly pushed my feet into the boots, which were too big, before following my aunt through the front door with a backward glance at Lily.

Morag led the way round the back of the cottage to the garden I'd looked down at earlier. Despite a gentle breeze stirring the leaves in the surrounding trees, the air was soft with the promise of milder weather, scented with herbs from the pots that lined the path to the allotment. The smell of rosemary brought a memory of my last Sunday dinner as part of a family: roast lamb with all the trimmings cooked by Mum. My parents and grandparents and me, crowded around the dining table, the air filled with chat and laughter, a Fleetwood Mac CD playing in the background.

No one knew that, hours later, after everyone had gone home, Dad would find fault with everything my mother had done, lifting his fist as she cowered by the fridge, before he gripped his left arm and dropped to the floor, face twisted with agony as he suffered a heart attack. I was fifteen. He was forty-nine.

I stopped walking and wrapped my arms around my waist, cold again. I should have worn a coat. 'Why didn't you come when Dad died?' I hadn't known I would say it until the words flew out. 'We needed you.'

Your aunt cares more about strangers in other countries than she does about her own family, Mum had said when I asked if Morag was coming to the funeral. *She'll be glad he's dead.* I shivered at the memory of her words, remembering that my mother had been glad too, despite her tears.

'I couldn't have got back in time.' Morag turned to look at me, her eyes narrowed. 'And Gail never needed me.'

You're sisters, I nearly said. *Family.* But I'd left too in the end, desperate to escape. Maybe Morag and I had more in common than I thought.

'Anyway, she had a new lease of life once he'd gone.' Morag's unnerving stare didn't waver. 'Best thing that could have happened to her, him dying.'

My throat felt constricted. I hadn't talked about my father for years. I tried to suppress an image of him, dying in the kitchen in my childhood home. 'He was still my dad.'

'I know.' Morag's gaze thawed. 'He loved you in his own way, but you and your mum were always on eggshells around him and that's no way to live.'

She was right, and she didn't know the rest; how he'd read me a bedtime story sometimes, doing silly voices to make me laugh while Mum cried downstairs. He'd pulled her hair once, demanding to know why she'd had it cut. All I wanted was to go and cuddle her, but I'd smiled for Dad and hugged him instead, knowing if I didn't, he would go and shout at Mum and make her cry even harder. It was ironic, really, that I hadn't chosen a better father for Lily after vowing I wouldn't end up with a man like my father, whose idea of love was controlling my mother's moods and actions.

I tried to summon a reply to Morag's blunt assessment, but she'd turned away and was surveying the surrounding land.

'I wanted you to see that you're safe here,' she said, and it took me a second to grasp that the topic of my parents was over. 'Woodland all round, the nearest road half a mile away, mountains that way.' She pointed to the tip of Snowdon, visible now beneath a drift of cloud. 'The security light comes on at night if anyone ventures too close to the cottage.'

It was the most she'd said in one stretch since I'd arrived. She must only chat with people when she chose to these days; had been a woman of few words even before she and my mother fell out.

I remembered the man's coat on the back of the chair. 'Do you have a ... a partner?' I said, stuttering a little. 'A boyfriend?'

She huffed out a sound that might have been a laugh. 'No, I don't have a partner, or a *"boyfriend"*.' She arched her eyebrows, giving the word quote marks. 'I'm very happily single,' she said, but something in her expression had shifted and her eyes were guarded once more. She was either lying, or had been through something she didn't to talk about. 'Look!'

Her gaze moved past me and fixed on a clump of bushes beyond the allotment, close to where the trees began. She stepped back and gripped my arm. 'Can you see?'

I squinted my eyes and beyond a cluster of daffodils caught a flash of reddish fur slinking low to the ground, a flash of white at the tip of a bushy tail. *A fox.*

'She comes regularly.' Morag spoke in an excited whisper, eyes brighter now. 'She's quite tame but will be nervous to see someone new.'

'She?' I couldn't help smiling, even as the fox's gaze met mine, sharp and knowing. It was as if it could see inside my head and read my thoughts. 'How do you know?'

'She had cubs a few weeks ago, through there in the woods.' Morag pointed. 'I was gathering mushrooms and came across them. She's usually friendly but I thought she was going to attack me.'

'Protecting her young.' The vixen turned and slipped silently back the way she'd come. 'That's what mothers do.'

Morag swivelled her eyes to me. I forced a smile as I swung round to look at the building behind us. Its grey stone walls and pitched slate roof looked somehow forbidding from this angle. 'The smoke.' I pointed to the chimney. 'Someone could see. They'd know you're here.' *Know I was here.*

Morag folded her arms. 'I thought you said it was over?' She wasn't fooled. 'I don't want any trouble at my door.'

'It is over, but …' I couldn't articulate the feeling I had, that Patrick might have changed his mind. 'It is,' I said with more conviction. 'Take no notice.'

'I won't light it again if you don't want me to.' I was surprised by how easily she relented. 'I have an electric heater we can use.'

'Morag, I don't want to be a nuisance. I—'

'You're not.' Her tone was firm. 'I want you to feel at home.'

'Thank you.' I felt perilously close to tears again. I thought I'd done all my crying, but being here, released from the agony of the past few weeks, was making me emotional. 'I should check on Lily.'

'I'll go,' Morag said firmly. 'You have a wander about. You look like you need some fresh air.'

I wanted to protest, explain that I needed to watch Lily, that I longed to hold her and make sure she was OK, but something in Morag's face made me think she needed this – to help me, or be with Lily, or both – as much as I needed her. And I had to learn to relax, to not constantly cling to Lily twenty-four hours a day. It wasn't healthy for either of us. We were safe now. I could afford to let go a little.

'Fine,' I said, a tremor in my voice. 'Thanks.'

'She's a lovely little one. Like you were.' Morag strode back to the cottage, leaving me staring after her, overcome that Lily had someone apart from me to love and look out for her now. *Little one.* Guilt rushed in. Lily also had a grandmother. The last time I'd spoken to Mum, I told her I'd met someone, that I thought he might be the one. She'd been pleased, almost gushing – thrilled at the thought of her daughter living a different life to hers. *You must go,* she'd urged me, when my friend Ana invited me to spend the summer working in her uncle's restaurant in New York. *Go and live your life, Grace. Don't end up like me. Get away from here.*

After everything we'd been through together, after all the ways I'd tried to protect her from Dad, after … She wasn't the same

31

after he died. She hadn't needed me anymore, and I could barely look at her. Morag was right. She'd had a new lease of life, had taken on more hours at the animal rescue centre where she'd volunteered for a few years – the only 'work' Dad would allow her to do – eventually taking over the running of it when the owner retired. The animals became her life, the other volunteers her 'family'.

Thinking about her made my skin feel itchy. I decided to give myself a week to settle in, to be sure we really were safe, and then I would call her. Whatever had happened in the past, she had a right to know about Lily. She would want to, I was sure, though my mind shied away from telling her I was staying with Morag.

I forced myself to keep moving, focusing on the orderly rows of kale and cabbages, a crumbling stone wall green with lichen, and an ancient oak, its branches bursting with buds.

Ahead of me, a flock of startled birds exploded from the trees. I let out a yelp, clutching my chest as I strained my eyes at the dense greenery. A shiver moved down my spine. There was something; a dark flicker. And again: a subtle disturbing of the light, then an absence of something – or someone – that had been there a moment ago.

Blood rushing, I stared until my vision blurred, my breathing shallow. It was probably the vixen, checking to see whether it was safe to return, retreating when she saw me.

The woods could hide anything.

I kept looking, my heartbeat in my throat. Only when I was sure there was nothing there, that my imagination was working overtime – I hadn't acclimatised to being in the country after years of city living – did I turn and run back into the safety of the cottage.

Chapter 8

Inside, Morag was still in her boots and jacket, staring at Lily as if she was a rare specimen – which, to my aunt, she probably was.

As I stood in the doorway, fighting the feeling I'd had of being watched, I caught an expression on Morag's face I couldn't decipher; almost fearful, as though Lily might suddenly morph into a monster. Then she stooped, hands on knees, and I realised she was checking that Lily was breathing. I'd done it often enough myself, seeking the rise and fall of her chest, my cheek to her nose, waiting for the tickle of breath on my skin that told me she was alive.

Morag straightened but kept her gaze on Lily. 'I'm used to living alone,' she said, out of the blue. 'I'm not very good company.'

A band of heat crept across my neck. 'I don't want to get in the way.' I'd been an idiot to think this would work. Morag had been kind so far, taken by surprise and probably sorry for me – or, more likely, for Lily – but we couldn't stay. 'Maybe you could ask around, see if anyone has a room I could rent.'

Morag darted a look at me as she shuffled her jacket off. 'I already said, you can stay as long as you want.' She moved towards the kitchen. 'I'm just warning you, I'm not much of a talker and I don't like being reminded of the past. I prefer doing things my way and like to be left alone.'

'You don't say.' On a wave of relief, I had an impulse to make her smile. 'I wondered why you were living alone in the middle of nowhere.'

She turned, the corners of her mouth lifting in acknowledgement. 'Your mum was the chatterbox, the sociable one.' She threw her jacket onto the table before switching the kettle on. 'We were chalk and cheese,' she said, giving her head a tight shake. 'Seeing you …' she swung round to grab the mugs we'd used earlier, still stained with coffee '… you're a lot like her.'

I'd never thought so but didn't want to risk upsetting Morag by contradicting her. Instead, I busied myself by unpacking the baby clothes from Annie, holding up dresses, tiny jumpers and sleepsuits, in varying sizes, refolding them while Morag made tea with real leaves in a pot.

'I can cook,' I said, as she took a packet of biscuits from the cupboard.

'I know you can.'

I smiled, aware of my facial muscles moving. I hadn't smiled properly for so long. 'I mean, I can cook dinners for us to earn my keep, at least until I get a job.'

'You're welcome to cook.' Morag dunked a biscuit in her tea and ate half in one mouthful. 'But how will you work with the baby?'

I knew better than to presume Morag would want to babysit. Anyway, I didn't want to leave Lily after what we'd been through.

'Hopefully, I'll be able to take her with me.'

Morag's eyebrows twitched as if to say *good luck with that*, but I could almost hear the cogs turning and I knew she was thinking of a way to help.

Lily slept on as I sat on the sofa with my mug of tea, suddenly overwhelmed with curiosity regarding my aunt, about whom I knew very little, yet had thought of instinctively when I knew I had to escape Patrick. Not my mother, but Morag – her polar opposite.

'Do you ever miss your old life?' I looked around for evidence of the career she'd had for nearly three decades, realising for the first time that there were no pictures, no sign of the press award she'd won fifteen years ago for her photo of a weeping, blood-soaked woman on her knees in front of a collapsing building in Iraq, soldiers firing bullets all around her.

She always loved taking pictures, Mum had said on the phone, calling to tell me about the award after seeing a mention in one of the newspapers. *Why couldn't she stick to family portraits, or weddings, like normal people?* I'd asked her if she was scared Morag would be killed or injured – which seemed a reasonable thing to fear – but her reply was upsetting. *In some ways, it feels as if she's already dead.*

'I don't miss it at all.' As Morag's expression darkened, I remembered too late that she didn't want to talk about the past. 'There's no glamour in watching people suffer,' she said, snapping a biscuit in half. 'It took me a while to realise just how much I hated it, how little difference I was making. The medics, they were the heroes. I was just taking pictures.'

'But you brought the horror of what was happening to people's attention.'

'Fat lot of good it did.' She drained her mug in a long swallow and placed it in the sink. 'I've work to do in the garden.' She reached for her jacket. 'Make yourself at home.'

Rebuffed, I guiltily watched her leave. I sipped my cooling tea, one eye on Lily, and tried to empty my mind. The day yawned ahead. For the first time in a long time, I had nowhere to be, no one to see, no job to go to. Nothing to do but care for my little girl, who was happily oblivious to my presence for the time being.

As the echo of Morag's words faded, I let myself luxuriate in the feeling of freedom, congratulating myself for getting here. I'd done it. I'd engineered a fresh start, found a safe haven for Lily and me. My limbs flooded with warmth, an unaccustomed light-ness flowing through me. I wanted to pick my baby up and dance around the room with her. Instead, I made do with gathering her up as she woke with a lazy yawn. 'Hello, moonbeam.' I smiled as her eyes found mine. 'How do you like your new home?'

I wished I could talk to Ana and explain why I'd left so suddenly, but I was worried Patrick might seek her out, wanting to make sure I'd left for good. It was better that she didn't know the details, only that I missed my family and needed to start over, however implausible I knew she must have found my texted explanation.

Ana invited me to join her in America after I left Langley college, where I'd completed a hospitality and catering course. She had extended family out there and her uncle Julio had asked her to spend the summer working in his restaurant in Manhattan while she figured out what she wanted to do. There was a job for me too, if I wanted it. Eager to get away, I hadn't hesitated. Neither of us had returned since for more than a fleeting visit. *Until now.*

Lily was fussing, letting me know she was hungry. I settled into the corner of the sofa and lifted my top, curling my legs beneath me. Lulled by her rhythmic sucking and the warmth thrown out by the fire, my eyelids drifted shut. In an instant, I was back there, a year ago; the night Patrick came into the restaurant.

I'd been running the kitchen for a while by then and was trialling a new menu. At the end of the night, the maître d' said a customer wanted to meet me, to compliment the chef. I walked out and there he was, alone at a table in the corner. He rose as I approached, tall and broad with sparkling dark eyes, and thick dark hair I could imagine running my hands through, wearing tailored trousers with a crisp white shirt. I'd been on dates in the past, had nursed a crush on a colleague, but hadn't come anywhere close to settling down, focused on my career – on my dream of owning my own restaurant – but when Patrick offered to buy me a drink, his lips curving into a smile, I'd felt a spark of interest.

'To thank you for the best meal I've ever eaten,' he said. It was cheesy but it worked – until I spotted the platinum band on his wedding finger. 'Just a drink,' he added quickly, smile fading when he saw me looking. For reasons I still couldn't fathom – I didn't think I was the type to get involved with a married man – I said yes.

I declined a drink but sat with him at the table in the corner, the conversation flowing while the restaurant emptied around us. He was a successful lawyer, planning to enter the race to become the county District Attorney the following year. He was the youngest candidate, at thirty-eight, and in with a good chance of winning thanks to a well-funded campaign, and his stance on gun reform. He'd come in to the restaurant on impulse after a colleague had raved about the food, and because he was tired after working on a big case – and, he confessed sheepishly, to avoid going home. In a spirit of confession, perhaps induced by two glasses of bourbon, he told me he'd married too young but had invested too much to walk away. He and his wife Elise owned a two-million-dollar house on East 71st Street, bought for them by her wealthy parents as a wedding gift, but their plan to fill it with children still hadn't happened after ten years of marriage.

'It's complicated. Maybe I just need a good enough reason to leave.'

Two hours later, he was in my bed in the apartment above the restaurant, and for the next two weeks, whenever he could get away, he would sneak up there after I'd finished work. Looking back, it was as if we'd regressed to being teenagers, madly in love with the idea of being in love. We couldn't be seen together because he was married, and if he was to achieve his dream of becoming DA, he couldn't be involved in anything potentially scandalous.

Maybe I thought on some level it would work itself out and we'd have a fairy-tale happy-ever-after, and maybe he did too, but it ended the evening he phoned the restaurant and told me Elise was pregnant.

'It must have happened during a trip to her sister's in Canada, a month ago.' Hearing how elated he sounded, wanting me to be happy for him, a door slammed shut in my mind. 'We'd given up trying,' he said, as though I was an old friend he wanted to share the news with. As if he hadn't told me in some detail about his wife's flaws – how she'd suffered two miscarriages in the past, that her chances of carrying a child full-term were small, that she was showing signs of liver damage from years of drinking – that she had a terrible temper when she was drunk. I'd resisted looking her up online after that first night with Patrick. I hadn't wanted to make her real, but felt I had a clear picture of her from everything he'd told me. Still, he was going to stay and make their marriage work, now that she was pregnant. He hoped I would understand. He thought I was special, he'd loved our time together, but he desperately wanted a family. He owed to his wife, his unborn child – and his future career, of course – to stay.

'I understand,' I said, because what else was there to say? 'I'm happy for you both.'

My eyes snapped open, the past receding in a flash. Something had disturbed me. The faintest sound, like the shuffle of feet on tiles.

Heart beating fast, I unlatched Lily who snuffled a protest and nuzzled my breast as I craned my neck to look around. I sensed that someone had been watching me, but it wasn't possible. The only way into the cottage was through the door Morag had walked out of and it was closed, the room empty. And yet … there was a faint scent in the air; something woody, grassy, as if the outdoors had been brought in.

I tugged my jumper down and sat Lily up, so I could rub her back. My pulse was racing. Stupidly, I wondered whether the cottage was haunted, another of my grandfather's stories coming back to me. There'd been a haunting – so rumour persisted – at the church where he married my grandmother. The ghost was a jilted bride who'd killed herself and stalked up and down the aisle, trailing chilled air and the scent of lilies. But I didn't believe in ghosts. A mouse then? More likely in an old building surrounded

38

by woodland. For a moment, I yearned for the city, the sounds of traffic, of people – my old life. Then I remembered why I'd left. I had to get used to different noises here and shake off the suspicion that Patrick might not have kept a flimsy promise to let us go.

As silence settled, I held Lily close, kissing her cheek and breathing in the scent of her scalp as she dropped her head on my shoulder. 'Silly Mummy,' I murmured, patting her back. My gaze scanned the room and the back of my neck prickled. I'd missed it before. The bathroom door, which I'd closed after my shower, was wide open.

*

He cursed himself for getting so close. For a second, he'd thought she must have seen him, just like the fox had earlier, scurrying past with a shifty glance in his direction.

Curiosity had got the better of him when he heard their voices. They probably didn't realise how far sound carried out in the open when the wind was blowing in the right direction, or when the air was still.

For someone like him, with his particular skill set, it wouldn't be difficult to stay hidden for as long as he wanted; to watch and wait. To find out more, before the time was right to make himself known.

It wasn't easy to drop out of existence these days, to disappear without a trace like he had. She'd done a good job. It had taken time and hard work to find her. Now he had, he wasn't going to rush in, guns blazing, risking everything.

She probably thought she'd never be traced out here, to the middle of nowhere, where there wasn't even a decent phone signal. It had been a challenge, even for someone with his exceptional tracking abilities, but he was here.

He wouldn't report back yet, though. He was enjoying himself too much, muscle memory kicking in – the thrill of the chase.

He moved a little closer. It was getting harder to stay hidden. Part of him wanted her to know he was there, to kick the door down, announce his presence.

To let her know she'd been found.

Chapter 9

I stopped myself from running out to ask Morag whether she'd used the bathroom after me, knowing how it would sound. It was the obvious explanation for why the door was open. Either that or a gust of air had pulled it ajar when Morag went outside. Even so, I couldn't sit still after checking the bathroom was empty, or throw off the feeling that someone's eyes had been on me. Once I'd changed Lily's nappy and settled her down, I decided to cook lunch, foraging through the fridge and cupboards for ingredients. Cooking was the only activity guaranteed to focus my mind.

'Have you thought about getting a dog?' I asked Morag, once we were seated at the table, thinking how easy it would be for someone to sneak up to the cottage during the day.

Morag looked up from examining her plate. 'Funny you should ask.' She dug a fork into her mushroom risotto. 'I was talking about that very thing at the pub a couple of nights ago.'

'Really?' I could hardly hide my surprise at the coincidence.

'Bryn said his uncle was asking if anyone wanted a sheepdog that hasn't taken to working on the farm.' I remembered Bryn was Annie's husband, the couple who owned the Carpenter's Arms. 'I said I'd think about it.'

'And are you?'

41

Morag ate a mouthful of risotto, pushing back the lock of hair that fell across her forehead. 'I thought it might be too much responsibility,' she said when she'd swallowed. 'I'm not like your mother, treating animals like children.'

I felt compelled to defend Mum again. 'She's done a lot of good at the rescue centre.' Maybe she'd been right to say Morag felt superior because her line of work was more important than protecting sick and unwanted animals.

'Exactly.' Morag's heavy eyebrows rose. 'Better than I ever did in my career.' Shock mingled with sadness. Her words were so heartfelt, I knew she meant them. I doubted Mum had any idea her sister felt that way. 'Gail has more patience than I do.' Morag dabbed the corners of her mouth with a sheet of kitchen roll. 'Still, at least Skip's a fully grown dog and doesn't need training.'

It seemed a good sign that she'd called the dog by his name. 'So, will you take him on?'

'I've seen him at the farm a few times,' she said. 'He's got a fierce bark.'

'Good for scaring people away.'

'You said that man wasn't coming after you.' Her eyes thinned. 'Has something happened?'

'No, it's not that,' I said quickly. 'It's just, out there ...' I looked at the window, where only small flashes of the sky were visible among the thicket of surrounding trees. 'It would be extra security, that's all.'

Morag's shoulders relaxed. 'We'd have to be careful with the baby.' Her eyes swivelled to Lily lying on a blanket on the sofa, curling and uncurling her fingers in front of her face. 'She couldn't be alone with a dog around.'

'Of course not.' I thought of Skip and his fierce bark and something loosened inside me.

Patrick was scared of dogs. He'd been badly bitten as a child by a neighbour's Dobermann. His calf bore a jagged scar where the dog's teeth had ripped his flesh. He'd needed stitches that became infected, requiring a stay in hospital. 'Something like that never leaves you,' he'd said when I traced the scar with my fingertips. 'I still can't be around dogs.'

'My mother wouldn't understand. She prefers animals to humans these days,' I'd told him.

As far as I could remember, it was the only time I'd mentioned my mother. Maybe I'd known even then our relationship wouldn't last, that it was better to hold things back. But if he talked to Ana ... I switched off the thought. Ana knew things had gone bad with Patrick, even if she didn't know the whole story. She wasn't stupid. They wouldn't be sharing any little chats, despite her early optimism that I might have found someone worth cutting down my hours at the restaurant for.

'I could pick up the dog today.' Morag's voice brought me back to the moment. 'He's used to living outside.'

Disappointment flowed through me. 'Oh, that's a shame. It would be nice—'

'He can't be in here.' Morag's tone brooked no argument. 'This place is too small to accommodate another body.'

'OK.' It was probably better that way. No one approaching the cottage would be able to get past the dog without us knowing about it. 'How do you call for help?' I said, voicing a worry that had been niggling at me. 'I mean, if you fell and broke your ankle, for instance.' We both knew that wasn't what I meant. 'You should get a mobile phone and keep it with you.'

'I don't need a mobile, I've got the landline.' Morag nodded at the ancient phone on the dresser.

I remembered calling her, the novelty of punching in an area code. Even Mum favoured using her mobile these days. At least there was a way to call the police if necessary. Which it wouldn't be.

He doesn't know where I am.

We ate in silence, the only sound our forks on plates and an occasional *ahh-goo* from Lily that made Morag's features soften and both of us smile.

43

'That was good,' Morag said when she'd finished, nodding her satisfaction. I thought she might ask how'd I'd learnt and prepared to tell her that Ana's uncle had taken me under his wing once he realised I loved to cook, leading me from food preparation to sous-chef in the steamy, stainless-steel kitchen of *Julio's*. How, despite the punishing shifts, the accidents – almost slicing off my thumb, spilling boiling water on my wrist – with barely time to sleep in the cluttered apartment above, which I shared with Ana and one of the waitresses for a couple of years, I knew I'd found my calling. How I eventually had the freedom to create my own menus, sourcing fresh ingredients from local suppliers, and was getting great feedback from customers, and glowing reviews like the one that brought Patrick to the restaurant that night.

But Morag didn't ask. She scraped her chair back, put our plates in the sink and ran hot water over them before reaching for her jacket once more. 'I'll see you later,' she said, leaving without further explanation.

Once more, I was left alone. Before Patrick, I was used to being around people, had loved the hum and chatter of work, the banter in the kitchen. There wasn't much time to socialise, but I'd got on well with everyone at the restaurant and enjoyed having a drink with Ana, or with the staff at the end of a shift, dissecting the day's events before slipping upstairs to plan menus, or unwinding with something on Netflix.

There was no television in the cottage, just a transistor radio shoved to the back of the countertop in the kitchen. When I turned it on, I discovered it needed new batteries.

How did Morag stand it? I'd always thought I was comfortable with my own company but realised now I'd rarely been alone.

After searching the cupboards of the dresser, I unearthed some battered board games that had come from my grandparents' house, and a pack of playing cards, but I wasn't in the mood for solitaire. I tidied the living room instead, shifting the baby items Morag had brought so they didn't dominate the tiny space, keeping up a running commentary to Lily as I placed her in the bouncy chair.

'This place is a lot smaller than you're used to isn't it, sweetheart? At least it's clean.' 'I wonder what your great-auntie does in the evenings.' 'Aren't you lucky, having all these nice new things?' 'Shall I fetch your teddy?' It was the only toy I'd packed; a small stuffed teddy holding a padded heart with her name on that Ana had bought her, and a cloth book I'd picked up in Walmart.

While Lily tracked a pattern of sunshine on the wall, legs pumping with excitement, I ran upstairs to check my money was still in the pocket of my suitcase. I couldn't quite rid myself of the image of a figure searching my belongings, however impossible it seemed.

Just because you're paranoid doesn't mean they aren't after you. Dad used to say that to Mum sometimes. He'd had a quote for most occasions, his favourite being *Don't let the buggers grind you down,* even though it was what he'd done to her.

The money was there, the notes reassuringly smooth in my fingers. Enough to last a while if my outgoings were low, though I intended to pay my way while I was here.

I knelt and pushed my case back under the bed, then pulled it back when it hit something. Bending, I peered into the dusty space, and to my astonishment saw that it was an air rifle. Stretching my arm under the bed, I tentatively pulled it out, recognising it immediately. It had belonged to my grandfather. He let me use it once when I was eleven, showing me how to shoot an orange on top of a barrel on a patch of land near their home. Mum had been horrified when she found out, especially as the recoil left me with bruising on my shoulder, which I'd worn like a badge of honour.

Standing up, I weighed the rifle in my hands, testing its weight. How had I even lifted it back then? I broke the barrel open. It was loaded with a pellet. Did Morag have it for sentimental reasons or protection? *None of my business.* I hastily closed the barrel and thrust the rifle back under the bed.

A howl from below brought me to my feet. *Lily.* I almost fell in my rush to get down the stairs, but she was quiet when I got there, one hand clutching the air. The teddy, which I'd propped beside her, had slipped to the floor.

'Here it is, here it is.' My breath came fast as I slipped it back, looking around as if expecting to see someone duck into the bathroom. 'This is silly,' I said in a jolly tone. Lily studied me, eyes wide, as if attuned to my mood. I forced a smile. The last thing I wanted was for her to pick up on my anxiety. There'd been enough of that since she was born.

'Let's go for a walk,' I said brightly. I couldn't stay in the cottage. I had no idea when Morag was coming back and it wasn't fair to expect her to entertain us. 'I can show you some of the country where your aunt grew up.'

My hands trembled as I dressed Lily in the fox-patterned all-in-one I'd brought with us, pulling the fleecy hood up over her hair before plucking the man's coat from the back of the rocking chair and sliding my arms into the sleeves. It smelt familiar, of soap and tobacco, and I realised it was my grandfather's; the one he was wearing in the black and white photo on the dresser. His 'best' coat, the charcoal silk lining worn but intact. For someone who professed to have no interest in the past, Morag was surrounded by it.

Once Lily was strapped in her carrier, she gave a squawk of delight that lightened my heart. It would be good to get out, do something normal, breathe air rich with oxygen instead of traffic fumes. I'd reacquaint myself with the weather, which could turn from sun to rain in a heartbeat. Maybe we'd see the fox.

I stepped outside and closed the door then paused. I didn't have a key. I couldn't leave the cottage unsecured, but couldn't face staying inside now I'd made up my mind to go out.

Bending awkwardly, I checked beneath a couple of plant pots to see if there was a spare. Morag was probably too safety-conscious to leave a key somewhere so obvious, but it was frustrating to find nothing there.

'Looks like we won't be going far.' I nudged the plant pots back into place. Ignoring a niggle of unease, I skirted the side of the garden and carefully made my way up a grassy bank at the farthest side of the cottage, pointing out clutches of buttercups and daisies to Lily. Her head was tipped back, her gaze widened on the view above, where clouds raced across the bright blue sky. 'Birds,' I said, pausing to point out a circle of darting starlings – or maybe they were sparrows. There were a lot of sparrows in Manhattan, and I'd once spotted a jay in the yard at the back of the restaurant, but it had been hard to hear birdsong over the cacophony of car horns, roaring planes, rattling trains and buses. Here, there was nothing to dim the joyful sound.

After cresting the bank, I walked on, enjoying the flex in my thigh muscles, but the unkempt grass seemed to stretch forever, with only more wild grass and towering trees ahead. The mountain view was as distant as ever and as Lily cooed and gurgled, I began to falter. I couldn't get lost. I hadn't thought to bring my phone, or any provisions for Lily. *What was I thinking?* Despite flashes of sunlight between the scudding clouds, the air had a chilly bite and Lily's cheeks were pink. I had to go back.

Turning, I half-ran in the direction I'd come, hands cradling the carrier so as not to jig Lily too much, my breath huffing out in bursts. 'It's OK, baby, we're nearly there.' I wondered whether she could feel the bump of my heartbeat.

As I carefully descended the bank, I caught a movement in my peripheral vision and froze as a figure came round the side of the cottage. Fear blocked my throat. A man was standing there, staring at me, a skinned rabbit dangling from each hand.

Chapter 10

As I scrambled closer, aware no one would hear if I screamed for help, the man spoke.

'*Rhaid mai chi yw'r nith.*' His voice was gruff, the words indecipherable.

'I don't speak Welsh.' It came out high-pitched. 'Who are you?'

'A friend of Morag's.' As he stepped closer, my arms closed more tightly around Lily. 'Ifan Jones.' His words were spiked with a heavy accent. 'You must be her niece.'

'How do you know that?'

The man's weather-beaten face split into a friendly grin. 'Word travels fast around here,' he said. 'I know your aunt was in the pub this morning, gathering things for the little 'un from Annie.'

'Right.' *He was a local, not a threat.* I took in his tall stooped figure, the collar-length, silver-streaked hair and wiry beard, the piercing blue eyes set beneath straggly brows. He wore a faded donkey jacket over stained overalls tucked into muddy black boots, but his teeth were white and his manner somehow assured. He looked about Morag's age, maybe a bit older.

'I told your aunt I'd drop these off for dinner.' He held up the rabbits but then became still, as though sensing my wariness.

48

'Apparently, you can cook.' His smile broadened. 'I wanted to meet the niece everyone's talking about.'

His words pierced me like an electric shock. I knew my presence in a place like this was unlikely to go unnoticed but hadn't expected people to be gossiping already.

'What are they saying?'

'Not much.' Ifan's ragged eyebrows knitted together. 'She's happy to see you, is all. Buzzing, she was, this morning by all accounts.'

'Well … that's good.' My mind reeled through my internet presence. If anyone looked me up, they'd find me linked to articles about the restaurant, which also had Facebook and Instagram pages dotted with pictures of me in the kitchen, and arty close-ups of plates of food. Nothing personal. I wasn't a big user of social media, had never been one to post selfies or keep the world updated with my daily thoughts and activities. There were no pictures of me in a couple, just the odd photo that Ana would tag me in from time to time, having a drink with the restaurant crew after hours, or on the beach at Coney Island on a rare day off.

There was nothing online to tie me to Patrick.

'I'm sorry,' I said, realising the man – Ifan – was waiting for me to speak. 'My aunt's not here right now.'

'Sorry if I scared you.' He waved an arm so the rabbit he was holding swung in an arc. I was glad Lily's face was averted. This wasn't the kind of wildlife I'd envisaged her seeing. I wasn't squeamish about meat, was in favour of the customer knowing its journey to the plate, but I'd never cooked rabbit – something to do with *Watership Down* and feeling sentimental about them. 'You've nothing to fear,' he added.

If you only knew. 'Does Morag mind you being here while she's out?' Maybe he had a spare key, was used to letting himself in.

'She trusts me.' There was a pulse of silence while we weighed each other up. 'I get it,' he said at last, raising his shoulders. 'You don't know me from Adam. I'll go away and let you get on.'

49

Something about his openness, his willingness to back off, made up my mind. I was a normally a good judge of character – or had been, before Patrick – and Ifan seemed decent.

'We've just been for a walk and got a bit cold,' I said, stepping past him to open the door. 'Come in and have a hot drink.'

By the time Morag returned, we'd worked our way through a pot of tea and the rest of the biscuits. After finding a plate to put the rabbits on and sliding it into the fridge before scrubbing his hands, Ifan had bonded with Lily.

'Reminds me of my daughter Rhiannon with those big eyes,' he'd said, holding Lily with ease, chuckling when she smiled, her fists punching the air. 'Now my Rhiannon's expecting a babby herself.'

He chatted easily, telling me about his three grown-up children, how he still missed his wife who'd died six years ago. He talked about the gamekeeping job he'd done for nearly thirty years and loved, before bringing me up to speed with village life, which sounded like something out of a film set in gentler times, when people looked out for each other and community was everything. 'You'll be welcome in Fenbrith,' he said. 'Practically one of us.'

I was happy to listen, letting his words wash away my tension, content to sit, bouncing Lily in her chair with my foot, relieved she seemed content.

Ifan asked me about myself but didn't push it when I said I'd come to Morag's for a fresh start and was focusing on the future. 'Your aunt's a bit of a mystery too,' he was saying, just as she walked through the door, trailed by a prancing black and white dog wagging its tail, tongue hanging out of its mouth. Ignoring Morag's half-hearted command to stay outside, he instantly sat at Ifan's feet and looked at him adoringly.

'Hey, you.' He ruffled the dog's silky head while Morag rolled her eyes.

'I'm regretting this already,' she said, seeming unsurprised to see our visitor. I guessed Ifan must drop by often and I wondered whether they were more than friends, despite her insistence that there was no man in her life. 'He won't do a thing I say.'

'He's a big softie,' Ifan said, letting the dog lick his chin. 'I've seen him up at the farm. Terrible work dog, but he'll be a good pet.'

'Just what I didn't want.' Morag looked so rattled I couldn't help laughing.

'He's gorgeous.' I crouched to pluck Lily from her bouncy chair before sinking my hand into Skip's soft fur. When he squirmed with pleasure, I felt a rush of warmth. I'd longed for a pet, growing up. 'Look, Lily, it's a doggy.'

Skip tipped his head to one side as if weighing her up and Lily eyed him solemnly then waved her arms.

'He likes you.' Tears pricked my eyes. Patrick was missing this. He'd never hear Lily's first word, see joy spread over her face, watch her take her first step; bank memories, like I was. He wouldn't take her to school, read her a bedtime story or comfort her when she cried. One day, I'd have to explain about him.

For a split second, the enormity of it struck me like a punch. Then I remembered the look on his face the first time he saw her; the quickly concealed disappointment. The way he'd hand her back after a cursory cuddle, claiming he couldn't stay long because he had an important meeting. *He didn't deserve to be Lily's father.*

Morag grabbed Skip's collar and attempted to heave him towards the door. He resisted with a mournful look until she let go, shaking her head as Ifan chuckled at her efforts. 'I bet my friend here gave you a fright, turning up out of the blue,' she said to me. 'I should have warned you he might pop round, but I'm out of the habit of telling anyone my business.'

It wasn't a dig, just a matter of fact. 'It's OK.' I didn't want her to think she had to modify her routine for me. 'We've been getting on like a house on fire. He brought rabbits.'

She nodded. 'Think you're up to making a casserole?'

'Sure.' I sensed she was subtly showing me off – *this is my niece, she's a chef* – and was moved again as I remembered Ifan's comment about her buzzing that morning, talking about my visit at the pub. 'I've never cooked rabbit before but I'll do my best,' I said, not looking forward to it.

'Were you planning on going somewhere?' She'd noticed Lily's outdoor clothes discarded on the sofa next to my grandfather's coat.

'We took a ... went for a walk.' I hoped I'd lose the little Americanisms I'd picked up. 'I couldn't find a key to lock up, so we didn't go far, then Ifan arrived and I invited him in.'

He was watching our exchange, one large hand resting on Skip's back.

Morag pursed her lips. 'I should have told you I keep a spare underneath the plant pot outside. What?' she said to Ifan when his eyebrows rose. 'I don't tell anyone that, not even you.'

'Well, now I know.'

'I looked under both plant pots.' I adjusted Lily in my arms. 'There was no key.'

It wasn't until Morag tensed her shoulders that I realised how relaxed she'd been, despite the dog's refusal to obey her. 'Are you sure?'

'Positive.' I looked at Ifan, suddenly uncertain. 'Maybe I knocked it out of sight.'

'Let's look again.' Ifan got to his feet, the bulk of him blocking the light from the window. We followed Morag to the door, Skip panting at our heels.

'Are you sure you looked properly?' Morag crouched and lifted the nearest pot.

I joined her, holding Lily tight, aware once more of the denseness of the trees bordering the land around the cottage. A rash of goose bumps rose on the back of my neck as I saw what Morag was holding between her forefinger and thumb. A small brass key, dulled with age and rimmed with earth, as if this was the first time it had been plucked from its hiding place. 'You can't have looked very hard,' she said. 'It was right there all along.'

Chapter 11

I couldn't be sure the key hadn't been ground into the soil and I'd missed it in my haste. I said nothing, suppressing a shiver.

'I'd better be off.' Ifan nodded at Skip hovering in the doorway as if worried that once he was outside, he'd never be let back in. 'At least you have this beast to protect you.' He let out a low laugh, shaking his head as he loped around the side of the cottage to where he must have parked a vehicle. The cottage was a long walk from the village unless he knew a shortcut.

'I reckon he knows something about this dog that I don't.' Morag eyed Skip with suspicion before turning her gaze on me. She seemed satisfied there'd been a misunderstanding about the key. 'You'd better hang on to this,' she said, handing it over. 'You OK?' Her dark eyes searched my face until I had to look away.

'I'm fine.' Pushing the key in my pocket, I glanced at the sky, which had darkened to a gunmetal grey. In the distance, a light mist shrouded the mountain tops. 'I'm just getting used to everything.' I mustered a smile. 'Still a bit jet-lagged, I think.'

'Looks like the baby needs a feed.' Face relaxing, she glanced to where Lily was snuffling at my chest, hand fidgeting with my top. 'I'll take her upstairs,' I said, glad to be back inside as the heavens opened and rain began falling in sheets. 'After I've fed her, I'll make a start on dinner.'

*

Upstairs, I shuffled back on the bed, needing to rest my head while Lily fed hungrily. Smiling, I studied her face, letting the fact of us being here sink in. Recalling the fright that Ifan had given me earlier, I shook my head. Something about him reminded me a little of my grandfather and I wondered whether Morag felt it too.

My gaze moved around the room, to the heavy beams overhead, the rough-stone walls unadorned with pictures or photos, the uncurtained window. The light had shifted but the effect was cosy, the patter of rain on the roof timeless and soothing. It reminded me of the time I came down with a cold while staying with my grandparents one wet summer. My grandmother had made a fuss of me, tucking me into their squashy bed, bringing warm milk and the television for me to watch.

As my eyes raked the dresser for the ring I'd left there that morning, I noticed a slip of paper lying on the floor. *A receipt?* Once I'd burped Lily and she was drowsing, I laid her on the duvet and swung my legs off the bed. Bending, I picked up the paper and held it to the window. Not a receipt; a note. As I read the roughly written words, fear whipped through me.

Keep her close. Anything could happen.

A chill stretched from my stomach to my heart. The scratchy words, written in blood-red ink, looked vaguely familiar. *What did it mean?* It had to be about Lily.

I leant across the dresser, pushing my face to the window as if the culprit might be out there, waiting to see my reaction. My vision was distorted by the rain-glazed glass, but I could see the wind had strengthened, lashing the tree tops, while crows circled the bank of dark clouds above. Everything was moving,

54

apart from … I looked harder, trying to see. *There*, between the trunks of two tall pines. I narrowed my eyes, heart bouncing off my ribcage. Was someone standing there, completely still? My breath misted the glass and I wiped it with my sleeve. Training my gaze on the same spot, I searched for a face. *Nothing.*

A hot wave of panic rolled through me. Had Patrick sent someone to frighten me after all? Make sure I stayed under the radar? If so, he must have planned it the second I left. Was this just the start? *But why?* I'd made a promise I intended to keep and thought that he had too. Had I completely misjudged him?

Moving away from the window, I unfolded the paper with trembling fingers and read it again. *Keep her close. Anything could happen.* A warning. Fear mushroomed. Someone had been inside the cottage. They'd come upstairs and left the note, which must have fluttered to the floor. *Someone had let themselves into the cottage while it was empty.* I doubted it was Patrick, he wouldn't – couldn't – risk being here. But he knew people – bad people. Or maybe he was crazed with grief and not thinking straight, but … no. That wasn't Patrick's style. I turned to check Lily, scrunching the note in my fist as if she might open her eyes and be able to read it.

'OK up there?' At the sound of Morag's voice, I gave a muffled screech. 'Grace?'

'I've got a headache,' I called back, dropping down on the bed. My limbs felt watery, my heart skittering in my chest. 'I think I'll take a nap.'

There was a pause, as if Morag could hear the tremor in my voice and was debating whether to come up, but to my relief, she simply said, 'Good idea. I'll take the dog out.'

Once the door had closed behind her, I ran down and tossed the piece of paper into the fire, watching it blaze and burn. When it was ash, I returned to the bedroom and lifted Lily into my arms. I squeezed her to me, stroking her hair. 'It's going to be OK,' I murmured, looking into her sleepy chocolate-drop eyes. 'I promise I won't let anything bad happen to you.' Her eyebrows twitched. She looked like she didn't believe me.

*

After bringing up Lily's Moses basket and laying her down to sleep, I tidied the room in a frenzy of activity, trying not to think about the note as I pushed the drawer back in the dresser and tossed my aunt's underwear in. When I'd finished, my energy was drained and I lay down on the bed, waking later with a jerk. Against the odds, I'd nodded off. Swinging onto my side, I stared at Lily in her basket in the fading light. She was napping on her back, her tiny hands curled into fists by her cheeks. *How long had I slept?* I couldn't hear Morag downstairs and sensed the cottage was empty. The gleam of a lamp in the living room bathed the ceiling in an apricot glow. Shifting my head, I saw a piece of paper on the bedside pile of magazines. I sat up with a feeling of dread and squinted at the neat, pencilled words. *Didn't want to wake you. Gone to the pub. Soup in the fridge if you're hungry. Dog's been fed. M.*

My thoughts leapt in time with my heartbeat. Was the door locked? What if whoever had left the previous note came back? Then I remembered the dog. Skip would bark a warning. Morag wouldn't have taken him with her.

I lay back down, stiff with tension.

It was evening, judging by the darkening sky through the window. There was no point getting up and cooking rabbits. The thought made my stomach turn. No point going downstairs at all; no TV, no radio, no internet. None of the usual trappings of entertainment to distract me. I could read one of the books I'd seen on the shelf downstairs, but found I didn't want to leave the sanctuary of my bed. And Lily looked so peaceful, like a little doll, her lips slightly parted as she huffed air in and out. I longed to pick her up and snuggle her against me but decided not to disturb her.

A clatter on the stairs made my heart bounce. Skip appeared at the side of the bed and looked at me with shining brown eyes.

'Hello, boy.' I held out a hand, which he took as a sign to leap on top of the covers, curling into the curve of my body with a sigh. He smelt faintly of biscuits, his warmth like a safety blanket. 'Sweet boy,' I murmured, my body finally relaxing.

I burrowed my fingers in the fur at his neck and tumbled into a dreamless sleep.

*

'You should come to the village today. I'll introduce you,' Morag said over breakfast the following morning. 'You can't stay cooped up here all day.' She seemed in good spirits, spooning sugar from the bag into a bowl of creamy porridge. The bedding she'd used was neatly folded into a pile on the sofa and I felt a pang of guilt.

'Isn't that what *you* do?' Matching her tone, I helped myself to some porridge from the pan on the stove and chopped an over-ripe banana into it. At some point in the night, I'd come to the conclusion that the note had been a test. Patrick was reminding me of my promise, showing me that – even from a distance – he had the power to keep a check on me. It was crude, and unlike the man I thought I knew, but maybe he hadn't believed I would keep my word. It was odd, when he had so much to lose, but the last few weeks had shown me a different side to him. Perhaps the real surprise was him letting me go in the first place.

I'd decided the best thing to do was keep my head down and stick to my plan – show him I meant what I'd said. As long as he left us alone, I wouldn't say a word to anyone. Ignoring the little voice that had whispered he might be willing to do anything to get his daughter back – to punish me for getting the upper hand – I'd finally slept again. 'How long have you lived here?' I asked Morag, as a distraction.

'Seven years, and I'm out more often than you'd think.'

'Good time at the pub last night?'

'Quiz night.' A smile touched the corners of her mouth. 'We won.'

'We?'

'The Carpenter's Arms. Four other pub teams were competing but we're easily the best.'

Her words gave me a wrench, thinking of Ifan's description of Fenbrith as a community, reminding me of the 'family' I'd left behind. *My people.* Here, I had no one. No, that wasn't true, I reminded myself, sitting at the table with my breakfast. I had Lily, and now I had Morag. And maybe, as her niece, I'd get a free pass with the locals and become one of them if I stayed.

'You were out for the count when I came back.' Morag eyed the creased top I'd spent the night in. I hadn't heard her return and Lily hadn't stirred either, though she'd fed voraciously on waking. 'I'm not a fan of the dog sleeping on the bed.'

'Sorry, I should have pushed him off.' I was unwilling to tell Morag how much safer I felt with the dog inside the house in case she wanted to know why. That I'd put an ocean and thousands of miles between Patrick and me, but somehow, he knew where I was. 'He didn't bark when you came in.' Worry scraped at my insides.

'No, but I thought he was going to bite me when I came up to check on you.' Morag gave Skip a dark look. 'It's like he thinks you need protecting.'

Skip was lying by the door, ears pricked. Was it true? I hoped so. Dogs were meant to have a sixth sense.

'Can I take him for a walk?' I said. 'Before we go into the village, I mean.'

'Be my guest,' Morag said dryly. 'So, you're coming with me?'

I made myself smile. 'As you said, I can't stay cooped up here.' I wasn't keen on the idea of meeting people yet, but didn't fancy staying at the cottage on my own. Plus, it would be an opportunity to get online and look Patrick up – see if there was any news. 'I used to go running in New York,' I said, wanting to change the subject. 'Early, before the day got going.' *Before Patrick.* Weird how my life was so clearly divided into *before* and *after*. No combining, which was what normally happened when two people got together, their befores and afters joining to create a future. But then, we were never really together. 'It cleared my head, set me up for the day,' I went on. 'Even when I hadn't had much sleep.'

'Sounds hideous,' Morag said briskly. 'Walking's kinder to your joints.'

'There was a park nearby. I mostly ran there, a few laps on the grass.' *A cop-out,* Ana used to say; not proper running at all. She'd done the New York marathon a couple of times, was training for the next one.

'Better scenery here.' Morag pushed her empty bowl aside. She was in her tartan dressing gown, her hair sticking out to one side. I felt a wave of affection. 'I'll keep an eye on the baby,' she said, resting her elbows on the table, her gaze travelling to the room in the eaves where I'd left Lily sleeping. Silence swelled. If I'd thought Morag might want more details about my life in America, again I was … *disappointed?* Did I *want* to talk about it? Maybe. The *before* part at least. Maybe I thought if I didn't, it was as if those years hadn't existed, the person I'd been extinguished. But surely it was better this way? A chance to begin afresh. *Lily's mum.* That's who I was now. The rest didn't matter. Keeping us safe was my priority.

'I'll be leaving at about eleven.' Morag scraped her stool back as she stood, the sound underscoring our conversation, making clear it was over.

*

Stepping outside without Lily felt wrong, as though I'd left a piece of myself behind. I told myself she'd be safe with Morag, that I had to learn to trust my aunt if we were going to be living under the same roof for a while. And I wouldn't be gone long. Besides, something told me Lily was safer in the cottage with her great-aunt than out of it with me. Try as I might, I couldn't let go of the idea of someone lurking about, waiting to snatch her.

Morag had reassured me that Skip was trained to come back when called, after I enquired whether there was a leash among the items she'd brought with him from the farm.

I tried it out as he ran ahead, clearly delighted to be outdoors, exploring somewhere new. He stopped to cock his leg, then returned to my side, looking up as though awaiting instructions. 'Good boy.' I patted his head. 'Go on then.'

As he pounded joyfully to the end of the vegetable garden where the trees led into the woods, I found myself smiling in spite of everything. I could only hope it would be as easy to 'train' Lily when she was older. It was hard to imagine a time when she would be walking, running; heading away from me. I hoped she'd always want to come back, that she wouldn't want to leave like I'd left my mother. The circumstances would be different, I promised myself as I followed Skip. I breathed deeply, feeling as if it was the first time my lungs had fully expanded in months. I would never give my daughter a reason to run away.

The thought of Mum made my stomach tighten. Having Lily … it had brought thoughts of her close, how well we'd once got on, the two of us against Dad. *Ganging up*, he'd called it, enjoying what he viewed as teasing, unaware we'd felt stronger and more able to cope with his moods when we were a team.

When Lily was born, I'd longed for Mum with a primaeval craving, crying as I fumbled with nappies and feeding, desperate for her advice, but something stopped me from calling her, just as it had when I found out I was pregnant; the same instinct that warned me not to mention it during our infrequent calls. Another week or two and I'd get in touch. Maybe even visit.

Pulling in a shaky breath, I concentrated on my surroundings. The air smelt earthy and sweet after last night's rainfall and the sky was a soft dove-grey. Beneath the wellington boots I'd padded with two pairs of socks, the ground was thick with mud, patches of grass bursting through. Blood surged in my veins as I picked up pace, a cool wind tugging my hair and whipping my cheeks.

The woods when I entered were dark, ancient and messy, with no designated paths that I could see. Dim light filtered through a canopy of leaves and I couldn't help imagining movements, flashes of eyes on me as I hurried after the dog, boots sinking into leaf mulch as I trod over tangled roots and fallen branches. Skip leapt nimbly over a dying tree stump covered with moss, chasing a squirrel that shot up a gnarled trunk and paused to look down, as if checking he was safe. The earth was churned, old roots pushing through. I had the sense of disturbing nature – that I wasn't welcome here. *The woods could hide anything.* Panic took hold of my insides. My breath came fast as I followed Skip, but it wasn't long before I reached a five-bar gate that opened into a wide, sloping field, a dazzle of daisies, where Skip was looping in circles, barking at the sky.

Blinking, I paused, drinking in the wild beauty of the view stretching into the distance; the valleys, hills and mountains – a kestrel gliding above on the breeze – and the cobalt glimmer of water in the lake that ran alongside the village. Sheep were studded on grassy banks like toys, the faraway sound of their bleating somehow ethereal. The world felt so much bigger here. In Manhattan I'd been hemmed in by tall buildings and other people, by cars, by … *things.* The city had its own beauty, which I'd learnt to appreciate, but nothing on this scale. There were no sounds here but the sheep and birdsong, and the wind blustering through the trees behind me.

I recognised another sound then, from childhood holidays: a steam train chugging through the valleys, its plume of smoke puffing in the air. That must have been the smoke I'd seen the day before, curling into the sky. It was too early in the year for

61

many tourists, but in another few weeks the place would fill with hikers and holidaymakers, taking in the scenery as I was doing.

Digging my hands in my coat pockets, I walked further into the field, inhaling a lungful of pure, clean air. Feeling a prickle at the base of my neck, I turned. Skip had doubled back into the woods and disappeared. 'Skip!' My voice sounded reedy and thin, lost in the space around me. 'Here, boy!' I tried to execute the complicated whistle my grandfather had taught me, using my fingers, but nothing came out. *'Skip!'* I yelled, cupping my hands around my mouth.

Suddenly, he was there, panting in the mouth of the gate, his head cocked as though wondering what the fuss was about. Relief thudded through me. I ran over, crouching down to ruffle his fur and kiss the top of his head. 'Where did you go, silly boy?'

As he whined and licked my cheek, I heard the sound of a twig cracking somewhere to my left. The woods were deeper there and the trees seemed to lean together, leaves whispering. My nerves jumped as I peered into the gloom, but Skip seemed unbothered.

'Hello?' *Idiot,* I chastised myself. People were allowed to walk through the woods without having to make themselves known. Only … it was so far from civilisation out here. 'Come on,' I said to Skip, a tremor running through me. 'Let's go.'

Straightening, I froze, spotting something in the churned-up mud by the gatepost: a set of boot prints, facing the field where moments ago I'd been standing, and beside the indented earth a glimmer of gold. Trembling, I reached down and picked it up, fear tightening my throat as I recognised the dull glint of sapphire.

My grandmother's ring.

Chapter 12

'Do people camp in the woods?'

Morag looked at me from the driver's seat of the van. 'Is that the start of a joke?' she said. 'Because I never get jokes.'

'No.' I made myself smile, knowing it looked unconvincing. 'It was a serious question.'

'I doubt it,' she said. 'I mean, they could, in theory. It's not part of the Forestry Commission, so they wouldn't need permission.' She shook her head, changing gear as she bumped the van onto the road to Fenbrith. 'I suppose if someone decided to pitch a tent they could, but it's too far from the pubs for most visitors and the weather's unreliable, especially at this time of year.'

'What about hikers?'

'Again, I've never seen any, but I don't spend much time in the woods.' She flashed me a quizzical glance. 'Why do you ask?'

'Oh, no reason, just that it's so nice out here. In the countryside, I mean.' I adjusted the seatbelt across Lily, pressed against me in her carrier. I needed to get her a proper car seat. 'I'm surprised there aren't any holiday homes out here.' If there were, the owner of the footprints could be holed up in one. 'It's an ideal spot for tourists.'

'There was a company a few years ago that wanted to set up one of those glamping sites, but it never took off, thank God.

I wouldn't be living there otherwise.' Morag seemed lost in her own thoughts for a moment, probably imagining the horror of other people encroaching on 'her' territory.

When I'd arrived back at the cottage, out of breath from stumbling over snarled roots, scared a hand was going to reach out and grab me, I'd almost blurted out the whole thing – the footprints; the ring now buried in my pocket, which I'd inexplicably found in the woods; the note I'd thrown on the fire that meant someone had been in the cottage. But something stopped me. Morag was in the kitchen where I'd left her, performing a makeshift puppet show for Lily, one hand stuffed in a sock, which she'd hidden behind her back as though embarrassed. A wave of relief had washed through me at the sight of Lily's innocent face, bringing tears to my eyes. I couldn't bring myself to utter the words that would change things. Not now I'd found a place to be. Nothing had really happened. I wasn't hurt. Lily was safe – for now. *Carry on as normal.* It wasn't a very good plan, but until I figured out a better one, it was all I had. Instead, I told Morag, as casually as I could, that I was going to take a shower and scrubbed myself under the stream of hot water until my skin felt raw and my mind had quietened.

'Don't get me wrong, I found it unbearably quiet at first.'

Morag's voice snapped me back to the moment, to being in the van with Lily breathing softly in my arms. 'Sorry?'

'Living here after …' Her jaw tightened, as if holding back the names of the places she'd been before. 'But the countryside's never really quiet when you get to know it.'

I looked at her profile, seeing the lines scored around her eyes, her mouth. A lived-in face; witness to unimaginable scenes. 'It must have been a big adjustment,' I said, trying to picture her moving among collapsed buildings shelled beyond repair, desperate screams ringing in her ears, broken and bloodied bodies strewn at her feet. I used to think of my aunt on Bonfire Night, or any time a volley of fireworks exploded in the sky like gunfire, wondering where she was. 'Where did you live between assignments?' I was ashamed that I didn't know, even though there was no reason why I would when she'd chosen to keep our contact to a minimum.

'I had a flat in London – Camden – but was rarely there.' A pulse twitched in her jaw. 'I shared with a friend, Jilly, a reporter. She was killed in an explosion in Iraq.'

I stared at her, shocked. 'God, I'm so sorry.'

'It was a long time ago.' Morag's hands gripped the top of the steering wheel as she accelerated. 'Came with the territory,' she said. 'It nearly got me too. I still have problems with my back if I'm not careful. We got too close that day.'

'We?'

'The television crew that Jilly and I had got in with.' Morag took a corner too fast and pressed her foot on the brake. 'Nearly all blokes back then, of course. We stood out as females, had to try to blend in.'

'Must have been hard.' I wanted her to continue. It was good to focus on Morag and not my own thoughts. 'How did you cope?'

She lifted a shoulder. 'We just did,' she said. 'I didn't think about it at the time.'

It struck me how far her world had been from mine, how I'd never experience the things she had. Morag knew what real jeopardy was, had lived with it for years. Now, she'd found contentment and I was in danger of ruining it. 'You shouldn't be sleeping on the sofa if you have a bad back.'

'It's fine,' she said. 'It's comfortable, don't worry.'

I looked at her properly. 'Mum couldn't understand why you didn't stick to portraits, or wildlife photography.'

Morag's bark of laughter startled Lily, who jerked under my hands. She turned to look at her great-aunt with saucer-eyes. 'I had a daredevil streak. Taking photos in a studio, or at a wedding, didn't appeal.'

'Mum was proud, you know, of how you got your job.' I remembered the story often told at Sunday lunch – until Mum fell out with Morag. About how her sister's winning picture in a national newspaper competition, of a bare-knuckle boxing match she'd infiltrated with a friend, led to the editor inviting her for an interview. 'She just didn't expect it to become your whole life.'

I thought I'd gone too far, until Morag said without rancour, 'She'd rather I'd been like her, but we were never going to be the best of friends. We were too different.' My mind dialled back to the day Dad died before quickly swerving away. They were more alike than they realised. Both possessed a determination to survive, but in different ways.

As the fields and hills gave way to grey-stone houses at the side of the road, I remembered how intensely green Wales was, how even the air felt green, the countryside as close as the buildings had been in Manhattan. In winter, those buildings funnelled frigid air that bit through clothing and trapped the fumes from congested traffic. Here, I remembered from visits to my grandparents' in Conwy, the cold was different; purer, cleaner. Mum would gulp it down like champagne, and we'd return from a walk with rosy cheeks and sparkling eyes, feeling more alive. Dad rarely came on a walk unless it ended at the pub.

'What made you want to retire?' I asked Morag as we drove past the sign for Fenbrith.

'It was time.' Her tone was even, but something about the way her knuckles whitened around the steering wheel told me there was more to it. I decided not to press her. I knew all about keeping secrets.

'So, how did you find the cottage?'

'By chance, out walking,' she said. 'I was looking for somewhere remote. It used to be a shepherd's home and was pretty derelict. I got it cheap and spent a bit making it habitable.'

'Do you ever go back to Conwy?'

She shook her head. 'No point.'

Mum had always claimed that Morag wasn't the sentimental type, but something about the set of her jaw told me that wasn't

66

true; that she stayed away because it was too painful to be in the town where she'd grown up, now that her family wasn't there.

'I'll get my stuff from the back,' she said, jumping out of the van as soon as she'd parked round the back of the pub and switched the engine off.

While she sorted through the boxes of vegetables she'd brought, I got out and walked to the pavement, jiggling Lily as I looked up and down the street, checking for … what? A figure hiding in the shadows?

The clouds parted, spilling sunlight across the rows of pastel-coloured buildings, bringing the place into focus. Apart from the creeper-clad pub, there was an old-fashioned bakery with people queuing under a blue and white awning, and a busy butcher's shop opposite, where a chalkboard on the pavement advertised 'home-made pies'. Next door was a florist's, silver buckets of daffodils arranged out the front, and slotted between a chemist's and a newsagent's was a shop displaying handcrafted gifts and knitting wool in the window.

On the corner, outside the village store and post office, a pair of middle-aged women in ankle-length coats were chatting. One held the handlebars of a black-framed bike with a basket on the front, her friend the lead of a glossy spaniel. Only the sight of a mobile phone in her other hand convinced me I hadn't travelled back in time.

'Are you going in?'

Startled, I swung round, breath catching in my throat. 'What?'

'I wondered whether you were going into the pub.'

I realised I was standing right outside, blocking the way. 'Sorry.' Tightening my grip on the carrier, where Lily was trying to look around, I stepped to one side.

The man stepped the same way. 'Oops.' He gave a soft laugh. 'Did you want to dance?'

Flustered, I moved the opposite way, briefly meeting a pair of smiling eyes. 'I am going in,' I said firmly.

'In that case, after you.'

He extended his arm and, moving past me, pushed the pub door open. I felt I had no choice but to duck inside, catching his spearmint smell of toothpaste as I stepped down two shallow steps into the dark interior.

The deep-set windows and timber-beamed ceiling didn't offer much brightness, but the atmosphere was cosy rather than oppressive. A stained-glass panel illuminated the bar, and the exposed stonework was hung with photos and paintings, candle-like sconces in between radiating soft light. Most of the floor space was occupied by chunky tables and pew-like seating. In front of a blazing log-burner, an older couple were sipping coffees on a wine-coloured sofa, a Labrador at their feet.

I thought of Skip, tied up outside the cottage at Morag's insistence, in case he chewed the furniture. Hoping he'd deter – or even bite – the intruder, should he pitch up again, I turned as the man joined me.

'Nice, isn't it?' He had to stoop to avoid hitting his head on the beams, his shoulder brushing mine. 'Sort of old-fashioned with a modern twist.'

'Lovely,' I said politely, fussing with Lily's hood so I didn't have to look at him.

'There you are.' Morag came in, boots clattering on the red and black quarry-tiled floor, a sagging box of vegetables in her arms. 'You find somewhere to sit while I drop these off and have a word with Annie.'

It sounded like an order. I found a table for two in the corner, partly concealed from view. I didn't want to stand out as the stranger in the village, though the couple by the fire were engrossed in their drinks and barely looked up. Perhaps they were visitors to the area too.

The door opened again and Ifan came in, rubbing his hands together as though to warm them up. He didn't notice me as he made his way to the bar where the stranger was leaning, waiting to be served.

I unstrapped Lily, holding her while I unwound the scarf that Morag had lent me – a long, stripy Dr Who affair. I placed it on the pew beside me before sitting down and laying Lily on top of her padded carrier on the table. She smiled and kicked and the sight of her rose-pink cheeks and bright eyes dissolved some of my anxiety. 'Hey, baby, you OK?' I tickled under her chin and was rewarded with a lopsided smile that took my breath away. The first time I saw it, I'd told myself it was probably wind, but there was no mistaking it this time. Smiling through a blur of tears, I unzipped her all-in-one, wondering when she would say *mama*. Not for a long time, according to the parenting websites I'd looked at, but I repeated the word a couple of times all the same, sounding it out while she blew bubbles.

'Cute.' The man was back, holding a pint of foaming beer. I studied him as I shrugged off my coat. He looked to be in his late thirties, his dark blond hair thick and longish, a covering of light stubble tracing his jaw. His eyes were an unusual shade of green and as they met mine, a strange sensation passed through me; as though I knew him. Then it was gone, leaving an unexpected fizz of warmth inside my belly. 'I don't normally drink this early in the day,' he said, as if reading disapproval in my glance. 'Can I get you anything?'

'I'm good, thanks.' I wasn't much of a drinker, mindful of how alcohol had affected my father, changing him from easy-going to unpredictable after a couple of glasses.

The man nodded at Lily. 'I'm guessing she's under age?' His lips were full and smiling but there was a tension to his posture.

'Just a bit.' I drew the baby carrier closer as Lily craned her neck to look more fully at the stranger. There was something outdoorsy about him – the navy, waterproof jacket, worn-in jeans, lightly tanned skin. As my gaze fell to his feet, I stiffened. My pulse started to race. He was wearing army-style boots caked in mud.

Chapter 13

'I'm surprised they let you wear those in here.' My voice was strained with the effort of sounding normal.

'Didn't realise they were in such a state.' I looked up to see him wince. 'I've got a hole in one of my socks, so I'll risk keeping them on.'

My mind spun. If the footprints had belonged to him, why was he here? Was this part of the plan? Was I supposed to act dumb? 'You don't have a local accent,' I said, deciding to play along.

'Neither do you.' He looked amused as he gestured at the seat opposite. 'Mind if I join you?'

I looked around, but there was no sign of Morag. I gave a reluctant nod, feeling outmanoeuvred. 'Are you here on holiday?'

'Are you?' He put his pint on the table and unzipped his jacket as he sat, playfully widening his eyes at Lily as she kicked and stretched a chubby arm in his direction. 'She looks like you.'

Despite myself, I was pleased by his comment. Morag had said the same thing. Of course, they'd never met Patrick. She had the same colouring as him, but I had dark hair and eyes too and I could detect my mother in the shell-like shape of her ears and slant of her nose. 'I'll take that as a compliment.'

'I'm Declan Walsh.' *Irish.* He held out a hand but I pretended not to notice as I drew a muslin cloth from my bag and dabbed at Lily's chin.

'Do you live locally?'

'Do you?' he fired back.

'Do you always answer a question with a question?'

'Only in pubs in the month of March, when talking to attractive women.'

Heat stained my cheeks. 'Does that happen often?'

'Now who's asking questions?'

My flush deepened. 'Doesn't seem like the best way to get to know someone.' *And a good way of avoiding answering.*

'We're talking, aren't we?'

'That's another question.'

'Is it?'

'Isn't it?' It was starting to feel like flirting, something I'd never mastered and had no time for, but despite the warmth of his smile, I sensed him holding back. If this was a game, if he was acting, he wasn't that good at it. Then he laughed. It was a good laugh, throaty and deep, and elicited a stream of excited babble from Lily that made him laugh again. My shoulders unclenched a little. Maybe I was overreacting. So what if his boots were covered in mud and he'd made a beeline for me? I was the only other person in the pub, apart from the couple in front of the fire. Now that I looked, the soles of their hiking shoes were muddy too. 'So, where are you from?' I said.

'Here and there.' Perhaps seeing something in my face, he leant forward and rested his elbows on the table, his expression opening up. 'If you really want to know, I grew up on a remote farm in Ballyfin in Ireland, with one sister, two parents and my grandmother, who came to live with us when my grandfather died. I left home as soon as I could to see the world, but I like to get back and visit at least once a year.'

'Your accent's not very strong.' I was suddenly reminded of

the night I met Patrick, right down to the tug of chemistry I was trying not to acknowledge.

'I've been away a long time,' he said. 'Where are you from?'

'Just outside London.' I kept it non-specific, glad he hadn't detected an American intonation in my voice. Then again, if he *was* here on Patrick's behalf, he'd know things about me already.

'On holiday?'

My smile vanished. 'Something like that.'

Declan's hand closed round his pint glass. His wrists looked thick and strong, a silver ring on the middle finger of his right hand; a Celtic knot of some kind. I wondered whether a woman had given it to him. 'Not married?' He looked at Lily who was staring at a print on the wall of a misty mountain, as though assessing its value.

I shook my head. 'You?' I thought of the platinum wedding band Patrick had worn, making no effort to conceal the fact he had a wife, and how I'd fallen for him anyway.

'Nope,' Declan said. 'Not met the right woman yet.'

'Have you travelled a lot?'

Was there a slight hesitation before he answered? 'I've been to lots of places. I was in the army for a few years when I was younger. It's a good way to see the world.'

'Army?' I felt a flash of surprise. He didn't seem the type somehow: hair too long, no power stance, no jargon. I was aware of mentally stereotyping. 'You were a soldier?'

'Geographic technician,' he said wryly. 'Best place to build a helicopter landing site? Most convenient route for a tank? Where would a missile do the most damage?' He executed a jerky salute. 'Lance Corporal Walsh at your service.' There was something regretful about his tone that reminded me of Morag. 'As I said, it was a long time ago.'

'You must have been all over the place.' *America?*

He took a sip of beer before replying. I wished I had a drink after all; something to do with my hands besides twisting Lily's muslin. 'Canada, Germany, Austria, Italy.' He shrugged one shoulder as though making light of it. 'Operational deployment to Afghanistan.'

I sensed a *but*. 'You didn't enjoy it?'

'It was fine for a while, especially the training. I was good at it. Then things got real. Providing key information to military commanders. I didn't like that so much.' He raised an eyebrow. 'Let's just say it brought home the whole killing aspect.' At least he wasn't pretending to be a hero. And it sounded as though killing was anathema to him – hardly the sort of person who'd willingly terrorise a woman with a baby, if he was telling the truth. 'I joined the army on a whim if I'm being brutally honest.' His mouth twisted in a self-deprecating smile. 'I thought it would be exciting. I'd had enough of school, of living on a farm, but I'd always loved geography, maps, being outdoors. I wanted to travel.' He paused and shook his head, the wall light catching glints of darker colour in his hair. The atmosphere and the lighting in the pub made it feel as though we were on a date. 'My mother was terrified I'd get killed and I wanted to be around to see my kids grow up one day.'

'And now?'

He took a breath, his tone lightening. 'I've moved around a fair bit. Can't seem to settle in one place. I look for work, stay a while, then move on.'

'And that's why you're here?'

As he met my eyes, my insides lurched again. 'I have a soft spot for Wales.' He grinned, revealing a set of even teeth. 'I met a girl on a camping holiday in Caernarfon with my family when I was fifteen. It was a memorable summer.'

Ignoring the implication, I said, 'Why Fenbrith?'

If he was fazed by my questions, he hid it well. 'I stayed in touch with the girl's brother.' He traced a finger around the rim of his glass. His nails were short and clean. *No trace of mud.* 'He still lives in Caernarfon with his wife and children, runs an outdoor centre there. Walking, climbing, mountain-biking, that sort of thing.' I relaxed further. I'd been to Caernarfon once on a daytrip with my grandparents. They took me to see the castle, whose walls encased the town. We'd eaten fish and chips on a shingle beach with a name I couldn't pronounce, and paddled in the sea. I couldn't remember where my parents were that day. 'Like me, Hugh's into outdoor activities. He knows a good route from here to Snowdon and that's where we're going today. We arranged to meet here at midday.'

'So, you *are* on holiday?' My tone had lifted. I saw something shift in his expression. Had he felt the spark of energy between us?

'More of a working holiday.' His gaze shifted to Lily. She waved her arms as though trying to take off and I dabbed her chin again. 'Hugh's looking for someone to guide hiking tours in the area and … well, I'm thinking about it.' I was aware of him subtly tracking my movements as I picked Lily up and nestled her warm body against my shoulder. 'What's her name?' he said.

'Little mouse, most of the time.' I discreetly sniffed her nappy area. 'What would you call a daughter if you had one?'

I said it to distract him, but he appeared to give it some thought. 'Of course, it would have to be a mutual choice, but I'd hands-down choose Cara, after my nan.'

'That's nice.' I swallowed the urge to tell him I'd named Lily after my grandmother. The ring, still in my jeans pocket, seemed to burn through the material and brand my leg. 'I prefer simple names.'

'Me too,' he said. 'You can keep your Zeramiahs and your weird spellings. There was a girl in my class at school called Emily but it was spelt with an a and two ees instead of an i and a y. She was forever correcting people.'

'I don't understand why parents do that.'

'Probably want their child to stand out.'

'And all children want to do at that age is fit in.'

'Exactly.'

I became aware of cooking smells trailing through the pub, of the world feeling almost normal – ordinary. The bar was growing busier. A group of anorak-clad ramblers were ordering drinks and asking about the menu. Twenty minutes had slipped by and there was still no sign of Morag. On cue, I spotted her emerging from a door marked private behind the bar, just as Declan said, 'Whereabouts are you staying?'

To buy some time I jiggled Lily as she grew restless. She was making a fretful noise that would soon escalate into crying. 'I'm sorry but I have to feed her.' My breasts felt heavy. Declan's eyes skimmed my chest and a flush of heat travelled through my body. I knew I looked unremarkable in the baggy sweatshirt I'd put on with my jeans – which I still hadn't got round to washing – make-up free, my hair shoved up in a topknot, but his gaze suggested otherwise.

'I should get going.' He drained his pint and got to his feet. Under his jacket, he was wearing a grey fleece over a white T-shirt. I felt an irrational urge to rest my cheek against it and feel the beat of his heart against my skin.

'Listen, if you'd like to meet for a drink sometime, give me a call.' He drew a business-like card from his pocket and slid it across the table. Lily's fists were flailing and caught me on the chin as I leant forward and picked it up. It simply read *Declan Walsh* above a mobile number in plain black font. 'Useful when I'm looking for work,' he said.

'I'm afraid there's no signal where I'm staying.' All the same, I dropped the card into my bag, attempting a casual smile. 'And I'm pretty busy with this one most of the time.'

'If you change your mind.' His gaze held mine for a moment longer, then someone called his name. He turned, raising his hand in a greeting. 'That's Hugh.' He looked back at me. 'Nice to have met you …?'

Aware he was waiting for me to supply a name, I looked at Morag. She was viewing our exchange with an inscrutable expression, her hands tucked under her armpits. 'You were gone ages,' I said, and Declan moved away with a nod in her direction. Pivoting towards the wall, I awkwardly arranged Lily at my breast as Declan passed the opposite window outside. Unguarded, his face looked unfamiliar; a stranger once more.

'I was watching you.' Morag sat where Declan had been moments ago. 'Looks like you've got an admirer,' she said. 'Fast work.'

Chapter 14

By the time I'd explained about bumping into Declan outside the pub, defensive under Morag's forensic scrutiny, Lily had finished feeding. I adjusted my top and rested her against my shoulder, gently patting her back. Morag looked about to say something but stopped as a smiling woman in her early forties approached, balancing two bowls and a basket of bread in her hands. A mass of curly blonde hair exploded around a zigzag patterned scarf.

'Lunch is served,' she sang. 'Hope you don't mind me choosing for you, but it's only vegetable soup and home-made bread and your aunt assured me you'll eat anything as long as it's nicely cooked.' Her accent was soft and lilting, her round face creased with laughter lines. She looked comfortable in jeans and a pink T-shirt, a black apron double-tied around her waist; at ease in her own body. 'Morag told me you're a chef, so I expect you'll be judging my food. You can tell me where I'm going wrong.' She spoke cheerfully, clearly confident about her cooking ability.

'It smells lovely.' My mouth watered as I admired the golden-crusted bread, cut into thick slices and accompanied by a pot of creamy butter, and the stew of colourful vegetables floating in herby stock. Steadying Lily, I wafted a hand above the bowl, inhaling the steamy scent of garlic and leeks. 'It's nice to be cooked for,' I said, thrusting away a memory of Patrick throwing chopped peppers into a pan with some prawns at midnight in my apartment, his shirtsleeves rolled up. *It's my mother's recipe, you'll love it, I promise.* 'People get anxious when they know I cook for a living.'

'Everything in the soup is home-grown by your aunt.' Annie looked at Morag as though seeing her in a new light. 'We were so excited when she told us her niece – and great-niece – had come to stay.'

'Thank you so much for the baby things.' I'd seen her eyes light up when she looked at Lily. 'I couldn't bring all her stuff with me,' I added, driven to offer some sort of explanation. 'I was going to buy what she needed when I got here.'

Annie waved a dismissive hand. 'Glad to be shot of it all.' Her casualness didn't quite convince. 'I'm pleased it's gone to a good home.' She cast Lily a yearning look. 'Wish my Gwynn was that age again, she's a total terror at the moment. The terrible twos have lasted nearly an extra two years, now.' Her tone grew wistful. 'Bryn's parents have got her for a couple of days to give us a break. She loves it there because they let her do what she wants.'

'Which makes her worse when she gets back.' Morag shook her head as she thickly buttered a chunk of bread before dipping it in her soup. 'They spoil her.'

'Ah well, we just want our children to be happy, don't we now?'

Morag paused before biting into her soupy bread, her dark gaze sliding to Lily. 'I suppose so.' She said it so quietly, I wasn't certain Annie had heard.

'Oh, I've got a car seat you can have too,' Annie said brightly. 'It tips right back so it's safe for a tiny one to sleep in if you're travelling. We only used it once to take Gwynn to Cornwall to see her great-grandma when she was a baby. She slept all the way, perfectly safe.'

'That's so kind of you.' I thought of visiting Mum in Berkshire. Not that I had a car. I hadn't driven for years, hadn't needed to in New York.

'You don't have postnatal depression, do you?' Annie's smile faded. 'I was terrible for a while. No one knew what was wrong with me,' she said. 'It's important to ask for help if you're feeling down.'

I remembered the numbness of a month ago, the constant flow of tears, the lonely hours of sleeplessness. 'I'm OK, but thanks.' I wasn't OK. The knowledge that I was being watched, probably followed, was like an icy prod in my heart. *How long is it going to go on for?*

'Well, if you fancy helping out here on a Saturday night, there's a job for you if you want it.'

It took a moment to realise that Annie was being serious. 'A job?'

'I had a chef but he was lured to the bright lights of Cardiff and I'm desperate for a night or two off, which might not be possible with the schools breaking up for half-term next week. We're always busy on a Saturday night, but once the visitors arrive …' She pretended to tear at her hair.

I laughed, allowing myself to breathe a little easier. Could I really stay, even work, here, in Fenbrith? Would it prove to Patrick that I was moving on, keeping my promise? 'I might take you up on that.' Laughter blossomed against a hum of chatter and clink of glasses. 'Thank you for asking.'

Annie nodded. As she turned to a customer trying to attract her attention, I picked up my spoon, flooded with a tentative sense of hope. If I didn't give in to the fear that threatened to overwhelm me, didn't react in the way Patrick must be expecting, maybe I could make it work here.

*

'I need to pick up some groceries,' Morag said, once we were back in the van.

'From the village store?'

'There's a supermarket a couple of miles down the road. They have the cereal I like.'

'OK.' Smiling, I settled back in my seat, replete after lunch, Lily burbling happily between us in the plush car seat Annie had produced. My little girl had been a huge hit at the pub, attracting smiles and questions about her progress while she responded with smiles as though trying to impress her audience.

Ifan had come over on his way out, to ask whether we'd enjoyed the rabbits, looking downcast when Morag told him we hadn't got around to eating them yet.

'Don't let them spoil,' he'd said. I had to resist telling him that, in my view, they'd already been ruined. I didn't want to sour the air of goodwill that sprang up once Morag had introduced me to a couple more locals, as well as Annie's husband Bryn, whose bear-like appearance was belied by an easy-going manner and gentle smile. He left most of the talking to his wife, but it was clear they made a good team and were well liked by their regulars. What had surprised me a little was how highly regarded Morag seemed to be, despite her less than sunny nature and refusal to be drawn into local gossip. I'd always enjoyed her sporadic visits growing up, but they'd been tainted by Mum's view of her sister as selfish, their father's 'favourite' – a woman only interested in doing what she wanted to do.

Isn't everyone, Gail? Dad remarked once, apparently amused by Mum's tears when Morag left straight after dinner because she had a plane to catch. *To be honest, I envy her.* On some level, I'd understood Mum resented being the one responsible for their parents, who knew which daughter to call whenever they needed something. *At least Mum got to do what she wanted in the end.* Sourness rose to my throat as Morag slowed at a set of lights and sped up again when they turned green, murmuring an apology when Lily's arms flew out. 'Got to get used to her,' she said. 'I'll slow down.'

The supermarket was on the outskirts of Caernarfon, a squat

building with a red-brick roof that seemed out of place after all the grey stone and slate I'd seen so far. The car park was crowded, people jostling trolleys and umbrellas as the rain returned, pelting the tarmac with a vengeance.

'Wait here, I won't be long.' Morag parked under a dripping oak tree at the furthest point from the store, in the only available space. She threw the hood of her jacket up. 'No point us all getting soaked.'

The van door opened, letting in a mist of damp air. Once Morag had jumped out, she was quickly swallowed by the deluge. The windows began to steam up, rain on the roof rattling like tiny hammers. Lily seemed fascinated, eyes tracking the sound, her mouth a perfect circle of surprise.

'You'd better get used to it, sausage.' I turned and clapped her hands together, smiling when her eyes met mine. 'It's even wetter in Wales than it is in New York.' I'd been surprised by how much it rained there, even during the summer. I remembered last year, when storms had caused havoc across the city, flooding streets and subway stations. Recalling the scenes, my mind flew back to a June day, when I was crouched in the toilets behind the kitchen at the restaurant, Ana staring at me with startled comprehension as rain battered the window above the sink. She'd swung by to invite me to her cousin's birthday party and was told I wasn't well.

'Why the hell didn't you tell me, Grace?'

'I don't know.' I slid to the floor, cradling my head in my hands. The signs had been there for weeks: tender breasts, a vague sick feeling, a metallic taste in my mouth that made tea and coffee undrinkable. When it finally registered, I did a test, then another in the bathroom upstairs, staring at the pink line until it blurred, wondering how it could have happened when I'd always been so careful. I hadn't told anyone yet, could hardly take it in. Apart from Patrick being out of the picture now he was back with his wife – *also pregnant. Well done, Grace. You picked a winner there* – I wasn't prepared for this.

'Are you ready to be a single parent?' Ana squatted beside me, the musky scent of her perfume making my throat close up. 'Or are you going to call him, tell him he has to step up?'

'You know I can't do that.' She was the only one who knew about Patrick, about why we were no longer seeing each other. 'His wife's having a baby too, remember?'

'God, what a creep.' Her lip curled with disdain. 'I don't care if he's going to be the next DA and all the grannies love him and he's got a lovely head of hair, or whatever, he's an asshole.'

'So am I for sleeping with him.' Sickness swirled through me. 'And, Ana, you can't tell anyone about it, ever. Or about this. About the baby being his.' I pressed a hand to my stomach. It was still flat; no hint of what was happening inside me. 'I don't want to be with Patrick and I *don't* want him to know.'

It wasn't as if he was going to leave his wife. She was an alcoholic, he'd told me, after the first time we slept together. I'd traced the contours of his face with my fingers, wanting to wipe away the pain that tightened his features. He'd known she liked a drink – a rebellion against a tightly controlled upbringing – but hadn't realised how much until after they were married. She hid it well, but her father had recently funded a secret trip to rehab. She'd quickly relapsed, leaving Patrick floundering, uncertain how to help. A trip to Canada to visit her sister had seemed like a temporary solution, a change of scenery, a break from everything. It hadn't worked. She'd carried on drinking until she discovered she was pregnant.

After he told me they were staying together, that she was a different woman now, that he knew this was what she'd been waiting for, the initial shock wore off. Once I'd had a good cry, I felt relieved. No more sneaking about, no more complications. I didn't want an affair, to be someone's mistress, to disrespect another woman. With my burgeoning feelings nipped in the bud I could get my life back on track. *If only he hadn't come back into it a few months later.*

Startled back to the present, I caught a movement on the driver's side of the van. I sensed a face staring through the rain and condensation, a shadowy figure moving past at speed. Pulse skittering, I jabbed the switch to open the windows but the engine was off. Morag had left the key in the ignition, but by the time I'd leant over to turn it on and lowered the window, whoever it was had gone. Maybe it was a shopper, though the spaces on either side of the van were empty now. I looked at the bank of trees in front, swaying against a backwash of grey sky. Craning my neck, I looked back at the car park, but saw only shoppers through the billowing rain, loading their car boots with bags, abandoning trolleys to the elements. I tried to pick out a parking attendant, but couldn't make out a uniform among the huddled figures and bobbing umbrellas.

Two children were running in circles and jumping in puddles like puppies. When one stopped and stared at me, I closed the window and made sure the doors were locked. 'Silly Mummy,' I said to Lily, who was examining her hand and started at the sound of my voice. I swiped my damp cheeks with my palm and waited for my heartbeat to slow.

I thought about Declan, a relative stranger in Fenbrith, finding me like a heat-seeking missile, determined to strike up a conversation despite my obvious reluctance. Why hadn't he stayed at the bar and chatted to Bryn and Ifan?

You have to stop this, said an unsparing voice in my head. *People are friendly around here. You're the one who stands out.*

Another voice, Patrick's this time, low and warm, his New York accent subtle. *You do know every man in here is looking at me, wishing they were sitting where I am, talking to you.*

Declan wasn't Patrick and even if he'd been an 'admirer' as Morag had put it, he hadn't asked for my number, or even where I was staying. *Unless he already knew?*

'Let's put some music on.' As I lurched sideways to fiddle with the radio, Lily grabbed a strand of my hair with a happy squeal.

'Hey!' I tried to relax as I freed myself, bobbing my head to an old ABBA song to make her smile. 'You're a cheeky monkey.'

I reached to the floor for my bag and pulled out my phone, freshly charged and solid in my hand. There was only one bar of reception, but I'd seen the 'free Wi-Fi' sign for the café inside the supermarket as we drove in. I could probably get online from here. It was time to look Patrick up.

Chapter 15

My palms felt slippery as I waited for the phone to connect. Morag could be back any second. I should have logged on straight away, had intended to look while we were at the pub but got distracted by Declan, then lunch. A part of me didn't want to read something in black and white that I wouldn't be able to unsee.

But now, I had to know.

'Hurry up, hurry up,' I muttered, turning it into a song for Lily, who was staring intently at the phone. 'You're not allowed one of these until you're at least seventeen.' I was filled with dread at the thought of the social media world I'd have to navigate with her in the future. With any luck, things would turn full circle and the world would revert to old-fashioned ways of communicating. The thought of her being bullied online made my blood run cold. Maybe we'd still be living in Fenbrith with Morag, in blissful anonymity, Lily oblivious to technology, content to live off the land, surrounded by wildlife with books for entertainment. At least her life wouldn't be complicated by her father's temper the way mine had been – as long as Patrick left us alone.

Finally, I was online. Adrenaline flooded my veins. My fingers twitched as I typed *Patrick Holden* into the search engine, spelling it wrong the first time.

Immediately, his image sprang up: a tasteful, well-lit headshot on his campaign website, conveying trustworthiness and quiet authority; a man guided by a strong moral compass. Seeing the faint laughter lines in the tanned skin around his coal-dark eyes, the Hollywood cleft in his clean-shaven chin, the thick dark hair I knew smelt faintly of limes, brought heat to the backs of my eyes.

I will not cry.

Pressing my lips together, I scanned for a newspaper article among the many links. Most of them detailed his race for the DA's position – *Patrick Holden on running for Manhattan District Attorney: "There has to be a sweeping overhaul of our criminal legal system."; The Race to become Manhattan's DA: Patrick Holden has what it takes … Patrick Holden, Manhattan DA race's youngest and most promising candidate.* My mind spiralled back to the body at the bottom of the stairs. His wife's death wouldn't be big news over here, but in New York there would have been quite a ripple.

When I spotted the sentence I'd missed the first time, my heart jerked. *Manhattan DA, Patrick Holden, 39, talks about the tragic loss of his wife.*

My limbs grew weak. Releasing a shaky breath, I pressed the link and brought up the feature on the front page of the *New York Times,* headed by a photo of Patrick caught mid-sentence, one hand outstretched as though in appeal. The photographer had captured the grief-stricken quality of his expression, the haunted gaze and crumpled brow. Leaning forward on the edge of a leather chair, shirtsleeves rolled up, one arm resting on his knee, he managed to give the impression of strength and resilience, of someone wholly reliable – even at his most vulnerable. The public would lap it up. Elise's death had catapulted him into their consciousness in a way no amount of campaigning ever could, and he'd been pretty successful at that. He would undoubtedly gain new fans, new supporters – new admirers.

Jaw clenched I skimmed the words underneath.

Patrick Holden, 39, campaigning to become Manhattan's youngest ever District Attorney next year, talked today about the tragic loss of his wife Elise, 36, eldest daughter of Clarence and Vanessa Boyd, founders of the Boyd Publishing Group. Elise tragically fell to her death at the couple's home last week. It's believed that she had been drinking heavily at the time.

'The shock of finding her body will never leave me,' Holden said, adding, 'It's true that my wife had fought a long battle against alcohol addiction, something those who loved her had tried to help her overcome. We'd like to ask for privacy at this extremely difficult time so her loved ones can grieve in peace. I will be taking some time out, but hope to be back soon, serving my community.'

Some filler followed about Patrick's New Jersey childhood, the youngest of three children, and the wrongful incarceration of his older brother, which led to his suicide when Patrick was eighteen, firing his ambition to become a lawyer, and how he'd worked as a public defender for some years, fighting for the underdog. He'd told me about his brother. I'd felt a kinship with him because we'd both suffered a family loss at a young age.

My eyes skimmed the article again. No mention of their child. He'd portrayed himself in the best possible light, giving the newspaper enough roughage – Elise's alcoholism – to satisfy their appetite for scandal (hers, not his) while retaining his integrity and all the sordid details. *What lie had he fed Elise's parents?*

My stomach felt hot with acid as I imagined how they must feel. Patrick had told me they didn't particularly like him at first, because of the nature of the cases he worked on and the long hours he put in, the pressure to win that meant he was permanently cupping the back of his neck to massage away the tension. They thought their daughter could do better, like her sister, whose husband had set up a tech company worth millions, but they'd come to respect Patrick's work ethic and determination to succeed. Of course, it wasn't his fault that Elise was an alcoholic, but there'd be no doubt in her parents' eyes that she'd be alive if she hadn't married him.

Insides fluttering, I scrolled down, a comment beneath the article catching my eye.

He probably pushed her. Have the police investigated?

My vision blurred as my mind crashed back to Elise, broken at the foot of the stairs, her long black hair thrown across her face. Patrick's conflicted features; the split-second brightness of relief. By then, I was sure he'd wanted her gone – had wanted rid of us both. I'd become part of the problem, one that could ruin his future. What if he'd seen this comment and thought I'd posted it, reneging on my promise? Feeling dizzy, I read on. Several people had leapt to his defence.

That's sick. He's just lost his wife, asshole.

Give the guy a break! I've met him a couple of times. He's one of the good ones.

Maybe he should look at diverting alcohol and drug-addicted criminals to treatment programs as part of his campaign.

I forced my breathing to slow. It was fine. Patrick had handled the tragedy. No one else knew about me, or Lily – or so I'd thought.

Just go, he'd said at the end, the arrangement of skin and bones in front of me transformed from the man I'd briefly imagined a future with, to a person I barely recognised.

And here we are. I'd left, yet he didn't trust me. Did he want Lily back, or was it that he didn't like me calling the shots? Maybe wanted to show me who was boss? It seemed so old-fashioned and Patrick was all about the future, about looking forward. It made no sense. But I hadn't imagined the note, the footprints, my ring in the woods. I just couldn't work out what he wanted.

Could I call him? My mind rejected the idea. What could I say? Reiterate I had no intention of changing my mind, that I wanted to be left in peace? He knew that already. Frustrated, I tuned back in to the lashing rain, to the radio playing 'I'm Free' by the Rolling Stones. I nearly laughed. I was supposed to be free, but felt anything but.

'Sorry I took so long. It was crazy in there.' Morag was back, filling the van with reusable shopping bags and the peaty smell of outside, shaking herself like a spaniel as she clambered inside, raindrops flying from her hair. 'How is she?'

She looked at Lily, who'd fallen asleep, with a complicated expression of love and something darker – the sort of look I'd occasionally caught on my own face; fear that everything precious could be snatched away any moment.

'She's fine.' Tears filled my eyes. Would there ever be a time when I didn't have to keep looking over my shoulder? When we were part of Patrick Holden's history? 'We're both absolutely fine.'

Chapter 16

Back at the cottage, I was filled with a surge of restless energy that Skip picked up on, barking and jumping around us as we put away the shopping – an eclectic mix that included a bag of lemons and jars of spices I suspected were to encourage me to keep cooking, and several packs of dried dog food. When the cupboards were full, which didn't take long, the rest of the items lined along the worktop and on a shelf fixed to the wall, I spotted the muddy pawprints Skip had trailed in.

'Shall I clean the floor? I can do the windows too if you like, while Lily's quiet.' She was awake in her bouncy chair, which I'd placed on the table out of the dog's reach. 'I'm not used to doing nothing.' And I needed a distraction.

'I don't need a housekeeper.' Morag softened her tone as she added, 'I suppose you can do the floor, but not much point cleaning the windows if it's going to keep raining.'

'It's stopped now.' The door was open, cool air drifting through the rooms, a spill of lemony sunlight on the tiles. 'I think it's done for today.'

'You're in a funny mood.' Morag watched with a frown as I picked up Skip and petted his ears with exaggerated daintiness,

90

making woofy sounds for Lily's benefit. Maybe if I acted fine, I'd feel it.

'I'm just glad to be here.' I put the dog down and reached for the plastic bucket I'd spotted under the sink. 'I can't thank you enough for making us welcome.'

'You'll be tearing your hair out with boredom by the end of the week.'

My smile felt more like a grimace. 'Believe me, boredom would be good.' I turned on the taps, trying to nourish the feeling of hope I'd felt talking to Annie at the pub. I realised how tightly coiled my muscles were. My temples throbbed as if I'd been grinding my teeth. 'Being able to appreciate all … this.' I swept my arm around to encompass the cramped little room – Lily waving her arms, Skip turning circles in the rectangle of sunlight, and through the open door, a patchwork of blue as the rainclouds cleared. 'I don't think I've properly seen the sky for months.' That much was true. In Manhattan, there were mostly skyscrapers if I looked up.

'Well, that's a tragedy.' Morag's mouth curved into a smile that made me think of a photo Mum had of them, dressed up for a rare night out together, arms around each other's waists, heads pressed together. *Boys never looked at me if I was out with Morag,* Mum had said, and it was easy to see why in that moment. 'You need to get out more,' Morag said now.

'I intend to.'

My fake enthusiasm seemed to make Morag uncomfortable, as if I was displaying some deeply unstable behaviour. 'I noticed you'd got Mum's ring,' she said unexpectedly. 'I saw it on the dressing table.'

Startled, my fingers went to the shape of it in my pocket. 'She left it to me,' I said. 'I take it everywhere.' The fact that I hadn't noticed it was missing, that it had been in someone else's hand – someone who hadn't meant me to find it – made me feel suddenly sick. 'You don't mind?'

'Why would I mind?' Morag's forehead rolled into a frown. 'I'm glad you have it.'

'I'm going to get a chain so I can wear it.' My voice sounded odd, pitched wrongly. 'I never wore jewellery at the restaurant, but now …'

She seemed to be waiting for more. When it didn't come, she looked at me oddly and nodded. 'I need to make a delivery to the farm where his nibs came from.' She nodded at Skip, who cocked his head. 'And a couple of other places.'

'You do home deliveries?' I said, grabbing the change of subject.

'People love their organic fruit and veg.' She ploughed her fingers through her hair, which seemed to be the closest she got to brushing it. 'I invest the money back into the business, if you can call it that.'

'It sounds exactly like a business.'

Morag looked grudgingly pleased. 'I tried to get into baking bread,' she said with a confessional air. 'Got as far as making a sourdough culture, but everything turned out either rock-hard or burnt. I don't have the magic touch.'

I smiled, picturing it. 'I'm a decent enough baker. Maybe I could make cakes as well, for birthdays, or offer private catering for dinner parties.'

Morag looked up from the cardboard boxes she'd plucked from under the table, her eyebrows high. 'You think people are throwing dinner parties in Fenbrith?'

My laugh surprised me as much as Morag. 'Maybe not all the time, but you never know. There are other places. Caernarfon's not far.'

'Do you drive?'

I deflated. 'I passed my test before I went to New York, but over there we either took the subway or caught cabs. Ana sometimes drove when we went out.'

'Ana was the friend you went to stay with?'

'That's right.' I was pleased she'd asked, after seeming

uninterested in my life there. 'Her uncle Julio owned the restaurant where I worked.'

Morag looked thoughtful. 'It'll be hard for you to get around if you don't drive. I could give you some refresher lessons.'

'You could,' I said. 'Or, you can be our designated driver.'

'I don't mind either way.' She lifted the boxes and patted her pocket for her keys. 'But you need to be independent.'

Was she warning me not to rely on her? 'I'll think about it,' I promised. *Being able to drive would be essential if I needed to make a quick getaway*. 'Morag, could … would you mind if I used the landline to call Ana?' I hadn't realised I was going to ask, but mentioning my friend had brought a strong craving to hear her voice.

Morag gave a curt nod. 'Be my guest.'

'I can pay for the call.'

'Don't worry about it,' she said. 'I'll see you later.'

Skip followed her outside and I left the door open, confident he would bark if anyone approached. Beginning to mop the floor I tried not to keep looking round, imagining someone sneaking up behind me. *Was that what Patrick wanted?* I didn't want to keep thinking about him, but maybe that was his intention.

I wished I'd asked Morag to buy some batteries for the radio, but made do with singing the ABBA song I'd heard earlier, checking Lily's expression and catching a smile.

When I'd finished mopping, I changed Lily's nappy on her changing mat, blowing raspberries on the soft domed skin of her belly. She grabbed at my hair and made cooing noises. I revelled in the sound, wanting to always make her happy. To let her know she could trust me to keep her safe. *Safe*. Such a simple word.

'You're the cutest baby in the world.' I took out my phone and snapped a couple of pictures once I'd dressed her. The forest-green of her jumpsuit made her eyes look darker, but the image quality was terrible, the phone a cheap model with a basic camera.

Maybe I could ask Morag for some lighting tips, and in return show her how to bake bread.

Lily grew excitable, kicking her legs and thrashing her arms around. I found a blanket in Morag's bedding pile and spread it on the rug, away from the draught from the open door, and placed Lily on top so she could wriggle about.

Next, I wiped all the surfaces with a damp cloth, careful to put each item back in the same place. As I worked, I turned my mind to the apartment above the restaurant. I'd carried on living there after Ana decided to study food science at New York University, choosing to share accommodation nearby with a couple of fellow students. The waitress we'd shared the apartment with initially had left to go travelling, so I had the place to myself. Ana's uncle hadn't needed the money so my rent was nominal and I'd been able to afford to change the furniture, do some decorating, make the place my own. Housed in one of Manhattan's oldest buildings it had plenty of character – high ceilings, ornate coving – and big windows with a view of the Hudson if I squinted hard. It was palatial compared to Morag's cottage. Although it had mostly been a place to sleep when I wasn't working, it came to feel like home; the smells and sounds of the restaurant as familiar as the ones I'd grown up with.

The queen-sized bed was where Lily had been conceived, the narrow kitchen where Patrick once cooked for me, the velvet sofa the place where he'd talked about his brother's death and – on one occasion – a trip we might take to England. I wished I had a better story to tell Lily one day, but at least I could honestly say she'd been conceived with something close to love.

In danger of becoming maudlin, I focused on wringing out the cloth before putting it away, then dried my hands. Kneeling down, I clasped Lily's tiny fingers in mine. 'You'll soon be crawling at this rate.' After spending some time talking nonsense to her, marvelling at how much more solid she seemed than just a week ago, I decided to prepare the rabbits for dinner and make a hearty stew.

With a bracing breath, I opened the fridge and took out the plate. *Odd.* There was only one rabbit there. Had Morag disposed of the other? It seemed unlikely, and I doubted Skip had managed to open the fridge door and help himself. I pondered for a moment, feeling my heart pick up pace, then found a casserole dish and a chopping board and began to prepare the meat, slipping into practical mode. There wasn't much, but it wasn't as if I was cooking for a food critic. With a heap of vegetables, it would be a satisfying meal.

The motion of chopping and slicing was as soothing as ever, taking me back to the early days at *Julio's* when prepping had been my job in the kitchen. I'd picked up several minor injuries – most notably, an almost severed thumb that required a trip to the hospital, my hand bound in a bloody tea towel while Ana propped me up and I tried not to faint.

Once I'd figured out how Morag's oven worked and the casserole was in, I cleared out the grate in the fireplace, sweeping cold ash into a bin bag. There was no reason not to light a fire now I was certain Patrick somehow knew where I was. It would be less expensive than using an electric heater. I scrunched up the pages of an old newspaper, arranged some of the logs in the hearth on top, and set it alight with a match.

Leaving it to catch, I stepped around the sofa to the telephone on the dresser, keeping Lily in my eyeline. My heart thumped with anticipation as I checked the time. Nearly 5 p.m. It would be lunchtime in New York. Ana, who now worked as a nutritionist for a public health company, would likely be out for a run, a habit she'd got into because she hated getting up early to do it before work like most New Yorkers, and believed the evenings were for socialising.

Ana's was the only number I knew by heart, apart from Mum's – I hadn't been given Patrick's – and it came to me easily. I picked up the handset, which felt cold and smooth in my hand, picturing Ana, long and lithe, her chestnut hair scraped back in a sleek ponytail, mouth on the verge of smiling. Then I realised I was imagining the girl she'd been when we met on our third day at secondary school. I'd been worrying about not having a best friend, head down, feeling close to tears. Ana was plugged into a brand-new, highly sought-after iPod and literally bumped into me in the corridor. She tugged one earbud out, her cheeks flushed, dark eyes shining, and without even apologising said, 'Listen to this, it's brilliant.'

That's how I'd been introduced to Pink and met my new best friend, Ana ('one n') Miller, whose mother was Spanish and who was so fun and friendly it was impossible not to love her. I was sure if she'd bumped into anyone else that day, she'd have become their best friend, but I was the lucky one; the one she'd stuck by through everything, not judging, even when I told her that Patrick was married and staying with Elise. She'd judged him, but never me. But even Ana didn't know the whole story and I knew I could never tell her. I just wanted to speak to her, hear her news, tell her mine – chat normally, like we used to.

I'd started pressing in her number when I realised there was no dial tone. *Weird.* It was definitely a working landline, despite the phone's antique appearance. I put the receiver down and picked it up again, pressed it to my ear. Nothing.

I traced the yellowing cord to the socket on the wall above the skirting board, checking it was plugged in. Maybe the telephone company were doing some work. It wasn't unusual, especially out here, for the weather to bring down the phone lines. I picked up the receiver and put it down a couple more times before admitting defeat.

Feeling thwarted, I lifted Lily up and went outside, calling for Skip. He bounded up from the bottom of the garden, stopping halfway to finish chewing something in his mouth.

'What have you got there?' I said when he reached us. It looked like an animal bone. He wagged his tail and swallowed before running around the side of the cottage. I followed, holding tightly to Lily, checking the stone walls for the phone wire that would feed into the building. The sun was still out, warm on the back of my neck, but as I moved into the shade thrown by the bank of trees at the back of the cottage, goose bumps pimpled my arms.

Glancing up, I noticed a thick black cable trailing along the side of the wall to a rusty connector box. 'Here it is,' I said to Lily, who was twisting in my arms. Looking closer, I froze. The cable wasn't attached to the box, where coloured wires poked from the casing. It had been neatly sliced across. Someone had deliberately cut the phone line.

Chapter 17

When Morag returned, I mentioned the phone line as casually as I could.

She shrugged, seeming unconcerned. 'I'll ask Ifan to take a look; he's good with things like that.'

'I think it's been cut.' It sounded too dramatic.

Morag frowned, one hand resting on the wall while she removed her boot with the other and gently nudged Skip away. 'It's probably corroded,' she said. 'That side of the cottage takes the brunt of the weather.'

'When did you last use the phone apart from when I called you?' I heard a thread of anxiety in my voice. Despite running inside and locking the door, leaving Skip to roam the perimeters – though all he did was whine and scratch at the wood – I couldn't banish the image of a shrouded figure, sneaking up to the cottage, gloved hand holding a pair of wire cutters.

Morag's frown deepened. 'I can't remember. Sometimes people phone with an order for fruit and veg, but not that often now I've got my regulars. I rarely call anyone.'

So, it could have happened before I arrived. It wasn't necessarily anything to do with me. *So why did I feel sick?*

'Why do you ask?' Morag kicked off her other boot, sending

it spinning across the newly cleaned floor. Skip chased after it, claws clattering on the tiles.

'I just think you should be able to ring for help if you have to.'

'Haven't so far.' Catching something in my expression, she added, 'I take your point though, especially with the baby here. We'll get it fixed, don't worry.'

After dinner, which Morag declared, 'Not bad at all,' clearing every scrap on her plate while I ate more slowly, I cleared up while she watched Lily and then shrugged her coat back on. 'I'm going to the pub.' It was a declaration of intent, no explanation, or apology for leaving me to my own devices. I wondered whether she went there every evening. I had the feeling that, like me, she rarely drank – there was no alcohol in the cottage and she'd stuck to water at the pub the day before – so maybe she liked feeling part of something at the pub. Maybe she hoped to see Ifan. *Maybe she was avoiding being alone with me.* I didn't want to ask and see her evade the question.

Once she'd gone, the van engine unnaturally loud in the fading light, I let Skip out before feeding Lily and bathing her in the kitchen sink, keeping one eye on the clearing outside, in case a figure appeared. I sat Lily up and supported her head, splashing her with warm water, glad I'd thought to pack baby shampoo and soap. Covered in bubbles, she smiled and kicked, blinking in surprise like she always did when I tipped her back gently to rinse her hair. I smiled, flooded with love. Life could be so simple, so perfect. This was all we needed – a roof over our heads, food in our bellies and each other. *Why couldn't he let us have that?*

After she was snuggled into her Minnie Mouse sleepsuit, dozing in the Moses basket, which I'd brought down so I could see her, I picked a novel off the bookshelf and settled onto the sofa with a blanket over my legs. I tried to absorb myself in a story about spies in war-torn Germany. It was ages since I'd had the time or headspace to read, but my mind, weary from a tangle of worry and fear, wanted to rest. My eyes kept closing, craving sleep. It was as if my body was making up for the hours I'd lost over the past few months; to Lily, who'd needed feeding every two hours, and the sickening burden of worry about our futures. My thoughts started drifting to Patrick, flitting from his face in the article I'd read, to the night he ordered me to leave, to the unexpected softness in his eyes when he found out I was pregnant.

I hadn't intended him to know. When he made his decision to stay with Elise something had shifted, like a veil being lifted. Deceit wore away respect. He'd deceived his wife, and me too, by telling me their marriage was over. She'd become real to me then, a woman who, despite Patrick's belief that she only cared about getting drunk as discreetly as possible, must love him deeply.

I didn't tell anyone I was pregnant, including Mum when she called for one of her irregular updates. Only Ana had known, after catching me that day in the toilets, and I'd sworn her to secrecy. As the nausea quickly passed, I carried on as usual, disguising the tiny swell of my stomach with baggier than usual clothes. No one I knew suspected, used to my single status and commitment to work. It hadn't occurred to them I was even seeing anyone, my brief affair with Patrick conducted in total privacy.

I hadn't wanted a baby, hadn't planned to fall pregnant. I didn't see a doctor. I didn't look on websites to see what stage it was at. I didn't try out names, buy bootees, or research the best pushchairs. I simply continued with my life as if I'd never met Patrick. When six months had passed, and Ana eventually asked what my plan was – adoption or single parenthood (it was somehow understood that a termination was off the table) – I said lightly, 'I don't know. I haven't decided yet.'

I wasn't hanging out with her family as often, when I wasn't working, not wanting them to see that I was pregnant. They were Catholic, her cousin Maria a midwife at Mount Sinai; they wouldn't understand.

I knew there was a baby inside me, that I was growing a whole new person, cells dividing, tissue growing, but it seemed abstract

– beyond my full comprehension. Right up until I felt a flutter beneath my ribcage, like a butterfly taking flight. I'd been in a cab on my way to meet a new supplier, overwhelmed with tiredness and trying to ignore a dull ache in my lower back. I gasped out loud, catching the driver's attention.

'Everything OK back there?'

'I just felt my baby move.' It had sounded strange, saying it out loud to a stranger. I laid a tentative hand across my stomach feeling slightly sick, not sure I liked the sensation.

'Your first?' The driver, stopped in traffic, turned, a smile on his leathery face.

I nodded, sitting back, my breathing shallow. I felt as if I'd been forced over a threshold into a different way of thinking that wasn't natural; wasn't the me I recognised. And this was just the beginning. Once the baby was born, a lifetime of caring for another human being would follow; a life of worry, dread and possible disaster; a life no longer my own. I'd started to cry, gulping sobs I tried to hold in with a hand pressed to my mouth as tears splashed down my face. 'I don't think I can do it,' I sobbed. The driver had somehow managed to pull over and hand me a pack of tissues from the glove box.

'The first's the hardest; it'll be easier next time around.' His voice was unbearably kind, his expression weighted with experience. 'I have four daughters and my wife, she was sick the whole way through each pregnancy. She wanted to kill me, but the second she held each of our girls it was all forgotten. It'll be the same for you, you'll see.'

I wanted so much to believe him, but the fear persisted, swelling whenever I felt another movement inside – my baby reminding me that he or she was there, waiting to meet me; waiting for me to decide his or her fate. And then, Patrick was back and everything changed again.

*

'Come to the market with me,' Morag said the following morning, looking as though she'd slept well. Her eyes were bright, her hair brushed back, the sofa bedding folded away in the dresser. I'd heard her come in the night before and tread softly to the top of the stairs. I'd kept my breathing even as I looked at her outline through my lashes, watching her watching us – probably longing to call Skip down off the bed where he'd taken up residence as soon as I climbed in. I hadn't stopped him. His presence made me feel safe.

'You can help on the stall or sit in a café, I don't mind.'

It was preferable to being left alone at the cottage, plus I could use my mobile to call Ana from the village.

'OK.' I nodded, biting into a slice of buttered toast, burnt on one side. Morag had made breakfast while I was feeding and changing Lily. 'Shouldn't you be there already, setting up?'

'Biddy's turn this week. She runs the post office, makes jam, honey, chutneys, that sort of thing in her spare time. We run the stall together. I don't have enough produce on my own.'

'I probably won't be much help, with Lily.'

Morag shrugged. 'You can get to know the place.'

'What about Skip?' He looked up sharply at the sound of his name and padded over to the table. 'It doesn't seem fair to leave him here on his own.' Especially as he was proving a less than useful deterrent. I thought of the phone line and how Skip hadn't barked once while he was outside. *Unless he knew the culprit?*

In the light of a new day, I was trying to convince myself that Morag was right and the ruined cable was weather-related, but my churning stomach said otherwise.

'We can take him with us in the van, I suppose.'

Skip's tail beat, as if he understood, and I gave him the crust from my toast.

'You shouldn't spoil him,' Morag said, as she rose from the table with her empty cereal bowl, but there was no heat in her words. 'I'm going for a shower.'

*

102

The farmers' market was in full flow when we arrived, the main through-road lined with stalls. There was an eclectic array of goods on display: foodstuff, garden plants, craft-ware and pet food.

Morag bumped the van carefully across the cobbles and parked beside a stall selling local produce, where a woman was sitting in a deckchair with a mug of tea. She was sixtyish, wearing a woolly bobble hat over her flame-red hair, and a green waxed jacket as though expecting rain. Although the sky was a watery blue, pale sunshine giving the illusion of warmth, downpours were forecast for later.

'Biddy, this is my niece Grace and her baby,' Morag said, once she'd jumped from the van. I felt compelled to clamber out too, once I'd transferred Lily from car seat to carrier. I submitted to an appraising look as Biddy placed her mug on the ground and rose to her feet. She was smaller than me, but wiry and broad-shouldered.

Apparently satisfied with whatever she'd seen in me, she switched her attention to Lily. 'She's a bonny one.'

'Her name's Lily,' I obliged, trying not to pull away when Biddy stroked a coarse finger across Lily's cheek, her wide smile revealing large, uneven teeth.

'Got a look of your aunt about her, poor bugger.' A raucous chuckle split the air. Lily twitched but didn't make a sound.

'Take no notice,' Morag said, but couldn't hide the gleam of pleasure that entered her eyes. 'I'll get my stuff.'

As she arranged her selection of tomatoes, potatoes, carrots, onions and cabbages on the trestle table, next to Biddy's jars of berry jam and clover honey, their colours jewel-like in the sunshine, I moved aside, hoping Biddy wouldn't bombard me with questions.

Instead, she surprised me by tilting her head and saying, 'You came at the right time, Grace.' Her eyes were round and intensely blue, reminding me of Ifan. 'It's just the lift your aunt needed.'

'Really?'

Skip sprang from the back of the van where he'd panted and whined throughout the short journey, demanding to be fussed.

'Oh, you've ended up with the runt.' Biddy snorted out another laugh as she stooped to stroke his ears. 'You really must have won your aunt over,' she said. 'The Joneses have been trying to find him a home for a while, but your aunt was very firm in her refusal.'

'What did you mean about her needing a lift?' My curiosity was piqued.

'She's not been her usual self lately.' Biddy lowered her voice as Morag came round the back of the van. 'There's been some trouble locally,' she said. 'Bored lads with nothing to do but make trouble. They broke into the gift shop a few nights ago, stole the takings, and smashed the windows in the pub a few weeks back. Your aunt's sure they've been up at the cottage.' My heart picked up speed. It explained the bolts on the door. Could it explain …? *No.* My spirits sank. The note, the missing ring. It was personal. 'Not even my cousin could put a smile on her face,' Biddy was saying. 'Just when I had high hopes they might actually, you know …' She winked and nudged me violently with her elbow. 'Oh, I'm so sorry,' she said, when Lily pouted and her face reddened. 'I didn't mean to upset the little one. I remember how hard it is when they're babies, never sleeping more than a few hours. When my two – I've got twin boys – were born, I don't think I slept through the night for two years.'

'Actually, she's only waking once or twice in the night.' Hearing the pride in my voice made me wince. As if it wasn't pure luck, but something Lily had mastered through hard work and determination.

'You're one of the lucky ones,' Biddy said. 'What about her dad? Is he in the picture?'

'No, he isn't.' I hoped my tone would deflect further questions. In New York, it had taken some time to adjust to how open people were with their feelings and emotions, their lack of reserve and willingness to talk, how nearly everyone was in therapy. Although I'd slightly resented Morag's reserve, I now found myself appreciating it.

'Well, a child doesn't necessarily need two parents to grow up well adjusted.' Biddy tugged her hat off and stuffed it in her pocket. Her hair was like the plume of an exotic bird, at odds with the whiteness of her skin.

'So, Ifan's your cousin,' I said. It explained the piercing blue eyes. 'He and my aunt seem to get on well.'

'I hope you're not discussing me.' Morag came over, her gaze on Lily whose eyes were teary as she took in her new surroundings. 'Leave her alone now, Bid. She's not used to old gossips like you.'

'Bloody cheek.' Biddy cuffed Morag's arm, but it was affectionate. Someone else who was clearly fond of my aunt.

'I think I'll have a look round,' I said. 'Unless I can help?'

'Two's company, three's a crowd.' Biddy's smile crinkled her eyes. Morag had turned to a man who was enquiring about the price of the cabbages. 'You don't want to be stuck here with us.'

'I think I'll get a drink in the café.' I pointed to a building opposite, with a sign shaped like a teapot above the door. 'I'll be back soon.'

'Oh, the Old Coffee Cup,' Biddy approved. 'Oldest café in Fenbrith. They do lovely Welsh cakes.' She grabbed Skip's collar as he made to follow me. 'He'll be fine now, off you go.'

The air inside the café was fragrant with coffee and pastries. I felt hungry after giving most of my toast to the dog. I'd always loved to eat, though I'd had to be careful at work when it came to tasting menus as it was easy to pile on weight, but for months I'd been forcing down food for Lily's sake, my stomach too knotted to accept more than a few morsels.

'Time for a treat,' I said to Lily, sitting down once I'd ordered a coffee and a couple of Welsh cakes that really did look delicious. Lily bucked and kicked her legs, emitting a high-pitched noise that turned a few heads.

I unstrapped her and bounced her on my knee, waiting for her smile.

Once the waitress had delivered my order, I settled Lily on my lap with a view across the street of people jostling around the market stalls. It was easy here, to believe everything was fine.

Drawing in a deep breath, I took out my phone and called Ana's number.

*

He couldn't believe how easy it was to get close without her knowing. The dog was no barrier. He'd always had a way with animals. Dogs in particular were easy to befriend as long as you gave them a treat. Skip. Hardly the name of a guard dog. A Rottweiler would have been better, but even then, he had tricks up his sleeve.

Seeing her at the pub, chatting and holding that baby as though she didn't have a care in the world … it made him angry. He knew he wouldn't report that. Not the sort of detail he'd be comfortable relaying.

Just biding his time now. Enjoying living like this, if he was honest; invisible, watching. Back to basics, doing what he was good at – stalking the enemy.

Cutting off the only means of contact had been easy. He didn't want her calling for help when the time came. Dropping the ring had been a mistake – unlike him – but he'd been startled by the dog. Good job he knew all about camouflage, about blending in.

Of course, two of them in the building made it harder, but that wouldn't stop him, not when he had a job to do. He was nothing, if not thorough.

Chapter 18

As the ringtone continued, I realised with a start that I'd forgotten about the time difference. It would be barely dawn in New York. Ana would be sleeping. She wore earplugs because the walls in her apartment were thin and her neighbours liked to party. Unless she was at Tom's place; the man who'd finally lived up to her romantic ideals by chasing a mugger who snatched her phone while she was out running, knocking her to the ground. Tom had not only returned with the phone, but saw her safely home and gave her his card in case she wanted him to give a statement to the police.

Instead, she called him and invited him out to dinner to say thank you. They'd been together for six months now – a record for Ana, who was usually disillusioned after the second date, swearing to be more distrustful of men, like me. She knew about my father, understood that he'd coloured my view of relationships and made me wary of picking the wrong man. Even though, in the end, I had.

Desperate to speak to her, I let the call go to her anonymous voicemail message.

'Hey, Ana, it's me.' Tears pricked my eyes. 'I forgot the time difference – sorry to call so early. Listen, I'm fine, Lily's fine. I just wanted you to know. And I'm so sorry I didn't say goodbye in person. I hope you understand, I had no choice. But it's OK, we're safe here. At least … we will be. I think. My aunt welcomed us, surprisingly. She loves Lily.' Ana had only met my baby once, right after she was born, her face tight with worry. 'I might even have a little job, in a pub. Cooking. God, I miss you, Ana,' I let out a laugh that was more like a sob, and the napkin on the table floated to the floor. 'Call me if you want to,' I rushed on. 'Ring this number. There's no reception at my aunt's so if I don't pick up there's a landline …' Too late, I remembered it wasn't working. 'Actually, I can't remember the number, but please call me, or I'll try again soon. Love you.' I just managed to garble out the words before getting cut off.

I clasped the phone and stared into space for a second. I imagined Ana waking and getting my call, trying to picture her reaction, knowing she'd have been thinking about me and wishing I'd phoned as soon as I arrived at Heathrow.

Lily wriggled against me. I pressed a kiss to her hair before bending to pick up the napkin, which fluttered in a draught as the door opened. As I dangled it in front of Lily, my mind still in New York with Ana, a familiar voice said, 'I don't suppose you fancy sharing those?'

My head jerked up. It was Declan, standing by the table, looking longingly at the plate of Welsh cakes.

My heart leapt. 'What are you doing here?'

'We're not going to start with the questions again, are we?'

'That's a question.' My tone was neutral but I couldn't prevent a rush of blood to my face. I'd never been a blusher, wasn't the type to go weak at the knees if a good-looking man so much as spoke to me. Before Patrick, I'd always be seeking the catch, the flaw, telling myself they were being nice because they wanted something, that it was better to take no notice. When Patrick had complimented me the night we met, I said, 'I bet you say that to all the girls,' and I hadn't been teasing or flirting. I'd believed it.

'So, are you willing to share?'

Declan was more rugged than I remembered, his eyes a darker shade of green, his smile a degree warmer. There was something of the land about him. I could imagine him rescuing a sheep, or felling a tree; living off-grid. *Living in the woods?* I surprised myself by saying, 'I was being greedy. I can't eat them both.'

'In that case, I don't mind if I do.' Declan pulled out a chair and sat down, picking up one of the sugar-sprinkled cakes and biting into it, miming a look of pleasure.

A waitress came over, practically preening. 'Can I fetch you a drink?'

'I'll have what she's having, please.' Declan pointed to my mug of cooling coffee. His manner with the waitress was polite. He seemed unaware of the effect he was having.

'Flat white,' I said.

When she'd gone, he finished his cake in two bites and dusted crumbs from his fingers. 'Are you going to eat yours?'

I adjusted Lily on my lap and reached for the plate. 'Sorry to disappoint you.'

I tried not to mind him watching me eat, but the cake felt dry in my mouth and was hard to swallow. I drank some coffee, Lily tracking the mug's journey to my lips. 'How come you're back in Fenbrith?' I said when the silence began to feel awkward.

The waitress returned with his coffee, but his eyes didn't move from my face. He waited until she'd gone, then leant towards me, palms facing up on the table. 'If I'm honest, I was hoping I might run into you.'

I felt a pulse in my throat as I searched his candid gaze. 'Why?'

'I liked our chat yesterday.' His smile was like sunlight parting the clouds. 'After I left the pub, I realised I didn't even know your name or where you were staying. I had a feeling you were never going to call me, so ...' He gave a shrug, eyebrows lifted. 'I knew it was market day and thought I'd hop over and have a mooch about, see if you turned up.' He looked through the window. 'I bumped into your aunt—'

'How do you know my aunt?' It came out more abruptly than I'd intended. Lily sucked her fingers, unperturbed.

'I recognised her from the pub.' Declan sat back and interlocked his fingers in his lap. He was wearing the same coat as the day before, a knitted sweater underneath that matched the colour of his eyes. 'I asked her where you were and the woman on the stall told me you were in here.'

Biddy. I remembered she ran the post office, probably loved a bit of gossip, knew everything about everybody and wouldn't be shy about passing on details.

'I have to say, your aunt was a bit cagey,' he said, adding before I could think of a reply, 'Not that I blame her. I could be anyone as far as she's concerned.'

Good for Morag. 'How was your hike?' I lifted Lily and patted her back, not sure whether I was soothing her or myself. 'To Snowdon?'

He grimaced. 'It's not half as much fun in the rain, though Hugh minded less than I did.'

'You have to get used to the rain around here.'

'You know the area well?'

'Everyone knows it rains a lot in Wales.'

'And it doesn't where you're from?'

Where did he think I was from? 'No more than anywhere else. You must have plenty of the wet stuff in Ireland.' It was so typically British to be discussing the weather, I almost smiled.

Declan nodded. 'Spent a lot of time with rain-draggled hair.' I had a sudden, vivid image of him as a boy, tearing around on a bike, hair streaming in the wind, eyes flashing with laughter. 'It could be raining on one side of the hills and blazing sunshine on the other,' he said. 'There'd be these amazing rainbows—' he made an arch with his arm '—and my grandmother had us convinced the pot of gold was always on the sunny side.'

He was easy to listen to, his accent lyrical. The sort of voice you'd never get tired of hearing. He picked up his mug, fingers brown against the white earthenware. While he drank, I studied his face, looking for … what? Some clue that he wasn't who he said he was? Would I have to live the rest of my life suspecting that everyone who spoke to me had a hidden agenda? The timing of Declan's appearance in Fenbrith was unusual but he seemed genuine, no trace of artifice in his face. *Even so.* 'Look, Declan … as you can see, I have a baby and—'

'Lily, right?' He put down his mug, a smile still playing at the corners of his mouth.

My hand stilled on Lily's back. 'How do you know that?'

'Have a guess.' Declan pointed through the window. The street was crowded, a queue at the fish stall, people chatting and smiling. A normal day. Better than normal because the sun was shining and everyone was in a good mood. 'Your aunt's friend mentioned it. She couldn't get over that her niece and great-niece had come to visit after all this time.' His gaze held a twinkle, but I saw a shade of sympathy there too. 'The downside of living in a small community.' He twisted his mug unconsciously – a small sign that he wasn't as relaxed as he seemed? 'Everyone knows your business. One of the reasons I couldn't wait to leave home.'

'What were you doing that you didn't want people to know about?' I hated the new sharpness in my tone. I didn't want Lily getting used to hearing it.

'Nothing that would frighten the horses as my gran used to say.' He paused, his gaze direct. 'Lily's a good name.'

I tried to relax. 'It was my grandmother's.'

'Doesn't it mean pure, innocent? Seems fitting for a baby.' Before I could comment, he added with a small laugh, 'Hard to imagine our grandmothers being babies once.'

Maybe it was the randomness of his comment, or comparing his reaction with Patrick's – *Lily's an old woman's name* – but some of my animosity drained away. He seemed nice – more than nice.

He's hot and he likes you. What's your problem?

If he bothers to ask again, I might say yes. That had been my mantra – until Patrick. He hadn't needed to ask twice.

'I wish my gran had got to meet her.' I slotted Lily back in her carrier, cradling her with one hand while I adjusted the straps, making sure her legs were dangling free. As her head drooped against my chest, I wondered whether she could hear my racing heart. 'I should get back.' I forced a smile as I stood up. 'It was nice to see you again, but I'm not looking for … whatever it is you think you want.'

'Whoa!' Declan lifted both hands, made a play of reeling back in his chair. 'Just give it to me straight, why don't you?'

The waitress looked over at me, her eyes flinty. *Let me have him, if you don't want him.*

'I just did.'

He shook his head and ran a hand though his tumble of hair. 'Look, I just thought if you're staying a while, maybe we could have a day out like tourists. Go up Snowdon on the steam train if you like and take a look at the view. I've heard it's quite something when the weather's nice.'

'Taking the train seems like a cop-out.'

'Not sure climbing a mountain with an eight-week-old baby is wise, unless you're experienced.'

'Nor is standing on top of one. I'm not keen on heights.' I imagined a strong pair of hands on my back, shoving me over the edge. A wave of nausea surged through my belly. *Elise, at the foot of the stairs. The look on Patrick's face—* Snapping off bad memories, I gathered my things together. 'Bye.'

'We don't have to go right to the top,' Declan persisted. 'There's a café near the summit, where the train stops. We could grab a drink and admire the view.'

'Fine.' I wanted to get away now. 'I'll give you a call.'

'You will?' He sounded sceptical. 'I won't have to come looking for you again?'

I paused, searching his face as I hoisted my bag onto my shoulder, careful not to jar Lily. 'Come looking for me?'

'I don't have your number.' His gaze didn't falter. 'We could

112

arrange a day and time now. I could pick you up, say … Sunday at 10 a.m.'

I shook my head, already moving away. 'Ten-thirty. Outside here. I won't wait if you're late.'

'I won't be.' His words followed me out onto the pavement where I stood for a second, catching my breath as though I'd been running, blinking in the brightness.

There was an old-fashioned toyshop next to the café. I plunged inside, a jangling bell above the door heralding my arrival. It was empty, apart from the woman at the till who looked engrossed in a crossword.

'Look at all these lovely things,' I said to Lily, closing my mind to my conversation with Declan.

The woman looked up and beamed. 'Oh, what a cutie!'

I ended up buying two board books, an animal-based activity mat and a ladybird wrist-rattle, paying with some of the notes I'd stuffed in my bag.

'Staying here, are you?'

I nodded, unable to face a grilling. On my way back to Morag, I paused to look in the gift-shop window, seeing a doorstop in the shape of a Cheshire cat – the sort of thing Mum would love. I couldn't remember the last time I'd bought her a gift. Maybe I'd come back and get it for her, take it with me when I visited.

As I made to move away, I caught a reflection behind me in the window like a ghost. A man in a waterproof, a gleam of dark blond hair, feet planted wide apart. He was looking right at me. *Declan?* My lungs felt chilled. Did he know I could see him? Slowly, slowly, I turned, but there was no one there. As I searched the pavement where he'd been, something occurred to me. How had he known that Lily was eight weeks old?

Chapter 19

'I didn't know it was meant to be a secret.' Biddy's cheeks were almost as red as her hair. 'Your aunt didn't say.'

'Didn't get a chance,' Morag murmured.

'It's not a secret, I just … I don't know the man very well,' I said. 'What exactly did you say to him?'

'Only, "Oh, you mean Morag's niece, Grace? She's in the café with that lovely baby of hers".'

'You didn't mention her name?'

'Well, he said, "What's her name again, the baby?" So, I said, "Lily." Your aunt was busy with a customer.' She looked confused as she glanced at Morag. 'If I'd known I wasn't supposed to say anything, I wouldn't have, but he seemed so lovely and I think—'

'It's fine.' Biddy's bewildered expression filled me with guilt. I shouldn't be interrogating her. Declan's throwaway comment about Lily's age had obviously been just that; a lucky guess. 'I'm being overprotective, that's all.'

'Oh, you can't be too protective with a little one like that.' Biddy's face cleared, back on familiar ground. 'Mine were permanently attached at that age. I breastfed them all until they were three.' She glanced at her chest. 'No wonder they're like a pair of deflated beach balls.' Her wheezy laugh drew amused stares, but Morag didn't smile.

'You're quiet,' she said, once we were back at the cottage. She was lighting a fire in the grate and stepped back as it sprang to life. 'Like I said, Biddy doesn't mean any harm, but she can't stop words spilling out of her once she starts.'

'Honestly, it's OK.' Morag had already apologised on the way back in the van, even though it wasn't her fault. I wasn't even sure it was Declan's reflection I'd seen in the window, and told her not to worry.

'Do you think you're in some sort of danger from Lily's father?' she said, facing me in the kitchen, still in her coat and boots. She kept glancing at the door, probably expecting Ifan to walk in. He'd followed us back to take a look at the phone line. 'Should we be worried?'

I shook my head. I couldn't say anything now. And Morag had nothing to fear. I was the one being targeted. If that looked like changing, I would leave. 'It's OK,' I said. 'He promised to leave me alone and I … I believe him.' I'd *wanted* to believe him. *More fool me.*

'Why so jumpy, then?'

'Habit, I suppose.' I wished I hadn't put Lily down for a nap. Without her in my arms, I felt insubstantial, as if I might blow away. Realising my hands were clenched, I unfurled them. 'I got used to looking over my shoulder for a while. After everything that happened it's sometimes hard to believe we're here.'

Morag's brow remained creased in a frown. 'Did he have you locked up or something?'

'No, no.' My chest tightened. 'Nothing like that, but I mean, there are more ways than one of being trapped.'

Morag's face darkened. 'Oh, I know that.' She sounded as though she was speaking from experience. 'How can you be certain he's not going to make trouble for you?'

I can't. 'Like I said, he's got a reputation to protect. I promised not to reveal certain things if he let me go.' I didn't want to go into detail – didn't think she wanted me to – but she clearly needed some reassurance. 'I read something online.' Her eyebrows rose. 'There was a piece in a newspaper that suggested he's moving on with his life.' *So why wasn't he?* I'd threatened to expose him, blackmailed him into letting me leave with Lily. Why risk me going to the police now? No one would be looking into Elise's death. Patrick's word, that it had been a tragic accident – a result of her heavy drinking – had been accepted. I had nothing to gain by reporting him.

Was I a loose end he wanted tying up?

'He must be important if he's in the news,' Morag said, but didn't ask who he was. 'Could he have sent someone after you?'

Hearing her voice my fears was a shock. 'I worried at first he might.' I decided to be honest about that. 'He knows people, could have had someone follow me here, but I was careful.' *So* careful. 'And he has too much to lose. His life is simpler without me and Lily. I doubt he'd risk everything he's worked for.'

'Is he a danger to the public?' Morag seemed curious, almost against her better judgement. 'You wouldn't want a man like that on the loose if—'

'He's not a danger to the public.' The thought was almost laughable. Patrick's job was to protect the public. As a prosecutor, he represented the state. He interviewed victims and witnesses, evaluated evidence to determine whether there was enough to open a case, to send someone to prison. He was held to a high moral standard, his background impeccable. He did most of his work in a courtroom, before a grand jury, was on call twenty-four hours a day. Since his brother's death, Patrick's whole life had been about making sure justice was done. The thought of him causing harm would have been funny, if I hadn't learnt that some people will do anything to realise their ambitions and to protect themselves.

The moral arc of the universe is long, but it bends towards justice.

It was Patrick's favourite quote, by Martin Luther King, Jr. But what about justice for his wife? Was it enough that he had to live with her death on his conscience? Was the thought of me being free, over here with his daughter, more than he could bear?

'You thought that man, Declan, was asking too many questions.'

'No, I … Look, Morag, it's been a weird time and I've been scared for months, since before Lily was born, and everything's changed so quickly.' The words came in a rush. 'I suppose I'm being vigilant because that's been my state of mind for a while.'

She nodded, but there was something in her expression that was hard to make out. 'So, you haven't seen or heard anything out of the ordinary?'

I shook my head, not trusting myself to speak. After a moment, I managed, 'Declan seems like a nice guy. I'm just not used to being—'

'Chatted up?'

I gave an embarrassed laugh, willing Ifan to come in. 'Do people still say that?'

'What else would you call it?'

'He wants to take us out on Sunday.'

'By us, I take it you don't mean me.'

I smiled. 'You're welcome to come too.'

'You're going then?' Her expression shifted again.

'You think I shouldn't?' Worry crackled across my chest. Had she picked up on something, just when I'd allowed myself to believe that Declan was genuine?

'I don't know.' Morag picked up the jar of blackberry jam she'd brought back from the stall and studied the label, handwritten in a looping scrawl. 'I think you're right to be careful.' Turning, she opened the cupboard and put the jar inside. There was a row of them, all unopened, and the thought of her buying them when she didn't need to was oddly moving. 'You can't stop living your life because of whatever happened.'

It was on the tip of my tongue to say: *Isn't that what you've done?* but I realised it wasn't true. Morag had made a good life here. She wasn't the recluse I'd expected. She had friends, a job of sorts, loved working in her garden. Ifan clearly thought the world of her, even if she didn't acknowledge the fact. And, for now at least, she had Lily and me. And a dog.

On cue, Skip bounded in and nosily lapped from his water bowl. Ifan followed and I couldn't tell whether the slight sag of Morag's shoulders signalled relief or disappointment that our conversation had been interrupted.

'*Ni allaf ei drwsio,*' he said, scratching the back of his head. 'I can't fix it. You'll have to get the telephone company out.'

'What do you think happened?' I asked.

Ifan's brow furrowed. 'Looks like it's been chewed.'

My stomach tightened.

'Wouldn't surprise me.' Morag started scooping coffee from foil bags into the cafetiere. 'Lot of squirrels around here. It wouldn't be the first time.' I remembered Skip, chasing a squirrel through the woods.

'You said it was probably corrosion.' The sharp edge was back in my voice. 'The weather, you said.'

'It could be that.' She started making coffee, evening out the measures with a knife. 'Or squirrels.'

'I'll put in a call when I get home, ask them to send someone out.' Ifan settled himself at the table and rubbed Skip's ears, seeming oblivious to the tension in the air.

Forcing myself to relax, I checked Lily in her Moses basket. She was still sleeping, her dark hair sticking straight up.

'What did you think of the rabbit?' Ifan looked expectantly from me to Morag.

'Tasty, thank you.'

'Very tasty,' Morag agreed.

Should I mention one had vanished? Imagining their confusion, I decided against it, my mind slipping back to suspicion. If Ifan hadn't taken one away and the dog hadn't eaten it … it could only be the same person who'd left the note and taken my ring.

The moment passed. Morag had plunged the cafetiere down and was pouring dark liquid into three mugs. A pigeon cooed outside and Lily sighed in her sleep. Skip circled the rug and flopped down, eyebrows twitching as he surveyed his surroundings. A log cracked in the fire and we turned to look at the leaping flames. It was an oddly domestic scene.

'You coming to the quiz night on Monday?' Ifan asked Morag, though he surely knew the answer.

'Don't I always?' She removed her jacket and leant against the worktop, cradling her mug, studying him with something approaching affection.

'I'll take my coffee upstairs if that's OK.' I was aware of a headache building at the base of my skull.

As I reached for the Moses basket, Morag said, 'We'll keep an eye on her, don't worry.'

I let my hand fall. I didn't want to offend Morag and didn't need to keep Lily by my side every second of the day, however strong the urge.

'Thanks.' I picked up my coffee instead, smiling at Ifan. He was watching me, as if trying to weigh me up. I realised it would be a mistake to dismiss him as a country yokel. There was a shrewd intelligence behind those bright blue eyes.

'Have some biscuits.' Morag pushed a packet of chocolate digestives over. I helped myself to a couple, feeling clumsy and self-conscious. Laughable really, when I'd confidently run a kitchen for several years, delegating tasks to staff and negotiating with suppliers.

Upstairs, I placed my mug and biscuits on the pile of magazines and sat on the bed. The pressure in my temples increased. I massaged my scalp with my fingertips, eyes flicking over the surfaces, the shock of finding the note fresh in my mind.

Sighing, I took my grandmother's ring out of my pocket and

wiped it on my jeans. It felt warm in my palm. I studied it for a moment, letting the stone catch the light as I'd done so many times in the past, then thrust it under my pillow out of sight. Stupid to have left it lying around in the first place. Thank God I'd found it. I glanced at the space on the dressing table where it had been and frowned. There was something there.

I stood up for a closer look, flicking the lamp on as I passed. Next to the brush and comb set on the shiny surface was a lock of fine brown hair, tied at one end with a thin elastic band. My hand flew to my throat. Baby hair?

Shaking, I picked it up between my thumb and forefinger. It was darker than Lily's, the same colour as the wood, which was why I hadn't seen it. It wasn't Lily's. It probably wasn't even real, had been put there to frighten me. I dropped it as though scalded, a vivid image rising in my brain of me hunched and running, always running, Lily clamped in my arms while I waited for the axe to fall.

A bolt of anger shot through me. I wouldn't let Patrick do this; ruin my life and Lily's. If he was expecting a reaction, I wouldn't give him one.

Then I thought of someone sneaking in, taking the rabbit from the fridge – leaving the note, the lock of hair, stealing my ring on impulse. A shiver trailed across my back. What if next time they took Lily? Maybe this person had gone rogue, was enjoying the game too much. It had nothing to do with Patrick's instructions. A chilling montage ran though my head, culled from thrillers and horror films: a mutilated bird on the door-step, dead roses delivered, a cat nailed to the gatepost. *Or dog.* Wasn't the family pet always killed by the baddie? Everyone knew that killing an innocent animal delivered the biggest emotional punch.

I moved to the stairs and looked over the balcony rail. Morag was seeing Ifan out, his voice a low rumble in the doorway. Lily had woken in her basket, legs kicking, while Skip whined at Ifan's heels. As he moved aside to let the dog run outdoors, Morag turned and looked up as if sensing my stare.

'I thought you were having a sleep.'

'Lily needs changing.' Plastering on a smile, I descended the stairs. 'I'll keep an eye on her now if you've got work to do.'

Morag gave me a funny look, as if my tone wasn't quite right, but followed Ifan out without a word.

I rushed back upstairs, picked up the hair from the floor and dropped it in Morag's underwear drawer. It was proof of sorts. If I needed it.

Chapter 20

'Are you going to the pub this evening?' It was Thursday. I'd cooked dinner – lamb cutlets with a mint and shallot relish – which Morag had eaten with enthusiasm, tossing the bones to Skip when she'd finished. Now she was flicking through a local paper that Ifan had brought, my reading glasses perched on the end of her nose.

'I don't have a drink problem, you know.' She glanced at me over the glasses, which she must have taken out of the sweatshirt pocket where I'd stuffed them the night I arrived.

'I didn't say you had.'

'I thought you might worry about that, because of your dad.'

It was Patrick's wife who sprang to mind these days when I thought about alcohol. I'd mostly blocked Dad from my mind. 'I know the signs of a drinker,' I said. 'I can tell you're not one.'

'Never developed a taste for it.' Her smiles didn't last long, I noticed. As if she wasn't used to exercising her facial muscles. 'I like the quizzes, the card games, that kind of thing.' She turned a page of the newspaper. 'There's usually something going on there, someone to have a game of dominoes with.'

'People still play dominoes?'

Her smile was slightly mocking this time. 'Lot of old boys in the snug in the evenings. They've no use for iPads, or Netflix or whatever.'

'Do you still speak Welsh?' She and mum had been fluent as children, but Dad had thought the language old-fashioned and didn't like hearing it from Mum. *Speak English, woman, like the rest of us.*

Morag shook her head. 'Sometimes, with Ifan. It's still there, but I'm rusty,' she said. 'I remember Gran trying to teach you.'

'I was rubbish.' I grimaced. 'I've never had a knack for languages.'

Morag hadn't referred to our earlier conversation once Ifan had left, busying herself on the allotment. When I went out with a cup of tea, Lily in her baby carrier, she'd thanked me and carried on turning the soil with a trowel, making it clear she wanted to be left alone. She hadn't noticed my eyes discreetly skimming the perimeters. I didn't want to challenge whoever was out there, draw them into doing something dangerous, but it would be foolish to not be extra vigilant. Maybe whoever it was would get tired and give up. *Or resort to more risky measures.* I couldn't relax, knowing they could come in the cottage whenever they wanted, move around Morag's home – which I was starting to think of as my home – touching my things. Lily's things.

For the first time, I remembered what Biddy had said about bored youths from the area looking for trouble, but this was different; more calculated.

'I can stay here if you prefer.' I started at Morag's voice. She pushed up the glasses and glanced at me again, eyes magnified through the lenses. 'Are you worried about being left on your own?'

It was almost a challenge, as though she was waiting to hear me say it. *If I did, would she stay?* 'Of course not,' I said. 'Carry on as though I wasn't here.'

'I don't think you want to see me doing a jig in the nude, or hear me playing the trombone.'

It took a second to realise she was joking. 'I'd pay to come to that show.' I finished feeding Lily and sat her forward on my lap, patting her back to bring up her wind. 'Didn't you used to play … something?'

'Piano.' Morag dipped her head to Lily's level and smiled, almost as though she couldn't help herself. 'I was terrible. Your mother was a much better musician than I was, could play a tune by ear.'

Out of nowhere a memory rose, of my mother sitting at the piano in the living room of my grandparents' house one Christmas, playing something classical – Mozart, maybe – while my gran and granddad waltzed around, smiling into each other's eyes. I'd begged her to play a Spice Girls' song, throwing out titles until Dad said, 'Let her play, Grace. It's beautiful, don't you think?' I sometimes searched for good memories of Dad, but they were all from before I understood that he was only nice in the early stages of being drunk, which didn't count.

'What was your special talent?' I said, slamming a lid on the past. 'Apart from photography?'

Morag appeared to give it some thought, taking off the glasses and tipping her head back. Her neck was long, elegant. Hardly lined at all. 'I wasn't a bad singer, I suppose.'

'Really?' The idea was pleasing, but I couldn't imagine it. Maybe in a hotel bar in a far-flung country or, more likely, in the shower. 'It's not too late to apply to go on *The X Factor*.'

'Very funny.' Her eyebrows twitched. 'I've only ever had the nerve to sing if someone's playing the guitar.' Her gaze settled somewhere over my shoulder. 'There was something about it I couldn't resist.'

'Did you know someone who could play?' *Someone special* was what I meant and she knew it. The shutters came down, her gaze emptying.

'I did, but it was a long time ago, in another life.'

'Have you ever wanted to get married?' I wasn't sure why I'd said it, knowing she hated personal questions, but I had an inkling the guitar-playing man had meant something to her.

'What do you want to hear, Grace?' Her tone was flat. 'That I had some great love affair but there was a tragedy I never got over and that's why I'm alone?'

'That's not what I want to hear.' I pulled Lily onto my shoulder, still patting her back. 'I shouldn't have asked, I'm sorry.'

Morag shifted her gaze back to the paper. 'There was someone, once.' Her tone was hard. 'It didn't work out and I wasn't interested in marrying anyone else. I was married to my job, I suppose. And here I am.'

'Thank goodness.'

She looked up, as though caught by surprise. 'You'd have survived,' she said. 'Probably gone back to your mother's.'

'I'm glad I had a choice.'

She shoved back her stool and rose, clearly uncomfortable with the topic. 'I'll get off then. Leave you in peace.'

When she'd gone, I washed up, then laid Lily on her new activity mat, pointing to the hanging zoo animals as I sounded out their names. I squeezed the lion's middle so he gave a gentle roar. Lily seemed fascinated, hands reaching out, eyes flicking from my face to each of the animals in turn. 'You're going to be such a clever girl.' I tickled her bare feet and watched her toes curl. 'I can't wait to hear your first word.'

I waited until it was properly dark outside before opening the front door. Skip shot out and looped around, lit by the security light. There was total darkness beyond. Above, the clouds swept across a high moon and wind moaned through the trees. I shivered, clasping my arms around myself, looking back to check Lily was safe.

If anyone was watching, I was exposed, standing in the glare of the light and the lamp from the room behind me. I waited for Skip to move out of range and when darkness descended, let the door swing almost shut behind me.

I scanned the area, trying to let my eyes adjust, gasping when an owl hooted close by. How did Morag stand it out here alone? In daylight it was fine, but in darkness the isolation was more obvious. It was why I'd been drawn to Fenbrith in the first place, but now it seemed horribly easy to become a target with no one around to help.

The air in the cottage was cooling, the fire dying to a deep orange glow. Lily gave a muted whimper.

'Skip!' I peered at the darkness enfolding the cottage. 'Here, boy!' Silence, then a rustling sound somewhere to my left. The hairs rose on my arms. 'Skip?' Maybe he'd got in the bin, or was snuffling through the compost heap where Morag scraped any leftovers. 'Come here!' A bark bounced through the blackness. Should I leave him there? What if he was hurt? Why else wasn't he coming back?

Checking once more that Lily hadn't moved, I ran out, blinking as the security light flicked into life. 'You'd better not be injured.' The sound of my voice was heartening, proof that I existed. *Injured.* The thought hit like a punch. 'Oh no.' I rounded the cottage at speed and stopped when I saw the dog by the bin, a guilty expression on his face, bones scattered around him. They were small like … like rabbit bones. Maybe he'd got hold of the one in the fridge after all. 'You've been a naughty boy,' I said, mock-sternly. He whined and sank down, ears flattened as if expecting a telling-off. 'What have you been up to—?'

A heavy shove in the middle of my back sent me flying, knocking the breath out of my lungs. The side of my head hit the wall and I crashed to the ground, the world tilting sideways, my arm twisting beneath me. Skip growled and barked. Feet slammed the ground, running away, then the dog was licking my face as I slid into blackness.

Chapter 21

I opened my eyes, pain ripping through my skull. *Lily.*

As I struggled to my feet, headlights swung into the clearing. There was a moment's silence after the van's engine died, then Morag raced towards me, swearing. 'What the hell happened?' She helped me up, firm hands beneath my armpits. 'You're bleeding.'

'Lily,' I managed. 'She's in the cottage.'

'I should hope she is.'

'Go and look.' My voice was a rasp. 'Please, go and check.'

As Morag let go of me, I slumped against the wall, shivering violently. I made myself move, one foot in front of the other, hands gripping the rough stone as I rounded the cottage to the open door. Nausea rose, as pain gripped my head like a vice.

'She's fine, don't worry.' Morag came out and I fell against her. 'The dog was here, guarding the place. Doing his job for once.' She steered me inside towards the sofa.

Lily was where I'd left her on the mat, gazing at the animals, but I couldn't let go of an image of someone lifting her up and spiriting her into the night.

'Don't cry, it's fine. You're both OK.' Morag's voice was brusque as I wept weakly, head lolling forward. I sounded like an injured animal.

'How long was I out there?' I managed, as Morag rummaged in a drawer in the dresser. 'She could have frozen.'

'It can't have been long; it's only nine.'

'You're back early.'

'Not much happening at the pub.' She went to the sink and turned the tap on. 'I thought you might want some company.' Before I had time to digest this, she was back. 'How did it happen?' She loomed close, dabbing at the gash on my temple with a wad of damp cotton wool. 'I nearly had a heart attack when I saw you lying there.'

A shudder racked my body and my teeth chattered. 'Skip,' I managed. 'He wouldn't come in so I went to look for him and I …' It was on the tip of my tongue to say I'd fallen and hit my head on the wall, but I'd been attacked. This wasn't a scare tactic. It was assault. 'Someone pushed me.'

Morag's hand stilled. 'Pushed you?' Her head drew back, her face blank. 'What do you mean?'

'Somebody shoved me really hard from behind.' Tears trickled down my face as I relived the shock. 'I fell on my arm.' I flexed it, wincing. 'Whoever it was ran off.'

'Where?'

'What?'

'Towards the woods, or down the track towards the road?'

I tried to think, keeping my eyes pinned to Lily as though she might vanish if I looked away. 'I … I don't know.' There was mud on my jeans and my socks were filthy. I hadn't even put boots on to go outside. 'Towards the road, I think.'

'I'm calling the police.'

'It would help if there was a working phone.' Hysteria bubbled up. 'This is what I was talking about, Morag. We can't be cut off from the world like this. It's dangerous.'

'Funny how it never mattered before you arrived.'

'What about the bolts on the doors and the rifle under your bed?'

Colour stained her cheeks. 'You saw that?'

'Yes, I saw it, Morag.'

She was silent for a moment. 'You promised me earlier there was nothing to worry about.'

I shrank down. 'I know, I'm sorry.' I pulled away from her, flinching as my head throbbed, wiping my cheeks with my palms. 'I didn't think there was.' I bent over and picked up Lily, wrapping her close, letting her sweet scent calm me. 'I honestly thought we were safe here, but …' *But he hadn't taken Lily.* He could have, while I was out cold. He could have killed me, but hadn't. Had he acted on instinct? He'd known Morag was out, had probably seen Skip outside, but couldn't have been sure I'd go out to look for the dog. Maybe he'd seized the chance to issue a final warning – a punishment for leaving Lily alone in the cottage. *Keep her close. Anything could happen.* 'I should leave,' I said. 'I thought I couldn't be found here but maybe I was wrong. I shouldn't involve you.'

'Hang on.' Alarm flickered over Morag's face. She sat next to me, her eyes on Lily. 'You don't have to go.' It sounded like *I don't want you to go* and my heart clenched around the words. 'Ifan spoke to the phone company. They're sending an engineer tomorrow.' She paused then seemed to make up her mind. 'I'm going to drive back to the village now and call the police from there.' She got up and moved to the kitchen where she threw the bloodied cotton wool in the bin. 'The reason for the bolts, the rifle – though I've had that a long time; it was your granddad's – is because there's been some violence in the area and no one's been caught. It's bound to be the same gang, probably high on drugs. Maybe they considered robbing the place, lost their nerve and ran.'

I stared at her, a ribbon of hope unwinding. 'Is that really likely?'

'I'm afraid so.' Her fingers drummed the worktop. 'There's not much for young people to do around here. Sometimes, they pile in a car and go looking for trouble. There was an incident at the farm, where his nibs came from.' We looked in tandem at Skip in front of the dying fire, his head on his paws. 'Throwing eggs at the windows, frightening the sheep, that sort of thing. When Jan, the wife, came out to confront them, one of lads shoved her and she fell and hurt her knee.'

The rush of relief was intense. As awful as it sounded, a group of bored youths, drunk or high, daring each other to cause mayhem, was better than the alternative. I tried to recall some details about my attacker: tall, I'd thought, strong ... *a man, not a teenager.* Hope shrivelled as fast as it had flared. It wasn't a random attack. I felt it in my bones.

'Does anyone else have a key to this place?'

Morag shook her head as she reached for the kettle. 'Don't worry,' she said. 'No one can let themselves in without my permission.' Her tone was pitched to offer reassurance, but all I could think was: *So how did the note get upstairs, and the lock of hair? How did someone steal my ring?* And what had happened to the second rabbit I saw Ifan put in the fridge? And the sound I'd heard the day after I arrived – someone watching me as I dozed while feeding Lily.

'I should never have left a key out there in the first place,' Morag was saying, pushing the sleeves of her jacket up. 'It was careless. I'd got complacent out here.'

'No, no,' Tears threatened. 'You shouldn't be made to feel unsafe because of me. Everything was fine before I came, and now—'

'It's nothing to do with you,' she cut in, moving briskly, dropping a teabag in a mug before pouring boiling water in. 'You didn't ask for this to happen.'

Didn't I? Hadn't I been asking for it since I threatened Patrick and ran away?

It was an effort to hold my head up. My hair felt sticky with blood, the skin tender around the wound. Lily was heavy in my arms. She strained as she filled her nappy and a foul smell filtered out.

Morag placed a mug of brick-coloured tea on the barrel-table.

'Here, drink this,' she said. 'I've put two sugars in for shock.' She frisked her pocket for her keys. 'I'm going to call the police now and I'll wait for someone to arrive. Will you be OK?'

I tried to nod but it was too painful. 'Yes.'

'Shall I ring for a doctor too?' She moved closer to look at my head, wrinkling her nose as the smell of Lily's nappy hit. 'It's stopped bleeding. I don't think you need stitches.'

'I'll be fine.' Tiredness was closing in, replacing shock. 'You don't have to go back out just to call the police.'

'Yes, I do.' Her voice was firm as she backed away. 'We need to get it on record. They can take a look around. Check no one's hanging about.'

What if involving the police provoked something worse? My assailant – and Patrick – might be banking on me being too scared to call them. Then again, a police presence might put them off, convince them I wasn't worth the trouble. But what if he was one of Patrick's criminals, given immunity in return for information? Someone like that might not care. They might even get a thrill out of evading the police.

I was too tired to think about it anymore and anyway, Morag was on her way out.

'Bolt the door after me,' she instructed. I managed a nod this time. She was clearly used to dealing with traumatised victims – people in a worse state than I was. 'I'll knock when I get back.'

As she left, I carefully laid Lily on her blanket and hauled myself off the sofa. My limbs felt stiff, as though my bones had been shaken and rearranged. Crossing to the door, I jammed the bolts across. The room spun as I bent to wrestle with the one at the bottom. It was stiff. Blood pounded in my ears as I wrenched it into place. It struck me afresh that Morag must have been genuinely worried about intruders getting in. I wished she'd mentioned the troublemakers sooner, but guessed she hadn't wanted to worry me, just as I was trying not to worry her.

Skip trotted to his bowl for a drink, claws clicking the tiles, then returned to his spot on the rug. 'Thank you for watching Lily,' I said. The words sounded silly as they landed but his tail thumped as if he understood.

A numbness settled over me as I changed Lily's dirty nappy then removed my clothes and stuffed them in the washing machine. With Morag's dressing gown draped around me, I sat at the table to feed Lily. Feeling her mouth tug my nipple, her tiny hand on my breast, brought fresh tears to my eyes. 'I'm so sorry,' I whispered, stroking her hair. 'I'll do better, I promise. It won't always be like this.'

I thought of Mum and felt a desperate need to talk to her. She must have fed me like this once, her hand cupping my head, heart overflowing with love. Had she worried for my safety? *Didn't all mothers?* And what about Dad? It was hard to picture them as brand-new parents, to visualise their lives before I was born, but I knew they'd been happy once, that Dad had been kinder. He'd doted on me, according to my grandmother. My grandparents must have seen what he was like when he'd been drinking but never said anything – not to me anyway, but Mum had been good at putting on a front, would have made excuses for him. His parents had died before Mum and Dad met. Maybe they'd had a troubled relationship too. Was that why Dad – an only child like me – had been the way he was?

Would I have to make excuses for Patrick one day? Make up a story for Lily? It wasn't how I'd planned parenthood, but I hadn't planned to be a mother at all, or even a wife. I'd never dreamed of a wedding, like Ana had in the past. Relationships were unreliable, made life harder to navigate. Better to stick to friendships. The future I'd imagined hadn't featured a family of my own; until Lily arrived.

After her feed I rocked her, softly singing, 'Baa Baa Black Sheep', the rhythm matching the throbbing in my head. When I'd snapped the fasteners shut on her sleepsuit, I held her tight and kissed her velvety cheeks. An ache bloomed in my upper arm as I tucked her into her Moses basket and a flame of anger ignited. *Let the police come.* I hoped they would find whoever was responsible and arrest them. Let word get back to Patrick. He would see that he couldn't control everything after all.

Please God, let this be the end of it. But even as I thought it, I knew whatever was happening wasn't over.

Chapter 22

Blue lights flashed across the ceiling, pulling me from a jittery doze as Morag knocked on the door. The sound was muted, as if she knew Lily was asleep beside me on the sofa and didn't want to disturb her.

Skip gave a low whine and jumped up, nose quivering while I unbolted the door with frozen fingers. The fire had gone out and the room was cold, though Lily felt warm beneath her blanket when I hurried back and touched her cheek. The dog ignored Morag, but greeted the officer like a long-lost friend. The officer introduced himself as PC Ewan Thomas.

'Thought about having him myself when I was up at the farm last week, but my wife wasn't keen.' He crouched inside the door to tickle the dog under his chin, speaking to him in Welsh. He was a big man, somewhere in his forties, with tightly curled dark hair going grey at the temples. His open, friendly manner was more friendly big brother than officer of the law, but once he'd risen to his full height, and opened his electronic notebook, he was all business. 'Could you tell me exactly what happened?'

Huddling into Morag's dressing gown, I sat beside the Moses basket on the sofa and haltingly recounted everything I could remember – which wasn't much – while Morag refilled Skip's food bowl before laying logs on the fire, rekindling the blaze.

The officer's eyes skimmed the side of my head but there was nothing much to see. I'd wiped the wound at the sink in the bathroom once Lily was settled, shocked by my appearance in the mirror: matted hair, red-rimmed eyes and a bruise developing above my cheekbone. I didn't want Lily seeing me like that, for the image to be filed somewhere in her memory, returning one day to haunt her.

'Do you have any reason to believe this was a targeted attack?'

I caught Morag's eye and shook my head, the pain in my temple dulled to an ache by a couple of aspirins I'd found in the dresser drawer. No point saying otherwise. I had no proof. Even if I'd kept the note, I wouldn't have shown the officer. I couldn't mention Patrick without breaking my word and besides, I had no desire to say his name out loud. Saying it would bring him into my life when I was so desperate to leave him behind. If my attacker was linked to Patrick and got caught, I was certain *he* wouldn't bring his name up either – but I knew he wouldn't get caught. He was too clever for that.

'I told you, it's the same thing that happened at the farm,' Morag said with a hint of impatience. She pushed her hair back, leaving a trace of ash on her forehead. 'I know you probably think it's a wild goose chase and a waste of police time, but I'd appreciate you taking a look around all the same.' Her voice was low and authoritative, as if she'd made up her mind that since he was here, the officer should make himself useful.

'I don't think it's a waste of time.' He closed his notebook and removed a torch from the belt around his hips. 'We'd very much like to catch these young offenders. They've been up to no good in Bala and Penllyn too,' he added, referring to neighbouring villages. When he turned, I saw *Heddlu* on the back of his jacket above the English translation *Police* and felt reassured by his presence, his commitment to do his job, though I doubted he'd find any evidence.

Sure enough, he was back five minutes later, shaking his head as he ducked through the door to find us exactly as he'd left us, staring at the fire. 'Hard to make out footprints on the grass, or which tyre marks belong to what vehicle, and nothing's been dropped or left behind that I can see.'

Whoever shoved me had used their hands, probably wore gloves. There was no weapon carelessly tossed aside to be found and analysed for fingerprints; no struggle that might have left DNA on my clothes or skin. No words had been exchanged, no car or bike screeching into the night. It might as well have been a ghost. Even Ewan Thomas looked uncertain, the line between his eyebrows deepening as he scanned the room. Maybe he thought I'd been drinking and, unsteady on my feet, had wandered out and tripped over, inventing the assault to cover my embarrassment. Maybe it was only Morag's presence preventing him from asking.

'They could be hiding in the woods.' My words were prompted by a need to convince him something had actually happened. 'Isn't it worth a look?'

He looked from Morag to me, his expression sheepish. 'Not tonight, I'm afraid.' He tucked his torch back in his belt. 'Not with so little to go on and no immediate danger. We don't have the resources. Anyway, they'll be long gone by now.'

'Not if they've set up camp.'

He shook his head. 'Unlikely. They'd need to be experienced and to know this area well. I doubt these youths have the capacity.' He met Morag's steely stare with a cheerful smile. 'Rest assured this will go on the record,' he said, turning his attention to me. 'I'm sorry this has happened to you, Grace. It's not the impression of our beautiful country we want to leave visitors with.' He flicked Morag a look. 'Make sure you get that phone working.'

'I'm on it.'

'Maybe you should get some Wi-Fi up here while you're at it.'

'No coverage,' Morag said coolly. I wondered whether it was true, or if she was still resisting connections to the outside world.

Ewan nodded. 'I'll send some community support officers up tomorrow to take a good look around.' He eyeballed Skip who'd rolled onto his back, tongue lolling out. 'He's not much of a guard dog from what I've heard.'

I exchanged a look with Morag. Seeing her mouth twitch, I had an answering urge to laugh but knew if I did, it wouldn't be long before I was crying again.

*

Friday passed without incident. Apart from the ache in my arm and cotton-wool feeling in my temple I was oddly calm, as if a storm inside me had blown itself out. I'd even managed a decent night's sleep, waking only once to feed Lily in a daze.

Morag didn't refer to what had happened, just suggested keeping the door bolted when she went outside after breakfast.

I was desperate for some fresh air, but made do with taking a stroll around the garden with Lily tucked against me, scanning the area where Skip had been in case I spotted something the officer had missed, but even the tiny animal bones had gone.

I scrutinised the trees around the cottage and the flattened ground at the side, but saw no tell-tale glint of wire cutters lying in the grass below the damaged phone wire. The weather, which had started out sunny, reverted to wind and rain and confining myself to the cottage wasn't hard. There was no sign of the phone engineer, but a pair of community officers turned up as promised – looking young enough to still be at college – and made a valiant effort to chat to Morag in the garden before disappearing into the woods, returning dishevelled and red-faced an hour later, one of them limping; nothing to report but a twisted ankle.

'They're coming back in shifts to keep an eye on things,' Morag said dryly when they'd gone. 'Nice kids, but I wouldn't put much faith in them catching a cold, never mind a criminal.'

While she carried on with her usual routine, disappearing

after lunch to do deliveries – perhaps needing to be away from me – I decided to cook. I baked two loaves and an apple cake and made a vegetable lasagne for dinner, forcing myself to stay in the present by singing to Lily, happy on her activity mat, and throwing a pair of balled-up socks for Skip while the loaves baked.

After we'd eaten dinner, Morag challenged me to a game of Monopoly while the wind howled outside, pushing at the window, and the fire leapt in the grate. It felt cosy, reminiscent of winter days when I was a child, but with the addition of the dog I'd always longed for. Morag wore red plaid pyjamas under her dressing gown, and I was wrapped in the throw from the bed upstairs, which smelt comfortingly of washing powder – the same brand my grandmother had used. Neither of us spoke much, as if by mutual agreement, sticking to safe topics – the rules of the game, the weather, Lily – not wanting to disturb the fragile sense of peace.

'Are you going to help out at the pub tomorrow night?' Morag said when she'd won the game. I kept yawning and forgetting the rules. 'It'll do you good to get out.'

'I'll think about it.'

Morag nodded, as if asking was a formality and she'd known all along I was keen to get back in a professional kitchen, to grab the opportunity I'd been given – a step towards building a normal life.

Chapter 23

The kitchen at the Carpenter's Arms was small but streamlined; updated a year ago, Morag had told me, to capture the tourist market and cater for locals who wanted an evening out that didn't involve nursing a pint in the snug. 'Not everyone likes seeing the old boys playing dominoes, darts and card games,' she said, as if she couldn't understand why.

Annie showed me around, pausing to stir a bubbling stockpot on top of a stainless-steel range. 'It's probably a lot smaller than you're used to.' I wondered what Morag had said to her. My aunt hadn't asked for details of my job. Maybe she'd made assumptions because I worked in New York, or had simply told people her niece was a high-flying chef.

'It is, but everything's newer,' I said. A familiar buzz of adrenaline kicked in as I admired the shiny equipment and gleaming surfaces, breathing in the cooking smells, enjoying the hum of activity that took me back to *Julio's*. I'd known the minute I set foot in his kitchen it was where I wanted to be. I missed it, I realised – even the punishing hours. I accepted I would probably never own my own restaurant now, with my name above the door, but I couldn't imagine doing a different job.

'It's a small menu, very straightforward, nothing fancy.' Annie was unapologetic, clearly proud of her domain, where a woman who looked like a smaller version of her, with the same wild curly hair fastened up in a bun, was chopping onions with great concentration, pausing to wipe her eyes on the back of her hand. 'My sister Bethan is standing in for the chef who buggered off to Cardiff, but she'd like to get her Saturday nights back and, like I said, I wouldn't mind the occasional break myself.' Bethan surveyed me with bloodshot eyes and nodded a friendly greeting. 'And this is my cousin's boy, Lewis. He does the clearing up, loads the dishwasher, and Daisy over there waits on tables with her brother Niall. He'll be in later. Bryn's in charge of the bar, so you probably won't see much of him.'

'Lucky her,' Bethan said, her tone teasing. They seemed close-knit, just how Ifan had described the people in Fenbrith. If they were curious about me, it wasn't obvious, beyond Annie enquiring what sort of food I was used to cooking.

'Anything really.' I thought of the eclectic menu at *Julio's*. 'I introduced some British recipes where I worked, but mostly Spanish, some Italian. I cooked for myself too, loved trying different things. I was always experimenting.'

You take after your mother, Dad had said when I took over making Sunday lunch aged thirteen, pleased with my puffed-up Yorkshire puddings and how easily the roast beef had sliced. *If anything, you're a better cook.* I'd taken it as a great compliment, not seeing the hurt my mother had masked with a smile for what it was.

'We do Bolognese and chilli.' Annie refastened her apron, blue eyes settling on my face. 'Our customers love it.'

'Mostly one-pot stuff.' Bethan pointed the knife she was holding to the range, where a delicious smell of rosemary and onions was rising from the pan. 'Easy, cheap and tasty.'

'You make us sound like a truck stop.' Annie shook her head as she stirred the bubbling concoction again. 'We only use the best ingredients, Grace. We've loads of five-star reviews on TripAdvisor.'

'I can believe it.' I knew how important reviews were, especially to a new venture relying on word of mouth to succeed. 'It all looks great.'

'So, where's that baby of yours?'

'My aunt's watching her in the bar.' I'd rather have kept Lily with me, where I could see her, but it was too dangerous; spills and breakages, hotspots and chemicals, all hazards in a working kitchen. I wasn't sure how to get through the evening without her and had resisted coming until Morag practically pushed me out of the door.

'Lots of mothers go back to work, and all you're doing is having a look round the kitchen this evening. I'm perfectly capable of minding the baby while you do that.'

'But she'll need feeding and changing and …' *She's barely been out of my sight since she was born, and I'm not convinced someone won't swoop in and take her if I look away.* 'It's too soon. Maybe if Annie still needs help in a few months' time.'

'You're planning to stay in Fenbrith, then?'

With Morag's words, the thought of putting down roots, however flimsy, had taken hold once more. Going out, exploring the possibility of working at the pub, making friends – Declan's face flashed into my mind – would make it harder to leave, to run away. I couldn't stay at Morag's indefinitely, but I needed a place to call home, somewhere Lily could grow and flourish, where we could be a family. Going to Mum's wasn't an option and I couldn't think of anywhere else I wanted to be, even with the possibility that someone was watching us; had hurt me. At least in Fenbrith, living with Morag, around people who were aware I existed, there was a modicum of safety. Better than being adrift, moving from place to place with someone on our trail, ready to strike without warning.

'Fine, I'll go,' I said. 'But you have to promise you won't take your eyes off Lily and you'll come and get me the minute she cries.'

'Can't you milk yourself so I can feed her? Not right now, but in future?' Morag's unexpected question had prompted a burst of laughter.

'I'm not a cow.' My smile faded when I remembered Patrick's comment as he caught me breastfeeding Lily. *At least pump and freeze if you won't use a bottle.* 'But I suppose I could. I brought the equipment.' I'd pushed it in the bottom of Lily's changing bag, just in case.

'I know. I saw it that first morning when I made the baby a bottle.'

'If you're going to keep watch you have to call her Lily instead of baby.'

A look had rippled across Morag's face then, something close to distress. It passed like a door being slammed. She looked away, making a performance of ordering Skip to lie down as he hovered at our heels before saying, 'OK. It's a deal.'

In the end, Skip had followed us out and into the back of the van and was now curled underneath the table at Ifan's feet.

'And your daughter?' I said to Annie, trying to remember the little girl's name.

Her face broke into a smile. 'Gwynn's upstairs with my mum,' she said. 'My mother's looking forward to having the occasional Saturday night off too.'

With the family seemingly desperate for a break, I heard myself saying, 'So, it would just be the odd Saturday night you'd like some help?'

'To begin with, but more hours if you'd like them.' Her expression was coaxing. 'I know it's not easy right now with you being a new mum, but your aunt's dying to make up for lost time and help you out.'

'It's more that I don't want to leave my baby with anyone.' Even my aunt, who was apparently dying to help. It was true that Morag seemed keen to interact with Lily, but the thought of leaving her, even for a few hours, was hard to bear. 'We've gone through a lot to get here,' I said, regretting my curtness. Annie was just being friendly.

'I get it.' She seemed unfazed. 'At that age, you could just sit and look at your baby for hours. I couldn't bear to put Gwynn down for the first six months, but running this place ...' She cast her eyes around. 'I didn't have much choice, but I love to work and our parents have been brilliant.'

'I could start next week and see how it goes.' *If nothing goes wrong before then.*

Annie's smile bounced back. 'Great,' she said brightly. 'Why don't you give Bethan a hand now, take a look at the menus, get a feel for the kitchen while your daughter's safe with her auntie?'

Daughter. I had a daughter. Sometimes the scale of it still took my breath away. *Of all the things my hands have held, the best by far is you.* The line rushed back from a card Mum gave me on my fifteenth birthday, six months before Dad died. She'd never been sentimental, scoffing at mawkish verses, preferring to give funny cards with quirky illustrations and cover the inside with kisses but that year, when I read it in silence, she said, 'It's true, Grace. Remember that.' I hadn't thought about it for years.

'I'll just check Lily's OK.' I walked back through the hubbub of the bar before Annie could respond. Lily was in her car seat on the table between Morag and Ifan, legs frog-kicking as she babbled for the onlookers who'd gathered to admire her. Morag looked animated, cheeks flushed, hands moving expansively as she talked. It was like glimpsing a different person – someone younger, more vibrant. She'd changed into a dusky pink sweater that flattered her colouring, and a pair of dark jeans. I imagined her long ago, a camera slung around her neck, holding court in some smoky bar in Islamabad.

Perhaps it was Ifan's presence, or Lily's, or maybe both, but it felt wrong to gate-crash the little group and risk Morag's guarded expression returning. I'd left my bag with her, a couple of spare nappies. Confident that she was fine without me for now, I returned to the kitchen with a stronger sense of purpose, time peeling back to when nothing had worried me apart from a hollandaise sauce curdling, or too much salt in the pesto.

After washing my hands and putting on the apron Annie handed over with a grin, I set to work, helping Bethan chop the pile of vegetables she was working her way through.

'Great bread, by the way,' Annie said. Morag had insisted on dropping off one of the loaves I'd baked the day before. 'If there are any more where that came from, I'll place an order,' she added, opening a sack of rice. 'Making bread's too long-winded for me.'

'Great.' Pleasure glowed in the pit of my stomach, melting the ball of tension that had taken up permanent residence since I was shoved. I couldn't bring myself to think the word 'attacked' or 'assaulted' anymore. It made what had happened more sinister – too real. Thankfully, nothing had occurred since. The phone line had been restored, the engineer coming and going without fanfare – *don't know what happened there, but should be right as rain now* – and the community officers, Alison and Owen, had been over again as promised, patrolling the area with great solemnity, Alison making light of her sprained ankle. I longed to sink into a sense of security, even if it was false – to believe that what had happened was nothing more than bad luck, or being in the wrong place at the wrong time.

'Do you know Declan Walsh?' I said, my heap of diced vegetables almost embarrassingly neat beside Bethan's roughly chopped pile.

'Can't say I do.' She looked at Annie who now had a stack of plates in her arms. 'Ring a bell?'

Annie shook her head, distracted. 'Lewis, can you put these somewhere, please?'

'He was in here the other lunchtime, waiting for his friend,' I persisted.

'What's his friend's name?' Bethan took a bite from a stick of celery and wrinkled her nose. 'God, I hate this stuff.'

'Hugh.' I tried to remember whether Declan had told me his

144

surname. 'He runs one of those outdoorsy adventure places in Caernarfon.'

'Oh, Hugh Williams.' Annie nodded. 'Nice guy. He and his wife have been over here for dinner. I don't think I've met his friend, though.' She widened her eyes at me. 'He was the good-looking one, chatting you up, wasn't he?'

My cheeks burned. 'He was just passing the time.' I wondered what they'd say if they knew he'd invited me out for the day tomorrow. 'I don't suppose you see many strangers in Fenbrith at this time of year.'

'A lot more from Easter onwards.' Annie passed the plates to Lewis. 'You'd be surprised how busy it gets in our little neck of the woods.'

'Proximity to Snowdon and the lake,' added Bethan. 'Having grown up here, I prefer it in winter, but we wouldn't have an income without the holidaymakers, so it's a bit of a love-hate relationship.' Her eyes grew big as she watched me chop parsley with muscle-memory precision. 'Where did you learn to do that?' Her admiring look was gratifying. 'You're like one of those chefs off the telly.'

'I was taught by a professional.' I was enjoying a rare chance to show off, more relaxed on familiar territory. 'I can dice an onion in thirty seconds.' I demonstrated and was treated to a round of applause. 'If you like, I can show you how to make grilled cheese. It might go down well at lunchtimes.'

'Isn't that what we call a cheese toastie?' It was Bryn, poking his balding head round the door, eyebrows raised. 'We already do those.'

'A grilled cheese sandwich is buttered on the outside and cooked in a pan,' I said, smiling.

'Ooh, I like the sound of that.' Annie lifted her chin in her husband's direction. 'What is it, Brynny-boy?' She exaggerated her Welsh accent. 'Speak up, man, or forever hold your peace.'

The noise level in the bar had risen, laughter drifting through.

I cocked an ear, attuned to Lily's hunger cry. She hadn't been fed for a while and my breasts felt full and heavy beneath my thin blue fleece – another Walmart special.

'Firstly,' said Bryn, 'I need Daisy.' He beckoned to where the young girl was standing by the dishwasher, smoothing the ends of her poker-straight black hair. 'Someone's waiting to order.' As she scuttled over, Annie said, 'And secondly?'

'What?'

'You said firstly, so what's the second thing?' She hurried back to the range and switched it on, rolling her eyes. 'Good God, man, spit it out.'

'Oh, right.' Bryn looked at me. 'Your aunt said to tell you that your phone keeps ringing.'

Chapter 24

I pushed through the heaving bar to the table where Morag and Ifan were chatting to an older couple. Lily had nodded off again, her head tipped to one side, a rosy flush on her cheeks. So much for my worrying the pub wasn't a suitable environment.

'You said my phone was ringing.'

Morag looked up, pleasure flashing over her face at the sight of me. 'I heard this weird noise, like a bird had got trapped.' She reached for my bag, tucked by her side. 'I realised it must be your phone but it stopped, then started again.' She gave me a meaningful look. 'Someone has your number.'

'It's OK,' I said, heart thumping hard. 'She's the friend I mentioned the other day, the one I was going to call.'

Understanding relaxed Morag's face. 'Ana.'

'I tried calling her when you were in the supermarket,' I said. 'I left a message, asking her to ring me back.'

'You could phone from home,' she said, so naturally it was as if I'd been living under her roof for years. 'Now it's been fixed.' She wiggled her eyebrows at Ifan – such an unusually flirtatious gesture I had to look at her glass and check it really was orange juice and not vodka.

'I'd like to call her back now, if that's OK.' I pulled the phone out as it started ringing again. No one had called me on it before. Morag was right: it sounded like a distressed bird.

'Take it outside. Go on,' she said when I paused and looked at Lily. 'She's fine.'

'She's gorgeous,' said the woman sitting opposite, lipstick gathered in the wrinkles around her mouth. 'Looks just like you.' She leant forward, peering at me myopically. 'Is that a bruise on your cheek, dear?'

'You think it was the same lot who attacked Jan at the farm?' I heard the old woman's companion saying as I hurried away, bursting through the door into the car park with the phone pressed to my ear. When it carried on ringing, I checked the screen and pressed the green handset button. 'Ana?'

'Grace, thank Christ! I've been calling for ages. I was starting to worry.'

It was so good to hear her voice, I felt like bursting into tears. As my two lives collided, everything that had felt normal moments ago receded. It was seven o'clock here, which must mean it was 2 p.m. in New York. I heard traffic sounds in the background, imagined Ana crossing the busy road to the ugly building that housed the health company where she worked, a cup of something healthy in her hand from the juice bar on the corner. Sometimes, she'd buy me one and bring it to the restaurant, but I could never manage more than a couple of sips. 'I didn't have my phone with me,' I said, walking to the van. The door was unlocked and I clambered in out of the biting wind. 'How are you, Ana? I've been desperate to talk to you, but the phone at my aunt's wasn't working and—'

'You didn't go to your mum's?'

'No, I ... I couldn't go back there, Ana, you know we don't get on and I thought it would be safer at Morag's. She lives practically in the middle of nowhere so—'

'What the hell happened, Grace?' Ana couldn't let me finish a sentence, the questions she must have had banked up all spilling

148

out. 'I don't get why you had to go so suddenly that you couldn't even tell me. I could have driven you to the airport. Hell, I could have come with you. I'm owed some time off.'

'Oh, Ana, if you decide to come and visit your parents some-time it would be brilliant to see you.' The image of her walking towards me was so vivid a smile broke over my face. 'We could meet up. I'd love that. I want you to see Lily. She's been amazing, Ana.'

An ominous silence was broken by the wail of a siren. 'He let you go then?'

'Only just,' I said. 'I had to … I threatened him,' I admitted. 'I said I'd tell people everything.' *Elise, at the foot of the stairs, eyes wide but empty, staring at nothing.* I hated that I couldn't share the whole truth with my friend, but I couldn't risk it. As much as Ana loved me, she might insist I go to the police. 'I didn't want him coming after us. I thought it was best to say as little as possible to anyone, to not leave a trace. That's why I got a new phone and didn't make contact straight away in case – oh, I don't know, in case … he has contacts, probably knows about tracking, that sort of thing.'

A great sigh gusted down the phone. 'Everyone misses you, Grace.' A tear spilled down my face at Ana's words. 'I wish you'd come to stay with us, or Julio. You could have gone back to work at the restaurant.'

'I'm not sure your uncle would have wanted me back after the way I left, and what with the baby situation.'

Ana made a scoffing noise. 'My uncle still says he'll never find anyone as good as you to run his bloody restaurant. He'd have come round to it, everyone would. You'd have loads of support. Everyone would love Lily. Julio would have treated her like his own grandchild.'

My heart felt bent out of shape. 'I can't come back, Ana. Probably not ever.'

'I get it,' she said after a heavy pause. 'I just wish so much that

I hadn't told him you were pregnant. I'll never forgive myself for that.'

I wished that too. I wished Ana hadn't found me in the toilets that day and put two and two together; wished I hadn't told her Patrick was the father. 'You thought you were doing the right thing.'

'It was totally messed up.' She sounded angry. 'I didn't know it was going to end like it did or I'd never have—'

'Ana, don't,' I cut in. 'It's fine, really. I like being here, more than I thought I would.' *In spite of everything.*

'I saw the news, Grace. I know from what you told me …' There was a loaded silence. I knew what was coming. 'Do you think he had something to do with his wife's death?' The background was quieter now. I guessed she was inside the Public Health building, with its over-conditioned air and the faint antiseptic smell that had reminded me of a hospital when I once went to meet her after work.

'No.' I made myself sound just a little bit outraged. 'I don't think that, Ana, I promise.' The lasagne I'd eaten earlier lay like concrete in my stomach. I didn't want to talk about it, to have the past rush back. 'He's not a killer – that's crazy.'

'It's just, with everything being so complicated and his wife being an alcoholic …'

Elise, I wanted to say. *Her name was Elise.* My chest burned with guilt and fear. 'The point is, Ana, I got away and I don't ever want to see or hear from him again.'

'What if he decides he wants to see Lily?'

'He knows he can't do that.' *Can he?*

'But—'

'He didn't even like her, Ana.'

There was another pause. I heard a sniff and guessed she was crying. 'I miss you.'

'I miss you too.' Tears rose again. 'Please tell me you're coming over.'

'Definitely. In the summer.'

'Oh, Ana, that would be great. You should see Lily. She's keeps trying to lift her head up already. I'll send you a picture, but my phone camera's awful. And I think you'll like my aunt. You never met her, did you?' I could see Morag through the pub window. The sight of her was like an anchor, holding me to the present. 'I'm so glad you called.'

'Me too.' She sounded anguished. 'Oh, Grace, did I ruin everything for you?'

'Don't make it sound like I didn't have a choice, Ana.' Tears scalded my cheeks. 'What happened made me change direction, but it's for the best. I like it here and I have Lily. That's all that matters.' I couldn't tell her what had been happening. She would only worry and blame herself even more than she already did.

'I wouldn't trust Patrick an inch.' Her voice grew faint for a second as she greeted someone in a lighter tone. 'Men like him don't like to lose,' she said.

Fear gripped my chest. 'He'd have more to lose by finding me.' In the pause that followed, a shiver ran down my back. 'What is it?'

'It's just … my uncle mentioned yesterday that someone had asked after you at the restaurant the day you left.' Ana's words came a rush. 'A man.'

'What do you mean?' I realised how cold it was in the van. I couldn't feel my feet in their cheap trainers. The tip of my nose was numb.

'Julio was helping out. He said a man came in and asked whether the tenant still lived upstairs.'

'What?' A couple passed the van, their laughter ringing in the air. I felt displaced, pain circling my temples. 'Did he say why he was asking?'

'No. He just asked if you were OK. Said he needed to talk to you.' *Patrick?* 'Did Julio tell you what he looked like?'

'I asked, obviously.' Ana's voice dipped again. 'I thought it might be Patrick but Julio said he was tall, white, maybe mid-to-late thirties with a beard.'

Not Patrick. Which didn't mean he hadn't sent someone to check I'd really gone. *Still lived there.* Not *worked.* Patrick knew I'd lived above the restaurant. 'What did Julio say?'

'He said the guy seemed worried. He told him you'd gone back to the UK with the baby. I know, I know,' she said when I swore. 'I told him he shouldn't have said anything, but remember my uncle didn't see any reason to be suspicious. He said, "What's the harm? She's gone."' He clearly hadn't forgiven me for deserting the kitchen he'd left in my hands, despite what Ana had said. 'He told him you wouldn't be back, were probably at the airport.' I closed my eyes. Julio might as well have given whoever it was my aunt's address. 'I'm so sorry, Grace.'

'Don't be silly, it's not your fault.' My limbs felt stiff and cold. In the light of the pub window a pair of moths fluttered in the light. I wanted to be in there, not having this conversation. 'It's not as if anyone knew where I was going,' I said. 'Don't worry.' I had to see Lily. I opened the van door and stepped out. Morag was craning her neck, looking for me. 'Thanks for calling, for letting me know.' I aimed for a normal tone that would reassure my friend. 'How are things at work and with Tom?'

'Fine and fine.' She brushed the questions aside. 'We're moving in together next month, but Grace, I'm worried about you. I think you should—'

'I'm fine, honestly.' I hurried to the pub, one arm around my waist, imagining two strong hands on my back and the sensation of falling. Patrick might as well be here, shouting warnings in my ear. Maybe it would help to talk to him, clarify that I had no intention of telling anyone – ever – about that day as long as Lily and I were left alone. Find out what he'd told Elise's parents and whether they were satisfied with his story. They loved their daughter and were far from gullible. They'd have insisted on details. Patrick was paid by the state to uphold the law. They'd be inclined to believe whatever he said – but as a mother myself now, I knew what lengths I'd go to for my daughter. If Elise's mum was the same, if she had some intuition that things weren't right, she might have decided to push further, get to the bottom of things. Could she be the one who'd set someone on my trail, employed a private investigator? Would there have been time between the inquest and me leaving New York? In her grief, would she have even been thinking along those lines?

Privacy to let the family grieve in peace, Patrick had said, implying things were settled and everyone just needed to be left alone. *I'll be taking some time out, but hope to be back serving my community very soon.*

Taking some time out.

I stopped, as though I'd slammed into an invisible wall. *Was Patrick here, in Fenbrith?* Dread tightened my chest.

I had to find out.

Chapter 25

I pushed into the pub, elbowing my way through a noisy group to get to Lily.

Morag laid a restraining hand on my arm as I reached to unstrap her. 'She's asleep.'

'She's due a feed,' I said. 'I'll do it in the toilets.'

'It seems a shame to wake her.'

The couple opposite stared at me. I imagined how I must look with my bruised cheek and trembling hands, my hair tossed about by the wind. 'You're right. I should let her sleep.' I tried to smile, tucking my hair behind my ears. 'It's really cold out there.'

Morag's eyes narrowed. 'Did you speak to your friend?'

'Yes, it was good. She's fine.' I started backing away. Skip poked his head from under the table and woofed. 'I won't be a minute. I just have to …' I nodded to the sign for the ladies' room and hurried away, heart banging. After checking the toilet cubicles were empty, I whipped up my top, unfastened my bra and quickly squeezed some milk into the sink. The relief was instant and I felt a little calmer. Adjusting my clothes, I studied my reflection in the smoky mirror, seeking some sign of the woman Patrick had met. This version bore little resemblance. My eyes looked too large, my face thinner, pale apart from the bruise, which had deepened to a purplish stain. I didn't even look like the woman who'd arrived at the pub a couple of hours ago, disguised with a coating of make-up and neatly brushed hair, determined to make a good impression.

After locking myself in the nearest stall, I pulled my phone from my jeans pocket and sat on the toilet seat as I logged onto the pub's Wi-Fi. I didn't have a number for Patrick, but I could call his office, at least find out whether he was in New York.

Bringing up his website – motto: *Moving Justice Forward* – I scrolled past the lists of signature projects and community partnerships, and a mission statement to remove guns from New York City streets – *an average of a hundred people a day die of gun violence in America* – until I found contact details. There was a number to call for general information. I brought up the keypad and pressed in the digits before I could change my mind.

'Patrick Holden's office, how may I help?'

My stomach lurched. 'I'd like to speak to Mr Holden, please.' The smell of lemon air freshener was overpowering and my mouth filled with saliva.

'Mr Holden's on compassionate leave until next Monday.' The woman's voice softened as she spoke his name. *Veronica,* Patrick had told me. He made of point of knowing everyone's name. He'd literally stepped into my world but I'd never been to his office, or met anyone there. Our affair had been so brief, separate from reality, from work. In a parallel universe, where Patrick wasn't already married, I'd have wanted to know more, know everything about him, but I hadn't dared look ahead, staying focused on the moment.

'Do you have a number where I can get hold of him?' I was aware of slipping into an American accent. The last thing I wanted was a message getting back to Patrick that a British woman had called and asked to speak to him. 'It's kind of important.'

'You have seen the news, I take it?'

I squeezed my eyes shut, forcing out an image of Elise's lifeless body. 'I have, yes.'

'Then you'll know he's attending his wife's memorial service today.'

I ended the call and let out a long breath. Patrick was in New York. He wasn't in Wales, waiting for the right moment to persuade me to hand Lily over. Had I really thought he could be? The idea of Patrick lurking in the woods, letting himself in the cottage, was absurd. Patrick, who had a fondness for cashmere and linen and hated the cold. He preferred swimming, being by the ocean on the rare breaks he took, his head too full of whichever case he was working on to think about anything much but winning and, lately, on stepping up his campaign to become District Attorney. Or, so I'd thought. Maybe he wasn't willing to forget about Lily so easily, to let her go without a fight. But the cost of having her in his life was too great and he knew it. So why not leave us alone?

Sounds rushed in. A whoosh of taps, female voices talking about someone called Bronwyn who'd suffered an allergic reaction to wool and developed a rash. 'I mean, who's allergic to *wool*?'

I quickly clicked off the website, wrists shaking. Resisting the urge to look for more news, I clicked onto Ana's Facebook page. She wasn't an avid user, tending to only post updates when she'd had a few drinks. There she was with Tom in a post from two weeks ago, both in running gear, looking as if they'd crossed a finish line under blazing sunshine. Tom had a beard and glasses and a broad, white smile. Although he didn't look it in the picture, he was a couple of inches shorter than Ana. They looked vital, happy, eyes crinkled with smiles, foreheads sheened with sweat. Ana's hair was shorter, just above her shoulders. She'd had it cut and I hadn't known. *This was just the warm-up,* she'd written underneath. She hadn't posted anything since.

Scrolling back, I landed on a picture of her and me in a group on a night out. Julio's sixtieth birthday, gathered around a long table in someone else's restaurant. Seeing my carefree smile as I raised a glass of champagne to the camera – I'd barely sipped it

– was like looking at someone related to me; the same shiny hair and dark eyes but confident, with an aura of self-belief; someone sure of her place in the world. A woman with a plan.

I'd met Patrick a few weeks later.

Some impulse prompted me to type *Declan Walsh* into the search bar. I didn't hold out much hope of finding him – he hadn't struck me as someone who'd bother with social media – but his image immediately leapt out from a long list of Declan Walshes. My heart skipped when I read *Worked at: British Army. Lives: wherever the mood takes me,* under a profile picture of him standing on a rock with a backpack, a vast blue sky behind, glancing over his shoulder at whoever had taken the shot. He had a full beard but his eyes pulled me in, recognisable even at a distance. His cover photo was a distant shot of a farmhouse set in emerald hills that could only be Ireland. *He was exactly who he'd said he was.*

His account was set to private, but he'd been tagged in a couple of photos, one by Shauna Cafferty. His sister, judging by her likeness to him in her profile photo, the same friendly smile. Beneath a faded shot of him as a gangly teen at the wheel of a tractor in a muddy farmyard, she'd written: *Remember when you nearly ran Dad over in this?!*

In the second, he was standing outside a bar, somewhere hot and dusty-looking, next to a deeply tanned man wearing khakis. One arm was slung around Declan's shoulders, the pint of beer in his other hand raised in a toast. *Good to see you, mate, stay in touch.* The man, Todd Bridges, looked like an off-duty soldier. Someone from his army days? Declan looked relaxed, smiling, eyes screwed almost shut against the blinding sun. His arms were folded, roped with muscle beneath the sleeves of his T-shirt, his hair pushed back off his forehead. I couldn't stop looking at him, scouring his features – slightly blurred as though the photographer had moved at the last moment – until a cough outside the door landed me back in the pub. Relief had made my legs feel stringy. Switching my phone off, I stumbled out of the cubicle, meeting the startled stare of a woman outside examining her nails. 'Sorry,' I said, holding the door open. She shook her head as if my appearance had alarmed her.

'I'm waiting for my friend.'

Back at the table, I fought an instinct to wake Lily just so I had an excuse to lift her out and hold her soft body against me, reassure myself she really was here with me; that she was safe. Morag watched me. 'Everything OK?'

I nodded, but the pub was too noisy, too warm. I felt over-emotional, teetering on the brink of tears. 'Do you mind if we go home?'

She didn't hesitate, just picked up her jacket, asked Ifan to say our goodbyes to Annie and followed me out, Skip close behind. 'Why were you gone so long?' she said when we were in the van, Skip panting in the back. 'I was about to come and get you.'

Lily was waking in her seat, beginning to cry. I shushed her, rearranged her blanket, pressed a kiss to her forehead. 'I had to check something.'

Morag started the engine, switching the heating on. 'And?' The whites of her eyes gleamed as she turned to look at me.

'And, nothing.' I made myself meet her gaze. 'Everything's OK.' I was tense, wondering what might be waiting back at the cottage. Hopefully, the presence of the officers had put paid to my stalker's plans, at least for now. 'I'm looking forward to a good night's sleep.'

'Me too,' Morag said.

It was a moment or two before some sixth sense alerted me to a vehicle behind us. I shielded my eyes as the beam of headlights filled the interior with bright light.

Morag was hunched over the steering wheel, squinting at the near-invisible road ahead. 'Could they get any closer?'

'That's what I was thinking.'

She adjusted the rear-view mirror to deflect the light and pressed on the accelerator. 'Road hog.'

'Maybe you should let them go past.' I rested a hand on Lily's blanket. Her face scrunched in protest as light seeped through her eyelids, and she twisted her head as if to escape the glare. 'What are they playing at?'

'Some impatient wanker,' Morag muttered, slowing down reluctantly. Instead of manoeuvring round, the driver behind slowed too as if keeping pace. My heart missed a beat. Someone was following us. The flare of headlamps filled the windscreen, highlighting a warning sign at the side of the road: a concealed left turn.

'Down there.'

'What?' Confused, Morag took her eyes off the road.

'Just turn!' As we reached a gap at the side of the road, I seized the steering wheel. The van slid off the tarmac, wheels skidding.

'Jesus!' Morag struggled with the wheel as the van lurched down a track with tall hedges on either side, barely wide enough to accommodate a bike. She slammed her foot on the brake and the engine stalled.

I blinked in the sudden darkness, the silence a roar in my ears. 'What—'

'Shh!'

I waited, expecting twin beams to swing into view behind us, for the purr of a 4x4 – I was sure that's what it had been, a flash of silver as we swerved off the road – but there was only blackness behind and a muddy track ahead, puddled with water that quivered in the glow of the headlights.

Morag looked shaken, her face pale. 'What the hell was that all about?'

'Don't you think we were being followed?'

'It wasn't my first thought, no.' Morag glanced over her shoulder. 'You shouldn't have grabbed the wheel like that. It's dangerous.'

Shame flooded my veins. What had I been thinking, with Lily in the van? 'I'm sorry. I don't know what came over me.'

Morag eyed me silently before gunning the engine. 'So much for you being fine,' she said, reversing back to the road. 'Maybe a decent night's sleep will do you good.'

Chapter 26

The following morning brought a reprieve from the wind and rain. Sun streamed through the kitchen window as I washed up after breakfast and, when Morag came in from the garden, the air had a cut-grass scent that made me think of summer.

'Good day for going up Snowdon,' she said, slipping her jacket off and pushing her the sleeves of her sweater up. She'd risen early – to walk Skip, she'd said, but I suspected it was to check for signs of anyone hanging about. I knew I'd spooked her last night with my insistence that we were being followed. In the warm light of day, it seemed improbable, yet I couldn't shake off the certainty I'd felt. Had someone intended to run us off the road, or just to scare me? *I'm here! You can't escape!* 'You should get some good views.'

'Are you sure you don't mind dropping us in Fenbrith?'

'If you're sure it's a good idea to go up a mountain with a baby and a man you barely know, who am I to argue?'

'You're the one who said I shouldn't let what happened stop me from living my life.'

'Says the woman who thought we were being chased by baddies last night.' She shook her head. 'Just be careful, that's all.'

'Declan seems genuine. I checked him out on Facebook,' I said. 'He's who he says he is.'

'Oh well, if you've looked him up on Facebook.' She rolled her eyes. 'You know you could go up the mountain with me if you want to do the tourist thing.'

I put down the pack of nappies I'd picked up. 'You have your life, Morag. I'm imposing enough as it is.'

'Maybe I'm happy to spend time with you.' She crossed to the sink and washed her hands, almost angrily.

My throat tightened. 'I'm glad you feel like that.' It was more than I deserved.

'We should go and visit your mum.'

'What?'

'Tomorrow.' Morag turned, grabbing a towel off the drainer. 'It's long overdue.'

I felt the colour drain from my face. 'But—'

'Tomorrow.' She threw the towel down and folded her arms. 'We'll drive to Berkshire first thing in the morning.' She looked at Lily again. 'It's not right, keeping this from her. If she knew you were here and hadn't been in touch …' She stopped and swallowed. 'She'll be upset.'

This concern for my mother's feelings was unexpected to say the least. 'Morag, I was going to call her,' I said carefully. 'I was waiting until I was on my feet again.'

'If you're up to going on a date with a stranger, you're up to seeing your mum.' Her tone was final.

'But … you want to come too?'

'How else are you going to get there?'

'I could take a train.' My mind shied away from the reality. Maybe I could think of an excuse before tomorrow, invent a sore throat or a migraine. I wasn't ready to face my mother.

'If you keep putting it off, you'll never get round to it, and maybe it's time I made peace with her too.'

My mouth fell open. 'Where's this coming from?'

'Life's too short, wouldn't you say?'

I regarded her, trying to organise my thoughts. 'That depends how you look at it.' I shoved a handful of nappies into Lily's changing bag along with a pack of baby wipes. 'It's too short to be around someone who makes you unhappy.'

'I think your mum would have left your father if he hadn't died,' Morag said out of the blue. 'Once you were at college, an adult.'

I busied myself lifting Lily out of her chair, kissing the tip of her nose. 'If I agree to go tomorrow, will you drop me in Fenbrith and stop giving me a hard time?'

'I thought you were going to bake some more bread.' She looked at the floor. 'Annie wants a loaf.'

'It wasn't an official order.' Was Morag jealous that I was going to meet Declan? 'There's plenty of time for that,' I said kindly – as though placating a surly child. 'It's just one day out, not even a whole day. And *you're* the one suggesting we swan off to Berkshire tomorrow.'

'Why don't you leave Lily with me today?'

'No.' I softened. 'No offence, Morag. It's not that I don't trust you with her, but it's too soon. I promise I will, but not yet.'

She nodded, as if it was the answer she'd expected, but I had a feeling there was a lot more she wanted to say. 'We'd better get a move on then.'

*

Declan was outside the café when I arrived, perhaps mindful of my warning that I wouldn't wait if he was late. My spirits lifted when he raised a hand and smiled, ducking to grin at Lily strapped in her carrier on my chest. The feeling was a welcome surprise after the sensation of dread I'd come to associate with Patrick.

'You're early,' I said, after Morag had driven off, revving the engine unnecessarily. She glared at Declan though the windscreen as she passed.

'Your aunt doesn't look too thrilled.'

'She's worried you're planning to push me off the mountain.' I was testing the waters with a flippancy I rarely deployed in male company. It felt too close to flirting. 'Just so you know, I now have phone numbers for the cottage and the pub so I can call if I need anything, and she'll be back here at four to pick me up.'

'Your aunt doesn't have a cell phone?'

It was odd to hear the Americanisation. 'Probably the only person in Wales who doesn't,' I said. 'She's not keen on connections.'

Declan laughed, shaking his head. 'Well, look, if I wanted to kill you, I wouldn't choose a popular tourist attraction on a Sunday morning, now would I?'

'You could make it look like someone else had done it.'

'We're going on a train that moves very, very slowly,' he pointed out. 'Unless we're right at the top, there's nowhere to bump you over the edge.' He studied me, head tilted in a way that made me glad I'd chosen the least hideous of my hooded sweatshirts to wear, under a padded jacket of Morag's, that didn't make me look too washed out. Shame my trousers were Morag's too, rolled up at the hem above my trainers. She'd grudgingly offered them when I revealed my jeans were still in the washing machine and I didn't know what to wear.

You need something suitable in case it rains. It can be brutal up there.

We're going on the train, not actually climbing the mountain.

Just take them, Grace.

They were waterproof and crackled when I moved, but glancing around, I didn't look too different to everyone else heading towards the little station, opposite a glittering lake where swans glided serenely on the surface.

'What happened to your face?' he said.

I realised he was looking at my bruise and felt like an idiot. 'I was running after a dog and fell.' I started walking, hoping he wouldn't ask for details.

'We're in luck, the railway has just reopened for the season.'

Declan fell into step beside me. 'We might have been forced to climb the mountain otherwise.'

'I'm sure we'd have been fine if you're as experienced as you say.'

'Hugh's the expert, but I know what to do in a snowstorm or an avalanche.' He gave me a sideways look, clearly teasing. 'I have mountaineering skills.'

'Shame it looks like you won't get to show me.' I glanced up at the wispy white clouds trailing across the blue sky. Around us, the range of mountains loomed, timeless and somehow reassuring, the peak of Snowdon clearly visible for once. 'Looks like spring has finally arrived.'

'Luckily, I'm good in sunshine too.' He seemed cheerful and the thought that it might be something to do with me was intoxicating. He looked good in his weatherproof jacket and hiking boots. I could easily imagine him scaling a mountain, all powerful arms and strong thighs, the wind ruffling his hair. 'I expect this will be a first for madam.' He nodded at Lily, who jumped as we entered the station and the waiting train let off a hiss of steam.

Her face crumpled, her bottom lip jutting out. I jiggled and shushed her, adjusted her in the carrier, making sure she was comfortable in her downy one-piece and woollen hat.

A smell of burning coal hung in the air, taking me back to bonfire nights and my grandparents' house where a coal fire permanently blazed in winter.

'It's a first for me too,' I said with a smile. 'I've never been up Snowdon.'

He clapped a melodramatic hand to his chest. 'But I thought your grandparents lived in Wales.'

'Yes, but we never quite got this far.' We joined the queue for the ticket booth. 'My father wasn't outdoorsy and Mum … I suppose when you grow up somewhere like this, you take the tourist attractions for granted.' Declan nodded but didn't comment. 'I remember my grandfather telling me the Welsh name for Snowdon means tomb,' I continued. 'Legend has it, the mountain is the tomb of an ogre who used to kill kings and make cloaks out of their beards. I was terrified at the time and my mum was furious with him.' I'd forgotten that memory; how Dad had chased me, screaming, around my grandparents' house, making 'ogre' noises while Mum pleaded with him to stop.

'Well, Wales *is* the land of dragons, wizards, King Arthur and the Holy Grail, or so I've heard.' Declan's lips were full and smiling, his eyes bright and warm. 'According to Hugh,' he added. 'He enjoys telling tales to visitors at the centre. Did you know the Devil is too embarrassed to visit this part of Wales?' I shook my head, amused. 'Something about saving an old woman's cow in exchange for a living soul, but she outwitted him with a loaf of bread.'

'What?' I couldn't help laughing. 'It wouldn't surprise me. The story, I mean. It's said that those who sleep on the mountain will awaken either as a madman, a poet, or never wake again.' He pretended to look scared. 'I came across that little gem when I was researching the area. It stuck in my mind.'

'Researching?'

Damn. 'My aunt … it's the first time I've visited her in years.' I kept smiling and tried not think of myself hunched in front of the computer at the New York Public Library, looking for details about Fenbrith, about how remote Morag's home really was. 'I wasn't that familiar with this part of Wales.'

'Where did you say you lived before?' We'd reached the front of the queue. Declan took out a card to pay, not looking at me.

'I'll get mine,' I dug a hand in my bag, heart racing.

'My treat.' He looked at the bag with raised eyebrows. 'There's a lot of stuff to cart around when you have a baby.'

Relieved by the change of subject, I said, 'Really, this is the best age to travel with her. It'll be much harder when she's older, especially when she's running about.' The thought of a day when Lily wouldn't need carrying was hard to visualise, but I supposed it was like that for all parents. You could only picture your child at the stage they were at. 'I didn't want to leave her behind today.'

'Well, I did invite you both,' he said gravely. 'Is she heavy?'

'Not now, but give her a few months.'

We headed past the gift shop and white picket fence, onto the departure platform. A large group of trainspotters were taking photos of the steam engine, which was attached to a single-coach. 'I'm impressed that you guessed how old she is.'

'Did I?' Declan leant close to the engine and studied one of the brass plates before looking back at me. 'She looks the same as my sister's baby at that age.'

'How many children does …' I almost said *Shauna*, remembering in the nick of time that I wouldn't know her name unless I'd looked him up online '… does your sister have?'

'Just the one at the moment. Ruby. She's going through the terrible twos.'

'I'd have liked a brother or sister,' I said out of nowhere. 'My mum couldn't have any more. Actually, that's not true.' I surprised myself again. 'By the time I was three, she understood my dad wasn't good at sharing her attention so decided to stop at one.'

Declan's eyes were loaded with questions, but all he said was: 'Having siblings isn't all it's cracked up to be.' I thought of the photo his sister had posted on Facebook, the fond memories it must have evoked, and suspected that wasn't true in his case, but appreciated he was trying to make me feel better. *Would Lily be an only child?* I couldn't think about that now. It was time to board the train. Declan gestured for me to go in front of him. As the queue shuffled forward, I got caught up in the throng of trainspotters with their cameras and felt myself being jostled, thickly clothed bodies pushing around me, too close for comfort.

'Excuse me.' Hot and panicky, I tried to force my way through the bottleneck, which seemed to tighten, hemming me in. 'Can you let me through, please?' My voice was high-pitched. 'I have a baby.' Terrified Lily was going to get squashed I pushed out my elbows to create some space. *Where was Declan?* Faces turned, disapproving, annoyed I was spoiling the fun. Reluctantly, the group parted, muttering unhelpfully.

I moved awkwardly past, shielding Lily with my arms, realising I'd gone too far when my feet reached the very edge of the platform in front of the engine. As I was about to turn and shout for Declan, someone barged roughly against my shoulder so that I teetered. I tried to steady myself, twisting my body away, but it was no good. Weighted with Lily in her carrier, I fell towards the track.

Chapter 27

Strong fingers closed around my arm and yanked me backwards. I slammed into something solid and stayed there a moment, eyes closed, arms around the solid bulk of Lily.

'It's OK, I've got you.' *Declan.*

My heart hammered, my mouth drying. *If I'd fallen …* Shock had frozen my movements. Opening my eyes, I checked Lily. Her dark gaze met mine, as if she too was making sure we were fine.

'Someone shoved me on purpose.'

'I wondered where you'd gone, then saw you being carried along with that bunch of anoraks.' Declan spoke at the same time and I wasn't sure he'd heard me.

I didn't repeat my assumption. I'd been surrounded by bodies, making a fuss, demanding space. It had been an accident; that was all. Thank God Declan had seen, that he had lightning reflexes, was strong.

Pulse slowing, I turned, my breath returning to normal. Space surrounded us now, the snappers moving off like a shoal of fish.

'Thank you,' I said, as Declan let go of my arm. I searched his face and saw quizzical concern in his eyes.

'Sure you're OK?'

'If you hadn't grabbed me—'

'Someone would have.' He glanced past me at the track. 'It's not a big drop, but with the baby …'

'Exactly.' I suddenly wished I hadn't come. I was cold in spite of my layers. 'Maybe this is a bad idea.'

Declan's smile returned. 'Too late now.' I glanced around, noticing the queue on the platform had cleared and the train was ready to leave. 'We'd better get on board.'

*

As we settled ourselves on one of the slatted bench seats inside the coach, I determinedly shook off the fright of almost falling in front of the train with Lily in my arms. At least it hadn't been moving, and Declan was right – it wasn't a big drop from the platform. Someone would have grabbed me if he hadn't. I was glad he'd been there though, looking out for me.

'So, where did you say you lived before?' he asked. The seats were narrow and his thigh brushed mine as he arranged himself, removing his coat and holding it loosely in his lap. 'Here, I'll put that underneath.' He took Lily's changing bag and stowed it under the seat. Across the aisle, a middle-aged couple smiled indulgently, probably assuming we were a family.

To buy a few seconds, I shifted Lily so she could look out of the window. Could I tell him the truth, or at least a version of it? My heart felt skittish. It would be odd if I didn't tell the truth and he found out later, but that was presuming we would meet again.

'I grew up in Berkshire,' I said, proud of my measured tone. 'Both my mum and aunt were keen to leave Wales as soon as they were old enough. It's the sort of place you visit, not live in, they used to say, though it's funny my aunt has ended up back here and the place where my mum lives now … well, it's not dissimilar to this part of the world.' I was aware of Declan listening intently, as if genuinely interested. Patrick had paid attention like that once, but it was a crucial part of his job to weed out information. 'She met my dad when he was on a stag night in Conwy, of all places. She worked behind the bar in a pub in the evenings, but was at college studying to be a vet. She loved animals, but my father persuaded her to leave and move to Berkshire with him. He was an accountant there, making quite a bit of money even then.'

I pictured my mum, falling for his charming patter, different to the boys she'd dated before, probably expecting to pick up her studies elsewhere, keen to live a different life away from the country she'd grown up in. Then she'd fallen pregnant with me and settled into a life of domesticity in suburban Maidenhead, miles from her family, with a man who'd convinced her he was all she'd ever wanted.

'So, that's where you were living before coming to stay at your aunt's?' Declan said. 'In Berkshire?'

We looked up as the conductor got on and asked for quiet so he could relay information about our journey and the importance of staying in our seats while the train was moving. I barely took his words in, a prickle of nerves passing over the back of my neck. I hadn't talked this openly to a virtual stranger for years – if ever. I glanced down at Lily, drowsy in her carrier, unbothered by her surroundings. *He's a new friend,* I imagined saying. *I think he's one of the good ones your auntie Ana believes in.* He'd saved us from falling and now I was opening up, which meant I trusted him.

Declan's hand nudged mine as he made himself more comfortable. My skin tingled with awareness. As the conductor finished speaking and the train lurched away from the platform, creating an excited ripple among the passengers, I threw Declan a smile.

'I lived in America for a long time.' I tried to make it sound as if saying it was no big deal, as if those happy times hadn't been wiped out by the events of the past year. 'Manhattan, actually.'

His eyebrows popped up and he looked at me with renewed interest. 'Let me guess, you were an au pair?' He glanced at Lily. 'You're obviously good with children.'

It was such an unlikely view of me – of the person I'd been

before Lily was born, when mothering wasn't even close to being on my radar – that I gave a disbelieving laugh. 'Actually, I cook. I'm a chef,' I said, looking for his reaction. 'I used to run a restaurant that belonged to the uncle of a friend.'

'Wow. *Really?* So, you never worked with kids?'

'No!' I laughed again at his expression, which was pure surprise. 'Is it so amazing? Chefs can be women too, you know.' I cradled Lily's bottom, feeling her twitch as she sank into sleep. 'I was pretty good,' I said, still smiling. 'People ate my food and even enjoyed it.'

'I didn't mean it like that.' He bumped me with his shoulder. 'Look,' he said softly. 'Isn't it something?'

I followed his gaze to a waterfall cascading over boulders between a canopy of trees, tumbling into a river below.

'It's lovely.'

People were taking pictures all around us. I thought about Morag. 'My aunt was a photographer,' I said, caught up in the moment. 'Not this sort of thing. I think she thought it too tame.' Declan was so close I felt his breath tickle my cheek. I kept my face averted, staring through the window. 'She took pictures in conflict zones, probably the kind of places you went when you were in the army.'

'Dangerous work,' he said, after a moment when I thought he hadn't heard. 'People have been killed in mortar attacks taking photos.'

'My mum worried about that, though she never said as much.'

'It's the sort of job that sounds exciting, like being a soldier, but it just brings home the futility of it all.'

'That's pretty much what my aunt said.'

As the train climbed, we fell silent, lost in our thoughts, eyes fixed to the scenery obscured briefly by smoke puffing from the engine. Gradually, I relaxed, letting myself appreciate the beauty of the changing colours as the sun poured iridescent light around gullies and into the valleys, highlighting the richness of

172

the terrain. It was so different to anything I'd looked at before. I had a sense of the untameable nature of it all, of being close to something mythical and understood the reasons people came up the mountain in their droves: fulfilment, escape, refuge, peace, adventure – or just for the conquest.

We passed plenty of climbers taking advantage of the good weather and promise of a spectacular view from the summit, some with all the kit, others in jeans and T-shirts.

'I hope the weather holds for their sakes.' Declan pointed to a gaggle of teenagers carrying Tesco bags, dressed more for a party than a five-mile trek to the highest peak in Wales. 'They clearly don't realise how cold and windy it'll be at the top,' he said. 'People don't see Snowdon as a proper mountain like Everest and come ill-equipped. The rescue team get over three hundred calls a year from idiots like that.'

On cue, we ascended into a curtain of mist and the temperature dropped by several degrees. It was a relief to finally get off the train and out of a bracing wind that threatened to knock us off our feet.

The visitor centre and café were set in a large, modern construction that looked like a feat of engineering, clad in oak and granite with panoramic windows. While Declan headed to the counter – *I think hot chocolate is the order of the day* – I wandered over to look at a wall hanging depicting the building of the centre, which had cost an eye-watering eight and a half million pounds. Lily stirred, snuffling and squashing her face into my fleece, her cheeks carnation pink. Outside, fog swirled around the windows. More people piled in, filling water bottles and queuing to order hot food.

Declan returned as I was carefully removing my coat and placed two steaming cardboard cups and a paper plate on one of the free-standing tables dotted about. 'The pasties smelt so good, I couldn't resist,' he said. 'They're enormous. You can share mine this time.'

His words were intimate, but something slightly formal had

entered his tone, subtle but unmistakable. Was he regretting bringing me here? Then he smiled and removed his coat once more. It was warm in the building, compared to outdoors. I felt the prick of perspiration in my armpits. Lily was nuzzling my chest, fingers grasping. 'She wants a feed,' I said, suddenly self-conscious at the thought of doing it in front of him.

'Shall I get them to heat up a bottle?' He bent to reach for the bag on the floor.

'Not necessary.' He straightened, looking mildly puzzled. 'I feed her myself,' I said, willing my face not to glow red. 'It's a perfectly natural process. You don't have to look.'

'You don't give her a bottle?' He seemed confused, almost disbelieving.

'Women do breastfeed.' I tried to laugh through a rising annoyance. 'Didn't your sister?'

'Yes, but …' He ran a hand through his hair, seeming to search for words that wouldn't come.

'Look, I can find the bathroom and do it there if it makes you uncomfortable.'

'No, no, of course it doesn't. I'm sorry. I don't know what I was thinking.' He gave a shake, seeming to return to himself, and held out his arms. 'Shall I hold her while you sort yourself out? We could go over there.' He nodded to a quiet corner by the counter. 'There's a seating area.'

I suddenly realised I was desperate for a wee, my bladder straining. 'Actually, if you wouldn't mind holding her for a moment while I go to the loo, that would be great.' I reminded myself he was an uncle, was used to holding a baby – had saved us from a fall at the train station – but it still felt strange to be handing her over. She looked tiny in his grasp, his fingers curling around her sturdy body, the other hand cupping her head. He held her in front of him, melting into a smile when she kicked and gurgled – a happy sound that drew smiles from a neighbouring table.

She's perfectly fine, I told myself, dashing for the toilets. I was getting better at trusting her with other people. Last night at the pub, and now in a café near the top of a mountain with Declan. It was a giddy thought that nearly prompted a giggle as I wondered whether I would only ever be comfortable leaving her with someone while I used the loo.

At least this time, I really needed to go. Luckily, there weren't too many people waiting, but I found myself washing my hands in a hurry, registering surprise that my reflection showed flushed cheeks and shining eyes, the lingering remnants of a smile.

My bruise was fading already.

*

I headed back, spotting Declan in the corner where he'd moved my bag and coat. He had his back to me, holding up his phone as though trying to get a signal. As I drew closer, I saw he was using the camera. Lily was pressed to his chest, facing forwards as he snapped a photo.

'What the hell are you doing?'

'Grace!' As he turned round, his phone fell to the floor and spun away. 'Christ, you made me jump.'

'Why are you taking pictures of Lily?'

She wriggled with a happy screech, whether at the sight of me or because she liked being in Declan's arms was hard to tell. I ducked down and retrieved the phone. 'Where is it?' I jabbed at the screen.

'Here.' Declan held out his hand and I thrust his phone at him.

'Hello, baby!' I forced a smile for Lily. 'Have you been a good girl?'

'She's been brilliant.' Declan bounced her. 'My mother rang just as you went. One of those WhatsApp video calls. My sister showed her how to do it. She happened to notice I was holding a baby.' He looked at Lily and rolled his eyes. 'She got *very* excited didn't she, little one?' He bounced his knees again. Lily's eyes widened with delight. 'She insisted I take a photo so she could show everyone what I'll look like when I'm a daddy.' He was still addressing Lily in a sing-song voice. 'Hey, take a look if you don't believe me.'

I was shaking as I looked at the screen. Sure enough, I could see the photo had gone to an Eileen Walsh, two blue ticks indicating she'd seen it. A message underneath read: *Oh, my GOD, the pair of you are so CUTE!!!*

I released a shaky breath. 'You shouldn't take pictures of people's babies without their permission.'

'You're right, I'm sorry.' He palmed his phone into his pocket. 'I didn't think. It was spur-of-the-moment, but you're right. I shouldn't have done it.'

He sounded genuine but something felt off-key. His tone didn't quite ring true and his eyes evaded mine.

'Actually, she does look really cute.' I forced a calmer tone. 'Would you mind if I took a picture of her too? I don't have many.'

He masked a look of surprise. 'Sure, be my guest,' he said. 'Just the baby, mind. You don't want my ugly mug in the picture.'

'Of course.' I rooted my phone from my bag and turned on the camera. 'I swear she's smiling,' I said, as cheerily as I could. I removed her woolly hat then took a snap before angling the phone slightly to include Declan's face as I took another picture. It was perfectly lit by the misty light flooding from the bank of windows. 'See?' Moving over, I clicked on the image of Lily and showed him.

'Beautiful.' He dipped his head to look more closely. 'Just like her mother.' His eyes met mine, his pupils dilated. I stared back, mesmerised by the intensity of his gaze. 'We've got about half an hour before we have to get back on the train,' he said, breaking the spell.

I gathered Lily's warm limbs against me as I sat down and discreetly fed her while Declan forked chunks of buttery pastry into my mouth, a personal gesture that felt oddly natural. The pasty was as delicious as it looked and while I ate I tried to hide the tension threading through my bones. When he asked about the restaurant where I'd worked, I squeezed the worry from my tone as I gave him broad strokes. 'What about her daddy?' he asked easily, once I'd run out of steam. 'He's missing out on this little one.'

'I don't really want to talk about him,' I said. 'I'm not being awkward just … he's not a good person, believe me. I don't want him in our lives.'

He studied me for a moment. 'I'm sorry.' He rubbed the side of his nose. 'I guess I take after my mother. She likes to get to the bottom of what makes people tick and I … well, I like you.'

Why? I couldn't stop the word from planting itself in my head as I blushed and looked away. I wanted to believe him, to not be paranoid, but still something felt off. When I'd finished my hot chocolate, I rose and said, 'I'm going to change her nappy,' not waiting for his response.

In the little changing room, I took out my phone and sent the picture I'd taken of Declan to Ana's number. *Could you ask your uncle if this is the man who asked about me at the restaurant?* My fingers kept slipping and I had to correct half the words. *He has an Irish accent.* Outside, I heard the final call for train users to gather outside. *Please let me know ASAP X*

Pushing my phone in my pocket, I opened the door.

'You forgot your bag.' Declan was outside, the bag dangling from one hand.

'Thanks.' I took it, knowing I looked flustered. 'I got her undressed then realised. Do I have time?'

'If you're quick.'

I changed Lily's nappy in record time, grateful she only needed a quick wipe, before popping her back into her clothes and heading outside. The mist had lifted and everyone was looking at the rocky slope leading up to the pyramid-shaped peak of the mountain. Stone steps curved into the side where a mass of people had gathered, waiting to reach the top. A couple was already there, posing for selfies.

'Takes away some of the mystery, doesn't it?' Declan said wryly. The wind was strong, thrashing our hair and whipping away his words. I had to lean close to hear him. 'Like those queues at Everest you see on the news, as if they're at McDonald's waiting to buy a burger.'

Sheltering Lily with my arms, I said, 'It would be even more popular if there *was* a McDonald's at the top,' and when he grinned and nodded, I wished I hadn't messaged Ana, that I wasn't looking for reasons to doubt him. That we really could be friends.

We didn't talk much on the journey back down. I wondered whether he sensed my reticence, or whether he'd got what he wanted – a photo of Lily. *Had he really only sent it to his mum?*

'There's nothing like this in Manhattan,' I said, twenty minutes in, pointing to one of the former slate quarries the area was famous for.

'This train was originally used to transport slate.' Declan added pointedly, 'I've done my Welsh research too.'

Was that a dig? He gazed past me through the window, a brooding set to his brow.

'Have you ever been to New York?' *Might as well go for broke.* 'I didn't think I could get used to living in a city, but I grew to like it.'

'Once,' he said, without hesitation. 'It wasn't somewhere I'd want to settle. I much prefer open spaces.'

'How long were you there for?'

'Not long.' He'd kept his coat on, hands pushed deep in his pockets. His legs were stretched in front of him, crossed at the ankles. He seemed relaxed but turned to look out of the window on the other side, where sheep were grazing at the side of the track. 'No ewes in New York.'

'When I told you earlier I'd lived there, you didn't say anything.'

'I didn't think it was important.' When he met my gaze there was something troubled in his eyes. 'Like I said, it wasn't my favourite place.'

'How long ago was it?'

'What is this, the Spanish Inquisition?' He pulled his head back, as if to see me more clearly. 'A lot of people have visited New York at some point.'

In my pocket, my phone beeped. Shifting Lily, who'd fallen asleep, I took it out and glanced at the screen, knowing it could only be Ana. My heart jumped as I read her message. *Just called Uncle. He said the man was American. What's going on? X*

My shoulders slumped as I put my phone back. If Patrick had sent someone after me, it wasn't Declan.

'Everything OK?'

'My friend, Ana.'

'Are you going to meet up with her while you're here?'

'She lives in New York. Works in the public health sector,' I said. 'She's got family in Berkshire, that's where I know her from, although her parents moved to Grimsby a couple of years ago, to be near her brother and his family. She's coming over in the summer, so we'll get together then. It'll be great to see her.' The relief of knowing he hadn't been asking after me at the restaurant released a gush of words, as though a dam had broken. 'She's met someone recently. They're thinking of moving in together. I've a feeling they'll get married. I hope it's here, though she's got a lot of family over there. She's half Spanish on her mother's side.'

'Nice to have a good friend.' Declan's face had subtly altered, the contours becoming less rigid as I babbled on. 'She sounds nice.'

'She is. I think you'd like her. Most people do.'

A thought planted itself in the centre of my mind. If Ana hadn't found Patrick and told him I was pregnant, I wouldn't be here, sitting beside Declan on a steam train on the side of a Welsh mountain with my daughter in my arms. As I looked at him and smiled, warm relief pushing away suspicion, another thought sneaked in – the kind I usually scoffed at. *Maybe this was where I was supposed to be.*

*

Taking a train up a mountain. Pathetic. He supposed it was a safer option with a baby, but couldn't resist giving her a little scare on the crowded platform. He failed to see the thrill of taking pictures of an old engine, but seeing the group of middle-aged men had given him the opportunity to push in where he wouldn't be noticed. Though part of him had hoped she would notice and run crying to her aunt. No one could prove anything. There weren't any cameras in this place.

He'd always been a risk-taker. Maybe that was why he was finding it harder to stay hidden, to keep his intentions private. He'd thought about going into the cottage again while she was there, just to see what she would do if she saw him. But he had a plan and must stick to it. He was overdue to give an update. Easier now, with a phone signal.

Even so, he would leave it for a while.

Until he'd decided exactly what to do next.

Chapter 28

Morag was parked outside the station and beeped the horn when she spotted us.

'Thanks for a lovely time,' I said to Declan, like a seven-year-old leaving a party.

'My pleasure.' Mild irritation rippled over his features when the van horn broke the thread between us again. 'Let's do something else soon. You have my number.' He mimed putting a phone to his ear. 'Promise you'll use it.'

'I only make promises to my daughter.' Seeing the good humour fade from his eyes, I added, 'Fine, I'll call.'

He half smiled. 'Don't overdo the enthusiasm.' He took his phone out. 'Let me send you the photo of Lily so you *actually* have my number.'

'That means giving you mine and I have a photo already.'

'Mine's better quality.'

'True.' Caving in, I gave him my number and his fingers flew over his screen. 'There you go.' Hearing the ping of a text from my bag I took my phone out and opened the photo attachment. He was right. It was a far better photo than the ones I'd taken. Lily was actually smiling, looking right at the camera. My lips curved in response.

'It's lovely. Thanks.' Morag beeped again, longer this time. 'I'd better go.'

'Me too.' He didn't move.

'How did you get here?'

'I borrowed Hugh's car.' He looked around, vaguely. 'It's in the car park round the back of the pub. Hopefully not vandalised.'

'I'd have said that's unlikely round here, but according to my aunt it's not.'

'Oh?'

'There's been some trouble with bored teenagers.' I nearly told him then about how I really got my bruise, about involving the police – how someone had hurt me – but Morag beeped again and kept her hand on the horn.

'Jesus,' I said, clambering into the van, trying to console Lily who'd woken and was grizzling. 'I'm not some teenager at a rave, Morag. It's mid-afternoon, not two in the morning.'

I said it with good humour and she responded with a grunt, thinning her gaze at Declan as we passed. He raised his arm in a static wave, watching until the van was out of sight and he was a tiny figure in the wing mirror.

'Had a good time then?'

I hid a smile, feeling even more like a teenager being picked up from a date – something that never happened because my father had forbidden me from going out with boys. 'Yes, I had a nice time. Snowdon's worth seeing. You should go up there sometime.' I didn't mention almost falling from the platform. There was no need to worry her when nothing had actually happened.

'You want me to ask around about him, get Ewan to check him out?' I realised she was talking about PC Thomas checking out Declan.

'God, no.' I wondered why it hadn't crossed my mind. 'It's fine, he's OK. He's lovely, actually.'

Morag pursed her lips but didn't comment. She'd been shopping and had invited Ifan for dinner. Still in good spirits, I cooked a stir-fry while they entertained Lily. Afterwards, we played a game of Cluedo at the table, picking at a box of chocolates Morag found in the cupboard. It was the closest I'd felt to being with family in a long time and I managed to hold on to a feeling of wellbeing.

It was dark when Ifan and Morag headed out. 'Chess club at the village hall,' she said. 'You're welcome to come.'

'Thanks, but I know nothing about chess except that I don't wish to learn.'

After they'd gone, I called Skip in and bolted the door. Morag would have to knock when she returned. After bathing, feeding and settling Lily, determined to get a routine going, I read to her from an ancient copy of *Anne of Green Gables* I found in the dresser until her eyes blinked shut.

I'd spotted a photo album in there while I was delving through, old-fashioned with a brown suede cover. After making a mug of tea, I sat on the sofa and flicked through the brittle pages, scrolling past images of my grandparents, my mum and Morag at different ages, even a few photos of me as a baby and as a gap-toothed toddler. None of my father, I noticed, though I clearly remembered Mum taking one of me on his shoulders, laughing behind the camera. I must have been about five. I could still recall the feel of his hair beneath my fingers, his strong hands holding me firm as he ran into the garden, excitement snatching my breath.

There was a batch of postcards from me, stuffed between the next two pages, held together with a rubber band. I was embarrassed reading the words on the back, which could have been from a stranger; bland and meaningless. Yet Morag had kept them all. I had a couple of hers too – *Bet you're glad you're not here!* on the back of an image of a sandstorm-swept desert – but to my shame had left them at the apartment.

As I put the postcards back and turned another page, a photo slid out and fell onto the rug. Skip shot over and sniffed at it before lying down again. I picked up the picture and turned it over. It looked to have been taken in the Eighties, slightly bleached out – a photo of a man, pale-eyed and high-cheekboned, perhaps in his early thirties. I knew Morag had taken the photo as surely as if she'd told me. He was sitting in what looked like a bombed-out room on a chintzy sofa with foam exploding from the cushions, wearing a padded vest and army-style trousers. *A soldier?* Someone she'd met out there, wherever it was. She'd caught him pushing a hand through a crop of silky black hair, gazing at the camera with knowing eyes and a smile that looked slightly cruel. He was good-looking, but something cold behind his wolf-like stare was unnerving.

Was he the someone Morag had been involved with? Why else keep the photo? I thought again of the letter I'd found tucked away in the picture frame. *Was this B?* Something told me Morag wouldn't like me looking at the photo, never mind asking her about it.

I'd just tucked it back and put the album away, disturbed in a way I couldn't pinpoint, when there was a knock at the door. I froze on my knees in front of the dresser. Skip looked up, a growl rumbling in his throat.

'Shh.' I pressed a finger to my lips, glancing at Lily to check she hadn't stirred. Skip ran to the door and barked when the knock came again. I glanced at the clock. Just gone nine. It felt much later.

Maybe it was PC Thomas with some news. I tiptoe-dashed to the window. The security light was on, a car parked just out of view, only the gleam of chrome wheel trims visible. I shrank back. Skip barked with menacing sharpness, but Lily didn't wake up.

I pressed my ear to the door. 'Who is it?'

'It's me. Declan.'

The air rushed out of my lungs. I shot the bolts back and swung the door wide, a palm pressed to my forehead. 'Christ, you scared me,' I said. 'What are you doing here?'

Declan held up my wallet. 'You dropped this,' he said. 'It must have fallen from your bag when you took your phone out at the station.'

'Thanks.' I took it from him. 'Not that there's much in there.' I peered past, straining my eyes through the darkness beyond the security light's glare. 'How did you find this place?'

'I asked at the pub,' he said with a shrug. 'Is that OK?'

'I'm not sure my aunt will appreciate them giving you her address.' Skip frisked around Declan's feet as if he'd never seen another human. 'You could have left my wallet at the pub.' I wondered whether he'd spoken to Annie. I couldn't imagine her telling him where Morag lived. 'Who did you ask?'

'The landlord.' He squinted, as if the sight of me was blinding him. 'I'm sorry, I shouldn't have come.'

He turned and started walking back to the car.

'Wait.' Suddenly, I didn't want him to leave.

He came back, hands in the pockets of the unzipped parka hanging from his shoulders. 'Hi,' he said, in a gesture of starting over. 'I really enjoyed our trip.'

'Me too.' I stepped outside, hugging my arms for warmth. 'I'm sorry about just now,' I said. 'It's just that my aunt lives here for a reason. She values her privacy.'

'I get it.' He looked around. 'It's not easy to find.'

'That's the point.'

'Doesn't she get lonely?'

'She has friends,' I said. 'But she chooses who to invite here.'

'You don't think she'd invite me?' He seemed to be searching for something in my eyes.

'She'll take some convincing,' I said. 'I'll have to work on her.'

He laughed quietly, seeming pleased. 'I hope you will.'

He came closer and propped his shoulder against the door-frame. Everything about him seemed brighter, sharper, his eyes more vivid.

'I should go back inside. Lily's sleeping.'

'You're not going to invite me in?'

'Definitely not.'

Skip woofed. He was sitting between us like a buffer.

'Sensible dog.' Declan lifted his gaze to mine. 'He must be reading my mind,' he said softly. The lamp from behind cast golden light and shadow across his face. My breathing grew short and a charge surged through my blood, as though I'd been plugged in. I wanted more than anything to grasp his hair, run my hands under his T-shirt and feel the curve of his spine. His mouth was inches from mine, his eyes on my lips.

'I … I have to go.' I clicked my fingers at Skip. He trotted inside and I followed, slamming the door before sliding the bolts across, as if Declan might be tempted to burst in and wrestle me to the floor. *Would I stop him if he did?*

I stood there, hands pressed to my mouth, heart thundering in my chest until I heard the car drive off, then sat on the floor with my back pressed against the sofa. Skip settled his head on my thighs while I stared at the fire, Lily sleeping beside me in her basket. *What was I thinking?* Hadn't I learnt anything from Patrick? But Declan was nothing like him. If I'd been able to compare the two of them a year ago, I wouldn't have gone near Patrick. I'd have known that his was the sort of love that came with conditions. It wasn't solid and sure, the kind I'd told myself was the only love worth settling for. The kind that didn't make unreasonable demands, wasn't cruel, didn't exact a price.

But I hadn't known Declan then and – I reminded myself as I stroked Skip's fur and kept staring at the leaping flames – Lily was all that mattered now: the only love that was truly unconditional.

Chapter 29

'Are you sure you want to do this? It's not too late to turn back.'

'As sure as I'll ever be.' There was a determined set to Morag's chin as she swung the van into the petrol station. 'And we're not turning back after coming this far.'

We'd set off on our four-hour journey to Berkshire at seven-thirty to 'make the most of the day' as Morag had put it. She'd risen early, packing sandwiches, apples, chocolate and a flask of coffee with the zeal of a scout leader. It was reminiscent of a road trip, though Morag's coiled energy suggested she was preparing for an ordeal, not travelling to see her sister, and my body was as tightly strung as a guitar string.

'It must feel strange after all this time,' I said when she got back in the van with a couple of packets of crisps.

'Of course it does.' Her jaw tightened as she thrust the crisps into the glove compartment. 'Your mum will be horrified. Why do you think I haven't called ahead?' She darted a look at me. 'She'd make sure she was out for the day if she knew I was coming.'

'I reckon she'll be pleased to see you.' Even as I said it, nerves circled my stomach. If Morag was filled with apprehension at what lay ahead, so was I. I'd spoken to Mum fairly regularly since leaving for America, and even visited four years ago but the visit had been awkward, filled with stilted silences, the gap between us seemingly too wide to bridge after such a long absence. I'd left earlier than planned, slipping away in a taxi just after dawn, glad to get back to work where I didn't have to think about what had gone wrong between us.

'She'll take one look at that baby and whatever happened between you in the past will be forgotten,' said Morag, seeming to read my mind. Lily was in the car seat between us for the long journey, tilted so she was almost lying flat. 'You mark my words. A baby …' She paused, focused on rejoining the busy road. 'A baby is healing.'

It was a very un-Morag thing to say. For a moment, my throat felt choked with emotion. 'She'll be upset that I didn't tell her about Lily, or give her the chance to see me pregnant, to come out to New York and be there when Lily was born.' *Would she have wanted to?* Since opening the animal sanctuary, my mother was wedded to her menagerie, to her life in Wokingham where she'd moved after Dad died, half an hour from our home in Maidenhead. She'd escaped from the town to countryside as if, like Morag, in her moment of crisis – or clarity – she'd yearned for more familiar surroundings, for the simpler life of her childhood.

'What happened between you two?' Morag asked.

I scrolled back to my father, collapsed in the kitchen, clutching his chest, and my mother a few weeks later with red-rimmed eyes, showing an estate agent around the house. Later still, Mum gripping my shoulders, her eyes blazing as she urged me to *get out there and live your life, Grace. Don't end up like me*. I hadn't argued, or challenged her; hadn't demanded answers.

'It's complicated.' I looked out of the window. The sky was a squally grey, rain splattering the windscreen. Hills and valleys had smoothed out to industrial estates and red-roofed towns as we headed onto the motorway. 'She was different after Dad died.'

'A good thing too.' When Morag fell quiet, I thought about all the knowledge she must have about my mother; about me.

'I should have done more,' she said unexpectedly. 'I could have helped, I see that now, but I was …' She lifted one hand off the steering wheel in an impatient gesture. 'I was on my own path to no good, even if I didn't know it at the time.'

I turned to look at her. 'Morag, did you ever want children?'

Her knuckles turned white as she fixed her gaze on the traffic ahead. 'I wouldn't have been a good mother.'

'You don't know that.' I shook my head. 'I didn't think I wanted children until I had Lily.' The shame still burned when I remembered how terrified I'd been during my pregnancy, how I hardly dared think about the baby I was carrying before she was born.

It's perfect, Patrick had said. *I can't believe you didn't tell me.*

'I got into a bad situation, like you did.' It took a second to realise Morag was referring to Patrick, as if my thinking about him had jogged her memory. 'A man I thought was good who turned out to be bad.'

'I saw a photo,' I confessed. 'In an album, last night. It fell out. I wasn't snooping.'

Her face paled. 'That was him.' Her voice lowered. 'Bernhard.' I thought of the letter I'd found. *B.* Bernhard. A love letter he wrote to her during happier times? 'I don't know why I kept that picture.' She sounded disgusted. 'Maybe as a reminder to never be that gullible again.'

'He … hurt you?' I thought of Dad and the ever-present threat of violence when he'd been drinking, filling the air like toxic smoke, sucking out the joy. Mum being extra careful to not tip him over the edge.

'Not exactly,' Morag said. 'I had to get away though. Just like you have.' She flicked me a look. 'So, I do understand.'

I wondered just how bad Bernhard had been. It was strange that my life and Morag's had followed a similar path, though I doubted hers had ended with a body lying at the foot of a staircase. 'Is that why you let us stay?' I swivelled to face her, nudging the car seat with my knee. There must be something about being in a moving vehicle that invited confidences; maybe a lack of eye contact, knowing that nobody else could hear. 'Because you knew how it felt to run from someone you'd trusted?'

'You're family.' She pulled into the fast lane, head turned so I couldn't see her face. 'Maybe I finally realised that family matters.'

There were so many things I wanted to ask her, but once she'd overtaken a couple of caravans in the middle lane, she slowed and switched on the radio. 'Could you pass me a sandwich?'

'Already?' I bent to rummage in the rucksack at my feet. 'It's nowhere near lunchtime.

'Driving makes me hungry. I didn't have breakfast.'

As she ate her cheese roll, her face inscrutable, I imagined a slew of memories rolling through her mind. What had Bernhard done that meant, after years of travelling and working abroad, she'd retreated to a corner of Wales and become a virtual recluse? And yet, she didn't seem unhappy. On the contrary, she appeared to belong. I understood more clearly now, her need to know I wasn't bringing trouble to her door. It sounded as though she'd had enough to last a lifetime, and explained her being unsettled at the possibility of troublemakers raiding the cottage.

As the radio continued playing hits from the Eighties, Lily woke up and started squirming, emitting hungry cries. Morag, cheerful again, pulled into the next services and got out to visit the shop while I fed and changed Lily.

As I settled her at my breast, her warm fingers curling around my thumb, I glanced in the wing mirror. A couple of cars behind, a silver 4x4 was queuing for the petrol pump. My breath froze in my throat. The bonnet of the car was visible, as if the driver had pulled out slightly to have a clearer view. *Of me?* It looked like the car that had followed us from the pub. I'd convinced myself I must have imagined the whole thing, but suddenly I wasn't so sure. Trying not to disturb Lily, I craned my neck to get a look at the number plate, so I'd know if I saw it again, but the driver pulled back in line as if sensing he'd been spotted. *Stop it.* I was being paranoid again. How many silver four-wheel drives were out there? I could see one ahead, pulling off the forecourt, another parked up while the driver inflated the tyres. No one had followed us from Fenbrith. Apart from anything, I'd have noticed sooner, especially on the quieter roads.

'Mummy's being silly again,' I murmured to Lily, focusing on her face, remembering a time – not long ago – when I'd walked up and down with her, not sure what day or time it was, the sound of her cries drilling into my ears. She was so much happier now, settled and content. And I would be too, if only I could be sure we had a future that didn't involve Patrick. And that I didn't have to see Mum. My heart rate doubled again. Lily stopped sucking as though she could feel it and let out a drowsy sigh. I hoisted her up and gently massaged her back, trying not to think about what lay ahead.

'Not far now,' Morag said, returning as I was settling Lily. Her words sent a shard of dread through me. I longed to tell her to turn back, that I couldn't go through with it after all. Memories rose like debris. I couldn't push them down, no matter how hard I tried. They eclipsed everything as our destination grew closer, until there was only one question in my mind. Would I would find the courage this time, to finally ask my mother the only thing that mattered: *Why did you kill my father?*

Chapter 30

A slab of oak with the words *Gail Roberts Animal Rescue Centre* painted in woodland green greeted us as we drove up the gravelled track. I'd seemed odd, Mum and me having different surnames now; another division between us.

Her home and workplace was a sprawling, one-storey barn conversion set in several acres, bought with money from the sale of the house in Maidenhead, which had been worth a lot more than my father had paid for it. Along with his life-insurance policy payout, Mum was set for life. She'd paid for my flight to New York and still transferred money every month to my account, where it sat untouched. Maybe, one day, I would use it to fund Lily through university. I suspected Dad would be turning in his grave to know the money he'd scrupulously saved over the years, while keeping Mum on a tight leash, had been used to help countless animals. Sometimes, I imagined her having a laugh about that.

My nerves pounded as Morag parked next to a Land Rover that had seen better days. Mum wasn't interested in material things. All her money went into the sanctuary. *To salve her guilty conscience?*

'I should find her first and prepare her,' I said to Morag. She hadn't moved since turning off the engine, her eyes moving across the low-slung building, taking in the elevated lawn at one side, and on the other, a yard stretching towards paddocks where several horses grazed. It hadn't changed since my last visit, though the horses were new. It didn't feel like home, but there were no memories of my father here, which was the point.

The sky had brightened, patches of blue among the grey. Puddles glistened, and rain dripped from the leaves of the oak trees standing sentry around the building.

'We should go with the element of surprise.' Morag opened the door and got out quickly as if worried she might change her mind. 'You see people's true feelings that way. No time to prepare a response.'

My mind shrank from the idea, but Morag was already striding away from the van. 'Wait!' I got out, grabbing the car seat. 'We should go together.'

She paused while I checked Lily over, playing for time. She looked adorable in the tiny floral leggings and pink top I'd pulled from the pile of baby clothes Annie had given me. Her gaze was somehow watchful, as if sensing this was a momentous occasion – that she was going to see her grandmother for the first time. *Oh God.* I shouldn't be doing it like this. I should have called Mum sooner, given her time to adjust, not turned up out of the blue with a baby. She thought she knew me. It would be a shock to realise I'd changed my stance on having children.

Just like your aunt, she'd said once, sadness in her eyes. *Maybe you'll change your mind one day.* I'd been annoyed that she couldn't see why, in my eyes, having children just tied people together and made them crazy. How many times had I heard my father say *I'll never leave you and Grace and you'll never leave me,* while my mother cried softly into a tissue? *We don't belong to you, we're not your property,* she said once, fighting back. Dad threw a full tumbler of brandy at the wall and Mum cut herself clearing it up while I told him about my day at school to make him smile.

As I caught up with Morag, I reminded myself that Mum was happy now. She'd eventually got the life she wanted, just like

Morag had – and like I would too. Three strong women who didn't need men to be happy. A new generation.

So why did I feel sick at the thought of seeing my mother?

I looked at Lily, letting love for her fill my heart, but couldn't banish an image of Dad on the kitchen floor of our old home.

I took a deep breath and straightened my shoulders, half-hoping Mum would be out and we could delay the moment, but there was a cry, then a shout and she was running towards us, hair flying, a dog at her heels that reminded me of Skip on guard at the cottage, waiting for Ifan to come and take him for a walk.

Morag stopped in her tracks ahead of me. I heard her say, 'I'm sorry,' then Mum was throwing her arms around her, burying her face in her sister's neck, laughing and crying and when she looked over Morag's shoulder and saw me standing there, her face crumpled again. Her gaze dropped to the car seat in my hands and she pulled away from Morag. Her hands flew to her mouth then stretched towards me. 'Grace.' Her voice cracked. 'Oh, Grace.'

Chapter 31

An hour later, Mum was still cradling Lily, eyes fixed on her heart-shaped face as Lily gazed up at her. 'I can't believe it,' she kept saying. 'I'm so happy, Grace. I just can't believe it.'

Morag had been right about the healing powers of a baby. It was as if the years I'd been away, the strained dutiful calls, the fact I'd failed to tell Mum I was pregnant hadn't happened; as if the past had been wiped clean and we were starting afresh from this moment. And it wasn't just Lily's presence. Before she'd even spotted me, as soon as Morag apologised, Mum forgave her. All she'd ever wanted was an apology, an acknowledgement that her sister had abandoned her family and left Mum to cope when their parents became old and frail. She didn't even ask why I'd gone to Morag instead of coming to her, as if she understood everything. *Only, she didn't.*

'I don't want to hold on to grudges,' she said now, finally lifting her head, rocking Lily instinctively as she must have done me, when I was a baby. 'I know I've been bitter.'

She was looking at Morag who – having been shown round the centre on a whirlwind tour, as if Mum was making up for lost time – was leaning against the worktop in the untidy open-plan kitchen, taking everything in with a clarity to her gaze that

I hadn't seen before. As if something had finally been put to rest that had bothered her for a long time. Which, I supposed, it had. Perhaps she wished she'd reached out years ago. 'But I want to put it all behind us now.'

'Me too,' Morag said simply. 'I'll make some more coffee, shall I?'

It was odd, seeing the two of them in the same room, juxtaposed over the photos I'd seen of them growing up, and memories I had of Morag coming to visit when I was little when she'd seemed brighter than her sister. They were more similar now, their differences rubbed away by years and experiences. Mum was more robust these days, her make-up-free face glowing with health, her trim body honed from the physical work of running the centre. Dad had liked her to keep her hair shoulder-length and blonde, insisted on her wearing skirts and heels, but she'd long since had her hair cropped and let it go grey and was wearing old boots with jeans, and a sweatshirt with a squirrel motif on the front – the kind of clothes Morag wore most of the time. Despite the lines mapping her brown eyes, she looked younger than she had years ago when the worry she'd tried to conceal behind layers of foundation and lipstick had weighed down her features and aged her. *Being a widow suits her.*

'She's such a good little girl,' she said, returning her gaze to Lily. 'She doesn't cry often now.'

'You once slept through a firework display.' Mum's smile was dreamy. 'I used to prod you sometimes to wake you up for a cuddle.' I wanted to hear more good memories, to ask so many things, but they would have to wait. 'You're not going back to New York?'

When I shook my head, happiness flooded her face. 'The restaurant?'

'I've left, but I'm hoping to go back to work part-time.' I glanced at Morag for reassurance, as if maybe now we were at Mum's she'd tell me I should stay.

196

'Local pub,' she obliged. 'Job there if she wants it.'

'That's wonderful.' Mum's gaze flicked to me. 'Come and have a look at the alpacas.'

'Alpacas?'

'They're like llamas, but smaller—'

'I know what alpacas are, Mum.'

She smiled, recognising my teenage tone. 'Someone reported they were living in terrible conditions so we brought them here. They were in an awful state but are doing really well now.'

My stomach dropped. She wanted to talk to me in private and I wasn't sure if I was ready. 'Lily will need feeding soon.'

'Morag can watch her for a moment.'

I wanted my baby back in my arms, as if holding her offered protection, but without waiting for a reply, Mum rose from the cracked leather sofa and crossed the wooden floor. All the furniture was ramshackle, chairs with frayed covers, a worn wooden table, paper piled in stacks on every surface, and the rooms all smelt of damp straw and dried animal food; a smell that reminded me of when Ana had a pet rabbit and would forget to clean his hutch.

Shelves bulged with books about animal husbandry, and there were photos scattered about of me at various ages, my grandparents, and one of Mum and Morag as children. None of Dad. He didn't exist in this place.

The dog that had followed Mum in – a grey lurcher with a limp called Max – was in his bed under the window, ears pricked, eyes big as he watched Mum's every move with clear devotion. He was one of the animals she'd adopted, along with a couple of feral cats she shooed outside to keep them away from Lily.

'Go,' Morag said, accepting Lily easily, laying her against her shoulder and resting her cheek on her hair. 'We'll be fine, won't we, little one?' She spoke with such tenderness, Mum looked briefly startled and stared at her sister until Morag turned away.

'Odd to see her with a child,' she said once we were outside, the air fragrant with rain and earth. Up here, the countryside seemed further away than in Wales, the shades of green more subtle. It was still beautiful though. It surprised me how at home I felt in the UK after being back for such a short time – almost as though I'd never left. 'Morag would never hold you when you were a baby. I think she was frightened of dropping you.' Mum's voice was tinged with regret. 'She was better when you were older and she could talk to you.'

'She seems pleased to be a great-aunt.'

'It's easier when you're one step removed. I suppose that's why grandparents get away with so much.' It was so different to last time I'd visited, when Mum had seemed brittle, too keen to please, treating me like a special guest, and I'd been defensive and closed off, wishing I hadn't come as old memories crowded in. There'd been so much to say, I hadn't known where to start.

Mum stopped as we reached the gate to the paddock, turning to face me. 'Why are you really back, Grace?'

I bit my lip, an urge to spill out the whole thing and cry on her shoulder almost overwhelming. 'I needed to get away from Lily's father.'

Her face changed, expression sharpening into alarm. 'Are you safe?'

It was the same thing Morag had asked. They both knew what it was like to be with someone who wasn't. 'Yes, I'm safe.' I sounded convincing and her shoulders dropped. 'Did you know Morag was in a bad relationship?'

Mum blinked, as if thrown by the change of topic. 'Your aunt was never any good at opening up. We never had gossipy conversations like you and Ana did,' she said, after a moment's pause. 'I suppose I thought of her as invincible, swanning off round the world, taking her award-winning photos.' That hint of something again ... jealousy, but faint, like an echo of something long buried. 'I envied her,' Mum admitted, a tinge of rose pink on her cheeks. 'She'd gone off to do what she wanted. I suppose it didn't occur to me that she might be like the rest of us, would ever suffer at the hands of a man. She never liked your Dad.' A hint of sorrow crept into her voice. 'She told me I was crazy to stay with him. I thought she'd have known better, would meet someone glamorous and elope, live happily ever after.'

I marvelled that she could mention Dad so freely. She hadn't referred to him during my last visit, but then, I hadn't given her the chance. She averted her gaze, staring across the paddock. The horses looked peaceful, manes ruffled by the breeze. In the corner the alpacas stood tail to tail like bookends, impossibly regal with their long necks. 'I wish I'd known she wasn't happy,' she said at last. 'We'd have had something in common at last.'

'It's funny how you both fell for men who weren't good, when granddad was such a nice man.' It was the first time the realisation had slipped into my head.

'That's probably why.' She nodded slowly. 'We took it for granted, thought all men were like him. We didn't look too deeply below the surface.' I wondered what it said about me that I'd tried not to repeat my mother's mistake, then fell for the wrong man anyway. 'It's awful, but I try not to think of the past these days. Helping these animals—' Mum looked at the horses again '—it puts things in perspective. They live in the present. I try to do the same.'

I felt a wave of something rising inside me. I gripped the top of the gate and Mum placed a hand over mine. 'It doesn't always work,' she said softly. 'I miss you so much, Grace. I hoped you'd come back one day.'

When I recoiled from her touch, she pulled back, shock widening her eyes. 'Why *did* you stay away so long?' Her words were halting, as if reading something in my face that she needed to question. 'That last visit was so awful. I knew I'd messed up, that you didn't want to be here,' she said. 'But when I told you, years ago, to leave, to get away … you know I didn't mean forever, don't you?'

I nodded, but my heart picked up speed again as the question I'd wanted to ask for so long, had tried to forget, had hidden so deep it felt as if my insides were being excavated, rose to my lips. 'Mum, that day, when Dad had his heart attack ...' Saliva rushed to my mouth. I thought for a moment I was going to be sick and swallowed. 'Why did you take so long to call an ambulance?'

For a moment, she just stared at me, then: 'What do you mean?' Her voice was faint, colour draining from her face.

'I was there, Mum,' I said. 'I came downstairs and saw him on the kitchen floor. You were ... you were just staring at him with the phone in your hand.' The memory zoomed in, as if someone had thrust a photo of the scene at me. Dad, looking up at her, his face contorted, a bluish tinge to his lips as one hand gripped his other arm; Mum still in her Sunday best skirt and blouse, an apron round her waist as she'd been washing up before Dad lost his temper and shouted about something she'd supposedly said at lunch to make him look silly, his anger propelling me up to my room to do my homework. She was gazing down at him like a puzzle she couldn't solve, one hand wrapped around the phone receiver, the fingers of the other worrying her bottom lip, a habit she had when she was thinking.

'Mum, he might have lived if you'd called the ambulance sooner.' The words came out like bullets, harder than I'd imagined. Mum stepped back, one pace, two, as if escaping a raging fire, then turned and strode away, faster and faster, arms pumping. I ran after her, through the kennel area filled with dogs waiting to be rehomed, where a red-haired woman I recognised from my last visit – Glenda – was chatting to a couple with a little boy, a clipboard in her hand. She looked round, startled, as we shot past.

'Mum, wait!' We were through the other side, in a yard round the back of the building, where a dozen chickens scratched in the dirt and a pair of geese flapped beside a pond. 'Mum, I begged you to ring for help and you ignored me.' She hadn't even glanced up, hadn't seen me on the stairs. I'd wondered afterwards whether the words had even left my lips, why I hadn't moved either, hadn't gone to her or my father, but I'd been so frightened, seeing him helpless for once, needing mercy and not finding any. It had felt as though my feet were glued to the carpet as I half-crouched there, shocked. Time had stretched and warped. Dad moved, tried to speak at one point. Still my mother kept on staring, pulling at her lip as if trying to decide what to do, or waiting to see what would happen.

Tears had blurred my vision. I ran back to my room, threw myself on my bed and pulled the pillow over my head, trying to block out what I'd seen, praying it was a nightmare I'd wake up from any second. Finally, I heard sirens, urgent rapping at the front door, voices filling the hallway and the sound of Mum sobbing. When I ran down, he was already in the back of the ambulance on a stretcher and I knew he'd gone. Was dead before they arrived.

I couldn't look at Mum when I went back inside. She was sitting, head bowed, at the kitchen table, a tissue pressed to her nose while our elderly neighbour boiled the kettle and uttered condolences, offering to make my dinner. I never talked to her afterwards about what I'd seen; hadn't told anyone. There was nobody I could unpick my feelings with during the following days and weeks, when I'd tried to convince myself I'd imagined it all, grief mingling with a terrible feeling that at last, a thorn had been removed from my heart and I could breathe properly.

In front of me, Mum spun on the spot a couple of times, raking her fingers through her short layers, looking anywhere but at me. Finally, with nowhere else to settle, her gaze fell on mine. 'I did it for you, don't you see?'

'What?'

She came forward and grasped my shoulders, her eyes swimming with tears. 'Do you think you would ever have left or had the life you have if *he* was still alive?' Her voice was low, steadier than I'd expected.

'Mum, I …' I shook my head, trying to break away, but her

grip strengthened. 'You would have stayed to protect me, like you always tried to do. That wasn't the life I wanted for you, Grace. His heart attack was a blessing.' Her words, though softly spoken, were pitiless. 'Of course, I didn't plan it, but—'

'You saw an opportunity.' Finally, I twisted away, feeling cold where she'd touched me, wanting her hands back there, pinning me to the moment. 'Why didn't you divorce him?'

She became still, her expression clouding as if she was back there. For a second, I hated that I was doing this, forcing her to relive that day, but I needed to understand. 'He wouldn't have let me go, Grace.' Her words were as clear as the chime of a bell. 'He said if I tried to leave him, he would kill me. I believed him.'

'Oh, Mum.' I pressed a hand to my mouth. 'I'm so sorry.'

'You've nothing to be sorry for.' She stepped forward, pulling me to her with strong arms. '*I'm* sorry. I'm so sorry you went through that, Grace, that you saw what happened. I had no idea. Why on earth didn't you talk to me about it?'

I thought back to how conflicted I'd felt, scared at seeing a side of my mother I hadn't known existed. How, when she sold the house and bought the sanctuary, blossoming into the person she was meant to be, it was as if the mother I'd known had died too. As difficult as I'd known her life was with Dad, I'd got used to it, my mother and I accomplices in some ways. The new mother, the one who urged me to leave, to not turn out like her, a woman capable of so much more than I'd thought … 'I was scared.' I folded my arms around her, childish tears falling. 'Everything changed and I was frightened. I had to get away.'

'Oh, Grace, my love. I'm so, so sorry.' She pulled back, swiping tears from my cheeks with her thumbs, her forehead resting on mine. 'I *never* wanted to hurt you, my darling girl. That was the very last thing on my mind. All this time, I thought … I thought you'd taken me literally, that you'd flown away to live your own life. You were happy, I could hear it in your voice when we spoke and I was happy for you. *So* happy. I told myself it didn't matter

202

if you didn't come back, because you'd made a life for yourself that was different from mine. That's all I wanted, but I missed you so much.' Her hands slipped down to mine and held them tightly. 'I wish you hadn't been there that day. You were *fifteen*, a child.' Her face contorted, as if the reality had finally hit her. 'I wasn't thinking straight. It was a shock when your dad ... when he collapsed like that, after all the shouting. The silence ...' She swallowed. 'I knew you were upstairs. I didn't even think to call you down. I hated that you felt you had to hide from him when he was being ... to hide from us.' Her face seemed to collapse. 'If I could turn back the clock—'

'Would you have called for help sooner?'

She closed her eyes. 'I don't know, Grace.' Her lashes were sparser than I remembered, or maybe it was the lack of mascara. 'I just wish you hadn't seen him – us – like that.' Her eyes slid up to mine, tears spilling over. 'It never occurred to me you'd heard anything, that you'd come to see what was happening.' Understanding flooded her face. 'No wonder you couldn't wait to get away.' Her voice wobbled. 'You must have hated me.'

'I didn't hate you, Mum.' I took a step back, wrapping my arms around myself. 'It was ... difficult. I didn't know how I felt.' I heard Lily's hunger cry from inside the house, as familiar as my heartbeat. 'He never got to be a grandad.' Tears blurred my vision. 'He was still my dad.'

'I know.' Mum wiped her cheeks with her fingertips. 'But you deserved better; we both did.'

'That doesn't mean he deserved to die.'

'No, you're right, but he wasn't a good person, Grace, you know he wasn't.'

He's not a good person. That was how I'd described Patrick to Morag and Declan. I'd deprived Lily of a father because I believed he wasn't a good man; the same reason Mum had deprived me of mine. 'He wasn't all bad.'

'No one is all bad,' she said sadly. 'I loved him once.'

I nodded, unable to speak.

'He might have died anyway.' She raised her chin. 'I asked the doctor afterwards whether, if he'd got help sooner, it would have made a difference ...' Her words trailed off. The truth was, we'd never know for sure. 'I'm so sorry,' she repeated. 'I really am, Grace.'

Was letting someone die the same as killing them? I still didn't know the answer.

After passing the cuff of her sweatshirt over her eyes, Mum added, 'If you decide you don't want me in Lily's life, I completely understand.' Her voice held a tremor. My revelation had shocked her, probably even more than she was letting on.

'I'm not here to punish you, Mum.' The years I'd stayed away had done that already. 'I just ... I had to say something.'

'It's more than I deserve. You being here.' Her chin trembled. 'Knowing that you ... that you ...' Her voice broke. She dipped her head, bringing her hands to her mouth. 'I wish I'd known.'

Closing the gap between us, I put my arms around her, felt her body tremble. I thought about why I'd come back, of what I'd left behind, and something released inside me, relaxing its grip. 'It's OK, Mum.' As she pressed her head on my shoulder it struck me. If I hadn't gone to New York in the first place – if it hadn't been for my mother's actions that day – I wouldn't be here now, a mother myself, my baby inside the house. 'Mum, I mean it.' Shifting, I grasped her fingers, thinking of all the times they'd held mine and how hard it must have been to let me go. 'We're going to be fine,' I said. 'It's all in the past.'

*

He sliced through the phone wire again and put his knife back in his belt. It would be too late by the time she realised, by the time she wanted to call for help. He had expected her to be a lot more careful, to not be so trusting. The key was gone now so he couldn't let himself in through the door but it didn't matter. The window in the bathroom was big enough to squeeze through.

They'd left early, wouldn't be back for hours. He'd overheard the conversation. He resented her having a day out. What right did she have to happiness after what she'd done? He fingered the little envelope in his pocket, containing the rest of the baby hair, dark and silken. He wondered what she'd thought when she saw it. What he had to do to really scare her.

The attack hadn't worked, or the note he'd left. It was as if she hadn't even seen it. He could have done worse, had been tempted that night outside the cottage, his hand feeling for his knife. But he wouldn't risk capture. The dog had been easy to pacify with the bones of the rabbit he'd eaten, but it was touch and go for a moment, the animal's teeth bared as if ready to pounce. Good job he could run fast, though he doubted he'd have been able to outrun the animal.

He'd watched the policeman come out and those idiot officers, knew they wouldn't find anything. Those idiot thugs who'd driven out and cased the cottage while it was empty had done him a favour. Now there was someone else in the frame, he could get away with more.

But he was tiring of the game now. The rain was hard to bear when it was so frequent. He had to be careful when lighting a fire that the smoke couldn't be seen, stamping it out quickly once he'd cooked. He daren't keep it going all night.

It was raining again now, but he would be nice and dry inside. He would have a look around while he was waiting for her to return. He didn't smell good and wasn't sleeping well. Maybe he would have a shower, a sleep. The old man had been over and taken the dog away in his truck. It was now or never.

He kicked leaves over the ashes of the fire, stuffed his rucksack where it wouldn't be found, and made his way stealthily through the trees.

Chapter 32

'That went better than I thought it would,' Morag said.

'Much better.' A freeing sense of relief brightened my voice. I'd confronted my mother and the sky hadn't fallen in. If only I'd done it sooner. Instead, I'd held on to a feeling of guilt, disguised as resentment. Guilty for feeling relief at my father's death. I'd missed him, but at the same time part of me had been glad he was gone. Guilty for not telling a soul what I'd seen that day. By staying silent, I'd been complicit. *You were only fifteen.* Did that excuse me?

'I thought she seemed well.' Morag's tone broke in, matching mine.

'I really think she is.'

We were back on the road, darkness falling, Lily asleep between us once more in the van. Mum had asked us to stay overnight, wanted me to stay longer. 'I've got a spare room and don't mind sleeping on the sofa.'

I was relieved when Morag insisted we leave, saying she had commitments and needed my help. Mum accepted it meekly, perhaps mindful of not disrupting the new bonds being forged. Back inside, with red-rimmed eyes and a new understanding between us, she and Morag had chatted about their jobs while I made a late lunch of ham and freshly laid eggs, the dog tracking my hands as I worked. They'd been surprised by how alike their lifestyles were. Morag asked about the chickens. 'I'm thinking of getting some, adding eggs to my delivery list.'

Mum wanted to know about her day-to-day life. She didn't mention Morag's old career, but exclaimed how their dad would have been impressed by her sister's allotment. 'Remember those roses he grew that he named after us?'

My aunt didn't talk about their parents, beyond admiring a cushion cover my grandmother had embroidered. I had the impression they were deliberately staying away from anything controversial but that other, more difficult, conversations would be had another time. Mum had said hesitantly, looking at me for permission, that she'd love to visit the cottage – she hadn't been to Wales for years – and Morag promised to stay in touch.

'What did you two talk about outside?' Morag said now. 'You were gone for ages.'

With a stab of regret, I said, 'We had a lot to catch up on.' I would never tell Morag about the part Mum played in my father's death, even though I had a feeling she would understand. It was Mum's secret to tell, not mine. I had enough of my own. *Elise.* The name was like a scratch in my brain. *If she hadn't married Patrick, she'd still be alive.*

'You both looked like you'd been crying.'

'We were,' I admitted. 'It was emotional.'

'Maybe it's true that time's the healer.' She sounded as if she was talking to herself. 'You have to be really dedicated to stay angry. Such a waste of energy.'

'You sounded angry when I asked about your job the other day.' I felt emboldened by her good humour and the success of our visit. 'Being a photographer, I mean.'

She changed gears as we approached a junction. I discreetly glanced behind for the umpteenth time. *No silver 4x4.* The reality of what I was going back to felt like a surreal bad dream and, for a moment, I wished I'd taken Mum up on her offer to stay.

'It wasn't just the job, not really,' Morag said. 'There was other stuff going on. I thought work would be an escape but it just seemed pointless in the end.'

'I suppose my job's pretty pointless.'

'Cooking for people is a nice thing to do; it gives pleasure.'

'It won't change the world.'

'Do you want to?'

I glanced at Lily, washed by passing headlights. Her eyes blinked open and closed again. 'Maybe this one will.'

When Morag didn't speak, I looked over and was shocked to see a glimmer of tears in her eyes. 'Don't mind me,' she said, brushing a finger across her lashes. 'I'm getting soppy in my old age.'

'Today's been emotional for us both.'

We were silent for a moment. It was raining again and the windscreen wipers moved with a hypnotic rhythm. With every mile, I felt closer to being home, despite not knowing what lay ahead.

'Do you want me to take over driving for a while?'

'No offence, but no thanks.' Morag flashed a smile. 'You haven't driven for years.'

'Thanks for the reminder.' I smiled back, but it was an effort. 'I'd probably end up on the wrong side of the road.'

'Talking of driving, we're getting low on petrol.'

Morag pulled in at the next service station. 'Want anything from the shop?' She got out, jacket flapping in the wind.

'Maybe some orange juice. I can't face any more coffee.'

As she fiddled with the petrol pump and unfastened the cap, Lily made a cat-like sound and stretched before sinking back into sleep. 'Did you enjoy meeting your grandma?' I whispered, stroking the crown of her hair, which rose with static. 'Someone else to love you nearly as much as I do.' Mum had been moved that I'd called Lily after her mother.

Your gran would have liked that.

I'm sorry I didn't use your surname. She's Lily Evans.

Mum hadn't blanched at the sound of her married name. *It suits her.*

The service station was brightly lit. I took out my phone, remembering I'd promised Declan I would call him. Had he been thinking about me? I tried to picture him going about his day and brought up the outdoor activity centre he'd mentioned on Google. There was a picture on the website of a man I assumed was the owner, his friend Hugh, kneeling on a paddle board on a lake, and another of a group of young people windsurfing. Hugh looked friendly and rugged, his weathered face creased with laughter lines. I wondered whether Declan would accept the job offer and found myself hoping he would.

I switched back to the search engine, my fingers moving across the keypad almost of their own volition, typing in *Elise Holden, memorial service, New York.* There was Patrick in a decent shot for the *New York Times* again – had he set it up? – standing with his head bowed, hands clasped in front of him. He was wearing a long dark coat, and a lock of hair fell over his forehead adding a sense of poignancy. Various people were gathered around; an older couple I knew from a previous search were Elise's parents, Clarence and Vanessa Boyd, and a straight-backed woman I guessed was Elise's sister, cradling a baby draped in a shawl. The image blurred in a haze of tears. *Elise would never raise a child.*

I shuddered, recalling the feel of Patrick's hands on my pregnant belly. Breathing deeply, I clicked off the website before I was drawn to look at anything else.

Morag was in the station shop, queuing to pay. I found a tissue and blew my nose. About to put my phone away, I felt the vibration of a text. *Ana.* My stomach plunged when I read her message. *Saw Uncle earlier and showed him the photo you sent to double check. He says he thinks it's the man he spoke to but with a beard. I'm worried Grace. X*

Outside, thunder cracked. Lily startled, her eyes flying open.

'It's OK, baby.' Light-headed, I found Declan's Facebook profile and took a screenshot. I enlarged it and sent it to Ana, my fingers fizzing with nerves. *This look familiar?* When it had sent, I looked through the rain-spattered windscreen. Morag was still queuing, probably swearing under her breath. It was mid-afternoon in New York. I knew Ana would send the image to her uncle right away. *Please, hurry,* I thought and: *Please, please don't let it be Declan.*

Morag was at the till when a message pinged back.

Julio says that's him. Who is he?

Saliva rushed to my mouth. *No, no, no.* If it was true, it meant Declan knew Patrick – but how? Hands shaking, I switched back to Google and typed in *Declan Walsh New York.* Maybe I'd missed something when I looked before. There was his Facebook link, but nothing else. I scrolled up and down a few times then typed *Declan Walsh, Patrick Holden, Manhattan, New York* and clicked on *images.* There weren't many. Until he started running for the DA's job, Patrick wasn't particularly newsworthy, but one picture stood out. Taken last year, he'd been attending a charity fundraiser. He was climbing out of his sleek back car outside the Waldorf Astoria, tugging down his tuxedo. His head was turned to the camera, a half-smile on his face, but it was the man holding the car door open that made me cry out. I pinched the screen to zoom in on his face. *Declan.* His hair was shorter, his expression unsmiling, but it was unmistakably him. Declan had been Patrick's driver.

My heart felt as if it was going to jump out of my chest. I almost dropped the phone when it pinged again. *Grace, I'm worried. You said the man was Irish, not American, yet this is the same guy? PLEASE call me.*

Morag was on her way back, shoulders bent against the rain driving across the forecourt. *Out now, can't talk, will call at 11 or ring me.* I stabbed in the number for the cottage, then threw my phone in my bag, grimly vindicated. Patrick had sent someone after me.

I just wished with all my heart it wasn't Declan.

*

He was tired of waiting. Where was she? He thought they'd be back by now. It had been fun, for a while, treating the place as his own. It was small, but that had never bothered him. He didn't care about things like that. There was a lot of stuff in the cottage, most of it old, none of it attractive. Even so, it made him sick that she was living such an easy life now, getting to do whatever she wanted without a thought for what she'd left behind, or the life she could have had.

He'd eaten, filling his mouth with food as he strode around, barely tasting it. He hadn't bothered showering after all. It was too cold in the bathroom. He'd had enough of being cold.

He tried to sleep for a while, lying on top of the bed where she lay at night. Was her sleep peaceful? He hoped not. She didn't deserve peace. She didn't deserve anything.

In his pocket, his phone rang. He didn't bother to answer, didn't feel like appeasing him anymore. It would be over soon. He'd tell him sorry, that it was for the best, that he'd done him a favour. The world would be a better place without her in it. He just had to be patient a little longer.

After checking the time, he moved upstairs to sit in the shadows once more.

Chapter 33

'You're very quiet.'

'I feel a bit sick.' *More than a bit.* My stomach felt like a washing machine on a spin cycle as Ana's message played on a loop in my head. Declan had known before I told him that I'd lived in New York. He knew Patrick. *He'd found me, he'd found me, he'd found me.* The words pounded in time with the windscreen wipers. Rain lashed down, drumming on the roof, thunder rolling overhead. A dagger of lightning split the sky ahead. It felt like the end of the world. *He found me, he found me, he found me.* Had he followed me from the airport? What was the plan? He must have been watching me all this time. He'd left the note as a warning, the lock of hair that wasn't even Lily's. *It was sick.* He'd been in the cottage. But why not just confront me? Why all the cloak and dagger, pretending he wanted to get to know me? Or was that the idea? Lull me into a false sense of security so I'd leave Lily with him, like I had yesterday, and when I wasn't expecting it, he would take her, return her to her father as instructed by Patrick.

Was Patrick calling my bluff? Maybe he'd devised a counter-attack if I went ahead and told people the truth, like I'd threatened. Or maybe he thought I wouldn't go through with it. Maybe I wouldn't get the chance. What exactly was the end game?

A headache began to pulse behind my eyes. My cheekbone ached. *Was Declan responsible for that too?* I remembered the powerful hands on my back, the force of the shove that sent me flying. My stomach rose, acid burning my throat.

'Your mum used to get travel sick because she insisted on reading in the car whenever we went anywhere,' Morag said. 'Used to drive your gran nutty when we had to keep stopping so Gail could throw up in a bush.'

I thought he liked me. I'd let suspicion override my instinct that Declan was a good man but my instinct had been wrong. *And yet … and yet.* The look in his eyes had seemed to shine a light on everything that was good about me, had suggested he liked being with me. And he could have taken Lily already if that was his intention. Was he here to monitor me, or scare me – make sure I toed the line?

If you tell one person a secret, it's not a secret anymore. Patrick had said that. I'd told Ana most of it, but knew she would never tell. The rest I'd kept to myself.

If I confronted Declan, told him the whole truth … My mind slammed away. He might not believe it. Patrick had power. He'd got to Declan first. What did he have over him? How had he persuaded him to come? *Was he dangerous?* I would have to pack up and leave tomorrow—

'—storm should blow itself out soon,' Morag was saying, digging her hand into a bag of crisps, the crackle of the packet competing with the thunder and rain. 'Nearly home now.'

Home. I twisted to unstrap Lily, lifted her out and tucked her against me underneath the seatbelt.

'You shouldn't hold her like that, it's not safe.' Morag spoke with a snap of worry.

'Neither's eating while you're driving,' I snapped back. I wanted to hold Lily, to feel the rise and fall of her breath, to inhale the baby-sweet scent of her. She was safer in my arms than anywhere else.

'You're right.' Morag crumpled the bag and shoved it under the dashboard. 'I'm sorry.'

'No, I'm sorry.' Guilt lit a flame in my churning stomach. 'I shouldn't have spoken to you like that.'

She turned quickly, trying to read my face but I stared ahead, arms curled around Lily. 'Sure you're all right?'

'Queasy, that's all.' If only I could tell her. 'I think I might have a nap.'

'At least put the baby ... put Lily down.'

I reluctantly strapped her back in and arranged her blanket, turning so I could watch her sleep, my head resting against the back of the seat. My mind felt dense and heavy, my thoughts growing sludgy. Thunder rumbled again but it sounded distant as the storm moved away. The rain was lighter, tyres swishing on the wet road.

'It's been a long day.' Morag reached over to place a hand on my knee. Her touch was warm, her presence like a fortress, solid and protective. 'There's a lot to think about.'

I would call Declan in the morning, I decided. Arrange to meet, just the two of us. Lily would be safe with Morag for an hour. I would talk to him. Tell him as much of the truth as I dared and take a chance he would understand and leave us alone, report back to Patrick that there was nothing to worry about.

Or ... I shifted, pain circling my head. *Or* I could arrange to meet him at a time and place that would give me a chance to run, to be gone before he realised I wasn't going to turn up, too late to come after me this time.

But I didn't want to run. And even if I did, there was nowhere to go apart from Mum's, where I'd be easy to find. *Ana's family?* I could stay up north with them for a while. I knew they'd make me welcome.

Loneliness engulfed me. I didn't want to run away. In a short space of time, Fenbrith had begun to feel like home; a good place to stay and raise my daughter. Despite everything, I didn't want to leave.

My eyelids drooped, grew heavier as the van sped through the darkness and Lily slept on, oblivious. I would figure it out in the morning.

*

'We're here.'

I jolted upright, wincing as my neck protested. Lily was awake, kicking and fussing under her blanket, eyes gleaming in the darkness.

'What time is it?' I stretched and yawned, a moment of peace before everything rushed back. *Declan.* Had he followed us up the motorway to find out where I was going? The other night, I hadn't seen the car properly when he turned up at the cottage. He'd parked too far away. *Deliberately?*

'It's just gone eleven.' Morag switched off the engine and flexed her arms. 'There was a lot of traffic on the A55.' I felt her gaze on me. 'You were out of it, mumbling in your sleep.'

'I was?'

'Lot on your mind, I suppose.'

You don't know the half of it. 'Something like that.'

'I'm pleased you and your mum are back in touch.'

'So am I.' With the heating off, the van's interior quickly cooled. I shivered as I reached to unclip the belt from around Lily's car seat. 'I'm glad you are too,' I said. 'Thanks for driving us. You must be shattered.'

'I must admit I'm looking forward to my bed.'

'Why don't you take it tonight and I'll sleep downstairs?'

'I've told you, that sofa's comfy.' She sounded tired but content. 'It's actually done my back the world of good.'

'If you say so.'

'I do.'

Was Declan here, waiting, watching? Or now he thought he had me convinced he was a good guy, was he resting easy in Caernarfon at his friend's place? A thought hit. *Was Hugh even his friend?* A spike of sadness lodged in my heart. I'd really believed Declan and I could be friends. Maybe more, one day.

'Are you coming in?'

Morag held out her hand to take the car seat. I handed it to her, remembering I was supposed to have called Ana at eleven. Maybe I'd leave it until tomorrow. I jumped out, a throb of pain lancing through my head as I landed. The earth had been churned up by the rain and ... I tensed as my gaze landed on what looked like a set of fresh footprints leading up to the cottage. Then I remembered, Ifan had arranged to come over and take Skip out.

'The dog's quiet,' Morag said, as though reading my thoughts. 'I thought he'd be barking the place down.'

'Maybe he knows it's us.' I look Lily's seat from her and Morag strode towards the cottage. I followed, treading carefully in the mud, trying not to imagine eyes trained on my back. The rain had stopped, but all around was the sound of dripping water. The clouds parted briefly, moonlight shining a path to the door where Morag had stopped, shoulders rigid. The security light hadn't come on.

'What is it?' As I drew closer, I saw why she'd stopped. The door was ajar, blackness around the opening.

My stomach felt oily with fear. 'Morag, don't go inside,' I hissed.

But she'd already pushed it wide and was stepping over the threshold, reaching round for the switch on the wall. Light sprang out. There was a moment when everything seemed frozen in time before Morag stepped back, a hand to her throat.

'Bastards.' Her voice was tight with anger. 'They've trashed the place.'

'What?' Gripping the car seat with both hands, I joined Morag in the doorway and stared at the scene of devastation. Drawers had been yanked out of the dresser, the contents strewn everywhere, the doors hanging off their hinges, shattered china all over the floor. The sofa cushions had been upended and slashed, the stuffing spilling out like innards. Books with their pages torn out were tossed about like confetti.

It was a similar scene of mayhem in the kitchen – flour dusting the surfaces, sugar gritting the worktops, eggs smashed against the tiles, yolks dripping. The fridge door hung open, food scattered, ruined, on the floor in a lake of milk.

When I saw the pages had been ripped from the photo album, pictures torn in half, and my grandfather's wall map on the rug, its frame splintered among the debris, I let out a cry. Surely this couldn't be Declan's doing. *Why, why, why?*

Only the fire hadn't been disturbed, flickering in the grate as if recently attended to, the dancing flames adding a sense of the macabre. I spun to see Morag standing among the wreckage, red splodges staining her cheeks, her eyes flashing with fury.

'Whoever did this could still be here.' My voice wavered as shock set in. I didn't want Lily seeing this, absorbing the air of menace. If we weren't alone, we could be in danger.

Morag shook her head. 'Bloody cowards, they wouldn't hang around.' Her voice was a growl as she stepped over the broken china to where the phone was lying, the receiver separated from the base. The cord had been yanked from the socket and she bent to jab it back in. I looked around, seeking signs that someone was there, eyes travelling to the shady area of the loft, the bedroom. A prickle of goose bumps ran up my arms, but no … there was nowhere to hide up there, and if the teenagers had done this I doubted they would have stayed. They couldn't have known how long we'd be away.

'I wonder if there's any damage upstairs and in the bathroom.' I swivelled to look at the door behind me, standing slightly ajar. Lily's gaze was wide, moving around the room. I thanked God she was too little to know what was happening.

The place even smelt different, something unfamiliar lingering, like unwashed bodies. I imagined vandals here earlier, admiring their work as if they were starring in an episode of a crime drama.

'Don't touch anything.' Morag's head jerked round. 'It's a crime scene.'

She picked up the phone and pressed the dial pad three times: *999*. Frowning, she pressed the numbers again then rattled the receiver pins, like I'd seen people do countless times in old movies. 'It's not working.'

Horror exploded in my chest. 'But it was only just fixed.'

'Listen.' She came over and jammed the receiver to my ear. Nothing but dead air. The room felt too hot, despite cool air flowing through the open door. 'No dial tone.' She made an angry sound and threw the phone down. 'Must have been the storm. I'll have to drive back to the village.' Her eyes were like coals, bluish shadows beneath. I wanted to cry, to hug her, to make all this go away. 'You'd better come with me.'

'I think someone cut the connection.' It felt like being sick as the words erupted. 'I'm not sure it's teenagers. I think someone's doing this because of me.'

'What?' Morag's gaze shrivelled. 'What are you talking about?'

'She's right.' The voice cut through the silence like a knife. A scream flew from my throat as I spun to see a figure at the top of the stairs, shrouded in shadow, Morag's rifle cradled in his arms. 'I did do it deliberately.' He allowed the words a moment of space before adding, 'No one's coming to help you.'

Chapter 34

Morag was breathing hard, both hands pressed to her heart. My stomach vaulted with shock at the look on her face.

'Go, Grace.' I hardly recognised her voice. 'Take the van and go.'

I tore my gaze away and looked at the man. Not Declan, after all, but recognisable as he came down one step, two, moving into the light. He was the man I'd seen in the photo: *Bernhard.*

Here for Morag, not me. *It had never been me.*

'Leave, now, Grace.' She made an anguished sound, like an animal in pain. '*Run!*'

My feet felt nailed to the spot. 'I'm not going anywhere.'

The man came closer, his movements stealthy. His pale eyes were cold and glittery, like broken glass, his silver hair cut close to his scalp, matching the stubble on his narrow jaw. He was dressed in combat trousers, a camouflage jacket and desert boots. Despite being thin to the point of emaciation, he radiated something powerful and dangerous.

'You probably should go.' He didn't look at me, his stare on Morag as if pinning a butterfly. 'I don't wish you or your baby any harm.' He barked out a mirthless laugh. 'Did you know she had one? *We* had one,' he corrected. 'A little boy. Isn't that right, Morag?' His accent was stilted, Eastern European, maybe

German. 'Have you talked about him, or do you still pretend he never existed?'

'Don't do this.' Morag's voice was hoarse. 'What do you want, Bernhard?'

'He got in touch with me.' The man took another step forward. 'The baby you gave away. He's all grown up now. Wanted to know about his mother. He managed to find me, couldn't find you. I told him I would do it for him. I've wanted to find you for a long time but you did a good job of disappearing.' Another edgy laugh. 'Although, when I put my mind to it, it was pretty simple.'

He seemed to have forgotten I was there, as though face to face with Morag at last, he couldn't stop the words he'd been saving up from tumbling out. 'I thought it would be fun to use my old skills,' he said. 'And a chance to pay you back for destroying my career.'

'You did that yourself.' Morag's voice was thick with emotion. 'You killed that soldier in cold blood. I watched you do it and try to cover it up. That's why I reported you.'

'I was doing my job.' His words were frighteningly cold. 'I went to prison because of you; my reputation was ruined.'

I was trying to absorb what he'd said. *Morag had a child?* A son? It seemed impossible, yet made a weird kind of sense. It explained her reaction to Lily, was perhaps the reason she'd made us welcome – a bittersweet reminder of her own baby. *Oh, Morag.* Why hadn't she told anyone?

'How did he find you?' Her vocal cords sounded strained. I could only imagine what it was costing her to mention him when I was certain she'd never spoken about her baby to anyone, what a shock it must be to hear her son had been looking for her.

'My name was on the birth certificate, remember? I made sure of that.'

I imagined a fling, Morag falling for Bernhard, discovering too late that he wasn't a man designed to be a father, that she'd made a catastrophic mistake – one that might ruin her son's life and her own.

220

'He must have known you were in prison, what you'd done,' she said.

'I told him you set me up, that it was all a mistake. He wasn't hard to convince. The poor guy is desperate to replace the old couple who adopted him with his real parents. Did you know they died several years ago, that he's all alone now?'

Morag was motionless, as if the slightest movement could create a landslide, a collapse so great she might never stand up again.

'You left the note.' My voice was too loud. He blinked as though remembering I was there. '*Keep her close.* You were talking about *me*.'

'Note?' Morag's head turned slowly as if it was too heavy for her body. 'What note?'

'I recognised the writing from the letter. The letter in the picture frame.' Her gaze was uncomprehending. I wondered whether she'd forgotten about it, until she suddenly dived for the painting lying face down on the floor beneath its hook. She tugged out the folded paper and hurled it into the fire. Bernhard watched with narrowed eyes, as if he had no idea what I was talking about. 'He left a note upstairs a couple of days ago,' I said. 'I thought it was for me, but it was meant for you.' I turned to him. 'You let yourself in when we were out. He took one of the rabbits from the fridge,' I said to Morag. I remembered the wisps of smoke I'd seen above the trees and how I'd convinced myself it was coming from a steam train in the valley. 'You were living out there.'

'A man has got to eat.' His grin revealed crooked front teeth. 'The dog enjoyed the bones.'

'Where is the dog?' I looked around as though he might be cowering in a corner.

'You'd better not have hurt him.' Morag spoke through gritted teeth.

'He's fine. A good boy.'

'Where is he?' I repeated, trying to hold Lily's car seat behind me, desperate for him not to see her, for her to not look at him and have his face imprinted on her brain.

'Not far,' he said dismissively. 'I'll set him free when I leave.'

'Why are you doing this?'

He switched his gaze back to Morag. 'It is a great game, don't you think?' His grin was terrifying. 'Yes, I left a message up there for you to find—'

'Oh my God, and the baby hair.'

'Baby hair?' Morag sounded bewildered.

His eyes swivelled back to me. 'Yes, and the baby hair.' He tipped his head towards the stairs. 'I didn't know she was sleeping down here.' His smile didn't touch his eyes. 'Your aunt never used to be so generous.'

'Don't talk about her like that.' There was a bite in my voice. 'You don't know her.'

'You're wrong. I know her well. You are very like her.' He cocked his head in Lily's direction. 'Except that you kept your child.' His eyes froze over again. 'Unlike her.'

'I did what was best for him.' The words sounded ripped from somewhere deep inside Morag. 'I didn't want him knowing who his father was. I wanted him to have a good life, to be with good people who would raise him to be a good person.'

'*Good, good, good,*' he mocked. 'What do you know about goodness?'

'A damn sight more than you.'

'He is waiting for me to report back.' Bernhard rocked on his heels, chin raised, a spark of something mischievous in his expression that made me see, suddenly, what might have charmed Morag once: a confidence, a swagger, maybe even a kind of charisma she couldn't resist. 'He'll be sad to hear his mama died.'

Fear tore through me. I felt breathless with panic. 'You can't believe you'll get away with it. You'll go back to prison.'

'I barely exist anymore.' His face was hard, as if cut from

222

stone. 'No one knows where I am. I will not be found and your word will mean nothing.' He was wearing latex gloves. I looked at them with a feeling of detachment, as if I was floating away, watching the scene from above happening to somebody else. 'It is quite annoying that you turned up, though it was fun to mess with you a little—'

'You tried to push me off the platform at the station.'

'You pushed her?' Morag whipped round. 'Grace, why didn't you tell me?'

'I hoped that she would.' Bernhard gave a crooked smile. 'Maybe she didn't want you to think it was him, her *companion*.'

Knowing he'd been there, watching Declan and me, waiting to hurt me to punish Morag ... it made my stomach turn over.

'Anyway, maybe another body won't matter in the scheme of things.' His tone was frighteningly casual. 'A burglary that went terribly wrong. Those boys, they have been up here before. They heard your aunt had a lot of money stashed away. They came to look for it while you were out and found this.' He raised the rifle, shaking his head. 'There was a scuffle, it went off, they panicked. These things happen. A local tragedy.'

'I don't have any money here and everyone knows it.' Morag took a step towards him. 'Please, Bernhard, you don't have to do this. Go back to whatever life you were living before Isaac found you.'

Isaac. *My cousin*. Morag's son.

As Bernhard focused his attention on her once more, I edged closer to the bathroom door, hand flailing behind me. When my fingers made contact with the wood, I pushed. Turning, I placed Lily's car seat inside. A cold blast of air hit me, the window flapping open. That was how he'd got in. I tucked Lily's blanket around her and shut the door, praying she wouldn't start crying until Bernhard was gone. Because he had to go. He couldn't be serious about killing us.

'When I have done what I came to do, I will go back and be with my son.' Bernhard's tone was gloating. 'I will be the father he has always wanted.'

My heart dropped through my stomach.

'You're insane.' Morag's face was bone-white. 'This is a game to you, just like being a soldier was. You enjoy killing. How many others?' Without warning, she lunged towards Bernhard and pushed him hard in the chest. Taken off-guard he stumbled back, staggering over one of the sofa cushions on the floor. As he shot out a hand to save himself, the rifle slid from his grasp. I hurtled forward, snatching up the gun as he twisted to reach for it. Jamming the butt against my shoulder, I pointed the barrel at him, hooking my finger around the cold, smooth trigger. 'Get out of here, now.' I swung the gun at the open door, then back to his chest. 'Run, or I'll shoot.' My voice had steadied, a calmness descending. I hadn't come all the way here with my daughter to wind up dead at the hands of a madman. 'I know how to use it.' I was aware of Morag breathing harshly.

'Grace …' Her voice was a growl. 'Don't do this.'

Bernhard held up his hands in supplication. He was on his knees, looking at me from under his lashes, the orange glow from the fire giving his face a devilish appearance.

'You won't do it.' His tone was arrogant. 'You are not a killer, any more than she is.' He jerked his head at Morag.

'Grace, put the gun down …' She stopped as the light changed, blue and red swirling across the room in a bizarre disco kaleidoscope.

The police.

Seeing it too, Bernhard's head swung in the direction of the door, perhaps calculating how long he had to get out. His gaze returned to me. Everything seemed to speed up. He rose like a cobra, pushing fast in my direction. Morag shouted '*No, no!*' the words mingling with the siren sound of Lily's cry and an unearthly roar from Bernhard.

I shut my eyes and squeezed the trigger, jerking backwards as agonising pain seared through my shoulder. As I landed heavily, my daughter's wails seemed to reach me from a long way off and all I could think was: *I'm sorry, I'm sorry, I'm sorry.*

Chapter 35

News travelled fast. Annie was outside the police station when we emerged an hour later, a coat thrown over her flannel pyjamas, to offer us a room at the pub.

'You can't go back home tonight,' she said, throwing an arm around Morag's shoulders. 'Ifan called to tell us what happened.'

She waited patiently while I made a quick call to Ana, to tell her that I was safe, running through the bare bones of what had happened.

'Christ, Grace, you could have been killed. Thank God you know how to handle a gun, which is not something I thought I'd ever say.' She sounded on the verge of tears. 'So, it was nothing to do with Patrick after all?'

'No.' It still hadn't sunk in.

'But what about the man in the photo you sent? Who is he?'

I promised her an update soon and rang off. I couldn't think about Declan right then.

I hadn't killed Bernhard. The pellet had penetrated his shoulder, deep enough to cause him pain and to give us a few precious minutes to escape – if the police hadn't turned up.

Ana had called them from New York. Worried about my message, and the fact I hadn't phoned when I said I would, she tried ringing the cottage. When she realised the line was dead, she got a bad feeling and phoned the police with a garbled story about me being in serious danger. It turned out Ifan had called them too. When he turned up to take Skip out, he was concerned the dog was acting oddly, running towards the woods and barking as if someone was there. He took him away for a walk and brought him back, then decided to drive up later to see if we were home. He had a look round and left, but couldn't shake the suspicion that something wasn't right. PC Thomas, worried the gang of teenagers were involved, drove out with a colleague to find Bernhard howling with pain outside the door, me crawling about inside among a sea of china, and Morag in the bathroom consoling a howling Lily.

'Ifan knows a bit about what happened to me back then,' Morag confessed, once Annie had left us alone in a guest room at the end of the landing, extracting promises to let her know if we needed anything. 'He knew I had a son.' She perched on the edge of the narrow bed, while I rested against the headboard on the other. Lily was peaceful after a feed, warm and sleepy in my arms, seemingly none the worse for our ordeal, but my throbbing shoulder was a painful reminder of what had happened.

'He was talking about missing his wife, how you learnt to work around the grief, and I found myself telling him I understood, that I lost someone too, but it was a choice I made so I didn't deserve to grieve.'

'Morag, that's not true.' I was shocked that she believed it. 'You obviously loved your baby.' I was still struggling to absorb the fact that my aunt was also a mother.

'Like I said at the station, I think I always knew Bernhard would come for me one day. I didn't want Isaac to grow up knowing his father was a murderer, that we might have to keep moving around once he was released from prison. It was easier to do it on my own, knowing my son was safe with a family who would care for him.'

'Mum would have cared for him, if you'd told her. Even your mum and dad.'

'Your father wouldn't have allowed it and my parents were too old. I didn't want to involve my family, maybe even put them in danger.'

She talked quietly, face shadowed by the bedside lamp, hands twisting in her lap. Exhaustion rolled off her in waves. 'I'd never planned to spend my life with Bernhard,' she said. 'He was a sergeant, leading a team of soldiers in Baghdad. I met him in a bar and I suppose there was something about him.' She pushed out a bitter laugh. 'Same old story,' she said. 'I broke my own rules by getting involved, even though I knew it would be short-lived, a fling. Everything out there was so bloody awful.' She broke off, face twisting with remembrance as I registered dimly the similarities of our stories. 'When he shot that civilian, I didn't even know it was him. I happened across the scene by chance, a soldier standing over a man who was pleading for his life. I took a photo as he fired the shot, another as he turned and saw me. That's when I knew.' She covered her face with her hands. I thought of the picture of Bernhard I'd found, the letter she'd kept, and knew she'd been in love with him. The shock of what he'd done must have been hard to bear. 'I knew I had to report him,' she said, letting her hands drop. 'There was something about how calm he was that made me think it wasn't the first time he'd done it. He liked the power.' My mind flew to Patrick, an image of him in a courtroom, holding someone's future in his hands. The difference was, he was on the right side of the law. 'My photographs helped convict Bernhard and, of course, he never forgave me.'

'I don't remember it being on the news,' I said. 'Mum never mentioned it.'

'I didn't tell her any of it. I couldn't.' Morag pushed at the skin around her thumbnail. 'The case was kept quiet because of his position, and because of the damage it would do to the army's reputation if what he'd done became public knowledge. He was sent to a military prison after a short trial.'

She tipped her head back, as if seeing it all play out across the ceiling. I tried to imagine her abroad, dealing with it all on her own. I hoped she'd had the support of her colleagues, of friends, but maybe she wasn't supposed to talk about it to anyone.

'When I found out I was pregnant, I … I thought maybe I *could* keep the baby, live a different life, but it wasn't me.' When her gaze landed on mine, it was filled with shame. 'It wasn't just about *him*. I was thinking of myself, too. I wasn't ready to be a mother and yet, ever since, I've regretted letting him go. I often wondered how it might have been if I'd kept him with me.'

The urge to reassure her was stronger than almost anything. Of all of us – Morag, Mum, me – she was the better person, her actions purer. 'You mustn't think like that.' I knew it was asking the impossible but said it anyway. 'By letting him go, you might have saved his life.'

She nodded reluctantly, as if needing to hear it but not quite believing the sentiment. I held Lily a little tighter. 'And it's not too late. He wants to meet you.'

'I don't know.' She shifted, stood up and paced the room, less sure of herself than I'd ever seen her, no doubt still in shock. 'He's told him terrible things about me.'

'There'll be work to do,' I acknowledged. 'But you're his mother, Morag. He needs you. Just tell him the truth.' *The truth.* I'd never tell Lily the truth about Patrick. Not the whole truth, anyway. 'He's your son and there's no reason now why you can't get to know him.' She stopped then and I watched the reality of it sinking through her, hope sparking a light in her eyes. 'Bernhard will go to prison and probably won't come out,' I said. 'Even if he did, he wouldn't dare come after you again.' She dropped back down on the bed, her face working. 'Is this why you stayed away so long? Why you never came to visit or stayed in touch? Because of what happened with him?'

'I was ashamed.' Her voice shook. 'I couldn't face my family knowing I'd judged your mother when I was no better, worse in fact, because I'd given my baby away. They would never have forgiven me.'

'I think they would.'

'Maybe I couldn't forgive myself.'

'You should talk to Mum. Tell her,' I said. 'She'll understand.' *More than you know.*

After sitting in silence for a while, Morag climbed into bed fully dressed and fell instantly asleep while I lay wide-eyed in the darkness, reliving it all, fitting the pieces together as Lily slept on beside me. Images blurred in my mind; Bernhard's arrogant features morphing into my mother's expression earlier that day as she cradled her granddaughter for the first time, knowing she'd looked at me with the same expression once. I cried silent tears, because she'd missed the chance to look at her nephew that way, didn't even know he existed, and because Morag had missed it all too, because of *him*. No man should come between a mother and her child, especially a man like Bernhard. I didn't regret firing the rifle. I only wished the pellet had pierced his heart.

The following morning, I looked at Morag across the table downstairs in the bar. Her face was pale but calm, the lightness I'd glimpsed in her gaze still there. Despite everything, I felt a burst of happiness for her. At least Bernhard had brought her son back into her life. I had a feeling she wouldn't shirk meeting him now.

'I still have the lock of hair he left,' I told her. 'It's in the drawer in the dressing table.'

Ifan turned up as we ate breakfast – taking it in turns to hold Lily – to say he'd found Skip tied up in the woods near where Bernhard had been camping out. The dog greeted us as if he hadn't seen us for years, seeming unaffected to have been tied up outside all night.

'Traitor,' Morag muttered, slipping him some bacon. 'Making friends with strangers.' Ifan was reluctant to leave her, I noticed, but Annie chivvied him out with Skip. 'Meet her back here in an hour,' she said. 'Give her a chance to eat and have a shower, then we'll all help clear up at the cottage.' Annie didn't know the full story and hadn't probed, but I knew it was only a matter of time before it all came out – the story of an ex-soldier on a revenge mission, staking out his former girlfriend, shot in the shoulder by the woman's niece. It would keep the locals gossiping for years, yet I knew they would be protective of Morag.

'Good for you,' Annie had said briskly, hearing about my part in the drama. 'You're allowed to shoot someone if they break into your property. He got what he deserved.'

As I sat across from Morag, empty breakfast plates in front of us, early sunshine streaming through the window, my mind turned to Declan. My throat grew tight. It was such a relief to know he wasn't the man in the woods, that he hadn't left the warning note and baby hair, stolen the rabbit or attacked me in the dark – but it didn't alter the fact that he hadn't been honest. He knew Patrick. He'd followed me here from New York. Worse, I didn't know what his plan was.

I dug out my phone, which was almost out of battery. My head felt as if it was being squeezed in a vice and my shoulder twinged whenever I moved. I felt dizzy with tiredness and delayed shock, but I couldn't put it off any longer. I had to talk to Declan.

I brought up his number and texted: *Hey, it's me.* It was hard to know what tone to strike. *Thanks again for the train ride! Are you free tomorrow? Pub lunch at the Carpenter's Arms midday? X*

Was the kiss too much? I deleted it, then added it back. We'd left things with the understanding that we were at the start of something. One kiss came across as friendly. For all he knew, I added kisses to all my messages. I wondered how much he *did* know about me. I supposed I would find out tomorrow.

He replied immediately, as if he'd been staring at his phone, waiting to hear from me. *You promised to call! X*

I *could* call him. Would it be better to ask him outright over the phone, rather than face to face? *No.* I had to look him in the eye. I wanted him to hear me out – to see my face and know I was telling the truth – but I wanted to do it somewhere public. After last night, I wasn't taking any chances. *Busy with Lily right now. She didn't have a good night. We'll be catching up on some sleep today X*

At least that was true.

Everything OK?

Just tired X

When he didn't reply, I felt a ripple of unease. Then: *It's a date. See you tomorrow X*

I stared at the kiss as if trying to solve a riddle. It didn't mean anything. Declan was here for a purpose, I reminded myself. I just had to find out what it was.

Chapter 36

When Ifan arrived to pick Morag up, I made my way through the pub with Lily. Annie followed us out the back to the stairs. 'I'm going to drive over to the cottage to help your aunt,' she said. 'If you need anything, give Bryn a shout, and help yourself to whatever you want from the kitchen.'

I turned to face her, knowing I looked a state despite grabbing a shower while Morag watched Lily before breakfast. I'd had to put on the clothes I'd worn the day before. 'Thanks for this,' I said. 'You're a good friend.'

'We care about your aunt.' Annie's tone was matter-of-fact, her smile sincere. 'That's how it works around here.'

There were sounds of a child running around in one of the rooms above, followed by a squeal and a thump. Annie winced. 'That's Gwynn, having one of her tantrums,' she said. 'Her granny's taking her out in a few minutes so you should get some peace.'

'There's no need.'

'Believe me, there is.' Smiling again, she wound a mustard-coloured scarf around her neck and untucked her hair. 'If she doesn't work off some energy she'll still be charging around tonight.'

When Annie had gone, I headed up to the bedroom with Lily

and changed her nappy on the bed, singing to her softly, tickling her feet to make her smile. Gwynn's shrieks and thumping feet reverberating through the walls was somehow reassuring; sounds of an uncomplicated life.

I tried to keep my mind empty as I crawled under the duvet, Lily tucked close to feed, as if my thoughts might transmit through my breast milk and taint her.

Worried about nodding off with her underneath me, I made a nest on the floor with the other duvet and a pillow, and watched Lily closely until her eyes drifted shut before climbing back under the covers and crashing into an exhausted sleep.

*

It was late afternoon when Morag came to pick me up. I woke with a start to see Lily gazing at the ceiling, gurgling to herself, and Bryn's voice calling that my aunt was waiting.

'I won't say it's as good as new,' she said back at the cottage. 'A lot of stuff was broken, but Annie's given me some plates and mugs from the pub and I've restocked the kitchen as best I can. Everything else can be replaced later.'

It was odd being back. The feeling I'd had of someone watching was gone. The trees were no longer sinister, hiding prying eyes, and the cottage looked tranquil and welcoming from the outside, with smoke curling from the chimney.

'I thought if I didn't come back right away, I never would,' Morag said, while I stood by the van, looking around me. 'I hate the thought he was here, that he'd been through my things, but I won't let him drive me out. I've been happy here.'

'I'm glad.' I wondered whether I'd feel the same. The memory of Bernhard materialising at the top of the stairs made my stomach shrivel. The sight of him with the rifle – had he intended to use that, or the knife the police had found in his belt? – was still too fresh in my mind.

Once inside, my fears subsided a little. Apart from the dresser being empty of china, the place looked much the same as it had. The cushions were back on the sofa, albeit upside down – 'Just until I replace it,' Morag said – and the rug and floors were clear. The kitchen looked cleaner than it had been before. The wall map was back up, pinned without a frame but otherwise intact, the ancient phone plugged in. 'He'd cut the wire again but it's being fixed tomorrow.'

'The photos,' I began.

Morag shook her head. 'I couldn't do anything about the those but your mum has an identical album.'

'She can copy them for you.'

Morag nodded. 'Ifan fixed the doors and drawers on the dresser. He's handy with a screwdriver.' She lifted Lily out of my arms and held her close, bouncing her gently as Lily dribbled and smiled. I noticed my aunt had colour in her cheeks and she'd washed her hair so it shone. She was wearing a navy sweater I hadn't seen before. The colour flattered her. Being around Ifan flattered her.

'Has he gone?' I glanced at the kitchen, though there was nowhere for a big man like Ifan to hide.

'He's coming back later.' Morag's colour deepened. 'Annie's cooking some food for us and he's bringing it over so we – you—' she smiled '—don't have to cook and we don't have to go out either.'

'That's nice.'

Skip snuffled around my feet and I crouched to loop my arms around his neck. 'We needed you last night,' I said, laughing as he licked my face. 'You could have given that horrible man a nasty bite.' It was better to talk lightly about Bernhard, not give him the gravity I was sure he thought he deserved. It was bad enough knowing we'd have to face him in court at some point. I imagined him in his cell, wondering where he'd gone wrong and what he could have done differently, then made him shrink in my mind, smaller and smaller, until he was gone in a puff of smoke.

235

'You did that already,' Morag said, picking up on my tone. 'You took a nice chunk out of his shoulder.'

'Not a big enough one.' I straightened, embarrassed suddenly under her laser-beam stare.

'Where did you learn to use a rifle?'

'Granddad showed me,' I said. 'He told me not to tell anyone, I was only eleven. To be honest, I didn't think I'd remember what to do, but I'd already seen it under the bed and saw it was loaded and … I don't know, it just came back to me. Muscle memory, I suppose.'

'He showed me too, but I didn't even know whether it still worked.' Morag widened her eyes. 'I never expected to use it.' She stroked Lily's forehead with her fingertip. 'Would you have killed him?'

I held her gaze. 'Not deliberately,' I said. 'Would you, in my position?'

'After what he did to that innocent man?' She pressed a gentle kiss on Lily's cheek. 'After all the killing I've seen?' She shook her head. 'Maybe he'd have deserved it but I couldn't have pulled the trigger.'

Her words confirmed what I already knew: she was better than Mum, better than me. My aunt had limits. I was more like my mother than I realised.

'I'm just going to put my phone on to charge and get changed,' I said. 'I need to get out of these clothes.' I hesitated. 'Is it OK to go upstairs?'

'There was no damage up there, but I changed the bedding anyway. I found your ring under the pillow and put it on the windowsill,' she said. 'I thought we could get it made smaller, so you can wear it in future.'

'I'd like that.' My throat swelled with tears. 'Did you find the lock of baby hair?'

'It was in the drawer, like you said.' Morag's eyes were shiny. 'I'd almost forgotten how dark it was. Like mine.'

'I bet he looks like you.'

She smiled. 'I don't care if he doesn't.'

Leaving her with Lily, I ran up to the bedroom to get my charger and check my suitcase, pulling it from under the bed. The money was still stashed away along with my passport. He hadn't even looked, maybe losing interest once he'd spotted the rifle.

I changed my clothes, pulling on clean underwear and a grey fleece with black jogging bottoms, before choosing a fresh pair of socks from Morag's drawer. When I was dressed, I plugged my phone in, breath faltering as the screen lip up. There was a message from Declan. He'd sent it a few minutes after our last exchange, just before my phone died.

We need to talk X

I blinked. Talk about what? Had he spoken to Patrick? Surely he wouldn't have added the kiss if something was wrong, but then again, he wouldn't want to alert me if it was. Had he guessed that I knew?

My shoulder ached. A bruise was developing, even as the one on my cheek faded, and the headache I'd slept off earlier pounded back. I grabbed Lily's carrier, strapping it on as I ran back down to Morag. 'I think I'll take Lily out with the dog.'

My aunt was pacing around with room with Lily, pointing out things, saying the words slowly. It brought me up short, seeing her as she might have been when her son was a baby. I wondered whether she'd met the family who adopted him and opened my mouth to ask just as she said, quietly, 'I wish your grandparents had met her.' She'd folded my grandfather's black coat and laid it over the back of the rocking chair, and I suddenly understood that she felt close to her parents here, surrounded by their things, and regretted being away from them during their final years.

'Me too,' I said gently. 'Gran would have been knitting up a storm.'

Morag punched out a laugh. 'I can't see me or your mother

getting busy with knitting needles, but I bet Biddy will have whipped something up the next time you see her.'

Next time. I liked the sound of it.

Smiling, I held out my arms. 'Come on, sweet pea. Let's get some fresh air and give Aunty Morag five minutes' peace.'

'Are you sure?' She was slow to hand Lily over. 'It looks like it might rain.'

'We won't go far.' I slotted Lily's arms and legs into the carrier and reached for a raincoat on the hook by the door. The baseball cap I'd worn the day I arrived was still there, like a relic from another life. 'I just need to clear my head for a few minutes.' I managed to zip the coat over the carrier, so just Lily's head was poking out, her hood covering her hair. Skip pranced on his hind legs, yelping with excitement.

'You can't not go now.' Morag gave the dog a despairing look. 'I'll make some fresh coffee,' she said. 'Thank God he didn't damage my cafetiere.'

Skip shot off as soon as we were outside. It was less blustery and the sky had brightened, deepening the green of the leaves all around. Nearby, a pigeon cooed and somewhere lambs were bleating. It was spring, I reminded myself. There might even be bluebells in the woods. Nature was doing what it did every year. If I was lucky, I'd be here next year to see it begin again. Maybe not at the cottage, but not far away. Somewhere I could decorate a nursery for Lily, do all the things I hadn't had the opportunity to do before. Once I'd spoken to Declan … maybe then, I really could put the past behind me.

I set off after Skip, past the neat rows of cabbages, chard and carrots, enjoying the sweet scent of compost in the air. At least Bernhard had left the allotment alone. I shuddered, imagining him watching Morag from the edge of the woods as she pushed her hands through the earth, tending to her vegetables while he planned his next move. He'd discovered where she kept her spare key, had let himself into the cottage more than once before she gave it to me. I knew it had been him, watching as I dozed that day while feeding Lily on the sofa. What would have happened if I'd opened my eyes?

'Hey, boy!' Skip was running back as if he'd heard something. I could hear it too. A car engine approaching.

I turned, heart leaping into my throat. A muddy silver 4x4 had pulled up next to the van. The door opened and Declan got out.

My hands automatically curved around Lily as I made my way back, stomach curdling with dread. 'What are you doing here?' I aimed for a friendly tone, but fear was blocking my throat and it sounded forced. 'I thought we were meeting tomorrow.'

'I had to talk to you.'

My heart thumped as though trying to break through my ribs. 'About what?'

'Hey.' Morag came out, a gingham tea towel in her hands. 'You found us.'

I remembered I hadn't told her about Declan's visit the night before last. It felt like a decade ago.

He was the one who'd followed us from the pub and when we visited Mum. I hadn't imagined the car at the service station.

'I need to speak with Grace.' He was wearing jeans with a grey hoodie, a black waterproof over the top. He looked tired, dark crescents under his eyes. His smile was thin.

'OK.' Morag glanced at me, eyebrows raised, then turned to go back inside. 'Call if you need anything.'

'There's nothing you can't say in front of my aunt.' I didn't want to be left alone with him.

Morag swivelled, her smile gone, and moved closer. 'You heard her,' she said to Declan, her tone no longer friendly.

He gave me an imploring look. 'You might want to do this in private.'

'Do what?' Morag looked from him to me. 'What's going on?'

'You didn't mention what happened last night.' His words were directed at me. His tone was light but I sensed something underneath, like pebbles at the bottom of a stream.

239

'What do you mean?' Lily moved against me. Too hot now, I unzipped the coat and her fingers fastened around my thumb. 'How did you know about last night?'

'News travels in a place like this.'

'But you're not staying in Fenbrith.'

'The police station is in Caernarfon.' His shrug was stiff. He was nervous, I realised, despite trying to appear relaxed. 'Hugh got wind of it, told me about a botched robbery up here, that someone got shot and a man was in custody.'

'It was someone I knew a long time ago,' Morag said at my side. 'A dangerous man.' She glanced at me. 'Grace saved my life.'

'Wow.' Declan's gaze softened. 'I had no idea.'

I felt a shot of heat behind my eyes, pressure building around my temples. 'I didn't. The police arrived. It was Ana who saved the day.'

Declan was looking at me oddly now, as if he couldn't work me out. I wondered whether he'd thought the supposed robbery was something to do with Patrick and had come to check up on me. But … Patrick had sent him, so it didn't make sense.

'Why are you here?'

He rubbed his forehead. 'When you messaged, I expected you to say something about what happened last night but you didn't even mention it.'

'I would have told you tomorrow.' I forced out a laugh. 'I made a date, didn't I? At the pub.'

'You know that I know Patrick.'

I felt the air being sucked out of my lungs.

'Grace?' Morag's gaze sharpened. 'What's going on?'

I stared at Declan. 'I thought it was *you*,' I said. 'I thought you were the one watching me, that you attacked me, left the note, that you were coming into the cottage when no one was here.'

'Grace, what are you talking about?'

Ignoring Morag, I continued. 'I know you only spoke to me that day in the village because Patrick sent you. What's the plan,

240

Declan?' I jutted my chin. 'Get me to fall for you, spill the truth and … then what? I don't understand what it is you want. I thought you liked me.' I hated how pathetic it sounded. 'I thought we could be friends.'

'Grace, I do like you.' He took a step closer, arm outstretched as if to restrain a wild horse, and looked at Morag. 'I am who I said I was.' His tone was more measured than mine. 'I'm Declan Walsh. I'm not here to hurt your niece.'

I backed away, holding tight to Lily. 'He's come to take my daughter back to Patrick.'

'But that's just it.' His hand dropped to his side. The look in his eyes was one of agonising sadness. 'You're not her mother,' he said. 'You're her nanny.'

Chapter 37

The silence following Declan's words was profound. My muscles felt weak, like melting candle wax, as his words ricocheted around my skull. *You're her nanny.*

'Grace?' Morag spoke at last, her voice tentative. 'Is it true?'

Blood pulsed inside my temples. 'Of course not.' I tried to swallow and felt like choking. 'Of course I'm her mother. It's … it's not what you think. I—'

'Grace, talk to me.'

As Declan advanced, I turned and ran. Skip barked, thinking it was a game as I headed for the woods, pulling up the zip of my coat as extra support for Lily.

Panting, I crashed along the path and through the trees, heading for the field I'd been in days ago. I had no idea where I was going after that, only that I needed to get away, to *run, run, run.*

'Grace!'

He was coming after me. I heard the crunch of boots behind me and tried to speed up, but couldn't move fast enough with Lily strapped against my chest. Scared I was jolting her too hard, that I might trip over a root, I slowed to a jog, pulling in painful breaths. 'I'm sorry, I'm sorry, sweetheart.' Sweat prickled my hairline.

When I looked at Lily, her eyes seemed full of reproach. *What was I doing?* I'd run once before. I couldn't keep running. I didn't even want to, but we weren't safe if Declan didn't believe me. If he was on Patrick's payroll, he might do anything, no matter what I said. I sank behind a tree trunk, pressing my cheek against the bark, which smelt of lichen and moss.

'Grace.' He was there, his hand cupping my elbow, his breath coming hard as he pulled me gently to my feet.

I looked at him through a haze of tears and saw only concern in his eyes. His face was pale in the greenish light edging through the trees and shadowed with worry.

Branches creaked around us, something rustling in the undergrowth. A gust of wind tugged my hair across my face. As if sensing something was wrong, Lily began crying, her mouth wide open, her eyes screwed up. 'Hush, hush, little baby, it's fine, it's fine, it's all fine, don't cry.' I bounced her, one hand on the back of her head, fresh tears pushing to my eyes. 'Please don't do this,' I said to Declan.

'Come back and talk,' he appealed. 'I promise I'm not here to hurt you, or to take Lily away. I just want to hear your side of the story.'

My side of the story. The story Patrick had cooked up and I'd gone along with. The stupid, stupid story I should never have agreed to. The story I thought had ended with Elise's death but clearly wasn't over. Wouldn't be over until the truth came out.

I wiped tears off my cheek with my wrist and stroked Lily's hair to soothe her as her cries subsided. A feeling of inevitability stole over me. 'I'll tell you, if you promise to hear me out.'

He made a sound, like air being punched from his chest. 'I promise.'

I followed him silently back to the cottage where Morag was waiting in the kitchen, her eyes fixed on the doorway. Her face was tense, her hair mussed as though she'd been running her hands through it.

'Sit down,' she instructed. Skip, clearly resentful his walk was over, padded to the rug and flopped down. 'I was talking to my niece.' The fact that she wasn't angry, was trying to make a joke, tore at my heart. I wished I'd been honest with her from the start.

'We've an hour before Ifan comes back.' She dragged over the stool from the kitchen and sat down, pointing Declan towards the sofa. He dwarfed it when he sat on the edge, forearms resting on his knees.

I took Lily out of her carrier, removed her hooded coat and checked her nappy was dry before sitting beside Skip on the rug. I stretched out my legs and laid Lily on my thighs. I wanted to see her face as I told the story, knowing it was the only time she would ever hear it.

The warmth from the fire was calming. I waited for my leaping heart to settle before taking a deep breath. The past rushed in like a tidal wave, pulling me back to the day Patrick reappeared and changed the course of my life.

*

'Can we talk?'

Not giving me a chance to respond, Patrick steered me down a side street, careful we shouldn't be seen together, as if everyone in Manhattan knew who he was and eyes were constantly on him. He told me once they probably were because of the cases he'd worked on; the families of criminals he'd helped put behind bars who might want to take revenge. A few years earlier, an assistant DA in another county had been mown down in a hit-and-run that was thought to be deliberate. The culprit was never caught.

'What are you doing?' I said, once we were sitting in a leather booth tucked out of view. He'd pulled a folder from his briefcase so it would look as though he was having a meeting. 'I haven't seen you for months and you just—'

'Elise lost the baby.'

The tiredness that had fogged my brain for days cleared in an instant. 'Patrick, that's awful. I'm so sorry. I know how much she wanted to be a mother.' In that moment, I meant it. Patrick had told me that having a child would save his wife, the fulfilment of a dream, a reason to stay sober. 'Was it a miscarriage?' I knew she'd suffered two already, that it was more likely to happen during the early months. I felt a twinge of fear, wondering whether it could still happen to me at six months pregnant. How would it feel for the life that had begun to grow inside me to slip away, to not exist anymore? I was frightened of giving birth and of what came next, but I didn't want to lose the baby.

'I think she'd been drinking again.' Patrick's face darkened. He looked tired, almost ill, his normally sleek hair dishevelled, pouches of tiredness under his eyes – older than his thirty-nine years. 'She promised she hadn't but I know the signs. She'd been feeling sick, couldn't keep anything down.' His voice was flat, as if to drain the words of emotion. It was odd to see him so powerless; odd to see him at all after believing we'd never meet again. 'She said she wished she could be put to sleep until the baby was born so she didn't have to deal with being pregnant.' Bitterness entered his voice, a frown wrinkling his brow. I wondered how much of what he was feeling was grief at losing his child and the fact that his wife was suffering, and how much was anger that the perfect marriage and family he'd planned had vanished.

'I was stupid to have got excited and pinned my hopes on it actually happening. It was too good to be true,' he said. 'And now she's regressed. Sleeping all day, not speaking to anyone. I'm fielding calls from her parents and the few friends she's got left, telling them she's still got terrible morning sickness. It's tragic when everyone was so thrilled for her—'

'Wait,' I interrupted. 'You haven't told anyone she's lost the baby?'

'She didn't want me to.' For a moment, he looked as though he might cry and I felt a surge of pity. 'She couldn't face telling people and, to be honest, neither could I. Not when things had been so good for a while.'

I pictured it, her family delighted that finally their daughter had a purpose. Her friends determined to rally round now there was something to celebrate. That things had reverted must seem unbearable. 'You can try again.'

Patrick shook his head, dropping his gaze. 'It might never happen. She doesn't think she can carry a baby full-term.'

Unsure what he wanted from me, why he'd sought me out, I said again, 'I'm sorry.'

He gave me an edgy look, building up to something. The slightly frantic way his fingers kept smoothing the folder was unsettling. That and the fact that he hadn't shaved for a few days. Two coffees sat on the table in front of us and I picked mine up and put it down again. 'What's going on, Patrick?'

'I thought …' He sucked in a breath, seeming suddenly unsure. Patrick, who was never lost for words, whose job depended on saying the right thing at the right time. 'Your friend Ana came to see me,' he said. 'She told me you were pregnant.'

'*What?*' It was the last thing I'd expected him to say. It felt as if an earthquake had rocked the café. 'When was this?'

'A couple of days ago.'

No wonder she hadn't answered my call last night. I'd rung to ask how her date with Tom had gone. She hadn't picked up, which wasn't like her. 'She had no right to do that.' My hands moved to the curve of belly beneath my loose dress. 'I wasn't going to tell you.' I lowered my voice, which had started to wobble. 'I don't expect anything from you, Patrick. I'm not planning to keep the baby. I'm considering adoption.'

'But, Grace, don't you see? It's perfect.' Reaching over, Patrick grasped my hand, the sleeve of his coat riding up to reveal his gold watch. He quickly let go, probably trying to not look round to check whether anyone had seen. 'It's brilliant news.'

'It is?'

'We'll have the baby,' he said. 'I mean, it is mine, isn't it?' He smiled his old smile, reassuring me he was being ironic; that of *course* he knew the baby was his and that I hadn't been seeing anyone since he went back to his wife, even though I had every right to. 'Look, Grace, it's perfect,' he said again and, for a crazy second, I thought he was going to say he would leave Elise, that we could start a life together with our child, and knew in that instant it wasn't what I wanted. I didn't want to be with a man who'd impregnated a woman while still married to someone else, a man who'd leave a wife who'd miscarried their baby and was clearly unwell.

Then he said, 'We don't need to tell anyone Elise has lost the baby. It's not unusual for her to not see anyone for months; it won't be difficult. In the meantime, stick close the truth. Tell people you're having the baby for a childless couple. You don't need to go into detail.' And that's when I realised. He meant for him and Elise to have my baby. 'You could give up working—'

'I'm not giving up my career.' Feeling as though I'd entered a parallel universe, I tried to digest his words. 'I love my job. I have to work.' But even as I spoke, I registered with a dull sense of shock that I hadn't immediately said no.

'I'll cover your living expenses—'

'I don't want your money.'

He nodded, one palm flat on the folder. I wondered whether there were documents inside, already drawn up – a contract, a business agreement. 'It'll be an informal arrangement so nothing can be traced back to me, but I'm sure that will suit you too,' he said. 'It'll be totally confidential. No one but us will ever know.'

'And, what? You just pass off the baby as yours and Elise's?' I could hardly believe I was saying it.

'Our names will be on the birth certificate, so … yes.'

My mind spun. 'Patrick, I … I don't know.' I picked up my coffee again but the smell made my stomach lurch. 'It seems wrong.'

'Isn't it better than strangers raising our child?' Both hands were on the folder now, his face animated. 'You could do anything you want afterwards. Open a chain of restaurants if you want. I'll invest—'

'I've told you I don't want your money.' Anger flared. 'How do you know I won't tell people about this? That Patrick Holden asked for my baby in exchange for a chain of restaurants?' I already knew I would never tell anyone about this. He knew it too.

'That's not you, Grace.' His voice was gentle. 'I know you.' He slid round without warning, onto the seat beside me, and rested his hands on my stomach. 'It's my baby in there.'

Mine too, I felt like saying, but it still didn't seem real. He moved back to his seat and looked at me expectantly, used to getting his own way. *If I say yes, I will never see my baby again.* A pinprick of something ominous pierced my disbelief. A premonition, maybe.

'What does Elise have to say about this brilliant plan?' I sat back and tried to steady my breathing. The baby chose that moment to move, as though protesting at my tone and racing heart. 'What have you told her?'

He had the grace to look guilty, drumming his immaculate fingernails on the table. 'I said I knew someone who knew someone who was pregnant and didn't want her baby, that she was happy to give it up for a price and sign a non-disclosure agreement.'

'And Elise is on board with that?' I shook my head, trying to picture it. 'She's an alcoholic, Patrick.'

'The only thing that will stop her is a baby.' His tone turned pleading. 'More than anything, Grace, she wants to be a mom. This is her last chance.' Emotion twisted his face. '*Our* last chance.'

I didn't bother to remind him that only a few months ago, he'd been in my bed, talking about everything that was wrong with his marriage. 'What if she can't give up drinking?'

As if sensing me weakening, he brightened. 'She *can* recover with a strong enough reason,' he said. 'She'll love the baby, I promise, Grace.' He kept saying my name. Wasn't that a tactic, to make me feel special? He was playing me. 'She was like a different person when she was pregnant. I know it's a cliché, but she was glowing. I'm sorry if that's hard to hear, Grace, but I know this is what she's waiting for. Her destiny, if you like.'

'And yours.' I gave him a hard stare, wondering how he'd kept this side of himself hidden – the side willing to do and say anything to get what he wanted. 'Looks good on the CV doesn't it?'

'Don't be like that, Grace.' His voice softened. 'It would be good for us all, don't you think? We all benefit, especially the baby.'

'If the baby looks like you, won't Elise suspect that you might have had a hand in its conception?'

'Of course she won't.' He actually looked hurt. 'I've never cheated on her before,' he said, adding quickly, 'Grace, you were different, you know that. I cared about you. I *care* about you. At least you know your baby will be with its natural father and will have a good life, have everything it needs. Grandparents who will love it. Our baby will have a good family, Grace.'

I used to have a family. What did I have now? A job I loved, one good friend, some great colleagues, and a home above a restaurant. It didn't amount to much. It was no substitute for a family. And I already knew I wasn't cut out for motherhood. Maybe he was right and this was the best option. He did have rights as the baby's father, but I didn't want to give in without a fight, worried about what sort of person it made me if I agreed to his mad plan. 'Wouldn't Elise want to meet me?'

Patrick shook his head, but I guessed he was the one who didn't want us meeting; didn't want his wife and the woman he'd made pregnant coming face to face. Maybe he suspected she'd know right away and didn't want to break her heart.

'Why not just tell everyone she miscarried and you've decided to use a surrogate.' I could hardly believe the words coming out of my mouth. An hour ago, I'd been concerned with staying awake long enough to visit my supplier and source some Scotch bonnet peppers for a private party at the restaurant. Patrick must have been waiting and followed me, I realised. 'A lot of celebrities do it; it's nothing to be ashamed of.'

'Are you kidding?' He took a swig of coffee, winced and pushed the cup aside. 'You know her parents are deeply religious?' I hadn't known that. 'And can you imagine the scandal? People don't want a messy story about surrogates, Grace; they won't want a DA who "paid" for his wife to have a baby by another woman. There was a long-held ban on surrogacy here and it's still a controversial topic. And even if I did suggest it and her parents accepted the idea, which they won't, they'd want to check you out, your family, your background. It would …' He sat back and released a deep sigh. 'It just wouldn't work, Grace, believe me.'

Oddly enough, I did when he put it like that. My mind was spinning so fast, I couldn't hold my thoughts together, could barely make sense of it all. 'So, it would be another secret you'd have to keep.'

'It would be your secret too, Grace. You can't tell anyone, not even your friend, however grateful I am that she let me know you were pregnant. If you tell just one person, it's not a secret anymore.' At that moment, I wasn't sure I'd ever speak to Ana again. 'You don't even need to tell her we spoke, just that you've made a decision about what to do.' Patrick sat forward, eyes glowing, in love with the idea. 'It's so perfect,' he said. He seemed to like that word, but nothing was ever perfect. 'I already can't wait to meet my son.'

'What if it's a girl?'

'It won't be.' He sounded so sure, as if it would come to pass simply because he wished it. 'It'll work Grace, I'm telling you.' This time, his smile reached all the way inside me, his special smile, the one I imagined he wore when he won a particularly tricky case. 'You just have to believe it.'

Chapter 38

'And so, I agreed.' I came back to the moment to see Morag and Declan listening with rapt attention. 'I carried on working until I got too big and my ankles became swollen and then spent a lot of time in the apartment. When people asked, I said I was carrying the baby for a childless couple, just like he suggested, and they accepted it.' I paused. 'It was harder than I'd thought, not telling the truth. It was a lonely time. Patrick got a burner phone that he'd call me from for updates, telling me to take this vitamin and that. He told me how excited Elise was to meet her baby, that she'd already stopped drinking and was looking after herself, had started decorating the nursery. That's what she said, apparently. *Her* baby.' I shook my head, recalling Patrick's barely contained excitement as he waited for his plan to come to fruition, how complimentary he was, telling me I was making a difference, saving his wife's life, their marriage. He insisted I go for a scan and email him the picture so he could show her. I went to the hospital alone, making my mind blank when I heard the echoey heartbeat for the first time, shaking my head when asked if I wanted to know whether it was a boy or girl.

'I don't even know what I was thinking by that stage, only that I wanted it to be over so my life could go back to normal,' I said, holding Lily's hands and squeezing gently. 'I'm so ashamed of that now.'

'Go on,' Morag prompted, a hardness in her voice that I knew wasn't directed at me. 'How were you supposed to have the baby and hand it over without anyone knowing?'

'He had this crazy plan to tell everyone Elise had the baby at home and they delivered it themselves. When I went into labour I was to go to the hospital, have the baby, and the next day get a cab to his town apartment, the one where he stayed when he was working on a case and didn't want to go home. Not the *actual* apartment but down the block, where he'd be waiting to take the baby to Elise.' I gave an incredulous laugh. 'It was stupidly cloak and dagger and sounds so ridiculous now, but he made it seem plausible, as if nothing could go wrong, and when Patrick puts his mind to something it just kind of … it works. I kept pushing the reality to one side,' I said. 'It was so far beyond how I imagined things turning out, like the plot of a soap. I just wanted my real life back, the one I was used to that didn't involve affairs or babies and it was actually, weirdly, OK – sort of. Until she was born.'

In the end, there'd been no long labour, no time to worry about pain relief or getting to hospital on time. I'd had a small bag packed for a week, had gone out and bought the basics, everything I thought a new baby would need. I'd toyed with the idea of an epidural as the date drew near and my fear of giving birth grew, but my labour started in the bathroom on a rainy night in January, waters pooling on the tiles. I'd got up to have a drink of water, but the low backache I'd suffered all day quickly gave way to a seething pain in my lower belly. I'd gripped the edge of the sink as it radiated up around my back and into my pelvis, shaky and sweating.

'I wasn't ready,' I said. 'I thought it was too soon, she wasn't due for another week.' There'd been no break between contractions. I panted through them in a panicked crouch, everything fading around me as some force beyond my control began to gather, making me push and push as I shook and cried for my mother. I lost track of time, but only fifteen minutes had passed before I felt a rushing between my thighs, a slipping sensation, and suddenly there was my baby, attached to a trailing cord, purple and streaky, her tiny fingers shooting out. When she took her first cry and I put her to my breast, a feeling of peace flooded into the space where she'd been.

'I called Ana,' I said, tears springing to my eyes as I remembered. 'She was the first person I wanted to tell and she came. She brought nappies, even though I had some, and a teddy for the baby, even though I'd told her I wasn't keeping it.' Ana had also brought her midwife cousin Maria, who was practical if disapproving. She helped me deliver the placenta, and cut the cord while Ana made sweet tea and cleaned the bathroom, still racked with guilt for telling Patrick I was pregnant. She'd done it because she was angry that he'd used me then gone back to his wife, and she thought I wasn't coping, that he should step up and support me.'

Maria had weighed the baby – *eight pounds, I don't know how you kept her hidden for as long as you did* – and when she finally bustled out, tight-lipped, I cried until I thought I'd never stop.

'I told Ana the truth then,' I said, addressing my words to Lily. 'I told Ana that the couple I was giving the baby to was Patrick and Elise. I knew she wouldn't say anything, because she felt responsible for telling him about her in the first place.'

'It's so great that you didn't need to go to the hospital,' Patrick said when I called him on his burner phone, after Ana had left and I'd spent an hour gazing in awe at my baby, amazed that my body had produced such a perfect being. She was wrapped in the lemon-coloured blanket I'd bought, a little white hat covering her fine brown hair. 'Clever girl,' he added. 'I'm so proud of you.' He sounded happy, excited and I'd felt buoyed up – almost as if we were a normal couple welcoming our first child, except I'd delivered her myself and he'd been at home with his wife. 'Elise can't wait to see her. She's so happy.'

I had twenty-four hours with Lily – her name was already there, as if it had been waiting for her to arrive – before taking a cab as instructed, feeling increasingly empty at the thought of handing her over. There was no formal agreement, I told myself. I could turn back. But I knew it wasn't that simple, that Patrick would find a way to take her. I tried to convince myself that once the endorphins wore off, I'd be relieved I'd let her go.

He'd been awkward holding her, had even said, 'Oh well, at least she's got my hair and eyes,' his breath misting between us, even though the car he'd turned up in was blasting out warm air. I hadn't missed his look of disappointment that she wasn't a boy, even though I'd told him right away. Maybe he hadn't taken it in at the time.

'You will get her checked out, won't you?' I said. 'You know about vaccinations, but they won't be for a while and she'll need to be registered.' None of these things had mattered to me before but were suddenly, vitally, important. 'You will be careful with her, won't you, Patrick?'

'It'll be fine, stop worrying.' His chuckle had landed like a slap. *Silly Grace. Probably hormonal, acting as though she's the only female to ever have given birth.* 'Elise will know what to do.'

I had a powerful urge to snatch Lily back. 'I want you to keep her name,' I said, trying to hold back the tears that threatened. 'It's the only thing I'm asking.'

He didn't look at me. 'It's an old woman's name.'

'Please, Patrick.'

'I suppose it's the least I can do.'

Hardly the endorsement I'd longed for. I suspected Elise would change it anyway.

'He said he'd be in touch, that I wasn't to worry.' I didn't dare glance at Declan or Morag. *I can never thank you enough for this,*

Grace. Patrick had looked at me then, a ripple of concern on his brow in the dim light of the car. 'We're good? You won't tell?'

'He made it sound like a game.' I recalled the sting of pain that he thought I might betray him. 'I kept looking at the pack of nappies when I got back to the apartment. I just felt so … *sad.*' My breasts, full of milk, had started leaking. I looked online, went out and bought a breast pump. 'It seemed wasteful not to save my milk,' I said. 'I thought maybe if I kept it, I could tell Patrick, and Elise could use it instead of formula.'

I looked up to see Morag staring at her hands. Her face was very pale and I guessed she was remembering a similar situation with her little boy. *Isaac.*

'I thought it would get easier, that once my milk had gone and the hormones settled, I'd go back to work and that would be that,' I said. 'But Patrick called in a panic the next day, said Elise wasn't coping. She didn't know what to do with the baby, she was out of her depth. He said I had to help, move in with them and help with the baby until Elise was ready.'

Even as I told Patrick I couldn't disappear from my life, I knew I'd drop everything to be with Lily again. 'He said I should tell everyone I was going away for a while, that I needed a break after having the baby. He said he'd pay me, anything I wanted, but it was never about money, I just wanted to see Lily. He didn't want to tell Elise I was her mother. He said I would be a nanny, trained in dealing with newborns.' I shook my head. 'The next few days were a nightmare because it was obvious Elise didn't know what to do and she was basically drinking as soon as she got up. He hadn't told me that bit. I doubted that she'd ever given up.'

'I saw you.' Declan's voice startled me back to the living room at the cottage. 'I came to the house to pick up Patrick. He had an important meeting downtown. He didn't come out so I knocked and Elise answered the door. She was wearing a nightdress and looked terrible. I heard a baby crying, realised she wasn't pregnant anymore. I said "Congratulations," and when I saw you, I asked,

"Who's that?" and she said, "The nanny." I was going to ask if the baby was a boy or a girl, because that's what you do, but didn't get a chance because she slammed the door in my face.'

I remembered that morning. Lily had been beside herself, red-faced and bawling, clearly starving. Patrick said she'd rejected the bottle Elise had tried to give her. I breastfed her, but she wouldn't settle. I'd been pacing round, breasts aching, head thumping, hormones raging. I'd just seen Elise in the kitchen pouring vodka into a coffee mug before drinking it in one long swallow. It was 8.30 a.m.

Can't you shut her up? she snapped when someone knocked on the door. My first impressions of Elise had not been good. Far from the recovering alcoholic desperate to be a mother I'd expected to meet as Patrick ushered me through the back door to the nursery they'd prepared, I was confronted with a sad-eyed woman who stank of booze, barely capable of looking after herself, never mind a baby. She was nothing like the striking, elegant figure, dark hair smoothed back in a chignon, that I'd seen in a photo online of her with Patrick at a charity event they'd attended with her parents a couple of years ago. While I understood Patrick's desperation to let his wife have the one thing he was certain would 'fix' her, I knew in my gut that the moment had passed – had maybe passed the day she miscarried their child. She hadn't even spoken to me, haunting the house like a ghost, spending most of the day in her bedroom with the door shut.

'I can't believe that was you,' I said to Declan, thrown by the strangeness of us almost crossing paths. 'I do remember Patrick saying, once, that he had a driver – someone he knew from way back – because he preferred to focus on work in the car while travelling, but I could barely remember what day it was that morning. I'd been up most of the night.'

Declan looked pensive. 'When Patrick finally came out, I congratulated him on becoming a father and he looked annoyed and kind of harassed. He said no one was supposed to know, that

256

I could probably see Elise was struggling. He kept fiddling with his tie. He told me they'd got a nanny in to help out for a while. I remember thinking there was no shame in having a nanny, but he asked me not to say anything. Her parents hadn't met the child yet. He and Elise were waiting until she felt better before making announcements about the new arrival. I said I wouldn't tell a soul. I mean, it was none of my business, but something felt a bit off and I didn't know why.' I was mesmerised, listening to his version of events. I could picture it so clearly, Patrick unusually ruffled in the back of the car – his sick wife and the mother of his baby living under the same roof – and Declan confused that his good wishes had been met with anger.

'When I dropped him back later, he thanked me but said my services were no longer needed.' He shook his head and rubbed a hand round his jaw. 'I sat outside the house for a while and saw you leaving. You looked as if you were crying. I don't know why, but I followed you. I saw you go to a restaurant called *Julio's*. You went round the back, upstairs, and came out with a bag. I thought perhaps that's where you'd lived before moving in with the Holdens to care for the baby.'

'It was,' I said, astonished that I'd had no idea my actions that day were being monitored. 'I was the chef there. I ran the kitchen, lived in the apartment above.' It was like talking about someone else's life. 'I'd gone back to get some things. I hated leaving Lily but had none of my stuff, I'd left in such a hurry.'

'I saw you go back to their house.'

'So, you were watching me, even then?'

'I guess I was curious,' he said. 'No offence, but you didn't look like the kind of nanny the Holdens would employ.'

'He hated relying on me,' I said grimly. 'But he knew there was no other way with the state Elise was in, not when everyone was expecting her to appear with a baby in a few weeks' time.' I thought of the days and nights that followed, all blurring into one. The panic in Patrick's eyes; how he didn't like holding Lily;

257

how he caught me breastfeeding and told me to stop, saying I should use formula or *pump and freeze*, so the baby didn't get used to me. But my milk was there, waiting for her, and Elise wasn't coping and I didn't want to give Lily a bottle if I didn't have to.

When I thought back, the weeks had taken on a nightmarish quality, the memories suffused with a charcoal haze. I only ever half-dozed, ears constantly pricked for Lily's cry. I couldn't read, or watch TV. I barely ate or showered, worried my baby would need me and I wouldn't hear her. If Elise decided she wanted to spend some time with Lily, I had to go to my room, a hotel-like suite where her parents stayed when they visited.

'They're in Canada with her sister, so no chance of them popping in,' Patrick said one night, passing the nursery on his way to see Elise. We were like ships in the night, as if now the baby was there and being attended to, he no longer had any interest in me as a person. I would sit rocking on the edge of the bed, cupping my painful breasts as I listened to my baby scream in another room, wondering how my life had been reduced to this, occasionally slipping down to the kitchen to grab food from the fridge, delivered by caterers because Elise didn't cook and Patrick was too busy. He told me to make myself at home, but I'd never felt more like an interloper than in their oddly soulless house.

I tuned in to hear Declan speaking again. 'In the end, I figured Patrick was stressed with everything going on – the campaign, the new baby, his wife being ill. I knew about her drinking,' he said. 'But I needed to find another job, was thinking about moving back to Ireland, so I put it to the back of my mind. Until I heard Elise had died.'

My head started buzzing. I shifted, adjusting Lily's position, careful not to wake her. 'You heard it on the news?'

He nodded. 'I suppose with Patrick running for District Attorney and Elise's parents being a big deal in publishing it warranted a good five minutes,' he said. 'I was shocked, I must admit. I called him.'

'You called Patrick?' My heart picked up pace.

'He sounded in a really bad way.' Declan's face was furrowed with concentration. 'I said I was sorry, asked if there was anything I could do. He said no. I said something about it being awful, the poor baby, something like that, and he said: "There's no baby anymore." I was confused. I asked him what he meant, but he said to leave it, to forget it.' Declan frowned, reliving his bafflement. 'I didn't want to push him. I thought he must be in shock and then I thought, oh God, what if Elise was holding the baby when she fell and it died too? But I couldn't understand why there was nothing on the news about it. I guessed they would have kept it quiet, that it was private, a family thing; they didn't want the press raking over it.' He sat back, then leant forward again. 'Then I remembered the nanny and went to the restaurant and asked if you still lived there. The owner seemed pretty pissed off. He said you were flying to the UK with the baby and wouldn't be back.' He sat back. 'The *baby*. The one Patrick had told me to forget.'

I straightened, easing the stiffness in my back. 'Ana told me the other night that someone had been asking her uncle about me,' I said. 'That's how I knew you'd followed me here.'

'Look, I know it sounds bad but—' he gave a baffled shake of his head '—I just couldn't work it out. I got it into my head you must have kidnapped the baby, run off with her, and that was why Patrick had acted so strange. I thought maybe you had something on him, were blackmailing him, though I couldn't think what it would be. He was so squeaky clean.'

'Why would any of it matter to you?'

'Patrick helped a good friend of mine from my army days.' Declan's gaze moved beyond me, looking into the past. 'He'd got into trouble, was wrongly accused of drug-trafficking. Patrick represented him in court, made sure his name was cleared, and he did it free of charge. I'd flown over to support him and wanted to thank Patrick in person. I thought he was a great guy. He seemed genuine, you know?' I did. 'When I said I was staying a while and looking for work, he gave me a job as his driver.'

'So, you felt like you owed him?'

'Something like that, I suppose.' Declan ran his hands over his face. 'Anyway, it kind of made sense that he wouldn't want a public fuss about the baby, but then I thought, what about Elise's parents? The baby was their grandchild. Surely they'd want to know where she was if she'd been kidnapped? I couldn't get my head around it.' He drew in a breath. 'It was a spur-of-the-moment thing, but I thought if you'd gone to the airport, I might find you, so I went straight there after I'd been to the restaurant.' His exhalation ended on a quiet laugh. 'I didn't see you, so I got on the first plane to Heathrow. God knows what I thought I'd do when I got here, but you were on that plane.'

My mind was racing, struggling to catch up. 'You were on the same flight?'

'I know, it's crazy. I felt like James Bond, or something. I thought maybe I'd confront you, take the baby back to her daddy, but … I knew there was more to it. You looked like a mother, but I couldn't forget Elise saying you were the nanny. I thought …' He rubbed the back of his neck. 'I don't know what I thought. I decided if I got to know you, I'd find out what the hell was going on.'

'The photo of Lily, was that really for your mum?'

Guilt crossed his face. 'I had some crazy notion about calling Patrick again,' he said. 'Asking for the truth about the baby, telling him I could help. I thought if he came clean, I'd send him the photo, tell him I'd found his daughter and could bring her back, like some great bloody hero.' He shook his head as though angry with himself. 'I did send it to my mum, though. She really is obsessed with me settling down and having kids.'

'But you didn't send it to Patrick?'

Declan's expression changed. 'At the café on Snowdon, when I asked about him, you said he wasn't a good person. It didn't fit with what I knew about him, but it made me think. Something had made you feel that way. I wanted to know what it was.'

'I'm not exactly a good person either.' Shame burned my throat. 'I agreed to the whole mad mess in the first place.'

'Grace, did Patrick have something to do with Elise's death?' Declan said it as if I hadn't spoken. Morag stiffened and I knew she'd been wondering the same thing. 'Because if he did,' Declan continued, 'you know you should go to the police.'

'He's right.' Morag's voice was steely. 'He can't get away with it just because he let you leave with the baby.'

My breath felt trapped in my chest.

'Grace, you can tell us.' Declan bent forward and touched my foot in an oddly tender gesture. 'Did Patrick kill his wife?'

Chapter 39

'He didn't kill her,' I said. 'Patrick's not a murderer.'

Morag and Declan exchanged looks.

'You don't have to be frightened.' Morag dropped from the stool to her knees, relaxing her tone. 'He doesn't know you're here.' She turned to Declan. 'I'm assuming you haven't told him you've been sneaking around after my niece.'

His cheeks reddened. 'I promise I haven't.'

'OK. So, you can be honest, Grace.'

Tears were rising behind my eyes. 'Patrick didn't kill his wife, I promise.' I lifted Lily and moved to sit with my back against the sofa. I could see Declan's beaten-up boots but not his face, nor Morag's. My top was twisted up around my waist and my arms felt leaden, but Lily was sleeping and I couldn't bear to put her down. 'When I said I was leaving and taking Lily with me, he tried to stop me.' I wanted to get it over with now. 'He said he needed her, that I had to stay because we had an agreement and what was he supposed to say to everyone expecting to meet the baby?' I swallowed the sour taste of bile. The fire was still blazing but I was cold all over and shivered. 'I knew by then that he didn't love Lily at all. He only wanted her so he could save face, save his career, and so he didn't have to tell the truth and be a lesser person in everyone's eyes. I was so angry and upset. I told him if he didn't let us go and leave us alone, I'd call the press and tell them we'd had an affair and that he'd tried to pass our baby off as his wife's.'

I took a breath, bracing myself to say the worst part. 'I said I'd tell the police he was angry because Elise wouldn't divorce him and he pushed her down the stairs.' I closed my eyes, face pulsing with mortification. I couldn't bear to see the disappointment in their eyes. 'I'm not proud of myself.' My throat had dried. I swallowed hard. 'Patrick wasn't very nice to her at times. He regretted their marriage and he cheated on her with me. He'd pinned all his hopes on her being a mother. He thought it would change her, but people don't change, not really. He was frustrated that she couldn't recover. He raised his hand to her while I was there, but she could be cruel too. He said she threw a knife at him once. Hardly the right environment for raising a child.'

I took another breath. 'She was ruining his future, I'm sure that's the way he saw it. His career means more to him than anything, but he's not a murderer. He puts murderers away. It would be abhorrent to him to kill someone, even in the heat of the moment.' The words were running out of me like water. 'I just thought if I threatened to throw out some suspicion about her death, about his reputation, imply he wasn't the good guy everyone thought he was, he'd willingly let me go. Her father would have withdrawn his campaign funding for a start. Anyway, I was right because he told me to leave. When he asked what he was supposed to tell Elise's family and their friends, I said he would think of something because he was good with words and—' I swallowed again '—I guess that's what he did.'

When I stopped speaking, the silence in the room was total. Skip stood up and walked to the door. Lily awoke, tipping her head to look for me. I wiped my leaking eyes on my sleeve. Morag was staring at the floor while Declan combed his fingers through his hair. Both of them looked as shattered as I felt. 'I can show you Lily's passport if you want proof,' I said finally. 'I have her birth certificate too. His name's not on it.'

'No need,' Morag said quietly.

Declan shook his head. 'You're right about it being a mess,' he said. 'But don't feel bad about it, Grace. You did what you had to.'

Morag nodded her agreement. 'He's not a good man,' she said. I had the feeling she didn't quite believe in Patrick's innocence; perhaps thought I was covering for him. 'I still think he got away lightly.'

'He's definitely not the good guy I thought he was,' said Declan.

'Well, I'm not blameless either.' I moved Lily to my other shoulder. She curled into me, solid and warm. 'I'll have to live with my decisions and so will he, but he's not completely bad. His work is important. It makes a difference and I know he'll be a good DA. His brother's death changed his life; it shaped him. I guess …' I caught Morag's eye. 'I guess we all have our reasons for doing the things we do.'

Declan reached down and stroked Lily's hair then traced his finger down my cheek. 'I'm sorry I wasn't honest about why I was here,' he said. 'That I doubted you.'

'I'm sorry too.' Morag raised her eyebrows at him before getting to her feet and looking at me. 'I just wish you'd told me you were worried someone had followed you here. You didn't have to keep it to yourself.'

'I know, I'm sorry.'

She nodded, signalling the conversation was over. As she went to the door to let Skip out, I said to Declan, 'Is Hugh really your friend, or was he a cover story and you've been staying at the pub all this time?'

He gave a flicker of a smile. 'I'm not that clever. I knew him way back, from that holiday in Wales I told you about. We talked about joining the army together back then, but he didn't and we lost touch. It was a good opportunity to make contact and we hit it off again. His job offer's real, too.' His gaze grew serious.

'Everything I said was real except why I was here,' he said. 'I could tell you were a good person, even if you didn't want to talk to me at first and kept asking questions instead. I knew there had to be a good reason why you were being evasive. I didn't want my suspicions to be true.' He paused. 'I was nervous.'

'You didn't look it.'

'I did some breathing exercises.'

'They worked.'

'And Lily really does look like you.' His smile lit a flame of hope in my heart. 'I'm glad you didn't kidnap her.'

'I wish Patrick wasn't her father—'

'You weren't to know how things would turn out,' he cut in, getting to his feet.

'I thought I was in love with him.' I felt a need to explain. 'It was wrong, but I believed his marriage was over. As soon as I knew it wasn't I was ready to walk away. I know now that what I felt for him ... it wasn't real.'

'It's in the past now.' Declan's voice was gentler than I deserved. 'What happened to Elise was terrible but Patrick didn't have to marry her. He didn't have to have an affair, and he definitely didn't have to take your baby.' He shook his head, as if the craziness of it had struck him all over again. 'He made his choices.'

So had I. My stomach clenched. For a second, I was torn back there, to that morning ... I dragged myself back to the present. The one thing Morag and Declan hadn't asked was: *Were you there that day? Did you see what happened?* assuming, perhaps, that I couldn't have been or I'd have said so. I would have talked about the trauma of seeing Elise's open, empty eyes and the look on Patrick's face – how, for a moment, he'd looked like a man given a reprieve from Death Row. I hoped they would never ask and I wouldn't have to lie.

Declan left as Ifan was arriving, refusing Morag's offer to stay and have some dinner. 'I promised Hugh I'd eat with him tonight, talk business.'

'You might be staying in Wales then?' I asked him.

'Do you want me to?'

'Do you want to?'

'Do you always answer a question with a question?'

Smiling, I walked him out to the car with Lily. 'You followed us,' I said. 'Did you go all the way to Berkshire?'

He didn't bother denying it. 'I thought you'd clocked me at the services,' he admitted. 'I felt so bad, I turned round and went back to Hugh's.'

'It wasn't the first time.'

'I tried to find out where you were living the night you left the pub but the roads round here are too quiet, especially at night. It was pretty obvious, I guess. I'm sorry I scared you.'

'How did you know I was in Fenbrith in the first place?'

'I'm afraid I followed you to the coach station.' He rubbed his jaw embarrassed. 'A classic case of "follow that cab". When I knew where you were heading, I hired a car. I watched you get off the coach outside the pub and thought you were staying there. I'd made contact with Hugh and he invited me over so I went, thinking I'd find you the next day, but when I came back you weren't there. I hung about, hoping to bump into you.'

My mind swam with this new information. 'At the restaurant, Ana's uncle said you weren't Irish. What was that about?'

'Maybe it was the James Bond thing kicking in.' He looked sheepish. 'It's pretty easy to slip into a New York accent when you're Irish,' he said, doing a convincing impression. 'Sneaky, huh?'

'Don't get used to it.'

He nodded. 'I won't.' As he opened the car door, he paused. 'You know, what really made me think I was wrong was when you breastfed Lily. I thought, you couldn't be her nanny if you were doing that. Unless you were one of those wet nurses, but that didn't make sense, either.'

'I breastfed her on the plane,' I said. 'Didn't you see?'

'I didn't dare get too close in case you spotted me.'

266

'I suppose you asking if I'd ever worked with children was another way of digging for information?'

'Let's just say, I'll never be a detective.' He rolled his shoulders, as though loosening tension there. 'Look, let's meet tomorrow at the café with the Welsh cakes. We'll start over. No secrets this time.'

No secrets. 'I'd like that.'

'Ten o'clock?'

'We'll be there.'

'Grace,' Morag called from the doorway. 'Your food's getting cold.'

Chapter 40

Morag drove us to Fenbrith the following morning. 'I'll be your chaperone,' she said. I knew it still rankled that Declan had entered our lives under false pretences, even though his motives had been pure. Perhaps after Bernhard, and everything I'd told them about Patrick, she was right to not trust men, though she'd seemed happy in Ifan's company the evening before. They hadn't gone to the pub after we'd eaten, but sat talking quietly long after I'd gone to bed with Lily, too mentally drained to summon new thoughts and make conversation. I knew they were discussing what had happened to Morag, not me. Perhaps she would never tell anybody my story, even Ifan. It was hardly one for the family archives.

'I'm going to make contact with Isaac,' she'd said over dinner, revealing he would be twenty-six in May, and had been adopted by a Scottish couple when he was a few days old. She'd given birth alone in a London hospital and returned to work a week later.

She'd been hoping Bernhard would reveal Isaac's exact whereabouts, maybe even a phone number, but he'd refused to speak once he was in custody, though a small envelope containing more baby hair had been found in his pocket. Morag believed his adoptive parents had kept it for him. 'He must have given it to Bernhard to give me.' She knew the name of the couple who adopted him. 'It won't be too hard to find him.' She could have made contact any time but had resisted; didn't even ask for a photo. 'I couldn't have coped,' she said while Ifan cleared away our plates and made coffee. 'It was better to make a clean break, except it never is. Not really.'

I'd thought of Mum, missing me all the time I'd been away, but letting me go because she thought it was what I wanted, glad that I was happy and safe.

'Will you tell your mum about what happened?' Morag said now as if tracking my thoughts, slowing to let a car pull out in front of the van.

'Maybe,' I said. 'I'm tired of keeping secrets.'

I'd slept deeply the night before but had woken with a heaviness in the pit of my stomach, knowing there was one last thing I had to do before I could really move on.

If Declan was surprised when Morag entered the café and sat down opposite, he didn't show it, greeting her easily, asking what we'd like to drink. 'My treat.'

He made a fuss of Lily, who looked bright-eyed and cute in a knitted jacket the colour of a strawberry milkshake – another of Annie's donations. 'I got her this from the store next door.' He produced a bendy giraffe and waggled it at Lily. 'It's ethical and good for teething.' He laid it on her chest and her little hands patted its head. 'Hey, you should get her swimming,' he said. 'They're never too young to learn.' He sat back in his chair and gave me a searching look. His hair looked freshly washed and he seemed relaxed, as if he'd slept well after coming to terms with everything I'd told him. In contrast, I was pasty-faced and hadn't bothered to comb my hair before coming out. 'What is it?' he said.

I was perched on the edge of the chair beside Morag, still with my coat on, Lily on the table between us in her car seat. 'I wanted to ask you something.'

'Shall I go?' Morag, halfway out of her jacket, made to push her chair back.

'No, no, it's fine.' My heart was thrashing now the moment had come. 'Stay.' I waited until the waitress had taken our order, giving Declan an extra-wide smile before sashaying away.

'Go on.' He sat forward, brow furrowed. 'Anything.'

I forced a calming breath. 'Do you still have Patrick's number?'

Declan's frown deepened. 'Yes, but I don't intend to ever use it again.' He reached into his pocket. 'Shall I delete it?'

'No, I …' I bit my lip. I had to do this. 'Could I have it? I want to call him.'

'What?' Morag stared at me aghast. 'That's not a good idea, Grace.'

'Why?' Declan's tone was more restrained, but his face showed concern.

'I have to know whatever was between us is really over, that I don't have to keep looking over my shoulder.'

'It is,' said Declan, at the same time as Morag cautioned, 'It'll only stir things up. You should leave it well alone.'

'Just a quick call to put my mind at rest.'

'It's not a good idea.' Declan was frowning again. 'I honestly think he'll leave you be. He's got bigger things on his mind.'

'I have to know what he told Elise's parents.' The words felt tight in my throat. 'About why there was no baby.'

'Why does that matter?' Morag turned to look at me properly, her dark eyes raking my face. 'You said he'd think of something. It doesn't matter what it was.'

'It does if he mentioned me, if he told them what really happened with the baby.' I took a ragged breath. 'Her parents are well connected and they have money. They might want revenge.'

'That's a bit dramatic.' Declan shook his head. 'Whatever he told them, he won't have implicated himself or you in anything shady. I'm sure it's over, Grace. Let it go.'

'Please.' I couldn't keep the desperation from my tone. 'I don't think I can until I know for sure.'

He was silent for a moment, trading an anxious look with Morag.

'I promise this will be the last of it. I'll delete his number afterwards and you should too. But I have to know.'

'Give it to her.' Morag sounded decisive, touching the back of my hand with her fingers in a show of support. 'It's about closure.'

'That's it.' My grateful smile quickly dropped away. The thought of hearing Patrick's voice made my stomach swoop.

'Fine,' Declan said, still shaking his head. 'But I'm not happy about it.'

Rising, I pressed a kiss on the tip of Lily's nose then headed down the street and round the corner, where I sat on a bench opposite a grey, gothic-looking church surrounded by gravestones. *Births, marriages, deaths.* It seemed like a fitting view.

It was 5 a.m. in New York. I had the element of surprise on my side if Patrick was sleeping, though I doubted he would be. Work was always a distraction. He'd be putting in more hours than ever. Even if he was at the office, I was confident a call from abroad would pique his interest.

My heart tapped a rapid beat as I pressed in the number Declan had given me. Patrick's personal number; the one I'd never been allowed to have.

As it connected, I rubbed at a stain on my jeans and saw my hand was shaking. A woman cycled by – the one I'd seen chatting outside the post office on my first trip to the village – a bunch of daffodils in the basket on the handlebars. She gave me a curious glance and I wondered whether I looked as nervous as I felt.

Three long rings were followed by a short delay, then Patrick's voice was in my ear, as close as if he was sitting on the bench beside me.

'Hullo?' It was soft, querying – not sleepy. 'Who is this?' I'd forgotten how American he sounded. *Foreign.* A stranger, almost.

'It's me.' The words emerged as a whisper. 'Grace,' I said, raising my voice. 'Please don't hang up. I won't contact you again after this, but I need to know, Patrick.'

The silence was so long, I wondered if he'd disconnected the call and I hadn't realised. 'Need to know what?' He wasn't angry or cold. He sounded … tired. 'What do you want from me, Grace?'

I tried to steady my breathing. 'Just to know what you told Elise's parents.'

He expelled a long breath. 'I told them the truth.'

'The truth?' Panic bubbled inside my stomach.

'The truth we decided on.' I burned with guilt at his use of *we* because it was true. I'd gone along with the lie. 'You didn't leave me much choice, remember?' he said quietly. 'I thought it best to come clean. I told them Elise had lost the baby but couldn't face telling anyone, and that she'd started drinking again. I said she pleaded with me to find her a baby that we could raise as our own, so I'd looked into surrogacy and found someone already several months pregnant, looking for a childless couple to raise the child.' I held my breath. 'I explained Elise wanted to get to know the baby before showing her to anyone, but at the last minute the surrogate changed her mind and decided to keep her.'

My lungs felt constricted. I stood up and circuited the bench, gulping in air. 'They believed it?'

'Why wouldn't they?' he said. 'It was true. I just didn't mention any names. To be honest, Grace, they were too devastated to want the ins and outs. They were angry with the "surrogate".' He gave the word quotation marks. 'But I know they were relieved too. Like I told you in the first place, the idea of their daughter raising a child that wasn't hers didn't sit right with them.'

'And they don't blame you?'

'Of course not.' Indignant now. 'They knew how hard Elise found it to stop drinking. They read between the lines regarding her fall; they're not stupid, Grace.' *Stoopid.* 'She had a high alcohol level in her blood.' He paused. 'They've been really supportive.'

'Lucky you.' I couldn't help it. 'You come up smelling of roses.'

'Grace, I don't blame you for threatening me, or for running away and taking the baby, I really don't.' *The baby.* As if Lily was nothing to do with him. 'When I think back, it was a crazy idea.

I don't know how I thought it would work. I was desperate, I guess, and desperate people do desperate things.' I didn't say that he hadn't seemed that desperate when he came to find me; rather he'd been happy to have found a solution to the problem of his wife. 'How is she, Grace?'

'You don't get to ask that.'

Another soft sigh. 'How are *you*?'

'I'm fine, happy,' I said. 'It's business as usual for you then?'

'Grace, I …' He hesitated, perhaps thinking it was no more than he deserved. 'I feel terrible, if it's any consolation. I'm ashamed of my actions. I'm working every day to do better, to be a better person, make the world a safer place.'

'That should be your campaign speech.'

He laughed, but it was a small, sad sound. 'I guess I'm not cut out for marriage and kids after all. I'll stick to serving my country in future,' he said. 'I wish you well, Grace, I really do, but it's probably best if you don't contact me again.'

'I won't,' I said. 'Goodbye, Patrick.'

I ended the call and deleted the number, knowing it really would be the last time we spoke. I had no idea what I would tell Lily about her father when she asked. Maybe I'd say I didn't know who he was. Would that be better than saying he hadn't wanted her? She would be surrounded by love; I'd make sure of that. She wouldn't for a single moment feel the loss of the man who'd fathered her. I thought of Declan then; a far better man for all Patrick's declarations about justice and serving his country. There were more ways than one to be good. I sat back down, letting Patrick's words wind through me. I felt another, stronger release inside, as if a tight band around my chest had finally broken.

Patrick hadn't needed to ask whether or not I planned to tell anyone he'd pushed his wife down the stairs. I never would, because now I knew for certain that I didn't have to.

And anyway, he wasn't the one who pushed her.

I was.

Chapter 41

I hadn't intended to do it. I was sleep-deprived, brimming with hormones, furious that Elise didn't seem to know what to do with Lily, angry with Patrick for bringing me to their home, for letting me believe she'd given up drinking – but angrier with myself for letting it happen.

I was struggling to pretend I was her nanny, a substitute until Elise was sober enough, interested enough, to take care of my baby. It shocked me that I'd ever thought I didn't want to be a mother. Now that Lily was there, so tiny and impossibly perfect, something had slotted into place. Already it was impossible to imagine my life without her. Being pregnant had felt all wrong, but everything I'd feared had fallen away once she was born. I *wanted* a baby to care for, to plan for. I wanted Lily.

In those foggy days at Patrick and Elise's expensive, three-storey, designer-decorated house, I tried telling myself it was my hormones, designed to make women love their babies, a trick to ensure they were looked after properly, making me feel that way. One night, I made up some formula and tried to give Lily a bottle, but she wouldn't take it, thrashing her limbs, her cries like a blade across my heart. I'd given in and breastfed her again, tears streaming down my face as I realised how naïve, how utterly stupid I'd been to think this could ever work.

Part of me was glad Elise wasn't coping. I couldn't bear to imagine what would have happened if she'd welcomed Lily with open arms and I'd never been allowed to see her again. Floods of panic surged through me whenever she was out of my sight, even though just keeping her alive seemed like a mammoth task. Patrick had immediately returned to work, and when he was out of the house and Elise had returned to bed, I treasured the time alone with my baby, even knowing I was making it harder to walk away.

I asked Patrick one evening, when he came to take Lily to Elise, holding her like a parcel that might detonate, if he thought he might change his mind.

'I could go, just slip out with the baby. No one would be any the wiser.'

He looked at me with tired, bloodshot eyes. 'Give it time, Grace, please, a bit more time. I know it's not easy, for any of us, but Elise will get there, I know she will.' I wasn't sure even he believed it anymore, but things had gone too far for him to consider giving up. 'Be patient.'

I couldn't. I started planning my escape that night. I would leave the country, but I needed a passport for Lily, which required a birth certificate. I knew she didn't have one yet because Patrick was waiting for Elise to be ready, had mentioned it to her twice.

Can't you do it on your own?

It'll look odd if you're not there, Elise. You're supposed to be her mother.

On the morning he went to his meeting, when Declan came to the house to pick him up and Elise had gone back to bed, I swaddled Lily in the carrier Patrick had bought for Elise to use, thinking that having the baby close would help them bond, and left a note in the kitchen. *Taking the baby out for some fresh air.*

Sweating with panic, I got a cab to the department of health

275

to register Lily's birth – *father unknown* – then to the Midtown Station office for an emergency passport, using a photo of Lily I took on my phone. At the New York Library, Lily nestled in her carrier against my chest, adrenaline surging through my veins, I used the computer to look up the Welsh village where my aunt was a recluse. *Fenbrith*. It looked nice, not far from Conwy where my grandparents had lived, where my mother and aunt grew up. When I got back to the house, Elise was still in her room, the note in the kitchen unread. Maybe if I hadn't heard her shouting at Patrick the following morning it would have all ended differently.

'I don't think I can love her, Patrick.' Elise's voice carried through the nursery wall. 'I'll always know she's not really mine. It's not the same as having my own baby.' The self-pitying whine in her voice told me she'd been drinking again. *Drunk, in charge of my baby.*

'Of course you will, just give it more time.' The same thing he'd said to me.

'You're a selfish asshole, Patrick Holden.' Something crashed to the floor. 'You only want it because it's good for your campaign. You don't know what it's like to not be able to carry a child. You don't get it. You could father a baby with someone else if you wanted to, but me?' Her voice climbed the scale. 'I'll never have my own baby and you think you can make it OK by giving me one ready-made?' *It. She'd called my baby it.* 'It's not the same, Patrick. I've tried, I really have, but I don't think I can do it.'

'Then try harder.'

'Pity it's not a boy.' Her voice grew snide. 'You'd be more hands-on then, wouldn't you? A replacement for your poor dead brother. That's what it's really about, isn't it?'

'You don't know what you're talking about.'

'It's fine for you – you're at work all the time. A baby's just an accessory, a campaign winner to you.'

'For fuck's sake, Elise, pull yourself together.'

Creeping out and peering round their bedroom door, I saw

her fly at him with an animal-like roar. He grabbed her wrists and pushed her. She flew into the wall and he stalked towards her, hand raised. I froze, my memory scrambling back to my father in the kitchen the day he died. Elise cowered and his hand dropped. He straightened his tie. 'Please make an effort, Elise. Your family is flying in next week. You don't want them to see you like this.'

In the nursery, Lily began to cry. I hurried to her, anger whipping through my veins as Patrick's footsteps clattered down the stairs, followed by the front door slamming and the sound of Elise's sobs. He hadn't even bothered to check on Lily.

When Elise came to the nursery a little later, she was pale but showered and dressed, though her jasmine-scented perfume barely masked the alcohol, or the coffee she must have drunk to disguise it. She hardly glanced at me in the rocking chair by the window where I'd been nursing Lily, trying to calm my racing heart.

'You have to go,' she said coldly. 'If I'm going to do this, I can't have help all the time. I need to do this on my own.'

My heart was thumping. 'You're firing me?'

'My husband will give you a good reference.' Her watery blue eyes narrowed, as if bringing me properly into focus for the first time, taking in my lank, unwashed hair and tear-stained face, the shapeless dress straining around my post-pregnancy stomach and breasts; realising I looked nothing like a baby-care professional. 'Give her to me.'

She came over and roughly prised Lily from my arms. 'I'll go and warm up some milk,' she said, leaving before I could respond, silky skirt swishing around her slim ankles.

'Wait!' I sprang up and ran after her, down to the kitchen. She was clutching Lily in one arm, opening the many cupboards, looking for a tin of formula. 'She's not hungry.' I was almost weeping, fingers itching to snatch my baby back. 'I just fed her.'

Lily started to cry, her little face screwed up and red. Elise

277

winced, as though the sound hurt her ears. 'It's not your call to make.'

'Babies have a routine.'

'Don't tell me what to do, Grace.' She tossed her curtain of hair, shifting Lily to her other arm like an annoying parcel. 'It's better for me to learn by trial and error.'

Not with my baby it isn't. 'Please, Elise. Let me take her.'

As Lily's cries escalated, the sound insistent, a ripple of disbelieving fury crossed Elise's face. 'This is your fault, feeding her on demand.' She jiggled my daughter with alarming ferocity. 'Why won't she stop crying?'

'Let me take her up to the nursery while you make her a bottle.' It was a suggestion borne of desperation, but Elise caved in and thrust my daughter at me.

'She'll never get used to me with you around.' Her voice was thick with anger. 'I want you out of here by the end of the day.'

'You should discuss it with your husband first.'

'What did you say?' Elise advanced, her pale lips an angry slash, eyes burning with rage. She shoved me against the fridge, her fingers closing tightly around my throat. I tried to avert my face from a stale waft of coffee breath, and from the fury tightening her face.

'Please, you'll hurt the baby.' My voice was constricted. She squeezed harder, then let go. I gulped in air, coughing as I checked Lily was unharmed. 'You're not fit to be her mother.'

'Who do you think you are, talking to me like you know me?' Fast as lightning, she grabbed a crystal tumbler on the worktop. I barely had time to duck before it sailed past my head and hit the doorframe. The sound of it shattering on the tiles was an assault on my eardrums. I stared in shock and disbelief at the mess. 'What the hell?' I glanced at Lily again, encircled in my arms. 'Don't you care that you could have hurt her?'

'You'd love that, wouldn't you?' Elise's chest rose and fell beneath her thin sweater. It had dropped from one shoulder, revealing her bony collarbone. 'Don't bother reporting back to Patrick; he won't believe you.' I doubted that was true, but didn't dare say so.

She stormed past, turning in the hallway, red patches on her pale cheeks. 'Clear up that mess, make her a bottle and bring her to me.'

I wept quietly as I crouched to sweep the glass into the corner with my hand, Lily – silent now – pressed to my chest. I sensed Elise watching but didn't look round, pausing only when I noticed blood, dripping from a stinging cut on my thumb.

When I'd finished, a badly applied plaster covering my cut, I found Elise in the bedroom, staring out of the window overlooking the quiet street. She'd fastened her hair up and pulled a white bathrobe over her clothes, though the temperature in the house was close to tropical.

I dragged my eyes from the rumpled bed she shared with Patrick – though I'd caught him coming out of a room down the corridor the previous morning, looking as if he hadn't slept.

'I should get her a pacifier for when she cries.' Elise's voice was neutral, as though nothing had happened. I noticed a half-empty glass of clear liquid on the nightstand and wondered whether it was vodka. 'Where's the formula?' she said when she turned, seeing only Lily cradled in my arms.

My fingers fluttered to my throat. I could still feel the imprint of her fingers. 'I'm not leaving her with you.' The thought of handing my baby to a woman who would never love her even a quarter as much as I did was too much to bear. I wanted to scream: *I'm her mother, can't you see? I'm not her nanny. Your husband DID father a baby with another woman. ME.* But I had to be careful. I had no idea how she would react after hurling the glass at my head. As far as Patrick was concerned, I was still happy to be lending a hand, waiting to rush back to my old life, go back to working at the restaurant – an idea that now seemed as ludicrous as launching into space.

'She's not very well; that's why she keeps crying,' I said instead, deciding I would wait until Patrick and Elise were sleeping that night and go. The sooner I was away from here the better. He could tell his wife whatever he wanted. 'Let me get her settled and I'll bring her to you when she's calm.'

'Just let me hold her for a while.'

'No.'

Propelled by my refusal, Elise rushed towards me once more. I backed onto the landing, my feet sinking into the deep pile of the carpet. She came after me, tugging the hem of my cardigan as I reached the top of the stairs.

'Give her to me, now.' Her face was colourless, her eyes wide and blank. There wasn't an ounce of compassion in her, I realised. 'She's my baby.'

'I heard you telling Patrick you didn't think you could love her.'

'Eavesdropping, were you?' She looked me up and down. 'Where did he find you anyway?' A crease appeared between her thin eyebrows. 'Are you one of his charity cases? Someone he thought deserved a second chance at life?' Her tone was puzzled and slightly mocking. I wondered whether it was the drink talking – she was swaying lightly as she spoke, one hand reaching for the banister post. Maybe she'd always been like this, or had drastically changed since Patrick met her. Maybe she'd have been a different person if she'd been able to have her own baby. I almost felt sorry for her, then remembered she'd said: *You only want it to boost your campaign.*

It. Not *her.*

'She shouldn't be with someone who doesn't love her.' I held Lily with one arm, holding out the other as Elise sprang forward as if to rip her from me.

'You're talking like you think she isn't mine.' Her long dark hair slipped out of the clip she'd fastened it up with and drooped across her face. 'Give me my baby.'

'No.'

As I turned, ready to run, she grasped my sleeve and pulled violently so I was forced to spin round and face her. For a moment, we were eye-to-eye. She clutched at me before I pulled away, causing her to totter. Her back was to the staircase. Surprise crossed her features as she realised there was nothing to grab on to and only space behind her.

As her hands flew out to grasp at me, her fingers caught the side of Lily's face. I grabbed her wrist, twisted it away and pushed hard. Elise lost her footing. As if in slow motion she went sliding, crashing, tumbling head first down the stairs, landing with a dull thud on the marble floor in the hallway.

I stared in shock as she lay there, expecting her to get up and charge at me again. When she didn't move, I slowly descended the stairs as if in a dream, Lily squeezed against me. When I reached the bottom step, Elise's eyes travelled to mine. She made a noise deep in her throat. With Lily tight to my chest and the sound of my heart pounding in my ears, I ran panting with fright to the phone in the hallway and picked up the handset, resting it on the table so I could press *911*. My finger shook as it hovered over the *9*. I jabbed it, then ran back to see blood seeping from under Elise's head. The life was fading from her eyes. With a terrified gasp, I hurried back to the phone and pressed the final *1*.

'What's your emergency?'

Patrick returned then, his appearance shocking in the stark white hallway. Maybe he'd thought of Lily and wanted to check she was OK, or – more likely – he'd come back to plead with his wife once more. I never got the chance to ask. He took in the sight of Elise on the floor and turned, wide-eyed, to see me with the phone in my hand and Lily in the crook of my arm. When I shook my head, a look that said: *It's over* smoothed out his features. A lightning flash of relief crossed his face before he ran to her. And he was right. It *was* over. *Case closed* as he might have said, if he hadn't been digging deep to find some grief for the tragic death of his wife. All I had to do was wait for the ambulance to take her away before telling him I was leaving with Lily and wouldn't be back.

*

As I deleted Patrick's number, I saw a text from Mum. *I hope you can find it in your heart to forgive me. I love you XX*

I love you too XX. It felt good to put it in words. I was looking forward to seeing her again, and for Lily to get to know her grandma. Smiling, I rose from the bench, pushing my phone in my pocket. The sun had emerged, bathing the church in a golden light so it looked like something from a fairy tale. It felt like a sign; permission to push down the memory of Elise for good, to seal her inside the space where my father had lain for so long, where she would stay buried forever.

'Lovely morning.' It was Biddy, holding the hand of a little boy with a crown of dark curls, carrying a bag of bread crusts. 'Got the morning off,' she said, smiling down at him. 'Thought I'd take my grandson to feed the ducks.'

'Good idea. I used to love feeding the ducks when I was a little girl.' *And Lily would one day, too.*

'I hear you're helping out at the pub on Saturday night?'

I returned her smile. 'That's right.'

'Bit of a come-down isn't it?'

I supposed it seemed that way to outsiders, from being a New York chef with a promising future to this, but it felt more like the real me; looking after Lily, staying with my aunt and working at the local pub. Building friendships. Getting to know Declan if he decided to stay. 'Actually, it's perfect,' I said. 'I hope you'll come in for something to eat.'

'I'll be there.' Her smile broadened. 'Give my love to your aunt.'

'I will.' I waved, then turned to make my way back to the café in the warm spring sunshine, where Declan and Morag were waiting with my beautiful, precious daughter. My darling Lily. *My family.*

Acknowledgements

There's a brilliant team behind every book, and I'm lucky to have such a great one at HQ.

Thanks to my wonderful editor Belinda Toor for her clever guidance, copyeditor Helena Newton, Helen Williams for the proofread, Anna Sikorska for the brilliant cover and everyone in marketing for spreading the word.

Enormous thanks to my lovely readers, the community of bloggers and reviewers, and to my friend Amanda Brittany for her support and feedback.

None of it would be possible without the support of my family, in particular my husband Tim, who never gets tired of listening to me rave about plot holes or making me cups of tea to keep me going.

Thank you.

Keep reading for an excerpt from
Your Life For Mine …

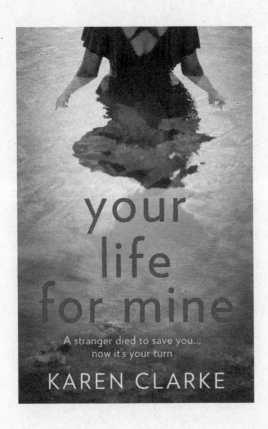

Prologue

After all the planning, I suppose it's natural to be looking forward to what's coming with a mix of apprehension and pleasure. Mostly pleasure, to be honest. The planning has been so meticulous, I haven't left room for anything to go wrong. I've been careful and patient – more than I'd ever have believed possible.

Knowing you're in London today, swanning about without a care in the world, simply brought home the fact that now – finally – is the perfect time to execute my plan to create maximum suffering. It's been a long wait, but that means the reward will be sweeter.

Time to get started.

Prologue

Chapter 1

The text came as I was getting off the train. I'd kept the volume at maximum since missing a call from my daughter's school a few days ago, and the vibration made me jump.

I fumbled my phone from my bag, ignoring the thrust of commuters keen to reach home after a hard day's work or, in my case, a hard day's wandering around London.

It was probably Vic, checking I was on my way home. He was throwing a surprise party for my birthday, and to celebrate us being together for six months, and although it wasn't a surprise (Vic knew better than that) he wanted to make it special.

Moving down the platform of Oxford railway station as the train pulled away, I pictured him in the kitchen with a checklist: food delivered, house tidied, cake baked – he'd been practising – my loved ones gathered and primed, eager to see my reaction. I'd been practising a look of joyful astonishment I hoped I could carry off.

I opened my messages, a smile hovering. I didn't recognise the number.

Enjoy your birthday, Beth. It'll be your last.

My brain froze. I read it again, heart beating unevenly. *Who is this?* I typed back, fingers slipping across the screen before hitting send. The response came swiftly.

You'll find out.

My heart rate accelerated as I tapped out a reply, not stopping to consider whether it was a good idea. *If this is a joke, it's not funny.*

No joke.

I glanced around, as if whoever had sent the message might be grinning with sinister intent on the platform, but the stretch of concrete was empty, sunshine glinting off the tracks. I'd been boiling on the train, but now cold fingers touched my spine, sending ripples of gooseflesh over my skin.

Who are you?

No reply.

With a plunge of dread, my mind barrelled back to a message I'd found on my car windscreen just after Christmas, *A LIFE FOR A LIFE* printed in big, black capitals on a sheet of plain white paper. I'd thrown it away, assuming someone had got the wrong car, or it was a religious thing, like the leaflets sometimes thrust at me in the street, offering salvation through Christ – but the words had still made me shiver and look around, just as I was doing now.

Another message buzzed in.

Bye, bye, Beth.

I dropped my phone as though bitten. Whoever it was had my name and number, yet no one I knew would do this, even as a joke.

My brain swooped around the possibilities.

'Everything OK?'

I spun round to see the station assistant watching me curiously.

'Fine.' I tried to smile but my face felt stiff as I bent to retrieve my phone.

'Have a nice evening,' she said, giving me a funny look.

'You too.' I stumbled a little as I hurried through the exit towards the car park. She probably thought I'd been drinking.

In my car, I switched on the engine to get the air-conditioning flowing and looked at my phone again. Nothing.

I tried to breathe through the tightness in my chest. I'd spent too many years feeling like this in the past. I didn't want to be pushed back to that place.

You know I can report you?

No response.

Perhaps one of my art -therapy clients was playing a prank. They knew my name and could have got hold of my number. It didn't make much sense, but neither did anything else.

Except … *A LIFE FOR A LIFE*. With a twist of fear, it struck me afresh that only someone who knew me well would know the impact those words would have.

I jumped when a text from Vic came through.

Are you on your way back?

I let out my breath. *Five minutes. X*

Love you. X

You too. X

I still couldn't say it back, even in writing. I'd been with my daughter's father Matt for seven years, had loved him deeply. My feelings hadn't died the minute he left, but Vic understood. It was one of the things I liked about him. He was a grown-up, who grasped that love was complex. He'd been patient, allowing my feelings to flourish at their own pace.

I manoeuvred out of the car park on autopilot, breathing from my diaphragm the way I'd been taught by a counsellor, but my skin and muscles were stiff with tension as I drove the short journey home.

When I turned into the street where I'd lived for the last six years, my shoulders relaxed a little. Home was a Victorian terrace on a quiet, leafy street overlooking the park near Hayley's school – a house we'd only been able to afford because Matt's grandfather died and left him enough money for the deposit. We would have to sell it soon. He needed a new place, where Hayley could go and stay, and Vic wanted us to buy somewhere together.

I switched off the engine, trying to picture the scene behind the olive-green front door; everyone hiding, waiting for a cue from Vic to leap out and shout 'Surprise!'. Hayley would love it. She'd been to several parties lately, running out with extravagant party bags, eager for her own birthday in October. *Five.* I had a nearly-five-year-old daughter I'd willingly die for. A daughter I'd fight to live for.

Enjoy your birthday, Beth. It'll be your last.

My breath caught when I detected a movement at the landing window, as if someone had been watching me and dipped out of sight. I stared for a moment, but the glass was opaque with the sun's reflection and I couldn't make anything out.

Getting out of the car, I tried to smooth the wrinkles from my flower-patterned, summery dress with a shaky hand. No point checking my face or refreshing my lipstick. If I looked too polished my guests might guess I was in on the 'secret' – if they hadn't already.

The air was thick with humidity, but I suppressed a shiver as I slipped my key in the lock and pushed the front door open, inhaling the smell of home; a mix of clean laundry, Vic's classy aftershave, and a heady waft of freshly-baked sponge cake. He'd neatened the hallway, lining up our shoes, putting Hayley's scooter out of harm's way and straightening our coats on the hooks along the wall.

He didn't live here full-time but came round most days, slotting easily into our lives – more easily than I could ever have imagined – but at times, it still felt wrong that Matt wasn't there, waiting with his guitar to burst into song the second I stepped through the door, his boots left wherever he'd kicked them off, something simmering in the kitchen as he experimented with new ingredients.

Placing my keys on the console table, I was hotly aware of my phone in my bag like a hand grenade. I waited for my breathing to settle. The silence in the house felt manufactured and somehow sinister. A sound, quickly smothered behind the living room door, conjured an image of strangers waiting to pounce. Swamped in sudden dizziness, I shot out a hand to steady myself, overcome by a suffocating certainty.

Somebody in this house wanted me dead.

Dear Reader,

We hope you enjoyed reading this book. If you did, we'd be so appreciative if you left a review. It really helps us and the author to bring more books like this to you.

Here at HQ Digital we are dedicated to publishing fiction that will keep you turning the pages into the early hours. Don't want to miss a thing? To find out more about our books, promotions, discover exclusive content and enter competitions you can keep in touch in the following ways:

JOIN OUR COMMUNITY:

Sign up to our new email newsletter:
http://smarturl.it/SignUpHQ

Read our new blog www.hqstories.co.uk

🐦 https://twitter.com/HQStories

fi www.facebook.com/HQStories

BUDDING WRITER?

We're also looking for authors to join the HQ Digital family!
Find out more here:

https://www.hqstories.co.uk/want-to-write-for-us/

Thanks for reading, from the HQ Digital team

If you enjoyed *And Then She Ran*, then why not try another absolutely unputdownable thriller from HQ Digital?

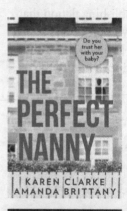